Michael and the Multicoloured Gospel

2ND EDITION

Mark Frew

Michael and the Multicoloured Gospel
2nd Edition

ISBN: 978-0-9954440-7-2 (paperback)
ISBN: 978-0-9954440-8-9 (hardback)
ISBN: 978-0-9954440-6-5 (ebook)

For those who have ears to hear
and minds to think

Chapter 1

The story of Lot and the cities of Sodom and Gomorrah is a curious one. Lot, who was Abraham's nephew, chose to live in these cities, cities inhabited by very wicked people. The Bible does not tell us whether or not the evil they committed was an entire collection of sins.

However, there was one sin which the inhabitants of these cities attempted to commit that would make these two cities an example for humanity for the rest of eternity and this was brought out in the story. Two angels were sent by God to tell Lot to escape from these cities because God was going to rain fire and brimstone on them so that they could be completely obliterated from existence. The two angels, who must have had the appearance of two young, very good looking men, lodged at Lot's place for the night, only to be harassed by the men of the city to partake in a male-only orgy. This was a dreadful sin that the inhabitants of these cities attempted to commit, a sin so repugnant in the sight of God that the only choice He could make was to completely annihilate them forever. Sodom and Gomorrah, therefore, became the symbols of the worst sin that a man could ever commit, embodied in the word *sodomy* today.

There were many cities at about this time and no doubt sinners lived in these cities where they stole, cheated or horrendously tortured and slaughtered innocent people, but God simply sat there idly and allowed these cities to continue to exist without His intervention. However, the very thought of men having sex together was just too abhorrent and intolerable for God to remain passive which is what stirred Him into action to obliterate Sodom and Gomorrah out of existence.

And this is the message that is brought out in this story or, at least, this is what is often highlighted as evidence against homosexuality. The story of Sodom and Gomorrah leaves us in little doubt that this is testimony to God's abhorrence of this sin.

But this is not the entire story. When we examine the story in greater detail, we find that this is not the only message to draw from this example. When the men of the city demanded Lot to send the angels out so that they "may know them", Genesis 19 tells us that Lot answered them,

> I pray you, brethren, do not so wickedly.
> Behold now, I have two daughters which
> have not known man; let me, I pray you,
> bring them out unto you, and do ye to them
> as is good in your eyes: only unto these men
> do nothing

In other words, the story reveals that Lot considered very strongly protecting the angels from having sex with these men but had no trouble allowing his own virgin daughters to be sent in their place. Lot was willing to allow his daughters to be raped in order to protect his guests. What the complete moral of the story of Sodom and Gomorrah, then, is that, sex between men is evil indeed, but raping women, or girls, is okay, even if it is committed against your own daughter.

A variation of this story appears later in the Book of Judges, chapter 19. In this story, a Levite – a type of priest – travelled with his concubine from his father-in-law's house in a city called Bethlehem-judah to return to his hometown in a place called Ephraim. During the night, they arrived at a city called Gibeah. An old man allowed them to stay at his place overnight. But later in the evening, the inhabitants of this city demanded that the old man send out the Levite so that they also "may know him". In the same way as Lot, the old man answered, "do not so wickedly" to this Levite. As it was with Lot, the old man had a virgin daughter but, in addition, the Levite had a concubine, and these women could be sent out to be sexually abused instead of the Levite. Where this story departs from the story of Lot is that this time, the concubine, who was as much a guest as the Levite, was sent out and, sure enough, the men of the city took advantage of her.

I have always tried to imagine what actually happened at that moment. I have tried to imagine what the Levite actually said to his concubine, "Come on! Out you go!" while pushing her out onto the street into the hands of this raging mob. After he had closed the door behind him and returned to where the old man was sitting, the two men probably continued their conversation where they had left off, then maybe played a game of cards and drank a night cap of goat's milk before retiring to bed. In the meantime, the Levite's concubine was out on the street screaming, "Oh, God! No! Please, no!" while the men of the city completely had their way with her.

In the morning, the Levite opened the front door to find his wife lying at the doorstep, probably her clothes nothing but rags now wrapped about her battered and bruised body. With what appears to be no sympathy for her ordeal, the Levite told his concubine, "Up, and let us be going," as if what she had endured throughout the night was a trifling matter. But when he discovered that his wife, in fact, was dead, the Levite sought righteous vengeance against the men of this city. In other words, had the woman survived the ordeal, the entire story would never have been told. There is no hint of accusation against the Levite's insensitive attitude towards his concubine. He comes out of the story squeaky clean. And, strangely enough, God did not think this city needed to be destroyed with fire and brimstone.

The conclusion we can draw from this is that, if the Bible speaks clearly and evidently against homosexuality in these stories, we must also draw the conclusion that the Bible also allows women to be expendable sex objects to be used as men see fit.

But none of the churches preaches this. Although I have heard them preach against the sin of Sodom, not once have I heard them mention the "righteous" act of Lot or the Levite. Are we really supposed to accept these stories in their literal sense as examples for us to live by?

This was how I was raised to view the Bible. After many years as a born-again Christian, I came to the conclusion that the Bible was not what I was originally told that it was. When I meet Christians today who try to convert me to the faith, I tell them that I left the faith long ago. The next question is always difficult to answer: Why? Why did I leave the faith?

Where do I start? There are so many factors which led to my decision. It was not something that happened overnight. I did love the Bible and cherish it as God's holy Word for many years but I cannot view it in this way today. The Bible is, in many ways, a beautiful book but it is impossible to claim that it is perfect.

The story of how I became a Christian is rather mundane. I was born into a Christian family. When I was much older and listened to the stories of how others in the church became Christians, I was often jealous of them. Many of them came from horrific backgrounds, from broken families or drug addition. Christianity brought serenity and stability into their lives but also brought hope and endurance to cope with the traumas they had left behind. Naturally, when these people had children, they ensured that their children were not exposed to the same traumatic experiences.

But for me, Christianity was the only life I knew. Ever since I left the womb, I was surrounded by a

Christian environment and didn't know anything different.

The story as to why I became a Christian, then, really begins with why my parents became Christians. My mother's story was rather simple. She had been a church goer all her life but later told me that during her childhood, religion was only the Sunday Service. Some time in her late teens she came to the realisation that there was more to Christianity than reciting prayers and carrying out the same ritual week in week out.

This was so different to my father's upbringing and it is surprising that my parents ever met at all, coming from completely different backgrounds. My father had a turbulent childhood, a life that was leading nowhere up until the time he was nineteen. He used to tell me stories of how, in his late teens, he would go out with his mates, pick up girls, get drunk and have, as he understood it within the Australian context, a good time. One night he was half drunk and, while standing above the cliff face of South Head in Sydney with a stranger in his arms, the chasm below him was as deep as the emptiness in his heart. After making love to this stranger in the bushes, the instant thrill of sex was swallowed up again by the emptiness that these cheap thrills, so he called them, could not fill.

There was a Christian at his workplace who my father and his workmates liked to make fun of for the sheer pleasure because the Christian was different and stood apart from the Australian societal norm. He didn't drink, smoke, swear, tell dirty jokes, he was always on time to work and always conscientious. My father told me that one day he played a trick on this guy. When morning tea arrived, someone told him that the boss wanted him. While he was away, my father removed all the cream from his cream bun, filled the cavity with axle grease and then replaced the cream over the top to conceal the grease. The Christian came back bewildered because the boss hadn't wanted him at all, picked up the cream bun, took a bite and seconds later was spluttering from the bad taste of the grease. My father and his workmates laughed and jeered at him saying things like, "God turned water into wine and now it looks like He turned your cream into grease!"

Despite the persecution that this Christian received from my father, this man did not sway from his faith. He didn't get angry. On the contrary, that afternoon, my father discovered that he had lost his wallet and hence had no money to get home. He asked all his mates for some money and this Christian was willing to offer him more than he needed. This ate at my father, how this man could continue to love and do good to others, even to those who did evil things to him.

What set my father's heart to change was the day that this Christian's mother died. My father and his mates found out about it and were very sympathetic towards him. But instead of showing any feelings of remorse or loss, the Christian kept a good face because, although his mother had died, so he explained, he had the confidence that she was with the Lord and that this parting was only temporary until the day he died himself and would be reunited with her in heaven. My father was struck by the fact that this man was not afraid of death and he pondered on this for a long time.

That year, the Billy Graham crusade came to Sydney. All my father's workmates heard about it and mocked and jeered the Christian all the more, asking if he was going to attend all Billy Graham's sermons. My father was one of the loudest of the mob and yet he himself went. He told me that it was on that night, after listening to the wonderful sermon, he could not stop himself from rising from his seat and come to Billy Graham's bidding and be saved. He told me that from that time on, the emptiness inside him was filled with something inexplicably wonderful, which he attributed to the Holy Spirit of God.

From that point on, my father's life changed. He immediately ceased from his aimless life, stopped drinking and smoking, abstained from sex until marriage and began attending church every Sunday. He said that the beautiful feeling that he had inside could not be contained and he wanted to share it with everyone. But his mates could not tolerate it and soon he was estranged from them. But he was prepared to sacrifice his friends for his new found faith, as he met new friends at the church he attended and at last met my mother. And from their union, I was born.

I grew up in Emu Plains, a small suburb literally on the western extremity of the Sydney Metropolitan Area, about 60 km from the centre of the city. Emu

Plains is a quiet, little suburb, built on the western banks of the Nepean River, officially on the opposite side of where Sydney ends. However, Emu Plains in some ways comes under the administration of Penrith, the suburb on the eastern bank of the same river, and hence holds a gasping last ditch to still be considered a part of Sydney.

When my parents moved out there, Emu Plains was still a series of orchards and farms but was slowly being developed to find new accommodation for the growing Sydney population. My parents were encouraged to move out of the inner suburbs, out of the choking masses of people living on top of one another, to embrace the open plains that this little suburb's namesake promised. It was also because land at this time was cheap and as my parents were newly married, this was all they could afford.

Emu Plains was a quiet place, dotted about with brick houses in an assortment of reds, oranges and cream, interspersed among an otherwise bushy woodland. My parents chose to build a house at the western end of the suburb, close to Russell Street, which was the last major street that the mighty Great Western Highway cut perpendicularly before making the courageous ascent into the Blue Mountains beside which Emu Plains comfortably nestled.

Life was grand as a child growing up here. Like many modern societies looking back at the illustrious periods of time that make their history, I look back at my childhood as some sort of innocent golden age where everything was good. At that time, my home was far from everywhere and it wasn't until I started attending school that I began to develop a close-knit network of friends with whom I would play.

Religion played very little in my life at this time. All religion was to me was the regular attendance at Sunday School followed by the church service each Sunday morning, which to me was more of an interruption to my regular riding of my bicycle or playing soccer with my friends. I hated going. I hated waking up on a Sunday morning to wear special good clothes that made me feel like a sissy boy that restricted me from running around like a little boy should. But as I was under the care of my parents, I had no choice but to comply.

My parents, my sister, Karen, and I attended the Church of England, which is now called the Anglican Church to separate its association from the English Commonwealth but still retain in some ways its original name. I was christened and confirmed into this religion and we attended a little stone church in the north of Emu Plains, St Mark's or St Michael's or St Stephen's Church of England, where the service was held. It was a quaint little building, established in 1869, a beautiful stone structure with a steeple, a bell that is no longer used, English-style hedges that surrounded it, and the cemetery, all these features reminiscent of the land from whence this tradition originated, that was so out of place with the eucalyptus trees and bottlebrush that grew some hundred metres away, with kookaburras and cockatoos looking down on this strange intrusion.

It was in this little church that I attended Sunday School, hearing stories of the great Bible heroes, of

Noah and the Ark, Daniel in the Lion's Den and Moses crossing the Red Sea. But of all the great people of the Bible was the greatest of them all, Jesus Christ, who died for our sins. The story was simple. We, humans, were destined for hell because we were all sinners. So God concocted a plan of salvation by sending His Son, Jesus Christ, to die for our sins. All sin was punishable by death, this death implying eternal torment in hell. Jesus was a sinless man so He did not have to die. But He did. And because He died, our sins were paid for and we could go to heaven. But to go to heaven, we had to believe that He died for us in the first place.

What a wonderful story this is that God should pay for all the sins of the world so that this responsibility was not left to us to find a solution. It was stressed over and over again that this salvation came by faith and grace only, and not by works.

I remember our priest telling us that this was what made Christianity superior to other religions because other religions never assured a place of eternal bliss after the grave. Other religions taught that if your good works outweighed your bad works, you'd go to heaven, and if not, you'd go to hell. But according to the Bible, just one sin condemned you to hell and hence all humanity, which has a notorious disposition to commit sin, was condemned. But by simply believing that Jesus died for our sins and arose from the dead, you were saved, despite what type of person you were.

We were taught that the Supreme Being of the entire universe was God. He was omnipotent, omniscient, omnipresent and all the omnis you could think of. An example of his omnipotence was the fact that He created the entire universe. Because He was omniscient, He knew everything from the beginning of time till the end, from the smallest quark to the largest galaxy. That He was omnipresent meant that He was all around us. Many bizarre questions were asked by my friends at Sunday School who then wanted to know if God was under the table, in the pencil case, in a shoe that had inadvertently been locked away in the back shed for three weeks and, yes, God was there, too.

But not only was God all these. He was also all-love and all-good. This meant that although He was almighty, He was not a despot. And being good, He did and said those things that were beneficial for all creation.

With such a wonderful picture of this Almighty Being, the obvious question came to mind: why, then, is this good and wholesome world that God created so full of suffering, pain, sickness and death, and why are His creatures, who were created in His image, capable of committing atrocities against their fellow humans? This was when we were introduced to Satan.

After completely ruining it for us in the Garden of Eden, Satan continued his rule of evil. He was the opposite of God, the anti-god, for what God was, Satan was not. Where God was all good, Satan was all evil, where God was all-love, Satan was all-hate, where God was all-truth, Satan was all-lies. Satan appeared to have about as much power as God, even being called by Paul in II Corinthians 4:4, "the god of this world". Satan, then, was the blame for everything that went bad on earth.

God and Satan were in constant conflict, the battle ground being the earth, the spoils of war human souls. Because God loved all humans, He was fighting so that they could be saved and live forever with Him in the next world, whereas Satan, who hated humanity as much as he hated God, only wanted men and women to be sent to eternal torment because of his spite towards God's goodness and love.

Because of our fallen state, we were refused direct communication with God because God could not associate with sinful beings. And this was where the Bible came into the picture. The only means of communication God had with us was through His Word, the Bible. Although written by men, it was really God who wrote the words, using these men's hands, pen and ink. Because the Bible was written by a perfect God, the Bible, therefore, was perfect also, containing neither mistake nor contradiction between its covers.

But because Satan hated God, he added to the temptations he inflicted on humankind the temptation to doubt the Bible and to question its infallibility. Anyone, therefore, who denied the infallibility of God's Word was in danger of hell fire. So, if anything in the Bible did not make sense, or seemed untrue, or if passages of one Scripture were contradictory to another, they were, in reality, none of these things, but rather, it was Satan trying to tempt us away from the Holy Scriptures in order to entice us away from believing any of it at all and thus paving the way for our eternal damnation. Wow! Who'd want to doubt the Bible with this type of understanding of it?!

But what is the Bible? To fundamental Christians, this is an absurd question. They would pull a book off the shelf with *The Holy Bible* stamped on the front and wave it in your face! Indeed, I remember the pastor of our church waving it in the air before all of us to convince us of its divinity.

The problem was that we were never told how the Bible came to be in the first place. We never learned about the history of the development of the Bible, or how that the earlier portions were originally written in Hebrew, later parts in Aramaic and the latter sections in Greek and, therefore, what we read in Australia today is only a translation. No-one in my church ever explained to me that there still exists a sect of Jews today who believe that only the first five books of the Old Testament, also known as the Pentateuch, are inspired by God, and all other books, including all the other books of the Old Testament, are spurious. In the same way, most Jews believe anything in addition to what the Christians call the Old Testament is an unholy addition to God's Word.

We were never told that, during the first three hundred years after the death of Christ, the New Testament did not exist in its current form but there were many books floating about after the resurrection supposedly written by the followers of Christ. Certain of these books, such as The Gospel According to Thomas, Barnabas, I Clement, Hermas and the Didache, were highly favoured and used as part of the New Testament Holy Scriptures in the early Church but were finally rejected, while other books, such as James, Hebrews, II John, III John, Jude, II Peter and the Revelation, were first disputed but later added to the present day Bible. In fact, what constitutes the New Testament are not the books and epistles that were written, or claimed to have been written, by the apostles of Christ, but the books and epistles that were agreed upon as being the Word of God by a democratic vote at the Council of Nicaea in 325 AD. In other words, those who believe that the Bible is the infallible Word of God do not put their faith in Jesus or the apostles but in a group of unknown men who, in the early 4th century, made the decision by a majority vote as to what Christians were allowed to believe were the words of Christ.

Nothing was mentioned as to how that for centuries the books Baruch, Tobit, Judith, I & II Maccabees and The Book of Wisdom, which constitute a collection of writings known in Christian circles as the Apocrypha, were considered as part of Holy Writ to all Christians until Martin Luther in the sixteenth century decided that they did not belong, a tradition that separates Catholics and Protestants today. A Bible-believing Christian's view of God and what He expects of us, therefore, can only be defined through the eyes of those who carved and restitched this divine library together than through the author of the very words themselves.

At this time, I didn't know all this. On the contrary, I was comfortable with the image of God, the Bible and the universe presented to me at my church until I reached my teen years, the age at which I discovered my homosexuality. But the word "discovered" is quite incorrect. I was always aware of my homosexuality from as early as I can remember. When I was about four years of age, I can still recall my fascination for the male body. Being at the beach seeing all those men bare almost all before those tender eyes of mine did marvellous things to my metabolism that I could not explain in words at the time.

At about this age, although I couldn't put my finger on it, I knew I was different to other boys. Pairing up of men and women in fairy tales, movies and comics, all these troubled me for some reason as I felt that I did not belong. Going to school, however, eased my anxiety for a while because boys and girls were sensibly separated from each other in the playground, and neither I nor my friends wanted to catch girls' germs, so we did our utmost to prevent any physical contact between us and them.

It was a long time before I realised that society abhorred men who loved men. This all started when I was introduced to the word "poofter". At first I didn't know what this word meant but I did know that whoever called you one was not paying you a compliment. There was something uglier, more hateful and more evil about these people because the term always projected forth from the lips with such venom. And for some reason it was always the scrawny, nerdy, effeminate and more childish boys of our age group who were forced to bear this name.

Eventually, somewhere down the line, I discovered what the term meant but I did not equate it with my own sexual feelings. A poofter was, after all, something negative and none of my friends would tolerate a poofter as part of their group. Poofters were men who had sex with other men, not in any beautiful sense, but only in some slimy, sleazy sort of way, in public toilets, in some deserted park, late at night, forcing it onto some senseless victim who just happened to ignore all our school teaching about never talking to strangers or about never walking through a park alone at night without parental guidance. And there was some feeling that it was contagious. You got the feeling that everyone around you was heterosexual except these loiterers. But if they caught you unsuspectingly and had sex with you or even just touched you, there would slowly occur a strange metamorphosis in you and soon you too would be doing the same.

It was when my male friends began showing greater and greater interest in the opposite sex that I noticed the vast chasm that separated us. Women became a constant obsession: breasts, vaginas, backsides, all these constituted a part of every conversation. Playboy and other pornographic magazines were scrutinised with lustful zeal in secret corners of the school. But the more they talked about women and the female anatomy, the more I realised how unappealing they were to me.

It took a much longer time before the Christian view of this practice became obvious. Homosexuals were sickly, perverted people, committing acts that could only come from the devil, and whenever Christians mentioned these types of people, which they hardly ever did, there was a sort of "them" attitude, as if nobody in the church could possibly have homosexual tendencies because such tendencies were so evil. In fact, the way it came across was that, although all sin is sin, homosexuality was more sinful than all the other sins.

I remember a little comic I read as a teenager called the Gay Blade, written by Christians against homosexuality, and by the end of it, you really were convinced that homosexuals were sick and depraved, and indeed, I believed it, even though I was one.

Because of the negative light thrown on homosexuality, even though I was aware of my physical attraction towards men, it took a long time for me to realise that I was in fact a homosexual. But when and how I finally associated my sexual feelings with the people whom the Christians and society taught us to hate I can't remember exactly, but I do remember that when I finally made this connection, I became completely disgusted with myself. I didn't feel twisted and public toilets didn't take on a new appeal, but the conflict between the external portrayal of homosexuality and how I felt within created a lot of anxiety.

Relief came when we had sex education. Because we were coming of age and entering puberty, we were warned of the physical and emotional developments that awaited us: pimples, pubic hair, mood swings and sex overdrive. When our sex education teacher asked what we would dream about when we had a wet dream, I remember the answer that came flooding back to him from the classroom was "Girls!" Our teacher went on to explain that as boys develop into manhood, their sexual organs begin to function and prepare for procreation by storing up an ever increasing supply of semen. When the supply was well saturated and no sexual encounter ensued, during the night, the mind used the dream state to create the object of our sexual attraction to bring on an erection and release the pressure from the system. Seeing that men enjoyed sex with women, the wet dream would be full of them. How relieved I felt at that time, knowing that when I had my first wet dream, the proper, clean, heterosexual orientation would at last be awakened in me and I would be like the rest of my male friends.

But that didn't work either. I can still remember my first wet dream as vividly as if it were yesterday. I remember in the dream lying on the beach watching the sun go down. There were swimmers and surfers coming out of the water and getting changed after a great day on the waves. I remember it was twilight. All the surfers were male and one of them started heading up the beach. But he was coming in my direction. When he reached me, I realised that he was naked and I knew I was as well but it didn't seem to worry either of us. I can still see that picture of a man, that well-built body, his healthy skin, his hairy chest and his sturdy legs. Eventually we were having sex and, right in the middle of it, I woke up. The dream, of course, was true to its name!

Naturally you can imagine how disgusted I felt about myself. And these feelings of disgust towards myself continued because I had many more wet dreams after that and not a single female was ever in them. I couldn't understand what was wrong with me but simply excused it with the thought that it was a phase I was going through that I would eventually grow out of. But, as you can obviously tell, I never did.

Chapter 2

When I was about eleven, I remember that my parents decided that the Anglican Church wasn't for them. I can't remember the details but there was some dispute between my parents and the leader of the church they attended, accompanied by a chance encounter between my father and another Christian in the neighbourhood. This guy told my father that the Bible was open for all of us to read and that we shouldn't wait till Sunday to read what it had to say. I suppose my father was bored with living on this cloud of salvation and wanted something more out of Christianity than the mere Sunday worship, and what this Christian had to say seemed to offer him just that. So he began to read the Bible for himself. And then he encouraged us to read it.

This Christian he had met was a member of a local Baptist Church and soon we were to leave this little piece of religious England for a church that was more in tune with the modern architecture of the time and area. I remember the Baptist Church was made of red brick just like our house and from the outside there was less of the traditional image of the church that I was used to except for a cross and the steep, arched rooves.

But there were more changes we had to become accustomed to. The priest was now a minister or pastor, the bread and wine were brought to us in our seats whereas before we had to go out to the front to eat and drink, the minister wore a business suit and not a dog collar, and we didn't have a prayer book but only the hymn book and our Bibles.

And the Bible was important, especially with Pastor Norman as our preacher. Oh, he was a fiery preacher, a real, modern, up-to-date, born-again, Bible Christian. His sermons flourished with quotations from the Bible and this came in such contrast with the sermons delivered by the priest in the Anglican Church who rarely mentioned the Bible at all. We heard more of the Bible in one of Paster Norman's Sunday morning sermons than we did the whole time we attended the Church of England.

Pastor Norman was so on fire for the Lord and really believed in the importance of reading the Bible for ourselves that it was hard for it not to catch on. His sermons were so powerful, you got the feeling that God Himself in all His awesome wonder was behind the pulpit. And he was a stickler for doing everything the Bible said because it was what God was telling us to do. His favourite saying was, "If the Bible says it, I obey it!"

For a long while, I believed that Mr Norman did everything according to the Bible no matter what and had the impression that he was as close to being God as any human being could be.

He taught Mum and Dad, who in turn taught me, that we should clear our minds of everything we had ever learned before about Christianity and just let the Bible speak to us, letting the Holy Ghost speak to us directly. He taught us that we shouldn't wait till

22

Sunday morning to hear what the Bible said from Pastor Norman. The Bible was, after all, our daily bread and we should read it as regularly as we ate a meal.

And so we did. Every evening after dinner, we had a family Bible Study. Each evening we read a chapter from the Bible and discussed it. Reading the Bible was so new. We were being enlightened because we read things we had never known were supposedly a part of the Christian faith.

I so admired Mr Norman (or Pastor Norman, since we called him both) that I wanted to be like him. He created within me the burning desire to love the Lord Jesus Christ and to cherish His Holy Book more than anything else in life. I thought it was such a beautiful message and I wanted to tell the world.

My fervent zeal for Christianity grew on me gradually so it is difficult to pinpoint an exact time when my secular, normal boyhood ended and my strict, zealous Christianity began. Like all my friends at school and in my neighbourhood, I did what boys normally did. We played sport, we rode our bicycles, we went for bushwalks and played games of make believe. I was also a fan of the latest pop groups that were out and knew all the words of the songs.

But there was something that my parents instilled in me that made me different to other boys – I didn't swear. I remember one evening blasting out with a swear word and my mother grabbing me and dragging me to the bathroom where she snatched a cake of soap and shoved it in my mouth. The theory was that if my mouth was dirty, it needed to be cleaned out and simple soap should do the trick. It surely did! After spluttering and crying and frothing at the mouth like a rabid dog, I learnt my lesson never to let come out of my mouth certain sounds that created syllables which caused my parents to react in such a violent way. My mother then went on to lecture me saying that neither Jesus nor the apostles would ever let such vulgar language pass their lips and that swearing was a grave sin.

It must have been when I reached Year 9, at the age of about 14 or 15, when I started to make a distinction in my life. I went to Nepean High School, which was the local secondary school in Emu Plains. I was an average student with no real flare at anything at the time. I had a few friends in the earlier years but one by one they left the area and by mid year, a guy called Gary was the only friend I had left. However, in the middle of that year, Gary also left because his father had gained a transfer in his job and so Gary and his family went to live in country New South Wales. So, I was left alone with no-one. Unfortunately, I never had the opportunity to make new friends because of an incident that would affect the way the other students viewed me as a person.

This was the age when my friends were showing signs that they were extremely sexually switched on just as our sex education teacher had warned us, when boys were discovering girls and girls, boys. Every opportunity was exploited to talk about sex so much so that any object which resembled genitals was something of a playground delight. Swearing, too, was very much a part of the school ground vernacular and of great interest at the time were the latest rock groups, like KISS, Pink Floyd, the Sex Pistols, the Eagles and so many others. But I had grown a strange aversion to all these things because all these things, so we were taught, were of the devil. I cannot remember if it was my parents or Mr Norman who had instilled these ideas in my head but they were expressing themselves in the way I reacted towards them.

I had managed to live my Christianity quite independently of school life and, really, moving in and out of these two worlds was quite normal for me. At school I was a school student but at home, and particularly on Sunday, I was a Christian. I never thought these two worlds were supposed to collapse into one but they did and the results were disastrous.

There was a group of three boys who used to sit at the back of my English class: Philip Casey, Wayne Ferney and Troy Krisston. All three were on the school rugby league team and the results of this expressed themselves through their bulky physique. They looked much older than the rest of the class. They were a rough mob, always untidily dressed and very vulgar in everything they said and did. Philip was a tall, redheaded boy with freckles which spotted his face like an overused pincushion. He was fortunate that he was so big because, despite this freak of nature, nobody wanted to pick on him. Wayne Ferney was a blond haired, blue-eyed, pale skinned Adonis. He had the perfect Aryan features that would have made Hitler proud.

And then there was Troy. He was a bit shorter than the other two and had slightly olive skin as a result of his Greek father. He once told me years later that his surname, Krisston, was an abbreviation and almost complete alteration of the surname his ancestors bore which was much longer and harder to pronounce. Despite his ruggedness, he had maintained certain handsome traits. I remember that even at that age, he had striking features, dark piercing brown eyes, a fine, pointed nose and unusually curly dark hair that dropped like springs from his scalp.

One particular morning, before the teacher had arrived in class, Troy strolled up to my desk and sat right on my exercise book in a rather intrusive manner, picked up a pen and began playing with it. This act obtained the attention of the rest of the class and a semi silence fell over the room which only highlighted my embarrassment. He turned around to look at me and, staring me right in the face, he asked, "Hey, Farril, do you swear?"

It took me by surprise. I had grown so accustomed to hearing others using swear words that I had no longer noticed it. I suppose Troy was expecting to hear me say, "Of course, I bloody swear!" But I didn't. For the very love of Jesus I could not use a word that would be offensive to His tender ears. Because of his question, by the suspended atmosphere that had built up around this moment, by a sheer gut feeling, something made me balk at replying. Being a Christian was all of a sudden a shame because I wanted to be like everybody else, to be an accepted part of my peer group despite my beliefs. I was thinking of just once using a swear word to get rid of him, or to be accepted by him, or both, when the passage in the Bible from Matthew 10:32, 33 came straight to my mind as if Jesus Himself were speaking to me:

Whosoever therefore shall confess me before men,
him will I confess also before my Father which is in
heaven.
But whosoever shall deny me before men, him will I
also deny before my Father which is in heaven.

My mind vacillated between two alternatives: do I swear to please Troy and get him off my back and then feel ashamed of Jesus, putting my salvation in jeopardy, or do I admit my beliefs and be laughed at? The fires of hell burned furiously before my eyes which made the right answer forthcoming. I told Troy that I was a Christian and as a Christian I shouldn't swear. Troy just leaned back and laughed out loud, and the class joined in unison with the laughter. He asked me if I went to church on Sunday and read the Bible and I replied that this was so. Troy and his mates down the back started jeering me with outbursts of "Praise the Lord!" and "Hallelujah!" and the class was in stitches.

And so, the mocking began against me and my beliefs. There were times when Troy and his mates would grab me and pinch my skin, telling me that they would not let go until I swore. But I was resolved not to swear and had to put up with the pain until they finally gave in to my firm resolution.

27

When I told my parents of my ordeals at school, I remember my mother telling me that I should rejoice and leap for joy for Jesus prophesied that His followers would be persecuted because of Him. What was happening at school was not somebody who held to radical beliefs which deviated from the norm but that I was a light to my peers, my peers were in darkness and Satan wanted to keep them that way. Since I had come along and stood up for the Saviour, Satan was not going to stand idly by and let me convert any of these sinners to salvation. Satan was going to make me pay by being scorned and persecuted. I would have to be really convinced of my beliefs to stand up against such opposition.

When I look back at it now, a lot of sadness weighs in my heart when I think about school. There are no fond memories to look back on and it is as if my entire youth has been stolen from me. My faith estranged me from my peers and I did not make any close friendships that would last after I had left school like friends of mine today tell me. But this was the price for being a Christian, although what I was later to realise, this was the price for being different, for not being a part of the norm.

Being a Christian was bad enough but it would have been nightmarish if my peers had known that I was gay. This really was my salvation at school because my religious beliefs gave me a plausible excuse as to why I didn't talk about women or appear to have any interest in sex. A plausible reason for those around me but that did not satisfy me within myself.

While my male friends and peers at the time showed more and more interest in women, I noticed that these same sexual feelings in me were directed towards men. Still the thought remained that this was only a phase I was going through. I recollected that at the age of about eleven or twelve, my friends were interested in their own anatomy but had seemed to have grown out of this interest and now they wanted to discover the opposite sex. They had passed out of this phase and so I reasoned that I was just a slow developer. But there were two occasions that really brought it home to me loud and strong that my sexuality, directed towards my own gender, was here to stay.

Because my peers thought I held to weird beliefs, I did not make any close friends and so, at recess and lunchtime, as soon as I had finished eating, I went to the library to read. This was my refuge from the cruel world we call school and books became my best friends.

One lunchtime I was making my way to my sol- ace from the crowd when I passed Troy and his friends in a group staring across the playground pointing and laughing. I didn't take much notice as I walked past but then Warren grabbed me by the arm.

"You're an expert, Farril," he said with a sinister look on his face.

"Yeah, Farril. We need an expert opinion," Troy followed through. "We're looking at the girls over on the girls' lawn and we want to know which ones you think have the best tits."

All Troy's mates were in stitches because they knew my stance regarding sex.

Just at that moment, the new English teacher appeared on the playground over in the distance. She was a young, blond woman and the boys thought she was something else. The sounds they made, fortunately well out of her earshot, left no doubts about what they thought of her.

But Troy did a very peculiar thing. He came and stood very close behind me and held me strongly by the shoulders, almost as if he were about to massage me.

"Now, look at the tits on that! I bet you'd love to be sucking on those nipples!" he half whispered in my ear and then began to explain to me what sexually explicit things I could be doing with her naked in bed. But as he spoke about the female anatomy, it made my skin crawl. The idea of breasts and vagina did not appeal to me at all. But as he explained what she could do to me, the description of the male body was exciting, invigorating. The whole scenario, Troy standing behind me, feeling his warm body, his hands touching me although quite roughly, talking about explicit sexual acts, all these things aroused me sexually. But it troubled me, also. A well of fear surged up in my body and I just burst out of his grip. As I stormed off, Troy yelled at me, "Hey, Farril! You're lusting! You'd better pray to God for forgiveness!"

This event troubled me greatly for the rest of the day and every time I saw Troy, I couldn't look at him in the face. There was something strangely wrong with what aroused me sexually, and Troy was the one who had caused it and it was as if Troy were a part of it.

Not long after this event, during one of our after dinner Bible Studies, we began reading Paul's letter to the Romans. The first chapter began with Paul's salutation to the Christians living in Rome, followed by praise to God and the Lord Jesus for the Roman Christians' conversion to the new faith. As the chapter unfolded, Paul began talking about those people who no longer worship the true God but turn away to worship created beings in the form of idols. But the concluding verses were to have the greatest impact on me where it was written:

> *For this cause God gave them up unto vile affections:*
> *for even their women did change the natural use into*
> *that which is against nature:*
> *And likewise also the men, leaving the natural use of*
> *the woman, burned in their lust one toward another; men*
> *with men working that which is unseemly, and receiving*
> *in themselves that recompense of their error which was*
> *meet.*
> *And even as they did not like to retain God in their*
> *knowledge, God gave them over to a reprobate mind,*
> *to do those things which are not convenient;*
> *Being filled with all unrighteousness, fornication,*
> *wickedness, covetousness, maliciousness; full of envy,*
> *murder, debate, deceit, malignity; whisperers,*
> *Backbiters, haters of God, despiteful, proud, boasters,*
> *inventors of evil things, disobedient to parents,*
> *Without understanding, covenantbreakers, without natural*
> *affection, implacable, unmerciful*

At first I did not pay attention to what had just been read because the King James Version was rather obscure – well, to me anyway. But to Mum and Dad, it was as clear as polished glass.

"So, *that's* why men and women become homosexuals!" my father said with confident delight. When he said that, I felt a cold chill run up my spine as I zeroed back onto the Scriptures while my father reread the passage aloud.

Here my father expounded that the Scriptures explained the origin of homosexuality and it confirmed his abhorrent feelings towards these despicable perverts. Homosexuals become that way, he explained, because they turn away from the Lord Jesus Christ and so God changes their natural attraction for the opposite sex to their own. But He doesn't stop here. Not only does He distort their sexual orientation contrary to nature, He distorts their entire sense of morality and code of ethics so that not only are their sexual acts loathsome, so is their character, to the extent that they become dirty, horrible, nasty, cruel, vile and despicable little creatures. And once God has done this to them, they are finished. Salvation is no longer for them but their life becomes just a matter of killing time until they are finally condemned in the next life.

I could almost feel my parents salivating as they related how homosexuals were doomed to hell. It was the first time I felt bitter hatred coming from those who believed that "he that loveth not knoweth not God: for God is love."

But I was terrified. While my parents thought they had stumbled across a new revelation, to me I had read the most dreadful curse against my very person from a book I had been brought up to love and cherish. I remember my sister, Karen, saying outrightly, "I couldn't imagine having sex with a woman! How disgusting!" I knew I shared my sister's sentiments, and yet she was blessed for hers and I was cursed for mine.

But I strove on, thinking that these feelings that lurked within me were not real, that it was impossible for me to love men like I was supposed to love women. It was only an illusion. There was an explanation.

But once again at school, Troy was there to poke a stick into my emotional beehive. There was another time when Troy and his mates hunted me down in the playground before I had a chance to escape to my bibliatic world. When they found me, they all stood around me like a pack of wolves around their prey. Troy stood in front of me in his intimidating manner and smiled. With that, he threw a pornographic magazine on my lap and told me he had bought it for me.

When I looked down, I saw the photograph of a naked woman sensually posed over a bed with her finger lustily sticking in her mouth. I looked at the woman and was instantly overcome by a sickening feeling of repugnance, at the same time afraid that I would be in big trouble for looking at pornographic material on the school premises, so I flung the magazine back at Troy.

Troy picked up the magazine, flicked through some pages and then placed the magazine back on my lap, saying, "We even got a picture of you with her!"

This time, the photograph included a naked man in as just a sensual pose as the woman. As I looked at the man's body, I became sexually aroused to the extent that I wished the woman were not in the picture. I examined the man's body from top to bottom, his thin waist, his muscular arms and his broad shoulders. All these facets sent signals to my brain to begin secreting hormones. Troy broke out in cruel laughter while I tossed the magazine at him and took off.

You can't imagine how that event affected me. It was just so obvious that men appealed to me and women did not. But I couldn't admit this to myself, I just couldn't. I didn't want to be a poofter, I did not want to be cursed. I did not want to be a nasty, horrible, loathsome creature that the book I loved and cherished condemned me to be because of my sexual orientation.

And the Bible had only complicated the issue for it said that I was like this because I had turned away from God and worshipped created beings. But when? I cast my mind back into my infancy but could not find a time when I did not love the Lord Jesus Christ nor cherish His holy Word. So it had to have been in my earlier childhood, earlier than I could remember when I worshipped created beings and rejected the true God.

But that didn't make sense either. The Bible also said that once God gave me these desires, I would no longer want to believe nor worship Him but instead would want to worship idols and yet I loved Him all the more. What was wrong with me?

It didn't make sense. I was confused and lost. And since we had read Romans chapter one, I knew I couldn't discuss my feelings with my parents. What were they going to conclude seeing they believed that the Bible was true and that they had never been confronted with what it was like to have sexual feelings for the same sex? Listening to the way they expressed their vengeful glee about the plight of the homosexual made it obvious that I could not turn to them for help. Nor could I talk to our pastor because no doubt he knew what the Bible said about homosexuality and he no doubt had the same feelings towards it as my parents did. And from the attitude often expressed by those around me at school, I knew that none of my teachers could be approached because even society hated it. I had nowhere to turn. I felt I had been unjustifiably cursed and I hated myself for it.

There had to be an answer and a cure since the whole world around me convinced me that it was a disease. I prayed to God to change me. God was full of love and compassion and, because He was all-powerful, He could change me. I thought that it was a curse for not doing enough for Him and hence I was resolved to completely dedicate my every moment to Him.

That was the only answer I had to content myself. After all, the Bible could not be wrong for it was inspired by a perfect God and therefore made no mistakes nor did it contradict itself.

Chapter 3

"Good morning! Isn't it wonderful to be here with the Lord on this glorious day!" This was always Mr Smithton's introduction to what we called the Announcements. This was a period of time just after the first hymn was sung in which the church was notified of different events that were to take place in the upcoming week. Usually it was to remind the congregation of what Bible Studies we could attend at various homes, who was getting engaged or married, death notices and so on, like a verbal bulletin board for the congregation.

This particular morning, Mr Smithton included in his announcements a voting sheet that the congregation could collect at the end of the service in order to elect elders and deacons of the church.

But the word "deacon" troubled me. I had never heard the word before. To me it sounded like the word "beacon" and every time he used the word, I visualised a lighthouse beaming its lights across the sea. Why did someone want to become a beacon?

And what was an elder? At school we were taught about tribal cultures where the elderly group of men and women passed on their experience to and were respected by the younger generation. Did they still exist in the church, in a religious institution which had progressed out of the jungle?

That evening at the end of our after dinner family Bible Study, I noticed my father had the voting sheet in his Bible and the lighthouse image instantly appeared in my mind. So I asked him what a deacon was.

"Oh, let's see. I've read about deacons in the Bible," my father answered and flicked through the pages of his Bible until he came to the passage in I Timothy 3: 8 - 12 which he then read out aloud. But the passage only listed the requirements that must be proved in a man before he took up the office and not what the position actually entailed. My father tried to use the cross reference in his Bible to find a portion of Scripture which most fully explained this position in the church but in vain.

"To be honest with you, son, I don't know. But I'll speak to Mr Norman about it next Sunday at church."

After saying this, I happened to look down at the voting sheet and see the names of the candidates for this position.

"Dad, how come Trevor Buchanon is listed on the voting sheet?" I asked.

"Well," my father replied, "I'd say that he feels led by the Lord to fill this role. He's a good Christian and a very fine young man. I suppose Mr Norman thought he would be a very suitable candidate."

"But, he's not married," I replied.

"What's wrong with that?" my father asked.

"In the Scripture you just quoted, it says, 'Let the deacons be the husbands of one wife, ruling their children and their own houses well'. The Scriptures say that one of the prerequisites for becoming a deacon is that deacons must be married and have children."

My father could only agree. And from the list of candidates, only one man was married with children.

And so it was with the list of elders. Some men on the voting sheet were married but did not have children and there were some men who were single, and yet when Paul wrote his epistles to Timothy and Titus, he told them to appoint elders in every church, and one of the prerequisites for becoming an elder was that the elders had to be married and have children.

It was agreed that maybe Mr Norman had overlooked this portion of Scripture. After all, we believed that although he was the minister of the church, he was not infallible, and that he was capable of making mistakes like everyone else.

My father eventually spoke with Mr Norman and after their discussion I was expecting my father to say that Mr Norman was indeed mistaken and would make the appropriate amendments. But my father did not have the same full-of-the-Holy-Spirit look on his face when he explained to the family what he had discovered.

How deaconship arose in the church, so Mr Norman explained to my father, was to be found in Acts chapter six. This portion of Scripture recounts a story of how, in the newly formed church after the resurrection, an argument broke out between what the King James Version describes as the "Grecians" and the "Hebrews". What I understood this to mean was that the Grecians were Jews who lived outside of Israel and therefore only spoke the *lingua franca* of the time, that is, Greek, whereas the Hebrews were Jews who lived in Judea and could still speak Hebrew, the language of the Old Testament. The Grecians complained against the Hebrews because the money that was collected from the congregations was given only to the Hebrew widows and the Grecian widows didn't get anything.

The Twelve Apostles explained that their function was to preach the Word and so they did not have time to worry about the monetary affairs of the church. This was to be the responsibility of other people. So, seven men were chosen to look after the distribution of the money in order to allow the apostles to freely dedicate themselves wholly to the gospel. These seven men, among whom was St Stephen, the first Christian Martyr, were the first deacons in the New Testament church.

To bring the meaning out, Mr Norman explained that in this passage of Acts, the words *diakonia* and *diakonein* were used in the original Greek which were translated in the King James Version as "ministration" and "serve" respectively. The term *diakonos* was the Greek word that was translated as "deacon" in I Timothy. The word *diakonos* in Greek literally means "servant", but in its anglicised form, it refers to a specific function in the church. All these words in Greek, *diakonia, diakonein* and *diakonos*, were related and had something to do with service and serving. This led to the conclusion that there were specially elected servants, *deacons*, who were appointed in the church to look after the monetary affairs where-ever churches were established.

This was a beautiful and new revelation from the Bible but it was obvious that my father was not ecstatic about this revelation, but rather troubled.

"However," my father continued, "Mr Norman said that the prerequisite for a deacon and an elder to be married and have children before taking up this office only applied to the time that Paul wrote to Timothy and Titus."

"But the Bible applies to us today just as much as then!" my mother exclaimed. It was the first time I had ever heard my mother express a strong opinion about the Bible or any other religious matter.

My father related how he had argued that this is what the Bible says and that the Bible applies to all of us in all times, not just at the time the New Testament was written. But Mr Norman replied that these letters were written to prevent polygamists, who were apparently quite common at that time, from becoming deacons and elders. This was why Paul had said that they must be the husband of *one* wife and not the husband of *a* wife.

My mother went into a fury. To her and to all of us it was clear that the Bible said that an elder and a deacon had to be a married man and that a single man did not fulfil this requirement. My mother could not understand what Mr Norman was on about. This man, who with great fervour told us that "if the Bible says it, I obey it", was now trying to side step a commandment of God.

But my father really put a cat among the pigeons when he related how Mr Norman said that women could also become deacons. My mother was livid! How dare the minister of the church even allow the thought of a woman taking on the function of a deacon.

But my father explained that it was in the Bible. He told us to read Romans 16:1 where it said, "I commend unto you Phebe our sister, which is a servant of the church which is in Cenchrea".

"Where on earth does it say that a woman can be a deacon in that verse?" my mother cried.

"Phebe was a woman," my father went on to explain, "and here Paul addresses her as a deaconess. The word *servant* in this verse is translated from the Greek word *diakonae*, which is the feminine form of *diakonos*, and could just as equally be translated as *deaconess*. Mr Norman explained that she was specially mentioned here as a servant of Christ when there were no doubt many other servants of Christ in Cenchrea and hence Paul must have been using the term in a more specific sense than what is translated. Mr Norman explained that she was not married which explains that deacons and deaconesses do not have to be married to take up this office."

"Really! And if a woman can be a deacon, why does Paul say that a deacon must be the husband of one wife? If a woman can be a deaconess, then she has to be a lesbian! And anyway, how does Mr Norman know that Phebe was a single woman? This man is supposed to be the leader of the church, teaching us to obey the Bible, and now he's reading things in and out of it. And so what if the Greek says it differently? We speak English, not Greek!"

This was extremely interesting to my ears because I had always believed that the Bible was originally written in English. I had always imagined the day Adam and Eve sinned, God escorted them to the gate where the angels were standing holding the flaming swords. God then told these first humans that, now that they had sinned, they could only communicate with Him through His Word. God then handed them a Bible written in King James English, bound in black leather, with all the chapter and verse arrangements, and sent them on their way. But throughout this discourse, I heard my father refer to the Greek language to embellish the argument.

"Dad, why did Mr Norman refer to the Greek language? Isn't the Bible written in English?" I asked.

"Yes, son, it is now. However, the Bible was originally written in Greek but has now been translated into all the languages of the world. In Judea, at the time of Jesus, everyone spoke Greek like we speak English today, and so the Bible was originally written in Greek. If Jesus had died in Australia, the apostles would have written the Bible in English."

This was absolutely amazing stuff. The Bible was originally written in another language. I asked my parents why, then, Christians didn't learn Greek and read the Bible in its original language, seeing the Holy Spirit wrote through the authors in the Greek tongue but nowhere in the Scriptures do we read that a translation was made under the guidance of the Holy Ghost. And this night's discussion proved this.

By knowing the Greek language, the relationship between the words *serve, ministration* and *deacon* were
obvious, but in English were not. But also, the word
diakonae in Greek had two meanings, and to choose
between the English translation of *servant* and *deaconess* was left up to the translator who may be, in fact,
leading us in error, preventing women from becoming deaconesses unjustly because the English word
servant does not encompass the same sphere of meaning as the Greek word *diakonae.*

My parents did not agree but maintained that the
English was just as inspired as the Greek. But I was
not convinced and so I decided to learn the Greek.

Some years after this event, particularly when I
had learned the Greek, I was more convinced that
learning Koine Greek - that is, the version of classical
Greek in which the New Testament was written -
should be an obligation for all Christians. All Jews
learn Hebrew and all Muslims learn Arabic which is
something that unites them as a whole and which fa-
cilitates communication between them. This also
eliminates the need for revised translations, an issue
which still creates problems among modern Christians as the traditionalists still hold tenaciously to the
King James Version, written in the English of 1611,
while others prefer more up-to-date versions such as
the Good News for Modern Man, the Living Bible,
the New American Standard Bible or the New Inter-
national Version, all in modern English but none of
them authoritative, only creating more confusion and
arguments because sometimes one verse is translated

slightly differently when compared with the other versions.

But I had another strong reason why I wanted to learn the Greek and no-one was going to keep me from it. After all, there was a strong possibility that Romans chapter one was mistranslated.

But this wasn't the only time that my parents and our minister failed to agree where the Bible was concerned. There was another time when we were studying St Paul's letter to the Corinthians during our family Bible Study when we arrived at I Corinthians chapter eleven.

In this chapter, Paul says that when a woman prays or prophesies she should wear some sort of head covering. It wasn't specified what type of covering it was but I guess from the context of the time and area, it was like the veils that Middle Eastern women wear today. The reasoning behind this practice is that, when a woman wears a covering on her head when she prays or prophesies, she shows that she is in subjection to the man, who is imperfect, whereas the man should not wear a head covering because he is subject to Christ, who is perfect. My mother recalled that in her childhood, a woman was forbidden to darken the door of a church if she did not wear a hat. She had thought that this was some sort of silly tradition but now realised that this was a commandment by God to all women because it said so in the Bible.

Not long after that, we arrived at I Corinthians 14. The bulk of the chapter was talking about the spiritual gift of tongues but it was verse thirty-four which stood out to us where it said:

Let your women keep silence in the churches: for it is not permitted unto them to speak; but they are commanded to be under obedience

At that time, women played a minor role in our church as there were no women preachers, women didn't preside over communion nor did they act as helpers to hand around the bread, wine and the collection plate. There were times when women did speak in church on special occasions though this was mainly to announce events that were happening during the week which really involved only the women. But now we were reading that, according to God, in church, women had to shut up! Mind you, we never resolved the issue even within our family if this meant that women were not allowed to sing the hymns during the church service!

It makes me laugh now at the stupidity of what occurred the following Sunday but it was no joke at the time. My mother had never been a hat wearer so she had to buy one the Saturday before. I'll never forget it! It was a big, pink, wide rimmed hat and when she wore it, it made her look like a lampshade gone wrong. But my mother didn't care. She was not there to make a fashion statement, she was declaring before all the church her obedience to God.

We arrived at the church and everyone stared at my mother as we entered. I mean, how could she have slipped in unnoticed wearing this outrageous headgear! Everything during the church service was going as normal until Mr Norman invited Miss Dempsy to make some announcements about up-coming women's meetings.

Miss Dempsy was a fat lady and always dressed up like a peacock. She loved to talk and made a simple announcement a major opportunity to give a great oration. She waddled up to the lectern, turned to the congregation and, in her loud, megaphonic voice, spoke at length about very little.

But while she spoke, my attention was diverted because from the corner of my eye I could see my mother's foot twitching furiously, building up tempo from *moderato* to *allegro non troppo* whenever Miss Dempsy emphasised a word in her dulcet tones. I tilted my head slightly just enough to see my mother's stone cold glare looking down at the floor and I could imagine what she was thinking: Miss Dempsy is sinning because the Bible says that women are not permitted to speak in church.

Finally, when Miss Dempsy had finished, she waddled back down the aisle and sat down with a humph in her pew. My mother felt as if she could look up again and I sighed with silent relief.

After the church service, we were all standing outside talking but those around us stared at the hat without saying a word. Something in their reaction made me sense that these people understood the real reason my mother was wearing the hat. It was writ-ten all over their faces. And when they spoke to my mother, their eyes darted up and down, trying not to look at the hat and yet having to but never daring to make a comment.

It was only Mrs Norman, the minister's wife, who had the courage to mention it.

"Hello, Mrs Farril," she said by way of introduction and entered into some petty conversation until she was able to address the issue that was foremost on her mind.

"I must say, you have a lovely hat on, but why on earth do you want to hide your pretty face?" she asked.

"Because the Bible says women should wear a covering in church," my mother replied very matter-of-factly. But Mrs Norman didn't like the answer and did not need to ask my mother where it said so in the Bible.

"But a woman's long hair is her covering," she snapped.

That was a stupid thing for Mrs Norman to say because her hair was short and fashionable and so she left herself wide open.

"Then, you'd better let your hair grow or wear a hat!" my mother replied.

Suddenly a big tennis match of words began and attracted all the onlookers.

"Paul was only telling the Corinthian women to wear a head covering when he wrote that!" Mrs Norman threw back.

My mother looked at the crowd and then back at Mrs Norman.

"Then salvation was only for the Corinthians also?"

Wow! What a backhand!

Mr Norman was close by and saw that his wife was in trouble and so he came to her rescue.

"Mrs Farril," he said as he approached the two ladies in combat. "You're not saying that because Paul told the Corinthian church that women should wear a covering that it applies today?"

My mother looked Mr Norman straight in the eye.

"So, it's not relevant today?"

"Mrs Farril, you have to understand the context in which Paul was speaking when he wrote that. At that time, it was a custom for women to wear a veil in church but we don't observe this practice today because it is irrelevant. Paul never told the women of other churches to do the same so he was only speaking to the Corinthian church."

My mother just stood and twiddled her fingers in an agitated manner. But now it was my father's turn to speak.

"So, what Paul wrote to the Corinthian church regarding salvation through Christ is irrelevant also?"

"Well, no," Mr Norman said with a sheepish laugh. "Salvation through Christ is a universal thing which transcends all time. But the wearing of a veil or a hat or any sort of covering is irrelevant. It doesn't take away from the gospel of salvation or the teachings of love. The whole reason why Jesus Christ came to earth was to set us free from rules and regulations. All we need now is to believe in Him and we are saved. You're starting to introduce rules into the church which have no meaning or relevance to the gospel of salvation and which will not change it in any way. I suppose you mean to say that women are to be silent in church as well."

"No," my father replied, "we don't but the Bible does, and we believe the Bible is the Word of God. Don't you? Aren't you the one who tells us each Sunday, 'If the Bible says it, I obey it'?"

Mr Norman shuffled his feet a bit as a murmur passed through the crowd.

"Again, Mr and Mrs Farril, you have to understand the culture of the day. The women and men at the time sat in separate parts of the church. Sometimes the minister would say something and the women would call across the room to ask what it meant. It made the church a shemozzle and so Paul told the Corinthian women to remain silent and to ask their husbands at home. But today it's different."

"So it's not relevant today, even though the Bible says so, and even though Paul does not say that this only applies to a particular church and a particular time?" my mother asked.

"Mrs Farril, you do not understand the context in which Paul was saying this. You're being too legalistic and saying that we must abide by the Bible to the letter. But we are free from legalism. The Pharisees were caught up in legalism before Jesus came, introducing laws and doctrines which governed every aspect of their lives. But we are free in Christ. Paul wrote explicitly to the Galatian church to tell them exactly that. But Paul went further by saying in Galatians 3:28 that there is now neither male nor female in

Christ. So, if the Bible tells us that there is neither male nor female in Christ, how can there be one rule for men and another for women?"

My parents glared at Mr Norman for a few moments and the crowd stood in suspense, waiting for a rebuttal. There was a moment of silence before my father spoke.

"So, if this is not relevant, where do we stop? Does this mean I am free, now, to commit adultery, to rob, to murder, to cheat? Are we now free to do these things also?" my father more stated than asked.

"Mr Farril, that's another matter altogether. The Bible is clear in saying that these are wrong."

"But how do you know that you're not being legalistic, accepting these are wrong because the Bible says they are wrong just like we are saying that women speaking in church and not wearing a head covering in church are wrong because the Bible says so? And how do you know that lying, murder, cheating and the like were only wrong to the churches to whom Paul wrote but the wrongness of these actions is no longer relevant to us today?"

The whole crowd waited pensively for Mr Norman's reply. First he coughed, then bounced on his heels, smiled strangely and finally said, "Mr and Mrs Farril, like I said, you have to understand the context in which Paul was writing. But a woman not speaking in church or wearing a covering is no longer relevant."

After saying this, my mother grabbed her handbag and pulled out a pen. She then snatched Mr Norman's Bible from his hand, turned the pages to I

Corinthians 11, drew a big line through the chapter and then handed back his Bible.

There was a communal gasp of horror from the crowd. Mr Norman's face went red and he cried, "How dare you!"

"Well, it's no longer relevant," my mother said coldly and calmly. Then she turned around and left.

It was amazing what effect this event had on the rest of the congregation. The following week, about half of the women came to church wearing a hat!

To this day, my parents still maintain that if a woman does not wear a covering to church, she is disobeying God. And if she continues to disobey God, she will go to hell. This is because the Bible says in Hebrews 10:26, 27

> For if we sin wilfully after that we have received the
> knowledge of the truth, there remaineth no more
> sacrifice for sins,
> But a certain fearful looking for of judgement and
> fiery indignation, which shall devour the adversaries

And if a woman is shown the Scripture in I Corinthians 11 but still continues to attend church uncovered, she will go to hell because she is refusing to wear a covering wilfully!

I can see it now! Fires are burning, people are screaming in pain in the depths of hell and a group forms to discuss their lives on earth. A group of thugs in studded leather and sordid women in fishnet stockings are talking, asking each other why they are there. Each tells of their sinful deeds, rape, mass murder, molestation, theft, and there is lady in a faded Sunday dress which is singed from the fires, bowing her head in shame.

"And what're you in here for, lady?" asks one of the thugs.

"Well," she sobs, "I didn't wear a hat to church."

These events created a real dichotomy. On the one hand, Mr Norman was telling us to obey the commandments in the Bible because these were the commandments of God but, on the other hand, telling us that certain commandments were irrelevant for Christians today. I could understand his point about the irrelevancy of veils and of women speaking in church because these things did not say anything about a person's character nor did they have an effect on other people. This, then, made me ask the question: if the Bible says that homosexuality is a sin, in which category does this sin lie, among the now irrelevant sins or the sins that are still relevant today? And then I thought further: who decides which commandments are no longer relevant and which ones still apply?

But my parents' belief in obeying everything in the Bible to the letter held sway in my thinking because this approach to the Bible was the most logical if I were to be a Bible-believing Christian. If the Bible was inspired by God, then everything written in it had to be obeyed irrespective of whether or not we thought particular commandments suited us because these commandments were decreed by the ultimate authority of the universe. And this divine authority was omniscient and eternal, which meant that His decrees were relevant at all times. After all, God was unchangeable and so it followed that His decrees were also unchangeable. This further meant that, if people were allowed to decide which command-ments they would follow and which they felt were no longer applicable, every one of us was then at lib-erty to choose those commandments we wished to observe and those we were happy to ignore. This would then mean that there would be no reason to follow any of the commandments in the Bible, to the point that there would be no need for the Bible at all in our lives.

When I see Christians today claiming that we must obey the Bible no matter what, I am always re-minded of the above event, and other command-ments in the Bible, such as Jesus' commandment in Luke 14:12 - 14 where He says

> *When thou makest a dinner or a supper, call not thy friends, nor thy brethren, neither thy kinsmen, nor thy rich neighbours; lest they also bid thee again, and a recompense be made thee.*
> *But when thou makest a feast, call the poor, the maimed, the lame, the blind:*
> *And thou shalt be blessed*

for Christians have friends and family over for din-ner despite what Jesus commands against this. I've never heard of a Christian organisation which tries to help people dealing with the problem of having their friends and relatives for meals and not the physically disadvantaged.

And in Matthew 6:6 where Jesus says

But thou, when thou prayest, enter into thy closet, and
when thou hast shut thy door, pray to thy Father which
is in secret

To follow this commandment, the benediction and other prayers made in church would have to stop because Jesus commands against open prayer. Again, there is no political party trying to vilify the rights of those who refuse to pray in the closet, those who want to come out in the open and be free to do so with pride.

But these are not the only issues that were argued within our church. Time would fail me to relate of all the arguments that Christians get knotted over, such things as whether baptism is essential for salvation or not, whether it is sinful to drink alcohol or not, are women allowed to wear jewellery, can a man grow his hair long, when Christians fast, does it mean that they don't eat anything at all or just certain foods, must we understand the six days of Creation literally or can we interpret them as six thousand years and marry the belief of evolution into it, will the world be made a peaceful paradise a thousand years before Christ returns or will Christ return first and so on and so on and so on.

For years I agonised over many of these issues myself because the Bible writers themselves did not agree on these issues - until I realised that these contradictions showed the humanness of the Bible.

Chapter 4

The rest of my time in the junior years passed as non-eventful and I really don't have many memories of this time. I can't even remember what I did during the holidays that separated Year 10 from Year 11. The whole period has been swallowed up with time.

But starting Year 11 began a new phase in my life. It was the beginning of my final two years where I would attempt to achieve the highest mark possible in the final exam, the Higher School Certificate. This exam was the most important exam that I would face because it would determine the destiny of my future career.

Beginning these final two years created a transformation in my life and the life of my peers. We were elevated in status because we had a section of the school dedicated to us away from the rest of the junior students, a section that was better kept, had park benches, trees and a well kept lawn. Our uniform was different also: boys now wore a white shirt and not blue as before, girls wore a light blue uniform and not the chequered outfit of the juniors. There was even a Seniors' Room, a special room for us in which we could hang out at recess and lunchtime.

This transformation from the junior to the senior years brought about some dramatic changes in the last leg of our adolescence. We felt older, more mature and better respected. It did not feel like eight weeks had passed since we had left school the year previous, it felt more like an eternity. The juniors seemed so much younger in comparison, the gap was so vast. It was as if we had blossomed out of a cocoon to begin a new development of our person.

During the junior years, I had made no close friends and so the first day back left me a little lost because I didn't know anyone well. But within a couple of weeks, I managed to get mixed up with a group of ten students. They were a great bunch of students and surprisingly tolerant. I had known them in the junior years but now they seemed different, older, wiser, more mature and more accepting.

Our group sat on a couple of benches that we squeezed together. We laughed, joked and had a great time. Another group formed not very far from us, Troy and his entourage being a part, but their group required four benches to seat everyone comfortably. However, there were only five benches on the seniors' lawn. So, whenever the recess or lunch bell rang, whoever was the first in either group to get to the seniors' lawn grabbed as many benches as was required for the group and clung to them with all their might until the rest of the group arrived. Oh, there were tug-o-war matches over the benches until the strongest won the bench and it was hilarious fun to watch or be a part of the battle. There were some very imaginable means of keeping all the benches in one group together that we were often in stitches of laughter.

But studying for the HSC exam itself was the most trying time of my school life, probably because so much hinged on the final aggregate. In my junior years, I studied for about one or two hours an evening maximum, but during the HSC period, I was up to all hours trying to keep abreast of homework, assignments and study. The relief, then, at recess and lunchtime of laughter, joking, talking and philosophising that my friends and I involved ourselves in was just priceless.

But my Christianity had to spoil it. At home a new fervour had developed from a result of our study of the Bible – the Second Coming of Christ. We were continually bombarded with the imminence of Christ's return and the need to keep preaching to the unbelievers until they were saved. Christ's return, so we were told and shown from the Scriptures, would be heralded by increasing natural cataclysms such as earthquakes, plagues and famine, an increase in human unrest leading to more and more wars, and the increase of false prophets and of people falsely saying that they were the long awaited Christ. These were occurring at this time which meant that the return of Christ was near.

Although we were waiting for Christ to return, we believed that even before His second coming, a miraculous event would occur called the Rapture. This was described as a moment in time when all the true Christians would be suddenly and mysteriously removed from the earth in a moment. This meant that, one day, the world would wake up and suddenly find the global population dramatically and inexplicably reduced. Millions upon millions of people would have simply vanished without a trace.

We believed that God would do this because He did not want His people to endure the last seven years of earth's history, called the Tribulation. These last seven years were so named because the Tribulation would be the worst period of time that the inhabitants of earth would have ever endured since the time the earth came into existence. During the Tribulation, Satan, in the form of a man, would take complete control of the world, demanding everyone to wear his mark on their palm or forehead, the number 666. Satan, who would be called the Beast in his human form, would finally muster up an entire army from all the world to fight the returning Christ at Mt Megiddo in Israel, or *Ar Mageddon*, as it is in Hebrew, and be destroyed by the brightness of His coming, to be resurrected and stand before the Lord at the Last Judgement, where the eternal rewards would finally be distributed. Because the signs of the times indicated that the Lord would return at any moment, it was urged that we try to save as many souls as possible, preaching the Word despite what opposition lay before us, to defeat Satan at his game.

It is difficult to remember the names of all the people in our group and what they looked like. I remember a girl called Sally. She was as rough as guts and her language was as course as P36 sandpaper. But she was very likable, with a bubbly personality and was a lot of fun. Sally sat next to me in my English class and she spent half the time in class scribbling on my notebook some really stupid and sometimes very obscene things. Although quite offensive to my pure Christian mind, I gained a secret pleasure from her attention which I consider today quite extraordinary considering my zealousness towards my faith.

Then there was Tony. I vaguely remember him as a sandy blond guy who had a quiet disposition. He was a serious student, quite smart, but not given very easily to joviality. He was excellent at the sciences and mathematics but was reluctant to help anyone who may have been able to benefit from his ability.

There was another guy, Darren, who I vaguely remember being tall with short, dark hair. From memory he was an excellent basketball player and had represented the school in a series of competitions. About the only other thing I recollect about him was that he was also in my physics and chemistry classes and I sat with him there.

Then there was Anne. She was a very small girl, so small that she earned herself the name Mouse, a name which she hated! She used to grow her hair out rather long which seemed to accentuate her shortness. What I do remember of her was that she was an excellent artist. I remember once that she did an assignment for art where she turned an ordinary piece of polyurethane foam into the shape of a man sitting down.

Then there was Kerry. How Kerry ever was a member of anyone's group is anyone's guess. She was tall and thin, with long flowing straight brown hair but with an awkward physique. She was extremely arrogant and opinionated although she could afford to be because she was one of the most intelligent students in the school. I don't know why she ever condescended to be amongst such average students that made up our group but in a strange sort of way, she ended up blending in and becoming a part of us.

I enjoyed this group of students. It was the first time that I felt that I fit in somewhere with a group of students and it brought out in me for the first time the desire to be social. I was finally part of a community and the library had since lost its appeal. It would have been better for me when I reflect back on that group if I had just remained a normal, teenage school kid. Really, I liked these people very much. I suppose this is what made the urgency to preach to them all the more pressing because I wanted this group to continue till the end of eternity.

I can almost remember distinctly how it all began as if I were still sitting there on the bench. There was one particular morning that Sally was late to join us at recess and she came bolting towards our group like a horse gone mad, bubbling with excitement. But as she approached our group, she tripped and in full velocity hurtled onto Tony's lap. Everyone just burst out laughing except Tony.

"Jesus Christ, Sally!" was Tony's only remark.

Sally clambered to her feet laughing but now I was angry.

"Tony, don't use the Lord's name in vain. It wasn't His fault."

Tony glared at me with daggers.

"Farril, why do you have to bring religion into everything? It's only a bloody word!"

"Then why don't you use one of the million other words in the English language? Why must you use this one?"

"Because I bloody want to!" Tony said angrily. "It's a free country!"

"But the Bible says - "

"I don't give a shit what the Bible says," Tony interrupted me.

Tony was now really angry with me.

"And who says the Bible is anything, anyway?" he asked.

"The Bible is everything! The Bible is the inspired Word of God," I replied proudly.

Everyone just rolled their eyes but then Darren took up the argument.

"Farril, you don't really believe that the Bible is infallible, do you?"

"Yes, I do," I replied confidently.

"But it was written by a bunch of men," Darren replied.

"It's true that men wrote it but it was really God writing through them."

"Oh, and says who?"

"The Bible!"

"Well, of course!" Darren said sarcastically. "But how do you know the Bible is the Word of God and not the Muslims' Holy Book or the Hindus'?"

"Because the Bible is," I replied, not able to understand why Darren could not accept such a simple fact of life.

"But how do you know that the Bible, the Muslims' Book and the Hindus' Book don't all say the same thing?"

"Because all the others contradict the Bible."

I said this with all authority when I had never read a word of the Koran nor the Vedic Scriptures. This was not just blind faith, this was stubborn closed-mindedness!

"But how do you know the Bible is right and the others wrong?"

"Because no other book talks about Jesus."

Darren humphed. I could tell he wanted to win the argument but I would not let him.

"But how do you know that Jesus is God?"

"Because the Bible says so!"

"But, Farril, you said that you know the Bible is true because it talks about Jesus but then you say that Jesus is God because the Bible says so. That's circular reasoning."

That hit me with a jolt but I didn't want to lose. Finally a solution came to mind.

"I believe by faith."

"C'mon, Farril," Darren said. "That's a cop out!"

"No, it's not. The Bible says in Hebrews 11:1 that 'Faith is the substance of things hoped for, the evidence of things not seen'. My faith is the evidence that the Bible is the Word of God."

At that moment, the bell went and we had to return to class. But Darren didn't say anymore and so I thought that I had won the argument and had convinced him of the truth. It never occurred to me that maybe he got tired of my narrow-minded responses which had no substance and so he had stopped asking questions to shut me up. But at the time, I felt proud of myself, knowing that up in heaven, Jesus was smiling over a job well done.

Then there was another occasion. This particular lunch period, the girls of our group were talking about the latest rock group, KISS. I remember many groups that were the rage whose music I never listened to at this stage because we were told that Satan was behind the music, feeding our brains with subliminal suggestions to take drugs, to be rebellious, to worship Satan.

As a digression, around this time, there was a major crusade where our church held a big bonfire and we threw all our secular music records and tape cassettes, playing cards, secular books and all sorts of trinkets that had been classified as evil, as we stood around singing praises to the Lord. Hence, all secular music became anathema to Christians. Throughout the eighties I did not listen to the radio to keep myself from being bewitched by Satan to turn away from the Lord.

On this particular day, Sally had brought along to school a magazine from her KISS fan club and the other girls were examining and talking about it. Soon everyone was involved and giving their feelings about certain of their songs. Suddenly, Sally dropped her magazine on the ground and I instinctively picked it up. But as I looked at a photo of the four singers in the group at some gig they were at, I was horrified at their painted faces and the evil aura that seemed to surround them.

"These are satanic!" I gasped.

Everyone began to laugh except Sally who got offended and snatched the magazine from my hand.

"Who cares what you think, anyway, Farril?" she snapped.

I didn't care that she was offended. She was in Satan's grip listening to this satanic music, worshiping the devil in the form of these four helpless individuals who had sold their souls to him. I felt that it was my duty to say something.

"They're satanic?" Darren said with half a laugh. "So, this is the devil's music?"

"Yes, it is," I said in all seriousness.

The whole group began telling me off as if I were an idiot and then they continued to look at the magazine.

"So, what music do you listen to?" Darren asked. "The hymns of Nat King Cole?"

Everyone started laughing while I sat there, except for one of the girls, a beautiful, red-haired girl, who was the quietest of us all. Her name was Ruth Carpenter and she seemed to smile with the rest of the group out of shyness. Something in her eyes told me that she smiled not because she saw the joke in Darren's comment but out of sympathy.

"He probably stands and sings while his mother plays hymns on the piano, enraptured by the music of God," Tony said and began to sing the hymn which begins with "Praise God from whom all blessings flow". When he had reached the third line, practically everyone in the group had joined in. I was overly surprised. This was a hymn that we often sang at church. When they had finished, to soften the embarrassment, I smiled and said, "Very good, choir! It's good to see that you're not irreligious after all."

"We're not irreligious, Farril," Darren said. "I go to church every Sunday but I'm not fanatical like you. I believe in Jesus so I'm going to heaven."

What? I thought. For all these years, I thought I was the only one who ever darkened the doors of a church or had anything to do with God because I was always made the laughing stock over my religion. But now these people around me were telling me that they go to church and believe in God - well, not everybody.

"I don't go to church because it's boring," Sally retorted. "You go and sit for an hour while you sing boring old songs from the Middle Ages and listen to some guy give a stuffy old boring sermon while it's sunny outside. I'd rather go to the beach. And it's such a waste of time when you can go away for the weekend."

"I go now and again because I believe God exists," Darren said. "It's not too bad and I have a lot of good friends there."

"Gee, I stopped going to church years ago. I believe in God but I don't have to go to church to prove anything," Tony said.

"Yes, I agree," I added. "Going to church makes you as much a Christian as going to a service station makes you a car."

Almost everyone agreed with this statement and it made me pleased that these people actually agreed with something I said on a religious topic. I felt, then, that this was an opportunity to lead the conversation to a point where all these wayward people could come back to the strait and narrow.

"Then, if you go to church, or at least believe in God, then you must believe in Jesus Christ dying for our sins and rising from the dead," I continued.

Again, almost everyone agreed whole-heartedly, except Sally who was preoccupied with her magazine and had switched off. This saddened me a bit but then the parable of the Sower came to mind. In this allegory, Jesus talks about a man who walks around his field sowing his seed, which was just a picturesque way of describing someone who walks around preaching the gospel. In the parable, it was inevitable that some of the seed fell on the wayside, that is, the pathway that separated two fields, which no doubt was often walked on and had become almost as compact as concrete. The seed, being clearly visible on this flat surface, was quickly taken up by the birds before ever having a chance to become a seedling. In the same way, I was preaching the gospel but the devil was taking these "seeds" away from Sally in her refusal to listen before she had a chance to process the information. But I continued with the rest of the group.

"Then you must agree that KISS or any rock band which does not glorify God in their singing is glorifying the devil and we should have nothing to do with them."

This was a logical conclusion for me but no-one saw my logic.

"Oh, Farril, don't be so dogmatic and fanatical. What's wrong with Rock 'n' Roll and rock bands? We enjoy it and it's not making us evil and worship the devil," Darren said and when he said "worship the devil" he snarled and pronged his fingers like a cat ready to strike.

"What do you think God wants us to do? Sit with our hands cupped together and sing hymns all the time and be bored?" and this time as he mentioned the cupped hands, he cupped his hands and sat in an angelic position looking up to heaven.

"No," I continued. "God doesn't want us to be bored. Being a Christian is not boring. But when we come to Jesus, Jesus expects us to want to glorify Him in everything we do, including the music we listen to. These rock bands aren't interested in God. They just want to glorify themselves and have us glorify them like gods when they are only men. Why do you think we call them Rock Idols if they are only people who want to entertain? We call them Rock Idols because they are idols that God told us not to worship. Satan has set them up to take away our minds from Christ and slowly and subtly lure us into his grip."

Darren haw hawed the idea.

"Oh, Farril, you're crazy and so fanatical. Go back to your hymns. You're living in the Dark Ages. I bet you believe that when you sneeze, the devil wants to take your soul and so you say 'God bless you'."

"No, that's not true," I said in defence. "God expects us to worship Him fully according to the Bible."

"Farril, drop the subject, will you?" Darren interjected without allowing me to finish my sentence. "You're a fanatic who wants to deprive people of life and fun with your crazy, stupid ideas. Why don't you just shut yourself away in the priesthood?"

I turned away frustrated but caught in the corner of my eye Ruth watching me intently. But when I turned to look at her, she turned away and looked at Sally's magazine with her.

Suddenly the bell went. Lunch was over and so we made our way back to class. I noticed that my friends kept a slight distance from me after a religious discussion which hurt but, true to the friends they were, as the afternoon rolled on, they were soon talking again to me as if we had just been having an argument to occupy the lunch break. Sally returned to her doodles in my notebook, Darren and Tony talked about the football and cricket. But Ruth, whom I knew the least in my group, stared at me across the classroom. But I only noticed it from the corner of my eye because each time I looked to see her staring, she looked away.

The evening after this event, during our family Bible Study after dinner, we began studying the second chapter of Paul's letter to the Ephesians. Although I had read this chapter many times before, on this night verses eight and nine struck a cord in my soul.

"Dad, here in this chapter, Paul writes that we are saved by faith only and not of works. Is this true?"

"Well, of course, son. No work we do will save us, only the faith that Jesus died for our sins and rose again from the dead. Why?"

"For the last number of years, practically everyone at school has made fun of me because of my faith. But today, I found out that some of my friends say that they are Christians. They say that they believe in God and Jesus and some of them go to church but at the same time they listen to satanic music, some of them swear and tell dirty jokes, and they make fun of me even though I believe basically the same thing. What Paul says in this chapter, therefore, means that they are still going to heaven."

My father gave me a condescending smile.

"Son, don't you remember what Jesus said in the Sermon on the Mount, in Matthew 7: 21? 'Not every one that saith unto me, Lord, Lord, shall enter into the kingdom of heaven; but he that doeth the will of my Father which is in heaven.' Jesus said that there would be many who would claim that they are Christians, even performing miracles in His name, but they won't make it to heaven because they don't do what Jesus says."

I pondered on this for a moment but I felt I was left in a little bit of confusion.

"If we don't keep the commandments of Jesus, we won't go to heaven?" I asked.

"Of course not," my mother piped up. "Jesus would not have given us the Bible if we didn't have to keep any commandments. But we have the Bible so we know what we are supposed to do."

I looked again at my father, then my mother, and then asked, "But doesn't it say here that we are saved by faith only?"

My parents looked at each other and my father answered the question with a bit of an embarrassed laugh.

"Yes, we are saved by faith but we show our faith by our works. James says in his epistle, 'For as the body without the spirit is dead, so faith without works is dead also'. So, we are saved by faith, but we show our faith by our works. If we do not do the works of God, we show that we have no faith in Him."

"Then, we're saved by works after all?"

"Are you saying the Bible is contradicting?" my mother said sternly.

"Hang on, dear. He's only asking a question," my father interrupted and then continued. "Yes, we are saved by faith but we show our faith by our works. Otherwise Christians could say, 'I believe Jesus died for my sins' but keep on sinning and still go to heaven while non-Christians would go to hell for committing the same acts. This isn't right, is it?"

"Then, what does Paul mean in Ephesians 2: 8, 9 when he says that we are saved by faith only and not by works?"

"He means that when we believe in Christ, we are saved at that very instant. But we show our faith by our works," my father replied, not really answering my question.

"Does this mean that even though my friends believe in Jesus, they are still going to hell?"

"We're not saying that, son," my mother said. "The Bible is. That's why Jesus told the parable of the Sower and the Seed. Remember how some seed fell on stony ground and for a while it grew but eventually withered away? Or the seed that fell among thorns and was choked by them and died? What Jesus is saying is that there will be some who become Christians but will not be able to cope with persecution like you receive at school or will be tempted by the world and then will stop believing and then die, that is, go to hell. Remember that Jesus said in Matthew 7: 13 and 14, 'Enter ye in at the strait gate: for wide is the gate, and broad is the way, that leadeth to destruction, and many there be which go in thereat: Because strait is the gate, and narrow is the way, which leadeth unto life, and few there be that find it.' Don't you see that what Jesus is saying is that the road of a Christian is tough? If all we had to do was believe we were saved by faith only and didn't have to keep any commandments, it would have been silly of Jesus to tell us that the road is strait and narrow, and everyone that says to Jesus, 'Lord, Lord' would enter into heaven irrespective of how they showed their faith in Him. Therefore, these friends who profess to be Christians aren't going to heaven because they are not observing the biblical commandments."

My mother raved on but I felt as if she were approaching the biblical texts with as much callousness as a science textbook describes how a nuclear bomb works and the scope of the damage without considering the emotional aspect of the involvement of people. To my mother, the people she was referring to were just nameless nobodies, a statistical mass, but to me they were a group of people whom I considered to be my friends.

When we had finished for the evening, I went to my room to study. But I couldn't study. There was something bothering me about that night's discussion which was causing a lot of confusion which I wanted clarified. I got my Bible out and plopped it on my desk. I began to ponder on what my parents and Mr Norman had preached to us, that 'all have sinned, and come short of the glory of God' (Romans 3:23), and 'there is none righteous, no, not one' (Romans 3:10) irrespective of whether we were Christian or not, which was why Jesus had to die for our sins.

But now I was listening to two conflicting views from the Bible, one that said we were saved by faith only, which made Christianity unique, and one that said we were saved by faith and works, which was like all the other religions. I thought if I examined the Bible in greater detail, it would resolve the confusion. I examined Paul's letters to the Romans and Ephesians, and compared these with James' general epistle.

Romans 4:1-5

What shall we say then that Abraham our father, as pertaining to the flesh, hath found?

For if Abraham were justified by works, he hath whereof to glory; but not before God

For what saith the scripture? Abraham believed God, and it was counted unto him for righteousness.

Now to him that worketh is the reward not reckoned of grace, but of debt.

But to him that worketh not, but believeth on him that justifieth the ungodly, his faith is counted for righteousness.

James 2:20 – 24

But wilt thou know, O vain man, that faith without works is dead?

Was not Abraham our father justified by works, when he had offered Isaac his son upon the altar?

Seest thou how faith wrought with his works, and by works was faith made perfect?

And the scripture was fulfilled which saith, Abraham believed God, and it was imputed unto him for righteousness: and he was called the Friend of God.

Ephesians 2:8, 9

For by grace are ye saved through faith; and that not of yourselves: it is the gift of God: Not of works, lest any man should boast.

Ye see then how that by works a man is justified, and not by faith only?

Romans 11:6

And if by grace, then is it no more of works: otherwise grace is no more grace. But if it be of works, then is it no more of grace: otherwise work is no more work.

James 2:26

For as the body without the spirit is dead, so faith without works is dead also.

I was completely horrified. Here were two passages of Scripture that were blatant contradictions and it was obvious that Paul and James did not see eye to eye on the same subject. Paul argued strongly that faith and works were two separate entities, the former by which we were saved, the latter having nothing to do with salvation. James, by contrast, argued that faith and works were so intricately bound together to the extent that it was foolish to separate them. But what horrified me the most was that both New Testament writers quoted Genesis 15:6 to back up their argument and yet both came to opposite conclusions.

I couldn't study for the rest of that evening. This was too traumatic an experience for me. But the only way to overcome the shock was to blame Satan. The warning had been given that Satan would try to make us question the validity of the Bible's claim to divinity and this was a major attack. So I just blocked the contradiction from my mind. Surely if I ignored it, it would just go away.

Chapter 5

Although our entire lives were based pretty much on the Bible and its teachings, my life was not completely monastic. Saturday nights were particularly entertaining at home and we usually passed the hours with a game of cards or Scrabble. Despite the crusade where we burnt everything that was considered satanic, my parents did not agree with Mr Norman that playing cards were of the devil. Therefore, our deck was spared and used Saturday evenings to play 500 or Euchre, my parents playing against my sister and me. As for Scrabble, I thought it was one of the most boring games ever invented and would have been delighted if it had been one of the evil objects on Pastor Norman's hit list during the bonfire. But my parents enjoyed playing the game and it at least brought us together.

These evenings were lubricated with wine or port, much to the chagrin of Mr Norman who viewed all alcoholic liquor as evil. His argument was that "Wine is a mocker, strong drink is raging" (Proverbs 20:1) which "biteth like a serpent, and stingeth like an adder" (Proverbs 23:32). My parents contrariwise argued that God made wine because it "maketh glad the heart of man" (Psalm 104:15) and that one of the first miracles of Jesus was to turn water into wine at the marriage of Cana as recorded in the second chapter of John's gospel. Also, Paul instructed Timothy to "drink no longer water, but use a little wine for thy stomach's sake and thine often infirmities" (I Timothy 5:23) which was an instruction not only to Timothy but to all Christians. Of course, my parents, not understanding the context of the times in which these portions of Scripture were written, were told by Mr Norman that the word "wine" used in Greek was in fact the unfermented juice of the vine, which was why we drank Valencio Grape Juice from Franklins to commemorate the blood of Christ at communion and not the real alcoholic stuff. Why, then, the study of alcoholic grape juice is called today oenology when it is the study of *oinos*, the Greek word for "wine", the same Greek word used in the New Testament when speaking of wine, Mr Norman was unable to furnish a convincing argument which supported his explanation. Nor could he prove satisfactorily that where the Bible spoke evil of wine, it was talking about the alcoholic variety, but when it spoke well, that it was merely grape juice. So once more there was yet another issue which further exacerbated the contention between our pastor and my parents.

Despite this family togetherness, my sister, Karen, always remained an illusive figure in my life, someone I never was really close to. We lived quite separate lives under the same roof, probably because of the large age difference between us. Probably also because we were the opposite sex and did not share the same interests, at least not anything that I could express openly!

Her wedding day was very troubling for me indeed. Although the marriage ceremony was filled with the usual pomp and fantasy, the reception was more earthy and familiar, and brought out strongly the disparity between what I felt within and how I was expected to feel without. Even though my sister is still quite an attractive woman, when the telegrams were read out in all their sordid imagery of the first night together, it was beyond my comprehension what excitement Peter, her husband, was going to get out of all this. But the way he drooled over the whole idea of breaking my sister's flower, as it was so delicately worded, made me realise that he seriously wanted to have my sister in a way that I could never want a woman. I could not understand Peter's feelings for Karen and it was a dreadful thought to know that this was expected of me in years to come, both from a Christian point of view and from society as a whole. Homosexuals could not fall in love and remain together with the one person all their lives because homosexuals were just sex machines, following an insatiable impulse without any regards to feelings of love, companionship and commitment for those they pursued.

But at that age, I had already begun to discover that this was not the case, for, although there were many boys at school, there was one guy in my grade whom I began to admire both with and beyond the sexual impulse. It became apparent to me one winter, that cold, dirgy, depressing time of the year. It was always so cold at school at this time of year and it seemed that I could never be warm enough in the draughty corridors and classrooms of our school. For a heater, we had large, metal box-like objects in each classroom which were only luke-warm to touch where we would huddle together to draw what little warmth we could get from them before having to return to our cold desks and chairs when the teacher arrived in class.

At the desk across from mine in my English class sat Troy Krisston. One morning he saw me shivering, despite the fact that I was wearing a jumper. Troy seemed insensitive to the cold and, when he saw me, he at first laughed, thinking I was putting on a show. When I told him that I wasn't, he took from his bag a coat and told me I could wear it since he didn't need it. You could have knocked me over with a feather. Troy hadn't stopped antagonising me over my faith, although it had lessened lately, but this act of kindness that I thought was so absent from him was just so unbelievable. When I put on the coat, I felt fine, but really, more than fine, because the coat not only warmed my body, the smell of his body in this article of clothing warmed my heart.

But this was not the only time that he displayed an open-hearted attitude towards me or to anyone else for that matter, for over time I would have in my possession pens, paper, books and so forth that had come straight from him. Feelings towards Troy were developing deep inside me that were beyond my comprehension, that neither the church nor society had a positive explanation for.

But I was not at school to fall in love with men. I was there to fight the Lord's battles against Satan and his demons.

Despite what I had discovered concerning salvation by faith and salvation by faith and works, I was just as adamant as ever that the Bible was the venerable Word of God. How my friends ever tolerated me I'll never know. During every lunch break, I always looked for an opening to preach the gospel even though I knew how my friends viewed this topic of Christianity.

I remember another time when I got into an argument over my belief. I don't know how we got onto the topic but I'm sure that if it wasn't related to religion in the first place, I would have somehow steered the subject there. Once my objective was achieved, Kerry blurted out, "Farril, why do you always have to bring up religion?"

"Because it's the truth and the answer to the world's problems," I replied.

"But, how do you know that God exists anyway?" Kerry asked. "You can't see Him and He is not perceptible to any of your five senses. So, how do you know He exists?"

"By faith, and because the Bible tells me He exists," I replied.

There was a murmuring among the group.

"That's not evidence," Kerry replied.

I was going to push the fact that this was evidence enough when I had an idea, which I took to be a revelation from God.

"Tell me, Kerry, do you believe oxygen exists?" I asked.

"Of course, I do," Kerry replied in a condescending tone.

"How do you know that oxygen exists? Have you ever seen it?"

"No," Kerry replied.

"Have you ever felt it, tasted it, heard it or smelt it?"

"Of course not!" Kerry retorted.

"If it is therefore not perceptible to your five senses, how can you truly believe it exists?"

"Because we'd die if we didn't have it, wouldn't we," Kerry said sarcastically. "And, anyway, it has been proven by science."

"Really?" I said with feigned surprise. "Scientists have seen oxygen?"

"Don't be stupid!" Kerry said. "Scientists have proven the existence of oxygen by experimental means. They have been able to isolate it and demonstrate that if you deny someone oxygen, they will die."

"And this is the same with my belief in God," I replied. "I cannot perceive God's existence by my five senses but believe by indirect means, and I know that we will all eventually die if we don't believe in Him."

My friends sneered at my explanation but Kerry continued.

"But how do you know that *your* God is the true God? I mean, there are so many gods and religions in this world. How do you know *your* religion is the true religion?"

"Because the Bible says so," I replied.

"Of course! How stupid of me!" Kerry retorted.

Again, another idea came to my head.

"Kerry, what year is it?" I asked.

"Nineteen eighty-two. So what?" she replied.

"And what does that mean?" I asked.

Kerry just stared at me mystified. I was really surprised because I had always thought that Kerry knew everything.

"Don't you know that this means one thousand, nine hundred and eighty-two years ago Christ was born? Don't you know the terms BC and AD? Don't you know that when we date things historically we use the terms BC, which means *Before Christ*, and AD, *Anno Domini*, which is Latin for *The Year of the Lord*? Our dating system indicates that Christ was so important that we count the years from the time of His birth. If Jesus didn't exist, our dating system would be based on a myth. But every time you write the date, you are declaring that Jesus is the Lord."

Everyone fell silent. But Tony brought up another wiry question.

"But, Farril, you believe that Jesus Christ is God, the Father is God and the Holy Ghost is God. That means that you believe in three gods. Then you say that there is only one God. That's Christian confusion for you!"

Everyone agreed with this but I wasn't fazed. I had an answer to that also.

"No, that's not true at all," I replied in all confidence. "Tony, what do you know about electromagnetic radiation? Don't you remember that when we studied optics in physics we were introduced to the argument between Huygens and Newton? Huygens believed that light was energy but Newton said it was matter. The argument at the time was that it was impossible for light to be both energy and matter at the same time but to this day we accept this paradox because light performs in both ways. Scientists cannot explain this and are resigned to accept this by faith. The same with the Christian. We believe that there is one God, and that there is the Father, the Son and the Holy Ghost. This seems contradictory but we just accept it by faith."

Everyone fell silent at my answer. I felt as if I had finally conquered over Satan and these people now did not have an answer to my responses and were left with rejecting Christ's saving grace if they did not believe.

But while I was at the tail end of my last comment, Warren and Philip, who were returning from the canteen, heard what I was talking about. Both of them stopped in their tracks and wandered over to the group. They stood and faced me behind the people on the bench opposite me.

"Don't tell me you're preaching again," Philip said with a sneer.

"Yes, I will keep preaching because I know that the Bible is the Word of God and that those who do not believe it will go to hell."

"But how can you believe in a god of love who is going to put His creatures in hell?" Philip asked. "Isn't that a little inconsistent? God is love and is going to throw people into hell?"

I sat back and sighed with superiority at these ignorant infidels who knew little about the "truth".

"No, it is not inconsistent," I replied. "You have highlighted one aspect of God and ignored other aspects of Him. For a start, it is true that God is a god of love. But He is also a god of justice. The fact that Jesus died on the cross and rose again from the dead illustrates perfectly these two aspects of Him.

Now, if God were only a god of love, He would not have died on the cross because, despite our sinful nature, He would let all human beings into heaven regardless of who we are. If God were solely a god of justice, again, Jesus would not have died on the cross. Justice implies that whoever does the wrong thing pays for the crime. If God were purely justice, we would all be sent to hell because we would all have to pay for our sins.

But these two aspects of God are beautifully met in the death and resurrection of Christ. Sin is still punishable by death, but the love of God is so great that He paid for the crime. Because Jesus was sinless, He did not have to pay for the crime, but now that He has, we don't have to pay for it. But we have to believe in Him.

If we deny what Christ has done for us, we are telling God that we want to pay for the crime ourselves. And as much as God knows that the payment for the crime is very heavy, He won't force us to accept His way of salvation. And you have all heard me tell you this and you are all now without excuse. When Jesus comes again, you cannot say that you never knew what Jesus has done for you."

I thought I had wrapped up that sermon pretty well. But Philip still wasn't convinced.

"You're not saying that you believe Jesus is coming again, surely!" Philip remarked sarcastically.

"Yes, I do."

"But they've been saying that for years," he replied carelessly.

Again, I sighed at his ignorance.

"This is another reason why we know we are living in the Last Days because the Bible says, 'There shall come in the last days scoffers walking after their own lusts, And saying, Where is the promise of His coming,' and you are fulfilling the Scriptures."

"Get off the grass, Farril," Philip said. "They've been prophesying the end of the world for years, ever since the Middle Ages."

Everyone mumbled something but I took up the argument.

"That may be true but never before have all the signs been coming to pass like they have today. Jesus prophesied that before His return, there would be wars and rumours of wars and earthquakes all over the earth. Watch the news on television. There is always some war going on somewhere and earthquakes seem to be on the increase."

Philip just looked at me and replied, "But there have always been wars since the beginning of time. The reason why we might have more wars today is because there are more people on the earth. As for earthquakes, you can't say that there have been more earthquakes today than ever in history. Seismologists have only been measuring earthquake activity in recent times. Also, the whole world hasn't been completely populated like it is today. How do you know there hasn't been a *decrease* in earthquake activity in Australia? White man has only been here for just under two hundred years."

That stumped me but still I had other cards to play.

"But one sign which really indicates that we are in the Last Days is that Israel would become a nation. Jesus said that before He returns, the Jews would possess their land and this finally happened in 1948."

"So, Jesus could come today?" Philip asked.

"No, not yet. There are still some signs which need to be fulfilled. First of all, the Temple of the Jews needs to be built in Jerusalem so that the Beast can enter and sit in the Holy of Holies and declare himself as God. And even before that, all the Christians of the world will be removed from the planet."

"Oh, really? How? Will they all just die? That would certainly bring some peace on earth!" Philip said sarcastically.

"No, they will just vanish in one moment, in the twinkling of an eye. Their sudden and mysterious disappearance will confound everyone and Satan will convince those who remain to blame UFOs or anything else to prevent them from realising the real reason for the Christians' disappearance. Notice how movies are conditioning us to think this way. Look at the story line of the movie *Close Encounters of the Third Kind*. In the beginning of the movie, there was a list of missing persons who had just disappeared without a trace and then, at the end of the movie, all these missing persons came out of the spacecraft. In the movie *The Quiet Earth*, people just suddenly disappeared without a trace because of a scientific experiment that went horribly wrong. The world will be able to draw on these stories to draw erroneous conclusions about how the Christians actually disappeared."

With that, everyone just cracked up laughing. I became embarrassed because as much as I believed in this with all seriousness, for the first time I heard how silly it really sounded. Philip mercilessly made fun of me, imitating the Twilight Zone theme.

But as much as I was embarrassed, I comforted myself with the thought that they laughed at Noah when he built a massive boat in the middle of the desert, miles away from the sea. No doubt Noah and his family were embarrassed by the jeering they had to face but their belief paid off when it began to rain.

Suddenly, a shoe came flying over in our direction and plummeted on the ground in the middle of our group. This stopped everybody short. We looked up and saw Troy hobbling over on one shoe while everyone in his group was chuckling. Troy came bowling over and crashed purposely on me in pursuit of his shoe and landed upside-down in my lap, his head very close to my crotch. He reached down for his shoe with his legs sticking up in the air. Most of his body weight was on me and Anne who was sitting next to me. Anne made a big fuss and complained, smacking Troy's bottom to get him to move.

"Oh, sorry, Anne," Troy said and leaned over onto me, putting both his legs over my right shoulder. I could feel his body weight on me, but despite the discomfort this brought me, I could feel the warmth of his body against mine and I was suddenly aroused. Everyone was again laughing both in Troy's group and mine. Troy reached for his shoe with one arm and with the other hand began stroking my leg.

"Ooooooh! Nice legs!" he exclaimed as he rubbed up my calf muscles and everyone laughed more. I was embarrassed but the embarrassment was increased because I could feel I was having an erection and was sure Troy could feel it, with his shoulder just on my thigh next to my crotch.

Troy began to get up and as he did, he put his hand heavily on my groin and it hurt. I recoiled and screwed up my face in pain. As soon as Troy was on his feet again, he said about his hand on my groin, "Sorry about that. But you won't be needing it anyway," and everyone laughed.

But I was highly embarrassed, wondering if he had felt my erection. Troy put his shoe back on and wandered back to his group while everyone was still laughing and I began to laugh with them. But while I watched him walk back to his group, I stared at him from head to foot.

In a matter of moments, I was back to reality. What was I doing looking at Troy like that, thinking sexual thoughts about him? Five minutes ago I was preaching faithfully and confidently the Word of God and suddenly I find myself lusting after Troy. What on earth was wrong with me?

That afternoon we had a physics class in the last two periods before going home. Like always, all my friends continued to befriend me although this time with an occasional taunt at my bizarre beliefs.

While I was setting up the retort stand to perform the experiment, Ruth wandered over to watch. I turned and saw her staring at what I was doing.

"How can I help you?" I asked.

She smiled and blushed.

"I...I don't know how to set up this experiment and you seem to know what you're doing. My physics partner is away and I can see yours is, too, so Mr Edwards told me to do the experiment with you this afternoon."

"Sure," I replied, "I'd be delighted."

I explained to her what we were doing for the experiment and she watched me intently. But it was one of those experiments that once you start, you have to sit for an hour taking time measurements at so many intervals. Hence, we had plenty of time to kill. We grabbed a stool each and sat watching the experiment when Ruth introduced the conversation from physics back to the lunchbreak.

"All that you were saying today at lunchtime, is it true? Do you believe all that?"

I was quite taken aback.

"Well, yes, I do."

"How do you know all about it?" she asked.

"It's in the Bible."

"You've read the Bible?"

"Well, not all of it. Only the New Testament."

"On your own?"

"Well, yeah."

"Oh," Ruth said. "I've always wanted to read the Bible but I think I would need my parish priest to help me, it's such a complicated book."

I looked at her strangely.

"It's not that difficult, really. I've been reading the Bible since I was eleven and I've never had any difficulty understanding it at all."

Ruth looked at me really strangely. She later explained to me that when she first heard me say this, she found this concept difficult to digest. Here was a fellow student of about the same age, doing similar subjects at school, of the same mentality, who experiences the same problems of growing up, saying that he reads the Bible. As far as she was concerned, the Bible was so complicated a book that it was reserved for holy men to read, study and then expound to the laity.

Because she had mentioned her parish priest, I immediately realised that she was a Catholic. This put me on guard because we had grown up to believe that the Catholics were wrong although we were never told why. It immediately set up a barrier between her and me, and the fact that I had read the Bible gave me a feeling of superiority and a greater sense of spirituality. But despite this, Ruth and I chatted for the rest of the double period, making light conversation and casual references to religion between discussions about the experiment.

Finally the last bell went. It was the first time that I was disappointed to go home from school because I was just getting interested in this conversation. We started packing up.

"Oh, Ruth," I said. "I wish you lived near me so we could walk home and continue this conversation."

"Why, where do you live?" she asked.

When I told her, she exclaimed, "Oh, Michael, I live only two blocks away from you!"

"But you catch the bus to school," I said.

"Yeah! How do you get to school?"

"I walk."

"Three kilometres?!" Ruth exclaimed.

"It's only about a half hour walk. And I enjoy the walk to and from school, and it's good exercise. Why don't you walk with me?"

Ruth pulled a funny face.

"It's a bit far, but I'd like to continue the conversation. Sure. Okay. I'll come with you. But I'll have to tell Anne that I'm not going with her on the bus today. Can you wait for me?"

"Yeah, of course! Meet me at the side gate. I'll be waiting for you there."

I grabbed my bag and went on my way while Ruth disappeared to tell Anne. I was busting with excitement. Wow! Someone was interested in religion like me. I stood at the gate and waited impatiently, excitedly, until I saw her come running across the basketball courts to the gate.

"Whatever do you do when it rains?" Ruth asked puffing.

"I get wet!" I said and laughed, and then we started our journey home.

We walked along my normal route home, first following a road past modern red brick houses with neatly cut lawns, and with flowers pouring out of the gardens and from the pots on the patio. We laughed and chatted as carefree as two birds. From there my way home led across a cricket field which led to a little creek which fortunately this afternoon was cheerfully gurgling as ever. I took her along the bank where I usually sat alone some afternoons on my way home from school and she sat down next to me.

"This is why I walk to and from school," I said smiling.

"It's so lovely here," she said freely.

"Yes, it's beautiful what God has created. I don't know how anyone could believe that something like this could have occurred purely by chance like they teach us in school. To me, this creek was placed here by God to especially make me happy."

Ruth smiled at me.

"No, I don't believe in evolution either. I believe that God created the world, too. When I see flowers, and trees, and birds, I thank God for everything that He has made. Can you imagine all those scientists lying on a spot like this and saying, 'Oh, thank you chance and evolution, for all this'. It would leave me cold and dry."

I was touched by Ruth's outlook on life, especially that she believed in God and Creation just like I did.

"Tell me, Ruth. Do you believe in Jesus?"

"Yes," Ruth said.

"Do you believe that Jesus Christ came in the flesh and is the Son of God?"

"Yes, of course, I do! I'm a Christian!" she said, this time with a little bit of suspicion in her voice.

Do you believe that because Jesus died and rose again from the dead, by believing this you will go to heaven?"

"Yes!" Ruth said and looked at me a bit impatiently. "Why are you asking me all these questions?"

"Well, you're a Catholic, and my parents and my church believe that the Catholic Church is not Christian. But so far, you have told me that you believe in those things which are the fundamentals of my faith."

Ruth chuckled a bit.

"That's funny because we were brought up to believe that you Protestants are led astray. But after listening to you at school talking about the Bible, I've grown quite curious to know what you believe. You have some strange beliefs but I asked my parish priest about some of the things you've said in the past and he agreed with what you say. Also, you speak so confidently about what you believe."

"Your priest agreed with me?" I asked.

"Yes, sure. Why are you so puzzled?"

"No reason," I said quietly.

But there was a reason. For all my childhood and growing up, we had been indoctrinated with the belief that a Catholic was a weird person, with weird beliefs who had weird church services, and for all intents and purposes was not Christian at all and was going to hell. But from all the questions I had asked Ruth so far, she believed the same things as I did and not only that, her priest agreed with what I had said in the past at school. I was a little perturbed and excited at the same time. Catholics are Christians after all, I thought, and because of that, Ruth was very much an equal in the faith.

But while I thought about this, my mind was diverted while I watched Ruth playing with a bracelet round her wrist made up of beautiful red beads.

"That's a beautiful bracelet," I commented.

"Thank you. They're my Rosary Beads," Ruth replied.

"What's that?"

"Well, when I pray, I keep a count of how many times I have said a Hail Mary and a Glory Be."

I looked at the beautiful beads and then asked.

"What's a Hail Mary?"

Ruth looked at me with a strange expression as if to say that everyone should know what a Hail Mary is.

"It's a prayer."

"How's it go?"

Ruth held one of the beads and quoted it to me:

Hail Mary, full of grace
The Lord is with thee
Blessed art thou among women
And blessed be the fruit of thy womb, Jesus.

Holy Mary, Mother of God
Pray for us sinners
Now and at the hour of our death.
Amen

I looked at her for a moment.

"And what's the other prayer?"

"Glory Be, and it goes

Glory Be to the Father, the Son, and to the Holy Spirit
As it was in the beginning, is now, and ever shall be,
World without end. Amen."

"What, so you start with a Hail Mary, then a Glory Be, then a Hail Mary, et cetera, until you've been right around the bracelet?" I asked.

"No, no," Ruth said laughing. "I start with the Pater Noster, then one Glory Be, then ten Hail Marys, then one Glory Be, and so on until I have finished."

"What's the first prayer again?"

"Pater Noster. And it goes:

Our Father, which art in heaven
Hallowed be thy Name
Thy Kingdom come
Thy will be done on earth as it is in heaven
Give us this day our daily bread
And forgive us our trespasses as we forgive them
That trespass against us
And lead us not into temptation, but deliver us
From evil.   *Amen*

And that's it."

When I heard her quote the Pater Noster, which I knew as the Lord's Prayer, it made me feel really weird inside. This was a prayer that my parents taught me when I was very young to say each time I knelt beside my bed before I went to sleep. This was a prayer that we recited at the benediction at the end of every church service. This was a prayer that Jesus taught His disciples to pray, a prayer that came straight from the Bible. And here I was listening to Ruth recite this same prayer word perfect, exactly how I had learnt and recited it for years. What was I to make of all this? As for the Rosary Beads, well, I knew nothing in the New Testament which spoke against them.

But then it was Ruth's turn to ask questions.

"When you pray, what do you say?"

I looked at the gurgley creek.

"Well, like you, I pray the Lord's Prayer. But generally, I just speak to God like I'd speak to my parents. I ask Him for help when I'm distressed, to help my friends come to the realisation that He loves them and wants them to be saved, and when all is going well, I tell Him I love Him."

Ruth looked at me sternly.

"You're not a priest or a holy man! What makes you so presumptuous that you can talk to God directly like that?"

That seemed like a puzzling question. This had been so ordinary for me.

"Well, the Bible teaches us that God is our Father. I couldn't imagine myself walking up to my earthly father if I needed his help for, well, like with my homework and then saying, 'Hail, Father, full of grace, blah, blah, blah', and then my father responding to me without saying a word, knowing exactly what I was really asking for."

Ruth just burst out laughing which was really surprising because I was being sarcastic about her mode of prayer. But then Ruth moved the conversation with a jolt to what I had been talking about at lunchtime earlier that day.

"All that you were talking about today, about the Second Coming of Christ, is that what your church believes?" Ruth asked.

"Oh, yes! Jesus Himself taught this before He ascended into heaven," I replied authoritatively. "Jesus told us everything that was going to happen before He returns so that when these events occur, those who have read the Bible will not be surprised and will not be afraid of what is happening because they will have known in advance."

Ruth looked a little stunned. She just stared out into the distance for a moment and then back at me.

"So, what is going to happen? What should we expect first?"

"Well, let me show you from the Bible," I said.

I dipped my hand inside my school bag and groped around until I had found my little Gideon's New Testament, one of the little red New Testaments which included the Psalms and Proverbs from the Old Testament, that were given to us in Year Seven. I told her all that I had read in the Bible and what I had heard at church about the signs of the Second Coming of Christ and showed her that the world events that we were currently experiencing matched up remarkably well with the predictions that led up to the finality of history.

When I had finished, Ruth gave a deep sigh of terror.

"That's frightening stuff, Michael. But is this really true?"

"Of course, it is. It says so in the Bible. But if you believe Jesus Christ died for your sins and rose again from the dead before all this happens, you'll be taken up in the Rapture and miss the horrors that will happen on earth."

"Well, I do believe Jesus died for my sins, so that must mean I'll go up in the Rapture, then," Ruth said. "Still, it frightens me to hear what you showed me from the Bible today."

With that, we decided to get up and go home. We scrambled up on our feet, dusted ourselves down, slung our bags over our shoulders and started our journey home.

When we arrived at Ruth's place, Ruth invited me to come in. We walked through her little picket gate and up the long driveway. Ruth and I were greeted at the front door.

"Hello, Mum. This is Michael. Michael, this is my mother."

"Hello, Mrs Carpenter," I said with a smile.

"Hello, Michael. It's nice to meet you," Mrs Carpenter said and returned the smile. "Would you like to come in for a cup of coffee? I've just boiled the jug."

I obliged and followed the two ladies into the house. While Ruth chatted with her mother, I stared at the interior of their house. They had beautiful furniture, a lounge setting of period style covered in green velvet, a matching dining set, and a beautifully ornate buffet and hutch containing striking crystal that sparkled under the light.

But my eyes caught more attention to the crucifix and other religious motifs scattered around the room. There was a statue of Mary on the cabinet and a large painting of the Last Supper, a copy of the original by Leonardo da Vinci, hanging on the loungeroom wall. There was a picture of Jesus and Mary with big valentine hearts superimposed on their chests and on another wall a picture of Pope John Paul II. I could feel the religiosity permeating throughout the house but it made me feel uncomfortable.

Mrs Carpenter fussed over me, offering me cakes and biscuits, and asking me questions about school and my family.

Eventually it was time to go. Ruth led me out of the front gate.

"Thank you for walking home with me," I said.

"I had an enjoyable chat!" Ruth replied.

"Ruth, I'd like to learn more about your religion."

"Well, why don't you come to Mass one morning?"

"Ooooh! I don't think my parents would approve if I skipped my church for Mass. Do you have a Sunday Night service?"

"No. But we do have a Saturday Night service."

"Oh, that would be perfect. I'll let you know when I'd like to come."

With that, I said good-bye and went home.

That evening, I decided to ask my parents about Ruth's version of Christianity. It had puzzled me all that afternoon because of the conflict between the negative light Catholicism was viewed in our church juxtaposed by what Ruth had told me about her beliefs. It puzzled me so much that I had to ask my parents what they thought about it. My parents were sitting in front of the television watching a movie and, when the advertisements came on, I thought that this was the opportune time to ask.

"Are Catholics Christians?" I asked with no introduction.

My parents swung their heads around.

"What makes you ask that, son?" my father asked.

"Well, there's this girl at school, Ruth Carpenter, and she's a Catholic. I walked home with her today and we chatted about our religions. Ruth confessed that she believes in the death and resurrection of Jesus and whoever believes that will go to heaven."

"Well, if they believe that, then they're going to heaven too, son," my father replied.

"No, they're not," my mother retorted immediately.

I looked at my mother with surprise.

"But why not?" I asked.

"Because they pray to Mary. Satan has clouded their minds to call to Mary for help and not to Christ. Anything that takes your mind off Christ and puts it on another is satanic."

I sat and thought about it for a moment.

"But Ruth told me that she prays to Jesus, the Father and the Holy Spirit. So, she must be saved."

My mother looked at me a bit coldly.

"Yes, son, I know," she continued, "but you can't mix up Christianity with another belief. Even Paul in his letter to the Corinthians berates the Corinthians by saying in II Corinthians 11: 4, 'For if he that cometh preacheth another Jesus, whom we have not preached, or if ye receive another spirit, which ye have not received, or another gospel, which ye have not accepted, ye might well bear with him'. If it were possible for the Corinthians to be deceived into believing another gospel and another Jesus then it is possible for people to be praying to and believing in another Jesus today. And it is obvious that the Catholics, who pray to Mary, believe another gospel and pray to a different Jesus than the one in the Bible."

I pondered on this idea for a moment.

"But Ruth seems like a nice girl and an example of how a Christian should live as well as believing in Christ. She's not like my other friends because she doesn't swear, or tell dirty jokes, or criticise religion in any way."

"Son, what the Catholics teach is unfortunately heresy," my mother replied again. "Satan deceives us subtly. He doesn't appear with big neon signs saying, 'Here I am! I'm the devil!' He presents ninety-nine percent truth and one percent lie. It's the one percent lie which will finally pull us away from Christ to believe another gospel. That's why we have the Bible so we can know what the truth is. Does the Bible tell us to worship Mary?"

I just sighed. No, I couldn't think of a verse in the Bible which said that we were to worship Mary. From reading all the New Testament, everyone praised and worshipped Jesus Christ but not once did I read about praise to and adoration of Mary.

"No," I finally said. "Ruth has also invited me to come to Mass on Saturday Night."

I was expecting my mother to fly off the handle but instead she just said, "If you want to go, sure. But you won't find the truth there."

"Mum, I'm not looking for the truth there. I want to know what makes the Catholic religion wrong and, if it is, show Ruth and her family so that they can be saved."

With this type of argument, I was able to quell my mother's fears that I might be wavering and about to become ensnared with the distorted Catholic view of Christ. And furthermore, my mother was happy to know that I was going to do this in an attempt to save Ruth from the devil.

That night, after doing some study, I went back over the conversations I had had with my parents about my friends and about Ruth. We had been brought up to believe that Christianity was unique because we are saved by faith only and that no work would save us. But when I told my parents that some of my friends at school said they believed in Christ and went to church, my parents said that faith was not enough but proved from the Bible that faith had to be accompanied by works to be acceptable to God.

Now I was hearing more of the fine print about salvation. Even though someone believed in Jesus Christ, that He died and rose again from the dead, and one acted like a Christian should, this person could be worshipping the wrong Jesus, even though the name and the action performed on our behalf was exactly the same. Certain things one entertained in one's mind about the nature of God or the nature of other biblical characters could play against you and you could be destined for hell because of it.

This was starting to confuse me indeed. What had originally seemed like a simple step to heaven was now turning out to be extremely complicated.

But I only knew a whisper of what the Catholic Church taught. What I did know was that the Catholics viewed the Pope as the head of the Christian Church whereas we viewed him merely as a man like everyone else. The head of the local church was called a priest whereas we called ours a minister or pastor. The Catholics addressed their priest as Father whereas we used the common terms Mister or Pastor. I had heard of things like confessionals, the sign of the cross, praying to Mary, all strange things shrouded in mystery, all because we had been told they were evil but it was never explained why.

Actually, I was at a fork in the road. Was Ruth a Christian because she believed in Christ, or not, because she followed erroneous practices? And if the Catholics indeed believed and prayed to the wrong Jesus, I needed to prove it and show Ruth so that she could be saved. And the only way I could prove it was to learn what the Catholics believed and find out if their teachings contradicted the Bible. So, I resolved to attend Mass and compare the Catholics' beliefs and practices with Scriptural teaching.

Chapter 6

When I saw Ruth at school again, I told her that I would be pleased to attend Mass with her one Saturday evening and we agreed on a date. This Saturday night arrived soon enough and I was quite excited to be going to Mass with her. At that stage, I had my driver's licence and my father allowed me to use the family car so I was able to drive to Ruth's place to pick her up.

The car chugged up along the Carpenters' long driveway and Mrs Carpenter came out to see who it was. When she saw that it was me, she brought me inside and began fussing over me extra specially which made me feel uncomfortable although pleased at the same time.

Mrs Carpenter made me sit down to a cup of tea and told me that Ruth was not quite ready, when suddenly, Mr Carpenter stepped into the room. I stood up to greet him. He was a big man, somewhat plump, with a crop of grey hair. Just by his demeanour, he came across as a man with a lot of confidence and, just by his presence, he was already in control.

"You must be Michael Farril," he said with an air of authority and extended his arm to greet me.

"I'm very pleased to meet you," he continued. "Ruth has spoken a lot about you and I'm delighted to finally meet this Michael Farril I've heard so much about. Please, sit down."

Mr Carpenter then extended his arm towards the closest chair.

"So, you study at school together, I hear?" he said as he sat back in his chair and made himself comfortable.

"Ah, yes. Ruth is in a number of my classes."

"And she tells me that you're a very bright student. And she tells me that you are very religious."

When he said this, I felt the blood rush to my head. I was aware of the antagonism between Protestants and Catholics, and so I was now on my guard.

"Well, yes, I am."

"Oh, that's good. It's good that a young lad like you has religion. I believe it's so important. I had religion at your age and it never did me any wrong. I know that because of my faith in God, I was able to get through many problems that I wouldn't have been able to if I hadn't had God's strength to guide me."

Mrs Carpenter was fidgeting in the kitchen and I wished Ruth would hurry up and come out so we could go.

"Ruth tells me that you are of a Protestant faith and that you know the Bible very well. You know, a lot of Protestants think Catholics don't read the Bible at all, but like you, my parents encouraged me to read it as well."

I expressed surprise in my face.

"Ruth tells me you are also interested in the Catholic view of the Bible and Christianity. As you no doubt are aware, the Catholic Church is the church which has preserved the oldest traditions of

Christianity and can trace its origins back to Peter himself. Ruth tells me you want to know more about Catholicism. Well, if you have any questions, I'd be more than delighted to answer them when you come back from Mass."

I wasn't really sure what to say to that. It completely struck me off balance that I was greeted with an introduction so forward and direct.

Mrs Carpenter came out of the kitchen with a plate of assorted biscuits and offered me one, then placed the plate on the coffee table.

"I don't know what Ruth is doing. I think I'll have to get her, otherwise you're going to be late," Mrs Carpenter said nervously but smiling the whole time.

"Ruth?" she called. "Are you ready, yet?"

"I'm coming," Ruth called in return.

Finally Ruth came out of her bedroom, emphasising her entrance with each step and drawing our attention to the beautiful apparition entering the room. I could smell her as she entered. She had a very beautiful dress on, with flowers and rose buds flowing carelessly from her shoulders to the hem of her dress. She had done her hair nicely, not overdone, and had a little make-up on. She looked and smelled like a bouquet. I just stared aghast at her. She looked like she was dressed up to go out to dinner, not to Mass.

"Do I look all right?" she asked me.

"Alright? You look fabulous!" I said.

I was even more embarrassed that Mr and Mrs Carpenter were so eager to fuss over me and ensure all my comforts were met, as if it were a first date. I finished my cup of tea and then led Ruth out to the car. I opened the door for Ruth, ensuring that all her dress was well inside the car before closing the door - a dying chivalrous act that my father had instilled in me - and then got inside myself and started the car. Mr and Mrs Carpenter stood on the patio and waved us good-bye with great beaming smiles.

We arrived at the church and I carried my Bible in with me just like I did at my church. But this night was filled with all sorts of surprises. My first impression when I looked inside the church building was how much the Carpenters' house was modelled after the church interior. There was a big crucifix at the front of the church with a smooth skinned Jesus hanging off it. There was a big statue of Mary to the right encaved in an opening in the wall. Along the walls hung friezes with depictions of the different stages of Christ's march along the Via Dolorosa.

As we entered, Ruth put her hand in the font and did a sign of the cross with the water. She then strolled sanctimoniously towards the pews while I followed behind. When she had arrived at one of her choosing, she stopped and genuflected. My eyes were too busy observing all that was around me that I didn't see her stop, and while she was in deep reverence, I walked right into her, she lost her balance and landed on the pew, her hands and legs spread out very unlady-like. The entire congregation looked around to watch the charade. I looked at Ruth. She had gone red and she just stared at me for a second before sitting down. Finally the service began with the altar boys who marched in, bearing a long, golden cross and singing some strange song.

The service was full of exercises. We stood, then sat, then knelt, then sat, stood, and this went on throughout the entire service that I felt that I was going to be exhausted before the night was out.

There was even a Bible reading that evening. But what annoyed me about the reading was that unlike in our church, the woman (who spoke in church, not wearing a head covering!) just began with the passage without announcing where in the Bible it came from and I had to search furiously through the Bible so that I could follow. I flicked the pages of my Bible noisily until I found the passage and, when I looked up, I could see a few people from the corner of my eye staring at me. So, eventually I put my Bible down and didn't touch it for the rest of the ceremony.

Throughout the whole service I looked around and observed what was going on, listening to what was said and done, and compared this with what I knew the Bible said as evidence of errors of this church. But I was more surprised by the similarities between our versions of a church service than the differences. Although there was more movement up and down in the pews than in our church, still, the congregation in our church stood up at least three times to sing the hymns. We also had a Bible reading and we also had a sermon, and communion, which the Catholics call the Eucharist. I could see how the Protestant Church was a reformed version of the Catholic Church service.

But the biggest shock came when we stood up for the millionth time to say another prayer. It was the Apostles' Creed. I had heard of it but I had never known its contents. I just listened to the congregation recite it:

I believe in God, the Father Almighty
Creator of heaven and earth
I believe in Jesus Christ, his only Son, our Lord
He was conceived by the power of the Holy Spirit
And born of the Virgin Mary
He suffered under Pontius Pilate, was crucified
Died, and was buried
He descended to the dead
On the third day he rose again
He ascended into heaven
And is seated at the right hand of the Father
He will come again to judge the living and the dead

I believe in the Holy Spirit
The holy catholic church
The communion of saints
The forgiveness of sins
The resurrection of the body
And the life everlasting. Amen

Because I didn't know the Creed, and I was only at the service as a spectator anyway, I just looked around the room, looking at all the blank, expressionless faces robotically reciting this prayer without thought. But I listened to the words and was astounded. The Apostles' Creed was everything I believed about God and Christ. Here I heard them confess their belief in each of the gods in the Godhead, the belief in Christ's death, resurrection and in His Second Coming.

"Well," I thought, "they must be Christians because they believe in the fundamental claim of faith in John 3:16 that Jesus is the Son of God, died for their sins and rose again from the dead."

While thinking on this, my eyes sailed across the room. Suddenly I lost my breath and my heart skipped a beat. For among this sea of expressionless nobodies was someone I knew very well: Troy Krisston. He was reciting the Apostles' Creed himself. I stared at Troy the whole time from this point on to the end of the service but he didn't see me. I didn't want him to see me either. This was one of the protagonists at school who for years had made fun of me because of my radical beliefs in Christ and the Bible, and now, here I was watching him mouth a confession for which I was the butt of a good joke. I watched him for the rest of the service, sing the hymns, recite the prayers and take the Eucharist.

At the end of the service, the entire congregation darted out of the church to their cars and were gone as soon as they could. I watched Troy disappear into the crowd and into the night.

Ruth detained me so that I could meet the priest. It didn't take long before no-one was left at the church except for a small crowd of about ten.

The priest was tidying up for the night. When he had finished, Ruth took me over to him.

"Hello, Ruth," the priest said with a beaming smile. "My word, you look delightful tonight."

He said this so sincerely and it was obvious that the priest knew her very well.

"Thank you," Ruth said blushing. "I'd like you to meet a friend of mine from school, Michael Farril. Michael, this is Father Hammond."

"Hello," I said, shaking his hand.

He beamed a smile at me too and he seemed from first impressions to be a very loving man.

"Hello, Michael. I'm glad to meet you. Are you a regular here? I don't think I've ever seen you here before."

"Oh, no," Ruth said for me and explained which church I came from and why I was here. I was expecting Father Hammond's facial expression to change from warmth to ice coldness and that he was going to say something like, "you Protestant scum", but instead I noticed a sincere pleasure in his face as if Ruth had told him I had simply come from another Catholic church.

"Well, I'm glad you could make it tonight. You are most welcome at any time, you know," Father Hammond said.

"Actually," Ruth said for me, "he's interested in our religion and would like to know more about it."

Father Hammond smiled at me.

"Well, any time you want to visit, the Presbytery is just next door. Did you want to ask some questions now?"

"Oh, no, but thank you, anyway," I said. "Ruth's parents have invited me around for dinner and we really should be going."

"Well, you are most welcome at any time. Anyway, Mr Carpenter is a very learned man and I'm sure he will be able to answer any of your questions for you. But if you want to see me at anytime about anything, it doesn't have to be on a religious topic, the door is open."

He shook my hand and walked off slowly and sedately.

We wandered over to the car in the cool of the evening. Ruth was as bubbly as a fountain but my mind was in a spin. While Ruth was pleased I had come to Mass, I couldn't cope with the confusion. For a start, there was Troy. I could still see him in the congregation, his lips moving at the confession of faith in the Apostles' Creed, and then I had flashbacks of him at school making fun of me because of Jesus and the Bible. I couldn't count the number of times Troy said or did anything to me on account of my faith, and here tonight I saw him confess the same fundamental faith.

I did the chivalrous thing again for Ruth, opening the door for her and then got in myself. Ruth babbled like a babbling brook with excitement all the way home. She couldn't stop talking but I just took advantage of the darkness in which to hide whatever facial expression may have revealed what I was really thinking.

My mind was in a spin. I claimed to be a Christian because I believed Jesus Christ died for my sins and rose again form the dead. But so did this room full of Catholics. Mr Norman had stated so clearly that, in Acts 16:31, Paul the Apostle clearly said that to be saved one simply needs to "believe on the Lord Jesus Christ, and thou shalt be saved," and not "Believe on the Lord Jesus, and believe this, and do that." But Catholics don't associate with Protestants and Protestants don't associate with Catholics and yet fundamentally, they are all going to the same place. Would there be religious war in heaven between Catholics and Protestants?

We arrived at Ruth's house and I was warmly received. I could smell the dinner which was a welcoming aroma. The Carpenters and I chatted a little bit and then we sat down at the diningroom table. But the ritual they went through before they ate came across as very strange. The meals were placed before us but, before we ate, the Carpenters did the sign of the cross, said a prayer, and did the sign of the cross before they touched the food. But it was the hurried way in which they said it that was quite strange to me. It wasn't done in unison. None of them had their eyes closed but their eyes were transfixed on the food while they raced to see who could be the first to get through the ritual. They did the whole procedure so fast that I didn't understand a word they said. It was like a magical formula they recited, a spell, a type of incantation before they could eat, as if the food were poisoned or there was a barrier between them and the food, and this special incantation broke down this barrier.

But then, how was this different for us? We always said grace before a meal. My father would always recite the same prayer before we ate: "For what we are about to receive Lord make us truly thankful for Christ's sake. Amen," and we were not even allowed to touch the food until grace was said. It hit me with such a surprise because, as I observed another version of Christianity with a critical eye, it only highlighted a similar practice of my own faith.

The meal was delicious and I commented on how nice the food was. After dinner, Ruth got up and brewed some coffee while Mr and Mrs Carpenter remained seated at the table relaxed. Mr Carpenter then opened the discussion about their version of Christianity which was so foreign to me.

"Well, how did you enjoy Mass tonight?" he asked me.

"It was very interesting indeed. It's very different to our church service."

"Ruth told me you had some questions that I could probably answer about our faith."

I began to feel a little uncomfortable. My back stiffened while I thought about it. There were so many things which our church had criticised the Catholic Church of observing that I thought if I started expressing these views it would cause some friction. But Mr Carpenter had asked the question and it sounded as if it were open for me to discuss any point that I so desired and how I viewed that point irrespective of how it sounded to Catholic ears. There were so many things I wanted to ask and as I looked around the room, I spotted the picture of the Pope on the wall. I pointed to the picture and began.

"Mr Carpenter, you and your family recognise the Pope as a great figure, as the head of the Christian Church, and any conclusion he makes on an issue becomes a commandment that all Catholics should follow. However, being a Protestant, I recognise him merely as another human being. Any commandment he gives is merely his opinion and must ultimately be weighed against what the Bible, the Word of God, says."

Mr Carpenter smiled and, in a commanding manner, leaned back on his chair.

"The Pope is the head of the Christian Church, this is true. But the Pope never says anything contrary to the Bible. Every edict he delivers to his Church is from God and is already weighed against the Bible before he delivers it.

But the position of the Pope is founded on the Holy Scriptures. Haven't you read in Mathew 16:18 what Jesus said to Peter, when Peter made the confession that Jesus is the Christ, the Son of God? He said, 'Thou art Peter, and upon this rock I will build my church; and the gates of hell shall not prevail against it.' See how the Church is built on Peter? The name, Peter, was given to him by Jesus and it means *rock* in Greek, and this is the Rock upon which Jesus built His Church. Peter passed on his authority down through the centuries by a succession of popes, an unbroken line which can be traced back to the first Rock, Peter. So, the authority of the Church is based on the Bible which you affirm to be the Word of God.

But Martin Luther and Henry VIII removed this authority away from Peter and all those who followed them to start new churches founded on new rocks which are not in the Holy Scriptures. Look at Henry VIII in particular: the Church of England is founded on a man who, when the Pope would not annul his marriage, broke away and decided for himself that he and all the descendants of the English monarchy would be the head of this church which he established. His church is founded upon a new rock of which the Bible is silent."

"But what about Martin Luther?" I asked. "He didn't say that he was the head of the Church. He said that the Bible was final authority and that Jesus is the Rock upon which the Church is built."

"My good friend, I don't mean to offend you but Martin Luther was a womaniser and wanted some nice nuns for himself."

I raised my eyebrows in horror. This was a hairbreadth short of blasphemy to me. I considered Martin Luther to be a great man of the faith, not because I was Lutheran, but because Martin Luther played a significant role in changing the perspective of final authority from the Church, that is, the Pope, to the Bible. Mr Carpenter noticed my discontent and realised that this was not evidence for discrediting the man. So he changed his tactic.

"Martin Luther went around telling people to stop listening to the Pope and to leave the Church that was founded on Peter. He then founded a new church which was founded on him, for the church which he formed is called the Lutheran Church because it is based on his teachings. He became the new rock in contradiction to the Holy Scriptures."

Mr Carpenter answered that question extremely well, quoting from the book which we had been indoctrinated to believe was the divine Word of God.

And the verse, when read in context, seemed to agree with what Mr Carpenter was saying. Immediately it made me worried. Could it be that I am already transgressing the Word of God because I reject the Church which founds itself on Peter? None of the Protestant churches had the history that the Catholic Church could boast about and, in this light, all had denied the Rock upon which Christ had built His Church. All I could do was agree and leave this question until I could research it later in more detail.

I sat there silent and so Mr Carpenter prodded me.

"Well, do you understand that?" he asked.

"Er, yes. But I don't know what to say to it. What you say is true and I cannot deny it. But be that as it may, I have other questions to ask which seem to indicate that other practices in the Church contradict what the Bible says."

Mr Carpenter laughed.

"Please! Ask away, and I will show you that all our practices are based on God's holy Word."

Ruth got up, went to the kitchen and started pouring the coffee into the assorted cups on the kitchen table, keeping an ear open to the discussion, and Mrs Carpenter sat with her head on the back of her fingers, her elbows on the table, and smiled sweetly while silently listening to her husband support their faith.

"Another question I have is with regards to Mary. You pray to Mary, but in the Bible, not once did the disciples or the apostles give praise to her. This was only given to Jesus."

Mr Carpenter lowered his furrow and leaned forward.

"Michael, no-one praised Mary in the Bible?"

This made me nervous. I had read the entire New Testament. I was as sure as eggs that no-one praised Mary. But his question obviously meant that my statement was unjustified and I waited for his explanation.

"My good fellow, haven't you read in Luke 1:28 what the angel Gabriel said to Mary before she fell pregnant with Jesus? 'Hail, thou that art highly favoured, the Lord is with thee: blessed art thou among women'. Mary later says of herself in verse 48, 'from henceforth all generations shall call me blessed.' So, we are not contradicting the Bible when we pray to Mary. For even an angel, which you must confess is greater than humankind, hailed her. Therefore Mary must have been recognised as higher than the angels, and who else is higher than the angels but God alone?"

Again, all my muscles tightened. I wanted to rend my clothes and cry "Blasphemy!" but how could I? How could I say he was blaspheming when he had just quoted the Bible to support his answer? But Mr Carpenter approached it from another angle.

"But also think about it this way. Jesus was in Mary's womb for nine months until He was born. During that time He was completely subject to Mary so Mary must have been someone very special indeed."

This to my ears was blasphemous. Mr Carpenter was implying that the Bible taught that we were to worship a mortal as if she had a status equal to God and, from his second explanation, even greater than God, for Jesus was subject to Mary for nine months. But I couldn't argue against it because I didn't know any verses in the Bible which contradicted this line of argument. But I knew something had to be wrong with this view of Mary if my parents and all the Protestants could confidently say that adoration of Mary was wrong and satanic.

I thought long and hard about it and finally was able to approach the question from a different angle.

"I'm not sure if I agree whole-heartedly that Christians are supposed to pray to Mary - "

"Even though the Bible tells us to," Mr Carpenter interrupted.

That made me angry but I kept my cool and continued.

"But why do you have a statue of Mary and of Jesus on church grounds when the Bible is clear that it is wrong to make graven images? Doesn't it say in the Ten Commandments in Exodus 20:4 and 5, 'Thou shalt not make unto thee any graven image, or any likeness of anything that is in heaven above, or that is in the earth beneath, or that is in the water under the earth: Thou shalt not bow down thyself to them, nor serve them: for I the LORD thy God am a jealous God'? It is quite clear that the Bible speaks against these icons which is why the Protestants do not have any statues in their churches."

I was expecting to see Mr Carpenter recoil back in horror not having an answer. But instead, he sat calmly, ready to give an answer for his faith. He smiled again in such a way that it appeared to me that he had answered this question to a thousand fundamentalists before me.

"Michael, what do you know about the Ark of the Covenant that Moses carried around in the wilderness and which was eventually taken to the Promised Land?"

I couldn't see how mentioning this Old Testament story had any relevance to this discussion but I thought I should answer his question.

"The Ark was a box which carried the Ten Commandments that God wrote for the Children of Israel."

"Describe the Ark to me. What did it look like?"

"It was a box, covered in gold, and the top of the box, I'd say was some sort of lid, had two angels looking at each other."

"That's right. Were the angels statues?"

"Well, no," I replied hesitantly.

"But if not, what were they? They certainly were not merely pictures. You have to admit, surely, that they were statues or graven images of some sort."

I nodded slowly, now realising the connection.

"Now, do you know the story in the Bible when the Philistines stole the Ark from the Israelites and, when this happened, the Israelites felt that God had deserted them?"

"Yes," I said.

This Sunday School story came to my mind which I later discovered was a story recounted in the book of I Samuel chapters 4, 5 and 6. Some time in the history of Israel, a race of people called Philistines suddenly appeared on the south west coast, in an area that is today the Gaza Strip, and took control of this area of land. To the Israelites, the Philistines were evil people, worshipping their own gods.

At one time, a war broke out between the Israelites and the Philistines and, during the battle, the Philistines succeeded in capturing the Ark of Moses and took it back to their part of the country. The Israelites were devastated because to them, God, who is supposed to be everywhere at the same time, had deserted them. For, as the story unfolds, it seemed to indicate that God's presence resided only in and around this box.

The story continues, how the Philistines placed the Ark in the temple of their god, Dagon, and in the morning they found Dagon lying flat on his face as if he were doing obeisance to the Ark. The Philistines were also afflicted with plagues until they realised that the Ark should be returned to its rightful place, back with the Israelites.

But the comparison was obvious: the Israelites had a graven object which represented God's presence, in front of which even another graven image was found lying prostrate, and the Catholics were now doing the same thing with a statue of Jesus and Mary in the church. Mr Carpenter continued with his questioning.

"Did the Children of Israel worship the Ark?"

That was a relieving question and I gave out an emphatic No!

"So, likewise, we don't worship the statue of Mary or Jesus. The whole commandment says that if you bow down and worship the image, this is wrong. But we merely have statues to remind us that Mary and Jesus are present and open to our prayers."

Again, what could I say? If I said that having statues in the church was wrong because the Bible speaks against graven images, I was confessing in the same breath that Moses was contradicting the second commandment of the Decalogue because Moses was the one who had the Ark made. But I considered Moses to be a prophet of God and so I didn't know what to answer. But, there was still something about Mary which didn't sound right and I had to clarify this.

"But Mr Carpenter, you say that you worship Mary. But when Satan came to Jesus in the wilderness to tempt Him, Satan told Jesus to bow down and worship him. But Jesus replied, 'Get thee hence, Satan: for it is written, Thou shalt worship the Lord thy God, and him only shalt thou serve'."

Mr Carpenter sat back and laughed gently in that fatherly way of his.

"I think you have misunderstood me," he said. "I don't think you understand what is meant when we worship Mary. She is not God. She is the Mother of God. We believe only in one God and we worship Him only.

But we don't always pray to God but sometimes we pray to Mary instead because she takes our prayers to God. When we pray to Mary, she takes our petitions to God for us because she stands between us and God.

You need to understand that Mary is the softer side and the female aspect in heaven. God sometimes can be very angry with us. You know what men can be like, insensitive to feelings. But women are softer. Don't you remember sometimes when you were younger and your father was angry with you and he was going to give you a belting but your mother stepped in his way and pleaded him not to be so cruel? Haven't you experienced times when your father has been busy and so you go to your mother with a question and she answers it for you? Well, it's the same with Mary and Jesus. Sometimes you sin against God and He gets angry and would punish you for your sins but Mary steps in His way and pleads with God to be merciful with you and not to treat you so harshly."

This again sounded blasphemous but I had no answer. I could see where the ideas had come from but I couldn't discredit Mary because Mr Carpenter had established the reason for giving Mary place in heaven on a verse from the Bible which I could not deny and I could understand the whole logic behind the subsequent arguments. All I could do was listen, store the ideas he was professing and pursue them in detail at a later stage.

Ruth came to the table with the cups and saucers tinkling in her hands, being the shy daughter of the host, and began offering the coffee around, nervously putting my coffee in front of me as if I were a lord from another province, not a friend from school. She next brought out a cake which she had especially made for the evening. Mrs Carpenter got up from the table, went to the kitchen and helped Ruth prepare slices of this delightful dessert and I could see the two ladies whispering among themselves with occasional glances at me. Ruth and her mother returned to the table to serve us.

When Ruth came over to the table with my slice of cake, I thanked and praised her politely for her effort. While she bent over to put the cake down, I noticed the medallion around her neck swaying before me and remembered that she had once said that it was her St Christopher medal.

That's right, I thought. Catholics believe in the saints. What are they and what's their function in the Church?

Mrs Carpenter and Ruth finally sat down and, while everyone commented on Ruth's delicious creation, I noticed Mrs Carpenter also had a medallion hanging on a chain. I pointed to it.

"Mrs Carpenter, who is the saint on your medallion?"

Mrs Carpenter looked up with surprise.

"Why, it's St Patrick, the patron saint of Ireland. I'm of Irish descent and still carry on the tradition that was brought down from my ancestors."

I looked at Mr Carpenter.

"Mr Carpenter, what function do the saints play in the Catholic Church?"

Mr Carpenter swallowed a mouthful of cake, put his fork down and leaned on the back of his fingers.

"The saints also look after us. They help God by answering our prayers for us."

"But, I thought God did everything for us," I protested. "I mean, I thought He listened to all our prayers."

Mrs Carpenter burst out laughing and it was she who was the one who answered the question for me.

"You can't expect God to do everything. While He is helping the starving millions in Africa, He can't also be helping us with our little, insignificant problems."

I was horrified with this explanation but I let her continue.

"So, the saints help us while God is looking after others. But you have to know which saints will help you. When I was pregnant with my first two sons, I prayed to St Xavier but both births were complicated. So, when I had Ruth, I prayed to St Christopher for help, and giving birth to Ruth was straight forward. So, I knew to pray to St Christopher when I was having a baby," and she leaned back and sighed.

"But Ruth was my last," she added, and put her hand on Ruth's and looked at Ruth with a smile.

What was this blasphemy that they were advocating? Since when did God need help from His creatures? God alone was the Almighty and could do everything. He did not need any assistance. He created the entire universe without help. So, why couldn't He solve all our problems and answer all our prayers? I was greatly horrified by the Catholics' limited view of God and wondered how they could call Him the Almighty.

But when Mrs Carpenter said this, I couldn't help but see a similarity between their concept of God and the concept purported by the ancient Greeks. The Greeks blatantly stated that they believed in many gods, where Zeus was the Father overall. But the Greeks didn't only pray to Zeus. Sometimes they called upon other gods and goddesses of the pantheon in times of need. But although there were many gods and goddesses in the Greek pantheon, Zeus was the Father and the highest of them all, holding the final authority.

In the *Iliad*, the ancient Greek story of the Trojan War, as an example, we read how the protagonist, King Agamemnon, decided to make war with the city of Troy to retrieve his stolen wife, Helen. However, he realised that he couldn't pray to Zeus for assistance because Zeus sided with the city of Troy. So Agamemnon and his people had to invoke other gods and goddesses for help, such as Poseidon and Athena. Mrs Carpenter's explanation of praying to the saints and finding the right saint who will answer our specific prayers just sounded exactly the same as this old Greek religion.

I could see then that Catholicism was just polytheism dressed up as monotheism where the Holy Trinity was equivalent to Zeus, and the saints were equivalent to all the other gods and goddesses. All Catholicism had done was take this Greek religion, reword and restructure it so that no-one could condemn a Catholic for being polytheistic because the Catholics would deny that they believed in other gods apart from the one God because they called the lesser gods saints.

By this stage, I was tired of asking questions and thought that it was time for me to be going home. I thanked Mr and Mrs Carpenter for having me over for dinner and thanked Ruth for taking me to Mass. All three got up with me and saw me to the door. Mr Carpenter gave me a hearty handshake.

"It has been a real pleasure to meet you, Michael. You are definitely a fine young gentleman and I'm pleased that you are a friend of Ruth's. It's good to see that a fine young lad is diligently searching for the truth. You are welcome at any time."

"Thank you, Mr Carpenter. And thank you very much, Mrs Carpenter, for dinner. It was extremely delicious."

"Oh, my pleasure, Michael," Mrs Carpenter replied with a smile.

I walked outside and Ruth came with me to the car. Before I got in, I thanked Ruth also for her hospitality.

"And you did a fine job with the cake!" I said.

Ruth looked away with a shy smile. She then turned back to face me.

"Thank you for coming to Mass, too. I was really pleased that you came. And I can see that my parents really like you a lot."

"Well, I really like them, too," I said. "Oh, well, I've gotta go. I'll see you on Monday. Study hard!"

With that, I got in the car and drove off.

What a night! It was such a mentally draining experience. As I drove home, I thought about the whole evening, how Mr Carpenter had answered practically all my questions to support his beliefs, using the Bible. But even so, I didn't agree with him. But why not? Why couldn't I agree with him when it was the exact same book we confessed to be the Word of God?

And then I thought about the Apostles' Creed and how it embodied our fundamental belief in the three gods in the godhead, that Jesus died and rose again, and that Jesus would come again to judge the living and the dead.

And then Troy came to my mind. I could not fathom that out. I could still see him reciting the Apostles' Creed and then see him at school mockingly saying to me things like "Praise the Lord" and "Hallelujah, brother!"

I drove up the driveway and stopped the car. With a deep sigh, I got out and went inside. When I walked through the front door, I could hear the television was on. I walked down the hall to the lounge-room. My parents were laid back watching TV. Both parents looked up with a smile.

"How was it, son?" my father asked.

I came into the room and sat in a chair opposite them. I fiddled around with my socks and then reclined back into the chair.

"It was interesting," I said with a sigh of exhaustion.

My parents paused, waiting for me to continue. And so I did.

"Well, for starters," I began. "They believe the Bible, too."

My parents just stared in expectation for more information. I leaned forward.

"Why aren't Catholics Christians?" I asked.

"Because they believe in the Bible and other things as well," my mother said adamantly. "You have to believe the Bible only."

"But Mr Carpenter demonstrated that every tenet of the Catholics' belief is based on the Bible, and I wasn't able to answer him."

"What do you mean, son?" my father asked.

"Well, let's start with the Pope. We believe the Pope is just a man but the Catholics believe he is the head of the Church. But they don't believe it for no reason. The Bible says in Matthew 16:18, 'And I say also unto thee, That thou art Peter, and upon this rock I will build my church; and the gates of hell shall not prevail against it'. Mr Carpenter explained that the name, Peter, comes from the Greek, *petra*, which means *rock*. In Greek, this verse reads, "thou art *Petros*, and upon this *petra* I will build my church.' It seems from this verse that Jesus was saying Peter is the Rock upon which Christ built His Church."

"That's not what that means," my mother spurted. "Peter is not the Rock upon which Christ built His Church. Christ is the Rock. Read the verse before it and see how it fits in context, not like the way the Catholics construe the Scriptures!"

I read from verse thirteen.

"'When Jesus came into the coasts of Caesarea Philippi, he asked his disciples, saying, Whom do men say that I the Son of man am? And they said, Some say that thou art John the Baptist: some, Elias; and others, Jeremias, or one of the prophets. He saith unto them, But whom say ye that I am? And Simon

Peter answered and said, Thou art the Christ, the Son of the living God. And Jesus answered and said unto him, Blessed art thou, Simon Barjona: for flesh and blood hath not revealed it unto thee, but my Father which is in heaven. And I say also unto thee, That thou art Peter, and upon this rock I will build my church; and the gates of hell shall not prevail against it'."

"See?" my mother said. "Because Peter recognised that Jesus was the Christ, Jesus told Peter that He would build His Church on the fact that He is the Christ. Why would Jesus build His Church on Peter anyway when later in verse twenty-three, Jesus calls Peter Satan? And later, when Jesus was betrayed, Peter denied Him three times!"

I didn't have an answer to this either, but then my father took up the argument where my mother had left off.

"If the Church were to be built on any of the apostles, it would have to have been built on Paul, because, at one time, Paul scolded Peter for sinning. Remember what Paul wrote in Galatians 2:11, 'But when Peter was come to Antioch, I withstood him to the face, because he was to be blamed' because, as Paul explains in verse 14, Peter 'walked not uprightly according to the truth of the gospel'. If Peter were the head of the Church, how could Paul stand up and say before everybody that Peter was wrong? Can you imagine a cardinal, or a bishop, or a priest standing up to the Pope and saying that the Pope is wrong and not walking according to the truth of the gospel? He would be instantly excommunicated!

130

And why does Peter himself say at the end of his second letter in II Peter 3:15 and 16, 'even as our beloved brother Paul also according to the wisdom given unto him hath written unto you; As also in all his epistles, speaking in them of these things; in which are some things hard to be understood'? If Peter were the head of the Church, why did he tell the Church to read Paul's letters? Not only so, Peter admitted that he found Paul's letters difficult to understand, as if Paul was the one delivering edicts to the Church. It would make more sense if the Catholics said that the Church was built on Paul and not on Peter! Again, can you imagine the Pope saying to the members of the Church how they should obey what a cardinal, or a bishop, or some priest has written to them, things that even the Pope himself finds difficult to understand?"

What my parents said made sense. But still, I couldn't help but agree with the Catholics' interpretation of Matthew 16:18 being a deliberate play on words to show that Peter was the head of the Church. So, I just nodded in agreement.

"But what about Mary?" I asked.

"What about Mary?" my mother retorted.

"Mr Carpenter explained why the Catholics pray to Mary," I said and explained to them the whole line of argument. My parents listened till I had finished but my mother sat fidgeting ready to explode when the last word of my final sentence had left my mouth.

"But Mary was still only human and needed her sins to be forgiven and paid for by Christ also. Christ didn't have to be subject to her. All the while that He was in the womb, it was His choice to be there and He could have changed the situation at will. But He chose to be born as a man because He could only pay for man's sins by becoming a man Himself. To become a man, He had to be born like one!"

I could see my mother's viewpoint. But I could see the Carpenters' viewpoint as well. Mr Carpenter didn't dream up his answer. He quoted the Bible, the Word of God.

But, again, I just nodded in agreement. I then talked about the family in general and told them in glowing terms what a nice family they were. But then I asked, "Apart from this, they confess that Jesus Christ died for their sins and rose again from the dead. Doesn't this mean that they're saved?"

"No," my mother snapped. "You have to believe the Bible and the Bible only. They may be good people but being good won't get you to heaven. You have to believe the Bible and the gospel of salvation only. They believe in another Jesus who is not in the Bible."

I did agree to some extent with this last statement because the Carpenters' view of God was limited whereas the God of the Bible was Almighty in power.

But when I went to bed, all these arguments fought a religious war in my head. What does it mean to be a Christian? Are Catholics Christians or not?

And what about Troy? Is he saved? He confessed the Apostles' Creed but then mocked me at school for the same faith I had in Christ. Was he saved or not? And if not, why not, when Mr Norman had proved from the Bible that it is not works that will ever save us, but faith only, which both Catholics and Protestants have.

But the other thing that troubled me was the marked contrast between Ruth and Troy. Ruth was sedate, polite, modest, a "good girl", whereas Troy was loud-mouthed and outspoken, always having a good time, who often swore and told dirty jokes. But every weekend, both Ruth and Troy worshipped the same God under the same roof and made identical confessions. According to the Protestant belief, both deserved to go to hell, according to the Catholic belief, both should go to heaven. If it had been left to me, all three of us would have gone to heaven together.

Chapter 7

The last year of school finally arrived. By this stage, Ruth and I had become close friends and we spent time at each other's places studying. When Ruth came to my place, my parents welcomed her and sometimes asked her to stay for dinner. We always continued our after dinner Bible Study and Ruth joined in. She never said anything but simply listened to our discussions. When I visited Ruth, Ruth's parents fussed over me as well and for a long while we left the conversation of religion to rest, although Mr Carpenter raised certain things from time to time.

The relationship between Ruth and me was becoming so strong that everybody began assuming that we were going steady, including the Carpenters and my parents. Out of everyone, I was the last to know. My peers were always referring to Ruth as my girlfriend and I would just laugh and say that we were just good friends. I couldn't see why it wasn't possible to have a friend of the opposite sex and not be going steady.

But there was a deep-seated reason which I didn't want to admit to myself: I wasn't in love with Ruth, I was in love with Troy. I didn't have it in me to make my relationship with Ruth go any further than a simple close friendship. But where Troy was concerned, I could have given him my soul.

When I sat with our group at lunch time or in certain classes, I found myself staring at Troy so much so that when I became aware of it, I became guilty and frustrated. I found myself getting jealous of Troy's mates because they got to enjoy his company more than I did.

And then Ruth herself began showing signs that she was in love with me. How was I to know? It wasn't natural for me to fall in love with a woman, it came naturally for me to fall in love with a man. But the more I thought of Troy, the more it made me feel guilty and evil because it contradicted my world view and I knew I would go to hell if I allowed myself to be led by my natural instinct.

I would never have made my relationship with Ruth any more than a simple friendship if I had been left alone. But I think my parents loved Ruth enough to see her as their future daughter-in-law. They noticed that whenever I talked about Ruth, there was nothing in my words which spoke of going steady, of our future lives together or of preparing for the wedding. And so, because she was a little anxious to help me along the way, my mother decided to give me a little push.

"You know, women like men to be romantic and have a hug and kiss from time to time, and be told that they are loved," she said to me one afternoon after school. We were sitting on the back patio having a cup of coffee while the last strands of light strained over the horizon.

When my mother said this, I thought she was making a comment about a lack of affection from my father that I was unaware of and so I just nodded. But then my mother continued.

"Well, you should show some affection to Ruth every now and again. You know. When you go for a walk, offer to hold her hand and give her a kiss good-bye and even say those magical words, 'I love you' from time to time."

That struck me from left field.

"Mum, I really like Ruth, but I'm not in love with her."

My mother smiled gently.

"Ruth is very much in love with you. And I know you're in love with her. You spend so much time with each other. But men usually have the habit of not really knowing how to express their love for their girlfriends romantically. And Ruth is a lovely, intelligent girl, and I can see that the Holy Spirit is working through you to finally win her over to the truth."

I was dumbfounded. I liked Ruth a lot. But I didn't love her, I knew that. There was no magic. I enjoyed her friendship, talking with her, learning about the differences between our versions of Christianity, talking about life in general. But as for loving her and expressing such love affectionately, I didn't have it in me.

When I had a chance to think about it later, I guessed this was God's way of curing my homosexuality. Of course, it all made sense. Satan was using Troy to lure me away from God and the Bible because my mind was enraptured in thoughts about him. But God had brought me a pretty young lady who really was searching for Him and, seeing I was spending so much time trying to convert her, this was bringing us closer together. But because I could not see it before, God had used my mother as the direct instrument to make me realise what He was doing without my mother really aware of the conflict going on inside me. So, I decided to do as my mother bid me and to begin showing affection to Ruth.

I really tried my best. I tried to hold her tenderly in my arms. I tried kissing her. But her lips to me were too soft and supple. I didn't like this at all. It excited her that I treated her in this way but, to me, it was a duty. My mother told me I was in love with her, my mother told me how to show it to her. It was God's indirect way of telling me to do this. But whenever I expressed my affection openly towards her, it was Troy I wished was there, not her. She had too many bumps in the wrong places.

I don't know how I managed to fake these feelings I did not have for Ruth but I managed to make them seem real enough for Ruth not to realise that my outward actions were in no way a reflection of what I felt inside. I was able to pull it off but still I felt as if there were a glass wall between her and me. As much as I tried to convince myself to the contrary, I didn't love her. The way I was responding to her signs of affection was mechanical, robotic, a concerted attempt to please God, my parents and Ruth, but inside I had no feelings. I knew that my true feelings lay with Troy. I tried to suppress my feelings and pretend they did not exist. But the more I tried to suppress and to bury them, the greater my love for him became and it made me all the more frustrated and miserable.

Then there was another event which stirred my restless soul within. At my school, Wednesday afternoon was reserved for sport. But one Wednesday afternoon, I managed to convince the teachers that I was unable to participate in sport that afternoon and therefore was granted permission to be relieved from physical exertion which allowed me the chance to finish a mountain of homework I needed to complete for the following day. But instead of going to the library or going home, I went to the Seniors' Room. This was a little room which must have once been used for something else but when the authorities found that they had no more use for it, they said to themselves, "Let's give it to the seniors."

I walked into this little room and there wasn't a soul there. That was great. I could do my work in peace. I pulled out all my work and began furiously going through it. I had been there for about half an hour or so when the door burst open. I jumped up with a start and when I looked up, there was Troy. When he saw me, he had a big grin on his face.

"What are you doin' here, you bludger? God'll be angry with you for waggin' sport!" he said.

He tossed his bag on the floor and came over to me.

"What're you doin'? The maths problems?" he asked.

"Yeah," I replied cautiously.

He came over to the desk I was seated at and stood really close to me. With that, my heart started pounding and I was scared he could hear it. He looked at my work uninvited which embarrassed me. I was expecting to hear his cynical laugh and to hear him say how stupid I was. But instead he pointed his finger at a problem I was doing and commented, "No, you've done this wrong."

With that he grabbed a chair and placed it right next to me, sat down and began explaining what I had done wrong. While he spoke, I listened, but I was first taken aback by his kindness to help. But what struck me off balance the most was that he sat himself so close to me that his shoulder was touching mine and although he was oblivious to the fact, the sensation was vivifying, sending me to the moon. Every now and again he would look at me and see if I had understood what he was explaining and I just stared at him and nodded.

He began flicking through the rest of my work and exclaimed, "You see? You've made the same mistake in all these questions. You know what you've done wrong..." and he continued.

As he ran his fingers gently down the pages, al-though it was nothing to him, to me he was running his fingers gently down my chest. I was frozen with a combination of pleasure and terror – while to him he was merely pointing out mathematical errors, to me he was pointing out how much he was in love with me. I tried to listen as he told me what he was doing but while he wrote and spoke, my eyes were trans-fixed on him.

I started with his hair. It was dark brown, thick and curly, like springs dripping from his scalp. His curls were so cute, I wanted to twirl them around my fingers.

My glance carelessly sauntered down his forehead to his beautiful brown eyes, like jewels, carefully polished and set in the sockets. My glance wandered down to his small nose, which was the correct size and shape, as if he who had set the mould was pleased with the result. From there my glance wandered down to his lips to watch his mouth move and speak wonderful things. And then to his neck, strong and sturdy, like a watchtower, strong and firm. I could feel myself kissing his neck, lying by his side.

He finished explaining what I had done wrong and turned to me.

"Do you understand?" he said, his eyes poised to welcome the answer.

"Er...yes," I replied, trying hard to come quickly back to normalcy.

"Any other questions?" he asked and stretched himself back with his hands behind his head as if he were opening his chest and heart to me.

"No...no. That was all," I replied.

Troy then got up from his chair and walked across the room to fidget with something in his bag.

"Damn, I forgot to bring my lunch today," he said disappointingly.

"You can eat mine if you like," I replied.

"What've you got?" he asked.

I took my lunch out of my bag, looked down at the thin sandwiches that I called lunch and pulled back the top slice of bread to examine the contents.

"Ham sandwiches," I replied.

"Yeah, they'll do. Why, aren't you eating?"

"I…I'm not hungry," I lied.

I wrapped the sandwich up and walked it across to him. To Troy, all he was observing was a fellow student walking across a room to give him a plain old ham sandwich. To me, I was gently pacing across a great hall, along a grand aisle, ornate with pillars and icons to offer my food offering as a sweet savour to my revered god.

Troy took the sandwich and began munching on it noisily. While to him I had done nothing but fed his appetite for the moment, to me I had performed a great task by quenching his appetite while I suffered in his place. While he munched away, I sat back down. Troy then began a new topic of conversation.

"Any cute girls in your church?"

I must have gone red. Troy laughed.

"Oooooh! I didn't think good little Christian Farril lusted!"

I paused and was unsure what to say but finally replied with the patterned response.

"No, we're not supposed to because the Bible says not to."

Troy's furrow dropped and he stopped chewing for a second. He had a strange look on his face and when he had swallowed that bite of sandwich, he asked, "Tell me seriously, Michael."

It was the first time I had ever heard Troy call me by my first name and it didn't pass unnoticed.

"Do you really believe the Bible is God's divine Word without error?"

I nodded and shyly answered in the affirmative while Troy attacked the sandwich with another bite.

"But why do you believe it? I mean, who told you?"

I stared at him.

"Can I quote from the Bible?" I asked hesitantly.

Troy stopped chewing for a second, looked at me and then laughed.

"Of course you can quote from the Bible," he said mockingly.

"Well, the Bible says, 'All Scripture is giving by inspiration of God'."

Troy was still looking at the sandwich when he replied.

"So, you believe the Bible is the Word of God because the Bible tells you it's the Word of God. There are other books out there that claim they're the Word of God as well. Will you believe them?"

"No," I replied emphatically.

"Why not?"

"Because the Bible doesn't say they are."

"Yeah, but be honest with yourself, Michael. The only reason why you believe the Bible is divine is not because the Bible says it is but because your parents and your church do, don't you?"

I was angry at him for saying that but also very astonished at his insight. When I thought about it, I could see that he was right and so I didn't answer him.

"And how do you know," Troy continued, "that the Bible has been faithfully transmitted down through the centuries intact without any additions or subtractions? I mean, how do you know that what you call the Bible today is the same as what the Christians of the first century called the Bible?"

"Because God wouldn't allow His Word to change through time," I said.

"But you only believe that because you firstly believe in the God of the Bible. All other religions would say the same thing about their holy books."

I thought about it for a moment and hated what he was saying. He seemed so carefree and careless about what he was saying. He was discussing the Bible as if it were a book open to debate. This was an approach to the Bible which had never entered my consciousness before. I had always axiomatically accepted the Bible as divine. There had never been any reason to go right back to fundamentals and even consider questioning the very foundation on which all my beliefs were based. Suddenly here I was engaging in a discussion which called into question the very reliability of the first principles of my entire belief system. From my childhood I had been taught that to do this was an extremely sinful thing to do so I could not understand how Troy could comfortably and unabashedly treat the Bible in this way. But he did, and it was extremely unsettling.

"The Bible is two thousand years old, Michael," Troy continued. "You can't seriously believe it has not been tampered with. But getting back to my original question, who says the Bible is the Word of God other than the Bible itself or your church and your parents who believe the Bible is the Word of God on the same basis as yourself?"

"I believe it is because it talks about Jesus Christ the Saviour," I replied.

"But who says that Jesus Christ is the Saviour?"

"The Bible," I said.

"So, the Bible is the Word of God because it says Jesus is the Saviour and you know Jesus is the Saviour because the Bible says so. You're not planning on becoming a lawyer, are you?"

I hated the way he kept tripping me up. And I hated what I viewed as hypocrisy in him. I had seen him at Mass confessing Jesus as Saviour and now here he was questioning it before me. Even to this day, I don't know how he was able to marry his criticism of Christianity and yet still attend Mass.

But what he was saying was right. My belief in Jesus was dependent on the validity of the Bible and I only believed the Bible was the Word of God because my parents and my church said it was. I realised for the first time just how flimsy and tenuous the basis of my faith had been and how that I needed more solid evidence to back up my belief. So I gave an answer that I thought would at least give some support.

"Well, the Bible is perfect from cover to cover," I said adamantly.

"Oh, so you've read it from cover to cover and you know it is?"

I hated him again for pulling me up. But all I could do was just shake my head.

"I've read the New Testament and the Psalms and Proverbs, and these are complete with no errors," I said. But as I said this, the question of being saved by faith only and being saved by faith and works came to mind and I knew I was lying. But to admit the contradiction was to say that Troy was right and I didn't want him to be right.

At this stage Troy had finished the sandwich and noisily screwed up the paper. He then flung the wrapping at the bin in the corner and got it in.

"I should have been a basketball player!" he mused.

"Well, what do you believe about God and about religion?" I asked putting the ball back in his court.

Troy leaned back in his chair with his arms behind his head.

"Oh, I believe in God but I don't believe the Church nor the Bible has the ultimate and final say on everything. I believe God loves us and wants us to be happy and enjoy this life, to be free to do what we want as long as we are not hurting anybody else. I believe in the Church and the Bible insofar as they are a guide but I don't stick rigidly to everything they say."

"But we're not free to do whatever we want. If we don't keep His commandments, we'll go to hell."

Troy leaned back his head and laughed.

"You don't believe in hell, do you?" and laughed again.

I sat and watched him for a moment, not knowing what to say at first. But then I finally spoke.

"Well, yes, because the Bible - "

"Says so," Troy finished my sentence for me. "Michael, listen to yourself. You believe in God because the Bible says so. You believe in Jesus because the Bible says so. You believe Jesus is coming again because the Bible says so. You believe in hell because the Bible says so. You even believe the Bible is the Word of God because the Bible says so. Your life and mind are so much wrapped up in the Bible that you've become a complete Bible-robot. You're not a human being but a walking program, not willing to think for yourself because you're scared that if you do otherwise you'll go to hell. You can't think for yourself, you can't make up your mind about any-thing. The Bible has completely robbed you of your individuality and your freedom to think that you have become mentally a slave to this book. It's inhu-mane.

Let me tell you straight. This business of hell is just a religious ploy that the Church invented so that the Church can take complete control over you. The Church tells you to do something or not to do some-thing and you'll obey it whether your reason tells you it's true or not because all you can see is the devil holding a pitchfork and stoking the flames. But it's all a load of crap."

I sat there motionless, just fidgeting with my fin-gers nervously because I was just so lost for words. But Troy hadn't finished.

"Tell me, Michael, I'm sure it says in the Bible that God is all-loving and all-powerful, doesn't it?"

I nodded my head.

"Well, if that's the case, why is there so much suf-fering in the world?"

"Because…because…Satan is the cause of all the suffering in the world, not God."

"Well, if Satan is the cause, where did he come from?"

I looked at Troy and didn't know what to say. There was a long pause. I was searching in my mind for Bible verses to provide Troy with the answer. I realised with all my reading that I had never actually read in the Bible about Satan's origins and I would later find out that the Bible doesn't provide any, or what at least is claimed to be the origins of Satan are ambiguous at best. But I had to give Troy an answer and so I eventually came out with what I had learned at church.

"Well, in the beginning, before God created the world, He created angels. Satan, who at the time was called Lucifer, was the highest of all the angels in beauty and splendour. But he got so puffed up with pride that he felt that he should be equal with God, even be God, and so God cast him out of heaven. In defiance, Satan became the god of everything that was opposed to God."

Troy looked at me squarely in the eye and with a sound of disappointment in his voice said, "Oh, Michael, you don't seriously believe all that bullshit?"

I just sat and stared at Troy. I was lost for words.

"Okay, okay," Troy then said, realising that my silence was the answer to his question. And so he continued. "Let's just say what you say is true. Tell me, if God is all-powerful and all-loving, how is it that an all-powerful God can be the creator of something which causes suffering and a being which is His enemy? I mean, if God is all-loving, He would hate suffering and, because He is all-powerful, He has the power to stop suffering whenever He pleases. Satan can't stop Him because God is more powerful than Satan."

This time I couldn't answer because I had no answer. I hated Troy asking me these questions which obviously proved the inconsistency of Christian doctrine. But Troy went further.

"I suppose you believe in the story of Adam and Eve frolicking around in the nuddy in the Garden of Eden."

I nodded slowly.

"Yeah, 'cos the Bible says so. I should have guessed. Well, let me ask you another question. Eve was tempted by the serpent, wasn't she?"

"Yes," I said.

"Tell me. If God is all-powerful and all-knowing and can see the future before it happens and saw the potential destruction that Satan could cause to humanity, why didn't God destroy Satan before He created the world? Then neither Eve nor Adam would have been tempted to eat the apple because, according to the Bible story, before Satan entered the picture, neither Adam nor Eve gave the commandment to keep away from the Tree a single thought."

Again, his question was sharp. But what could I say? I had never looked at it in this way. But this last question had far reaching implications than Troy realised. I knew that it said in Revelation 20:10 that God would in the end of eternity destroy Satan in the Lake of Fire. If God was eventually going to destroy Satan, why didn't He just destroy Satan in the beginning and spare all this present suffering on God's side and ours?

What was God really doing? Did God gain some sort of twisted pleasure in playing games with the devil, allowing Satan to continue to exist so that God could prolong this morbid game of strategy He played with the devil that God already knew He would eventually win, in the meantime making humankind miserable in the process?

But Troy was now in full swing.

"Let me ask you another question, Michael. Does the Bible teach that God is everywhere, occupying all space in the universe?" and when he said 'occupying all space in the universe', there was a lot of mocking contempt in his voice.

"Yes," I said cautiously.

"And does the Bible say so?" he asked.

"Yes," I replied.

"Can you quote a verse from the Bible that says so?" Troy asked.

I was surprised that Troy asked me so overtly to quote the Scriptures but I obliged.

"In...In Psalm 139 verses 7 to 10, David writes, 'Whither shall I go from thy spirit? Or whither shall I flee from thy presence? If I ascend up into heaven, thou art there: if I make my bed in hell, behold, thou art there. If I take the wings of the morning, and dwell in the uttermost parts of the sea; Even there shall thy hand lead me, and thy right hand shall hold me'."

"Well, Michael, I've heard you talk a lot about Jesus' Second Coming. If Jesus is God, and He's going to come back, from what place in the universe is He going to leave when He returns if He is everywhere? If He's everywhere, isn't He here already?"

I gasped in horror. What could I say? No answer was forthcoming. At first I wanted to say that Jesus is here only in spirit but that, at His second coming, He will return in a bodily form. But then, the Bible was clear in saying that God is a spirit and that, when Jesus resurrected, He took off His physical body like an article of clothing and put on an incorruptible spiritual body that would endure forever. Any way I tried to look at it, it led to a dead end.

Troy sat there and waited for an answer but I had none to give. So, he offered his own explanation.

"That's why you can't believe the Bible is God's venerable Word without error because it does not hold consistent beliefs. For every explanation, there is another question raised. Despite how beautiful a book the Bible may be, it was written by men and so it will have mistakes in it.

Michael, you have to realise that the Bible was written at a time when people didn't know how to explain what was going on around them. It is just a book of the interpretation of certain people's views of God in the past, but views change."

I just sat there dumbfounded. I saw errors in my belief that I didn't want to see. However, I didn't agree with Troy's last statement.

"But the Bible is applicable to all time. What the Christians believed in the first century and what Christians believe today is the same. That's why we can be confident that the Bible is the Word of God.

Christians still believe in the same Bible as they did when the apostles first wrote it, without having to update it. It has remained constant."

Troy just smiled and looked around this little room.

"Michael, what about the idea that the earth is at the centre of the solar system? Remember what we learned in physics when we studied astronomy and about the history of the ideas of the solar system? Aristotle proposed the idea that the earth was at the centre of the universe, which sounded feasible at the time because every day and night, everyone saw the sun, moon and stars circle around the earth which implied that the earth remained stationary. And, after all, if the earth moved, any object that was thrown into the air would land somewhere to the west. It was simple and it was logical.

The Church held to this belief because it had a theological point to it, for the earth was where God concentrated all of his attention.

When Copernicus proposed from scientific observation that, in fact, the sun is at the centre of the solar system, the Church did not like this at all, although Copernicus got away with it because he simply said that this was a theoretical model. However, later, Galileo pushed the idea further, claiming that this was not merely hypothetical but the actual reality of how the heavens move, and for saying this he was put under house arrest for the rest of his life. The Christians didn't like what Copernicus and Galileo were proposing because what they claimed contradicted the Scriptures. These days, everybody believes

Copernicus and Galileo so obviously the Bible is wrong."

"It's not true! The Bible does not say that the earth is at the centre of the solar system," I cried out in despair. "The Church may have made a mistake, but not the Bible."

"But the Church pointed to the verse in Psalm 93:1 where it says, 'the world also is stablished, that it cannot be moved.' Because the Bible said the earth was stationary, for Copernicus and Galileo to say that it moved was to say that the Bible was mistaken, and to the religious authorities, this meant that these astronomers were evil and satanic. But try asking Christians today if they believe the sun orbits the earth and they will laugh in your face, not realising that their Holy Book tells them otherwise."

"You're wrong! It's not true! The Bible is true and makes no mistakes! The Bible is the Word of God without error!" I cried out, almost like a mantra.

I was close to tears and was shaking. Troy must have realised that he had gone too far with his anti-Christian exegesis and noticed how badly it was distressing me. He came over to me and put his arm around my shoulder.

"Michael, I'm sorry. I didn't mean to get you so upset. Are you all right?"

This was a moment of moments for me. Troy gave me a hug and I planted my face into his chest. The feeling of his body close to mine and the sound of his heartbeat was a memory I would treasure for a long time afterwards.

"I'm sorry, Michael," he said by way of an apology, "I didn't mean to get you so upset. I just hate seeing you so trapped in your faith to the point that your mind is not free."

I just nodded. Troy then pulled out a crumpled up handkerchief from his pocket and began to wipe my eyes like a caring father would do to his beloved son. I have no words to describe the feelings going on inside me at that moment. Here was the man I loved giving me special attention, something that I had thought he was totally incapable of doing. I still don't know to this day why he behaved in this tender manner towards me.

After putting his hanky away, he then held my shoulders and looked at me with a gentle smile.

"C'mon. Let's forget about this religious discussion and talk about something else. Okay?"

And so we did. We chatted for what seemed like hours. We talked about what we hoped to do when we left school, what we hoped to get in the HSC, what we do on the weekend, anything and everything. It was one of the most treasured memories of my life. It was the one and only time that I didn't have to share him with anyone else. And he seemed so out of character.

But when the final bell went, we parted. It was the second time I hated its sound.

When I walked home, all I could think about was Troy and that afternoon only strengthened my original feelings for him. If it were in my scope to do it, I would have wrapped the moon in silver gossamers, tied it up with scarlet ribbon and given it to him on a golden platter, my love for him was so deep.

But his arguments against Christianity and the Bible caused me to doubt my faith even more. I didn't want to doubt but those questions he threw at me went over and over in my mind. As much as I tried to convince myself that the devil was behind all this and that the devil wanted me to go to hell because he hated me, Troy's questions had a lot of validity in them. They were not stupid questions nor did they sound like they came from someone who was evil. They showed up more inconsistencies in the Bible that demanded answers.

Seeing my parents were such strong believers in the Bible and since they were so much older than me, naturally I thought that they had been confronted with the same questions and the same problems in the Bible so had contented themselves with logical answers that gave greater substance to their faith.

And so, later that evening, I put the question to them. I had finished my homework and study for the evening. While my father was watching television, my mother sat next to him crocheting. I came out and flopped into one of the lounge chairs.

"Had enough, son?" my father asked with a smile.

"Yeah, I needed a break."

My mother continued crocheting with a vengeance.

"How was school today, then?" he asked.

"Oh, all right. I skipped sport to finish some homework and a friend of mine, Troy, helped me with some problems."

"That was nice of him," my father said.

There was a pause and then I came straight out with the question.

"I know the Bible is the Word of God, but how do we know that it is?"

My mother pushed her crocheting on her lap with a punctation mark and returned with, "Because it is! It's the Word of God!"

That put me on guard and I knew I had asked a dangerous question. But I had to have an answer.

"But, I mean, how do we know? And how do we know that what we call the Bible now has been transmitted to us exactly how it was written in the first place?"

Now it was my father's turn to get hostile.

"The Bible is the Word of God. We know it has been transmitted successfully over the last two thousand years because God ensured that it would be. It's the Word of God because it says so."

I paused for a moment out of fear of my parents' reaction to my questions but there was no solid foundation for the claim. My parents sounded just like the programmed robot Troy accused me of being.

"Yeah, but how do we know that the Bible is the Word of God?"

"Because it tells us that Jesus died for our sins. Don't you believe that?" my mother said, full of the wrath of God. "You should not be tempting God with questions of doubt! Don't you remember what happened to the Children of Israel when they questioned God? The earth opened up and swallowed them!"

I was filled with terror. God was going to open up the earth and swallow me because I had asked a question about the faith I loved and cherished. I wanted an answer to give Troy but also to satisfy my own mind as to why I believed the Bible's claim to divinity.

But I didn't dare ask any more questions after that. My mother resumed her crocheting and my father buried his head back into the television. So, I got up, went to my room, plopped onto my bed and stared at the ceiling. The question bounced around in my head: "But who says the Bible is the Word of God?" I hated the question but I had no answer. I hated doubting but now serious questions had been asked which required answers.

And I was in love with Troy. I was in love with a man. While I lay on the bed staring at the ceiling, I entertained the image of Troy when he was sitting beside me helping me with the maths problems and then when he was holding me against his chest. The beautiful, passionate feelings that all this engendered in my soul filled me with inexplicable euphoric feelings which I knew was love. I was madly in love with Troy and I knew it. But while love was supposed to be a beautiful thing, I hated myself all the more because of it.

Chapter 8

My love for Troy was full on since that afternoon in the seniors' room but Troy's attitude towards me had not changed one iota. Although he continued now and again to taunt me over my religiosity, it was nothing like he used to and I noticed more now that despite his rough side, there was a nicer side to him. Not only was he very handsome, he was enviably intelligent and was always in the top classes in all the subjects he was studying. But he never lauded this on himself. Rather, if anyone had a problem they couldn't work out in any subject, he would have all the time in the world to help out, even for me.

Subconsciously at first, I began asking Troy to help me with problems particularly in mathematics when I knew that if I really had thought about the problem I could have got the answer myself. Every time I asked Troy a question, he had no qualms about helping me out. It came to such a point that I began to feel disappointed if I could breeze through a series of mathematical problems without assistance.

Poor Ruth! If she had only known that if I could have had it, I would have dropped her for a man! But not just any man. I wanted Troy the way I could have Ruth.

And if Troy only knew! The more I saw of Troy at school and the more I pondered on those couple of hours when we were together alone in the seniors' room, the more it moved me to be with him, to want him. Each day when I woke up, Troy was on my mind. I couldn't wait to get to school just to see him. Once there, at least I could see him and maybe even talk to him. There were times when I did say a few words but to me even the most trivial and mundane conversation with him left a sweet savour in my mouth. The least attention he paid me was something beautiful to place in my box of treasures, those sweet memories locked away in the secret chambers of my soul. My yearning for him was so strong. But God's Word said that to love a man like I loved Troy was wrong. But why? Who was it hurting?

To try and overcome my true feelings for Troy, I entertained Ruth like a boyfriend should. I really worked hard to learn to love a woman how a man was traditionally supposed to. I took Ruth out to dinner on various occasions. They were pleasant evenings, just the two of us. Everything about the outings made me feel that I was doing the right thing: opening the door of the restaurant to allow her in, watching the waiters and waitresses treat us as a couple of lovebirds, having a slow dance on the dance floor. When I drove her home, kissed her good night and told her that I loved her, all these were the traditionally right things to do. As long as I complied with this traditional norm, I felt that I was doing the right thing.

Everything around me felt right but not inside me. I knew that what I was doing was not me. The person performing was a robot programmed by society, by my parents, by my God, but the real me inside was someone else, a spectator. I tried to fight it. I desperately wanted to be "normal", to really be the person I was acting out. I wanted to have the "normal", expected feelings for Ruth that instead I had for Troy. And it was frustrating and torturing me. What was wrong with me?

The confusion that it created in me! This gravitational pull, this electromagnetic force that attracted me to Troy was considered by the world around me as evil, wrong, licentious, perverted, lust, but if Troy were substituted by Ruth, these same feelings became righteous, good, noble, normal, love. The nature of the attraction was the same but by merely changing the gender of the object of this attraction decided whether this emotion, this feeling, came from the throne of God or from the dungeons of hell.

This orientation came from within. It was a part of me. There was no decision making process, no choice. If a choice had existed, I definitely would have chosen Ruth over Troy, but the attraction towards Troy was a part of me, against my consent. I was thus condemned to feel this way for Troy, doubly condemned by a world and a God who hated me because of it.

But I was determined not to give up. Surely if I continued to play the part of the boyfriend with Ruth, the "normal" heterosexual stimulus would somehow be absorbed into me by osmosis. But the more I fought against my sexual attraction to men, the stronger the attraction became.

The problem, so I convinced myself, was that I was not doing enough for God and so He was punishing me. Romans chapter one told me that these desires came from God as punishment for disbelieving. So, if I had these desires, I must not be doing enough to show that I believed in Him and His Word. And I was not showing Him I believed because I was not trying hard enough to convince Ruth of the errors of the Catholic faith. So I resolved to further prove to Ruth the truth of the gospel.

The time to tell Ruth fair and square that she was in error finally arrived. I planned my argument and was ready to show her systematically that the Catholic Church had erred in its teachings as the Church developed through the centuries. I chose to tell her after school beside the creek where we would be on neutral ground with no influence from her parents nor mine.

As we strolled out of the school and began our journey home, Ruth was relaxed and carefree with me as she always was. Ruth was never lost for words and she was happy to talk about everything and anything this afternoon as she ever was. Usually I joined in. But this afternoon, I found it hard to relax and join in with the conversation. The weight that was hanging over me to tell Ruth about the errors of her Church was so heavy and cumbersome that I just couldn't enjoy our simple walk home like I usually did.

As we approached the gurgley creek, Ruth was calm and relaxed but I was quivering and twitching, preparing to show Ruth the errors of her belief. The pressure was so great that I felt like forgetting the entire affair. But then Satan came to mind. I felt as if Satan didn't want me to tell Ruth. Satan wanted Ruth to remain induced in error and finally send her to hell when she died. I didn't want that. I wanted Ruth to go to heaven. And Jesus said that I was a light to her and so it was my Christian duty to tell her whether she wanted to hear the truth or not.

We finally sat down in our usual spot by the creek with a large eucalyptus tree behind us. Ruth placed herself gently on the ground and sighed with satisfaction. I sat down near her but I was twitching and quivering nervously.

"Aaaah! It's always so lovely to be here," Ruth said with contentment.

I smiled in agreement but the pressure inside was so strong. I had to push ahead and tell Ruth what was needed to be said.

There was a slight pause. Ruth stared at the creek while I looked at her in the serenity of the moment. I didn't want to spoil it. But I had to, for righteousness sake. If Ruth were in a burning house, wouldn't I run in and save her? She was destined to enter a burning eternity and I knew that this was the moment to save her.

"Ruth," I said.

"Yes," Ruth replied.

"Ruth, I've been studying the Bible and the beliefs of the Catholic Church and I have found a lot of things which the Catholic Church teaches which are wrong. And I feel so strongly that I have to tell you."

Ruth just turned towards me and gave me a sweet, lazy smile.

"Yes?" she asked.

This was my cue.

"Well, Ruth. First of all, I have to ask you. Would you agree that the Bible was written by the followers of Christ, I mean, those who spoke with Jesus and followed Him around in Israel?"

"Of course," she replied.

"So, wouldn't you agree, then, that the Bible should be the foundation of any church that claims that it is based on the teachings of Jesus Christ?"

"Well, of course," Ruth said with a little bit of suspicion.

"Therefore, would you agree that if the Bible says something and the church says or does the opposite, we should reject the practice of the church for the teaching in the Bible?"

"I suppose that would be right," Ruth said.

"Well, let me ask you a few questions and show you some verses in the Bible and see if the Catholic Church is doing things or believing things which are not from God's Word."

Ruth stretched her legs out as if she were ready to hear what I had to say and discount my criticism of her church.

"First of all, you call your priest 'Father', don't you? That's his title, isn't it?"

"Yes," Ruth answered.

"Well, it says here in Matthew 23:9, 'And call no man your father upon the earth: for one is your Father, which is in heaven'."

Ruth's expression changed a bit.

"Let me see," she said.

She read the verse.

"But that doesn't mean we can't call a priest 'Father'."

"But, Ruth, what else could it mean?"

Ruth looked at the verse and then at me.

"Michael, what do you call your father, then?"

"Since I've known this verse, I call him 'Dad' and not 'father'. According to the Bible, I can call no man my father except God. But the Catholic Church encourages you to call your priest Father which is in conflict with Jesus' own words, the Jesus to whom you supposedly pray."

Ruth read the Scripture and then said, "It doesn't mean that. I'll look it up in my Bible when I get home."

"But, Ruth, don't you think your Bible will say the same thing?"

"Yes. But my father, I mean, my 'Dad' can explain to me what this really means."

I just looked at Ruth for a moment. What else could that verse mean other than what I was just confessing? So, I left it and moved on.

"Ruth, let me ask you another question. In the Catholic Church, is a bishop supposed to be or allowed to be married?"

"Of course not. He must take a vow of celibacy when he enters the priesthood."

"But, Ruth, it says here in I Timothy 3:1, 2, 'This is a true saying, If a man desire the office of a bishop, he desireth a good work. A bishop then must be blameless, the husband of one wife'."

Ruth was a little flustered at this verse.

"Yes, but that's not referring to the same thing."

"But what's it referring to?"

There was a pause.

"Ruth, can't you see that the Bible says a bishop must be married and the Catholic Church teaches the opposite? If the Catholic Church bases its teachings on the Bible, then it must follow what the Bible says and, in this, the teaching of the Catholic Church is in direct opposition to the Bible upon which it is supposed to be founded."

Ruth looked at me with a hostile glare, obviously lost for words, but I let it sink in before I continued. Ruth looked at the Scriptures again and just said, "I'm sure there's an answer. I'll just ask my 'Dad' when I get home."

Again, how else could this verse be interpreted in any other way than that it meant that a bishop must be married? However, again, I left it at that and moved on to another point.

"Ruth, your father supported a very good argument about your adoration of Mary but I want to show you what Jesus said about His own mother. There's a story here in Matthew 12: 46 - 50 which says this, 'While he,' Jesus, 'yet talked to the people, behold, his mother and his brethren stood without, desiring to speak to him.' Now, first of all, notice how it says that Jesus had brothers, which therefore means that Mary wasn't a virgin all her life."

"But Jesus called all His followers His brothers," Ruth said.

"No, Ruth. The Bible teaches that Jesus had brothers and sisters, that Mary had children by Joseph after having Jesus. In the next chapter, those who listened to Jesus queried amongst themselves and said 'Is not this the carpenter's son? is not his mother called Mary? and his brethren, James, and Joses, and Simon, and Judas?' See how the Bible names Jesus' brothers, which shows that Mary was not a virgin all her life like the Catholic Church teaches."

Ruth looked at the verse a little flustered.

"They're all names of the disciples," she snapped. "You're just being picky."

"Ruth, there was no disciple called Joses."

"I'm sure it doesn't mean what you think it means."

I just stared at Ruth and then flipped my Bible back to Matthew chapter twelve.

"Continuing where I left off, the Bible goes on to say, 'Then one said unto him, Behold, thy mother and thy brethren stand without, desiring to speak with thee. But he answered and said unto him that told him, Who is my mother? And who are my brethren? And he stretched forth his hand toward his disciples, and said, Behold my mother and my brethren! For whosoever shall do the will of my Father which is in heaven, the same is my brother, and sister, and mother.' See how when Jesus' real mother, Mary, came to see Him, Jesus more or less discredited her in favour of His followers. So, if we are His followers, we deserve more honour than Jesus' physical mother according to this Scripture."

Ruth snatched the Bible from my hand.

"Where does it say that?" she snapped. She looked at the verse and I could see the horror in her eyes.

"It doesn't mean that!" she shrieked.

But although she said this, I could see her re-reading the verses over and over again.

After a few moments, I just said to her, "But Ruth, tell me honestly. Does it really make sense the way the Catholic Church views Mary and Jesus? Your father said that Mary is in heaven and that she's the softer, gentler side of God because God is a man. Because of this, God is harsher and more willing to punish. But this doesn't make sense when we consider Jesus when He was on earth. I mean, tell me, when Jesus was on earth, who did the prostitutes and tax collectors go to for forgiveness, Jesus or Mary?"

Ruth kept looking at the Bible.

"Ruth?"

But Ruth had clammed shut.

"It was to Jesus, wasn't it? And when the woman was caught committing adultery, it was Jesus to whom she turned for help, wasn't it, and not to Mary."

Ruth just sat there, her lips quivering. But now I was in full swing.

"Remember also the story of the prostitute who washed Jesus' feet with her tears and dried them with her hair. She knew she could go straight to Jesus and not to His mother first.

And what about Zacheaus? He climbed a syca-more tree to see not Mary, but Jesus, and it was from

Jesus, not His mother, where he felt he could find compassion and forgiveness.

And what about the Syro-phenician woman? She did not ask Mary to speak to Jesus but felt she could go straight to Jesus for healing.

Even on the cross, one of the criminals crucified with Jesus did not beg forgiveness by asking Jesus' mother who was there to witness this event but knew he could go straight to Jesus.

So, if Jesus was able to love and forgive on earth without any intervention from His mother, how much more can Christ in His glory pour out love and forgiveness from heaven without any intervention from Mary?"

Ruth became hostile.

"I don't want to hear any more of this. You're wrong!" she said adamantly.

I could see the cold steel in her eyes.

"Ruth, I didn't mean to get you upset. But this is what the Bible is saying, not me."

Ruth started raising her voice.

"I don't want to hear any more of this. All you're doing is being picky and making assumptions which are not true. My father was right. You Protestants are deceived by the devil and it's Satan in you who is trying to make me doubt my Church and discredit Mary whom the angel Gabriel called Blessed. But you're wrong and blinded by Satan and I don't want to hear any more of it."

Ruth threw my Bible back at me, stood up, grabbed her bag and angrily slung it over her shoulder.

I stood up.

"Leave me alone. I don't want to talk to you any more."

"But, Ruth!" I said.

"Leave me alone," she snapped and began walking off.

I grabbed my bag and began following her.

"Leave me alone," she shrieked and began running off.

When I arrived home, the misery must have been written all over my face. My mother asked me why I was so upset and I explained what had happened.

"Don't let it worry you, son," my mother said in an attempt to comfort me. "This is what Jesus and the apostles had to go through when they told people the truth. They were even estranged from their friends. Look what happened to Jesus. Even His disciples abandoned Him at his darkest hour. But Jesus is preparing you to stand up for what is true despite how close you are to these people."

From then on, Ruth avoided me and was only polite but aloof. It was very noticeable the change in our relationship and I could feel that everyone was talking about it behind our backs. It was very discomforting and I found it difficult to concentrate on my schoolwork both during class and at home.

But one afternoon, Troy decided to make a big show of it in our mathematics class. Ruth wasn't in this class so she was spared the embarrassment.

The teacher had gone out for a moment and, once gone, Troy yelled to me across the class, "Hey, Farril! You and Carpenter had an argument and are on no-speaks at the moment? What was it about? Carpenter was not sexually pleasing?"

Everyone just cracked up and I was doubly embarrassed because this statement had further reaching innuendos than Troy realised.

"C'mon, what happened? You can tell your mate, Troy," Troy added.

I just sat there trying to hide in my work. But Troy must have twigged onto the basis of the problem and he became very hostile.

"Farril, don't tell me it was over religion. Can't you just leave everybody alone to worship any god they bloody well want to? It's none of your bloody business who anyone worships and who do you think you are trying to convert everyone to your religion? Do you think you're the only one going to heaven and only those who believe in you will go there too?"

I didn't know what to say to that. And how could I argue with Troy after our discussion in the seniors' room? And the fact that I had done something that made Troy hostile towards me was most disconcerting.

I walked home alone that afternoon, which gave me a lot of freedom to think. In some ways, this cut off from Ruth hurt. She was my best friend and it was now that I realised that she had been my only true friend. Now I had nobody. But in another way, it was a relief. I no longer had to live this lie that I was in love with Ruth and the reason for the break was easily swallowed by everyone, particularly my parents who were sympathetic towards me.

But Troy was angry with me. I couldn't cope with that. I felt so sorry for what I had done that I wanted to apologise to him, to show him that I had no intention of making him angry or upset with me in any way. But then, I hoped that Troy would see that I was now free and, if he wanted me, I was all his. And I wanted him something bad. But to Troy, I was just another student and it wasn't long before this small storm passed and he was friendly with me again.

Till the end of the year, Ruth kept her distance and everyone got used to the idea that we were no longer going steady. Even throughout the duration of the HSC exams, Ruth had nothing to do with me. There was no last minute study together, there was nothing, and it really hurt.

Both Troy and Ruth were in my last exam. But after the last exam, one thing hit me that I had never thought about before: this was the last time I would ever see Troy again. Though I should have been overcome with ecstasy because the last exam was now over, this sudden realisation struck me flat.

At the conclusion of the exam, I went over to talk to Troy to treasure one last moment with him but he was cheering with some of his friends about having finished the HSC forever and I heard him arranging with them to meet at the pub to have a drink to celebrate. When I heard that, I felt all the more jealous and depressed. I knew they wouldn't ask me to join them because they knew that I would turn down the offer because of my religious beliefs.

I saw Troy's mates disappear into their cars and drive off whereas Troy headed towards one of the school buildings for some reason. I wanted to pick up some assignments and so I followed him. But once inside the building, I couldn't see where Troy had gone. So, I just wandered to one of the staff rooms where lay a big box full of manila folders of assignments we had done earlier in the year. I scrounged through the pile until I found ones with my name on them. I didn't even bother to look at what mark I got but stuffed the folders into my bag frustratingly and walked out of the building.

When I reached the seniors' lawn, I heard a female voice call me. It was Ruth. What did she want now?

She came running over to me panting and then said to me, "Michael, can you wait here for me? I want to pick up some assignments but I want to talk to you. Can you please wait here?"

"Yeah," I replied both idly and hurt.

"Do you promise? Please? I need to talk to you."

"Yes, okay, I will!" I said angrily.

Ruth smiled and ran off. I went and sat on one of the benches. It was the bench that Troy had always sat on. I sat and stared at the school. I had been at this school for six years. Suddenly the struggle of school had come to an end. The six years seemed to flash through my mind in an instant.

As I looked across at the main school building, I suddenly saw Troy walk across the lawn towards the front gate. He didn't see me but I watched him go. I watched him the whole time as he walked through the gate and began walking up the road while I wept inside, knowing that as soon as he was out of sight, he was out of my life forever. From that day on, I never saw him again and have no idea what ever became of him. I still reflect on him today as my first true love upon which all my other relationships would be compared.

I saw Ruth come out with a handful of folders and her bag in her other hand. She smiled gleefully and came rushing over to me as if nothing had ever been wrong between us. When she made it over to me, she started packing her folders into her bag.

"Thank you for waiting," she panted, as she delicately put the folders neatly into her bag.

We had finished a morning exam so there was a full afternoon ahead of us. Finally Ruth packed her bag and she was ready to go.

Ruth apologised profusely for being so distant for so long and explained that she had something really important to tell me. She had wanted to tell me before but felt it could wait until the HSC exams were over.

We left the school and walked towards our homes. We stopped along the way and took up our old traditional position on the bank of the little gurgley creek. I sat down on the grass and Ruth sat a little across from me and stared out across the oval, with a gentle, peaceful smile on her face. Finally she spoke softly to me.

"Michael, I've been thinking a lot about what you've said about Christianity and the Bible, and how that the Bible was written by the followers of Christ. So, I decided to read it for myself. All those things you said to me were there and so I knew you weren't making them up. Michael, I don't know if I believe in the Catholic Church anymore but I do believe the Bible and believe in Jesus Christ as my Lord and Saviour."

I was shocked and sat still for a moment.

"Whatever do you mean?" I asked.

"Michael, you've shown me in the Bible how that the doctrines of the Catholic Church, the fundamentals, are not from the Bible. I thought about what you said about the Bible also. It was written by the followers of Christ who knew Him personally so the Bible should be the foundation stone of the Church. Any doctrine should be compared against the Bible. Any doctrine which is against the Bible should be discredited because it would have come, not from Christ, but some other person, and therefore be their opinion. I've decided to read the Bible for myself and let God teach me directly."

I was elated. Suddenly all my contentions about my unspeakable love became unimportant because of a soul that was now released from the clutches of Satan and brought into the glorious liberty of the Word of God.

"Michael, before I met you," Ruth continued, "my religion was my life like it is to you and I considered myself a Christian. But to me, Christianity was an institutionalised religion, made up of buildings, a hierarchy of priests, bishops and cardinals, an endless list of hymns, prayers and rituals, all of it so cold and lifeless. God Himself was like a tyrant who looked at our sins and would only listen to us when we confessed our sins to the priest. He's a cold God, so far away in the sky.

But the way you talk about God, He seems to have a warm heart and truly loves us. You've stripped away all the ritual and everything that is more or less the institutionalised God and made God into a personal friend. I remember once how you said that you praised God and told God how much you loved Him which is so unlike what I'm used to and it is that love which draws me out of this institutionalised religion."

She paused a bit and then looked up at me.

"You know, I've never felt so free before. I feel as if a weight has been lifted off my shoulders. I feel as if chains have been removed from my feet. I feel as if I have been a caged bird and someone has opened the door and I have flown free."

She paused once again and began playing with a blade of grass.

"The only thing is that I don't know how to tell my parents. Both of them are well entrenched in their faith and would not know how to cope if they found out. But, Michael," she concluded, by sitting up and looking me right in the eye, "I don't care. God is on my side. I know what I believe. Martin Luther was once a Catholic and he stood up to the Pope when he saw that the Catholic Church was wrong. I know I am no Martin Luther, just an eighteen year old school girl. But if it's for my sake and my sake only, I'm going to stand up against all odds for I know God is on my side."

I was caught up very much with the moment. It was so exciting to hear someone confess that the faith I adopted was right. It gave me a stronger sense of believing. Satan had been conquered at last, at least for one person, I thought. I was so moved by the moment that I couldn't help telling Ruth I loved her.

I walked her home and then went home myself. At the dinner table I told my parents how God had vanquished Satan that day and how Ruth was about to face a heavy trial for her faith. My parents said many negative things about the Catholic Church, how it has blinded the eyes of the people for centuries and how it was up to us as soldiers of Christ to stop Satan where we could.

But things turned out worse than I could have imagined. I'll never forget the night Ruth appeared at the door. It was a terribly stormy night and raining heavily but it could not hide the bruise to Ruth's left eye or the blood pouring from the cut in her lip. It was shocking to see her turn up on the doorstep drenched, with a heavy suitcase, in tears and a complete wreck.

My father brought her inside and my mother appeared with towels and a clean change while I tried to salvage the contents of her bag in the best possible way.

After she had settled down and drunk a cup of strong, hot tea, though weepy and trembling, she related how her parents finally discovered that she had become a Protestant. Her father burst into a rage and began howling and bellowing at her, demanding an explanation as to how she could depart from God's

Holy Church and then cursed our family for deceiving her away from it. Mr Carpenter somewhere in his rage slapped and belted her, and demanded that she leave home that very night despite the weather. Having nowhere else to turn, she came straight to us.

Some time later that evening, when she had calmed down and our family had prayed, Ruth's second eldest brother and his girlfriend came around to pick her up. Mrs Carpenter had rung him and guessed correctly where Ruth must have gone. Ruth's brother was a big guy, like a big thug and, while there, he related how he had been through a similar ordeal when he came home one day and told his father he thought religion in general was a load of baloney and this event just concreted his opinion. My parents and I were just grateful that there was someone in her family who was able to be of some support in this time of need.

It was a dreadful night which tore at my heart, confirming my belief at the time of the error of Catholicism. But time would show me how this was not unique to Catholics but was a common reaction by the followers of any sort of religious idealism. As the years rolled by, I read and heard stories of Protestants becoming Catholics, Catholics becoming Mormons, Jews becoming Jehovah's Witnesses, Christians becoming Buddhists, and the terrible way the parents reacted, cutting their children off like some sort of post-natal abortion, cutting them out of Wills and banning them from any family functions, and encouraging other members of the family to have nothing to do with them.

And I was to experience the same when my parents found out that I was gay.

But through all of it, one thing was comforting. These people were religious. After all, had they been homosexuals, these acts would have been immoral.

Chapter 9

And that was school. The only pleasant memories that I retain of this period of my life is my silent, lonely, unrequited love for Troy, and the loss of my closest friend at the time, Ruth. Troy and Ruth both marked my thoughts about my faith and my view of the universe.

Troy's exegesis against Christianity gave me a lot to think about during the intervening period between my last HSC exam and when I finally received my results in the mail the following year. And from Ruth I learned that people have their prejudices which we will probably never be able to change.

Eventually I found out years later that Ruth now attends the same church as Karen and Peter, and it was through Karen that I found out what finally happened to her. After I last saw her, she went to her brother's place to live for a while. Her original plan was to go straight to university but, because her parents had banished her, she could not afford to go so she worked for two years to earn the money. She eventually went to Mitchell College in Bathurst to study and finally became a teacher.

She is now married and has three children, and her husband is apparently a very nice man. Karen has told Ruth about me, about my sexuality, my rejection of the Christian faith and about the distance this has placed between me and my parents. Karen told me that Ruth was, at first, quite shocked by this turn of events. However, she told my sister that she sympathises with me because she can relate to what I went through. After all, it took five years for Ruth's parents to at least speak to her. Ruth understands the pain of being rejected by one's parents due to a difference in perspective of the universe. To Mr and Mrs Carpenter, for a Catholic to become a Protestant is a very grave sin indeed, worse than most sins, and this was enough for them to feel justified for casting their daughter from their presence and not feel guilty for doing so.

Ruth's story reminded me of the joke I heard once at school where a Catholic nun approaches Mother Superior and says, "Holy Mother, I'm leaving the convent to become a prostitute." Mother Superior, full of rage, screams at her, "What did you say?" The nun, without batting an eyelid, repeats her statement. Mother Superior then begins to fan her face with her hand in relief and replies, "Forgive me, my child, for my misunderstanding. I thought you said you were leaving to become a Protestant." The irony of the joke is the peculiar stratification of sin viewed by religious idealists.

It was awful knowing that Ruth was cast away from her parents as if she had died all because the universe in her mind had changed. That she had still retained her loving and kind personality did not in her parents' minds make up for her rejection of the Catholic Church for another. Despite the fact that the fundamentals of Catholicism and Protestantism are the same, beyond the differences between the two branches of the same faith, she still believes in the basic teachings of love that are common to both and to all faiths. At least now her parents communicate with her, probably at arms length. But deep down in their hearts they are laden with deep sorrow because Ruth has committed in their eyes almost the worst sin possible for a Catholic to commit.

And so it has happened to me. To my parents, I have committed and am committing the gravest sin possible in the eyes of a Christian all because I have chosen according to my nature to spend the rest of my life with a man and not a woman. My belief in God or the gods may be different, but the teachings of love and the equality of humankind I still find fundamental and right, and are only reinforced by my understanding of the essence of all faiths, creeds, ideologies and philosophies.

Homosexuality only fits into this scheme of things as something that is, that it is neither good nor bad. It does not change the character of the person, it just is. Sexuality only dictates who we like having sex with.

Looking now from the outside in, I see that Christianity has a rather morose and sterile view of sex and sexuality, where chastity and virginity are next to godliness. By contrast, humans are sexual beings, and sex with whom we like to have sex with in its right place is a beautiful thing. How the Christian faith has developed its clinical approach to sex and feels it has a monopoly over sex is all the more peculiar when we discover the origins of Christianity.

But it would be years before I came to this view of the world. Although Troy had challenged my faith, my faith still had quite a strong hold over my mind and it would take years for me to free myself from this. I knew by this stage my sexual orientation despite the fact that I attempted to portray the opposite view. It was not safe to tell anyone I had homosexual tendencies especially when around the time I left school, AIDS had exploded onto the scene.

AIDS was the homosexual disease, the gay plague, the scourge of God. Only homosexuals caught it, which pointed to an obvious conclusion. Society loved it because it supported their oppressive view of homosexuality. To be gay meant to have AIDS, which fuelled more hate for and fear of this sexual phenomenon.

And it was especially welcomed by the ministry. The fiery condemnations against homosexual practices poured liberally from the pulpit. This was the curse of God and homosexuals were receiving the recompense of reward that was suitable for their depravity.

I can still see the hostile, mussolinic stance that Mr Norman adopted as he gleefully approved God's judgement on these outcasts of society. Had these unsuspecting evil doers sought the Lord's mercy and repented from their evil deeds, they would have been spared the unspeakable trauma these sufferers were forced to undergo on their road to death. The idea that was conjured up was that the mere sexual act between two people of the same sex, and it was stressed more between two men than two women, caused God to look down from heaven with disgust and deal out His judgement, and the victims were struck and doomed to a slow, inhumane death. AIDS showed no mercy nor forgiveness as it was incurable, even if the victim fell on his or her knees in repentance.

I don't know what the Christians think now of the curse of God that got out of hand, spilling over into the heterosexual world, even going so far as to afflict innocent children. But at the time it was still only a gay disease and it was a horrible thought for me. The Bible taught that God punished those who turned away from Him by making them gay and now He was doubling the curse by afflicting them with a horrible plague because of their evil doing, even though their evil doing was given to them by God in the first place. And then God would send them to an eternal torment in the next life. It was obvious that this God of love absolutely hated homosexuals, even though He Himself was the author of this sexual phenomenon. It was a sin He just could not tolerate.

Because of the mass hysteria that ensued from the outbreak of AIDS, I was under the impression that I was in danger of catching this horrible disease even though I wasn't having sex. The simple fact that I was sexually aroused by men made me a potential target.

Even at that time, I couldn't understand why God singled out this sin as the most hideous. If James in his epistle said that all sins, great and small, were viewed equally by God, why didn't a plague break out against those who murder, or cheat, or gossip? I mean, why weren't women who didn't wear a head covering to church afflicted by some hideous disease of the scalp, or unmarried men who became deacons afflicted with some scourge of the hands when they handled the church's monetary affairs? Why did God, who viewed all sins as hateful, hate homosexuals so much, especially when He made them homosexuals in the first place?

But the fear of AIDS was strong enough to keep me from accepting my homosexuality and to continue to believe the faith despite the events with Troy and Ruth at school. There was no way that I would become a casualty. And to prevent this from happening, I applied myself stronger to reading the Bible, looking for answers to counteract Troy's arguments against the faith and to find out from the Bible how to change my sexual orientation, to find a cure for that which was not a disease.

But what further was there to read? I had read the entire New Testament several times almost to the point that I knew it by heart. And the answers I was looking for were not there. Where else could I turn?

When I looked closely at my Bible, I noticed that there were in fact two parts, the Old Testament and the New Testament. But we were never encouraged to read the Old Testament because it was only written for the Jews. Only the New Testament was relevant for the Christian. Even this was an inconsistency in my church because sometimes we read from the Psalms and the Proverbs, which were in the Old Testament, as well as other bits and pieces like the Story of Creation and the Ten Commandments. The Old Testament was viewed as an antique piece which gave the Bible its bulk but was not really there for the Christian to read. It was written for the Jews, the antagonists of Christ, and was no longer relevant for the Christian.

Because of my zeal for the Bible, I had to know what the Old Testament said. After all, we were told that the Bible was the Word of God, all sixty-six books of it, and since thirty-nine of these books were in the Old Testament, they were equally worthy of being read. When I compared the thickness between the Old and New Testaments, I noticed that the Old Testament was twice as thick. Why, then, wasn't it twice as important?

My expectation when I opened my Bible to Genesis chapter one was that I was embarking on a boring, tiresome story that would have my mind wandering by the time I had reached the second page. But nothing could have been further from the truth. The Old Testament was a complete treasure trove of stories which gave Christianity more meaning than ever I thought it would.

The first three chapters began with the story of Creation, one which all of us who have had any exposure to Sunday School or church will know. God, who has existed for all eternity, decided one day to create the universe. In six days it was completed, the last thing created was an earthly being made in His image: man. And because woman was made from man's rib, the two of them together were special creations in the image of God. On the seventh day God rested and it was for this reason that the current week is made up of seven days.

God's special creatures were placed in the Garden of Eden where they were free to eat of every tree, except the Tree of the Knowledge of Good and Evil. But the snake tricked Eve into eating of its fruit. Eve in turn gave the fruit to Adam to eat and hence the first sin was committed, changing the nature of Adam and Eve into sinful beings, a nature that would be passed onto all generations like a hereditary gene. Adam's punishment was that he and all his male descendants forever afterwards would have to work hard to make a living, woman's punishment was that for her and for all women who followed her, giving birth would be painful and that the man would rule over her, and the snake was punished by having its legs removed so that it was forced to slither along the ground and eat the dust of the earth, a punishment that extended to all the descendants of this reptilian creature and which is still evident today.

Adam and Eve were evicted from the Garden of Eden and so the history of sinful humankind began.

Adam and Eve bore Cain and Abel. Cain killed Abel, which was the first murder. Adam and Eve then had a third son called Seth and then, glibly stated, they had "sons and daughters". Of course, the difficulty with this story was that the only way humanity could fulfil the commandment to be fruitful and multiply was for brothers and sisters to marry, incest later being condemned as a sin.

The descendants of Adam and Eve multiplied and so did their sin. So, God was sorry that He created them and decided to destroy them all. But because Noah found grace in God's eyes, he and his family survived the ravages of the Flood, the story we are all familiar with, only to emerge from the Ark and start again. From Noah's sons, Shem, Ham and Japheth, descended all the peoples and nations of the world.

Again, humanity increased and so did its sin. As the people multiplied in number so did their power. In their quest for domination not only of the earth but also of the heavens, the human species decided to build a great building, the Tower of Babel. While the tower was still under construction, God came down from heaven and was astonished to see what humans could achieve when they worked together as a team. Not pleased with what He saw, God decided to prevent the humans from achieving their aim. To create disunity, God decided to "confound the languages". The next morning, the humans woke up to find that they no longer spoke a common language. Suddenly the peoples of the earth were multilingual and hence could not understand what each other were saying. So, the building of the tower was left unfinished. The humans then left the city of Babel and became dispersed throughout the rest of the globe.

Despite this miraculous event, the human species continued to sin. But out of all the humans in the world, there was only one who worshipped the true God. This was Abram, later to have his name changed to Abraham. The relationship between God and Abraham developed into such a strong friendship that God lost interest with the rest of the world. It was as if the great empires that existed at about this time, the Egyptians, the Assyrians, the Chinese, the Olmecs, the Aztecs and the Mayas, were going on their merry way while God looked on with casual indifference.

But the Bible tells us that God loved Abraham and him only. To establish a lasting relationship in Abraham's honour, God made with Abraham a covenant, a religious agreement which is probably like our modern contracts, that He would especially give a section of the globe to him, which extended from the Nile River to the River Euphrates. But because Abraham's existence was only temporary, God extended His promise to include Abraham's descendants forever. The requirements of the covenant were that Abraham and his descendants had to keep the commandments of God and the male descendants had to carry a permanent memento of this covenant in their flesh – they had to be circumcised.

Abraham bore Isaac and Isaac bore Jacob. God reinstated His covenant with Jacob, changing his name to Israel, meaning *prince of God*, which was why the later generations were called the Children of Israel, or the Israelites. Jacob had twelve sons and each son formed his own tribe which eventually developed into the Twelve Tribes of Israel.

Out of all his sons, Jacob loved his son, Joseph, the best, and because Jacob openly showed his love to Joseph, Joseph's brothers, out of jealousy, secretly sold Joseph into slavery. Joseph ended up in Egypt and went from being a slave and a prisoner to the second most powerful man after Pharaoh because he had correctly interpreted Pharaoh's dream about the seven years of plenty to be followed by seven years of extreme famine.

The seven years of famine arrived and Jacob and his family were starving in the land of Canaan. They went to Egypt to buy food, discovered Joseph, and migrated there. Jacob and his sons and his sons' families were given the land of Goshen to live in, a region somewhere near modern day Cairo. And that was where the book of Genesis ended.

The Book of Exodus explained that as time went by, the memory of the great deeds of Joseph were forgotten and, out of fear of the increase of Israelite population, the Egyptians made the Israelites their slaves. But God had not forgotten His promise to Abraham and so He raised up Moses to lead His people to the Promised Land. After various miraculous plagues that Moses was able to conjure up, the last being the death of all the firstborn throughout the land, Pharaoh let the Israelites go.

After the miraculous passage through the Red Sea, God, through Moses, led the Children of Israel to Mt Sinai where Moses had earlier seen the burning bush, to again reaffirm His covenant with the Children of Abraham and to newly teach the Israelites His commandments, especially the Ten Commandments written on stone.

When I reached the opening of the twentieth chapter of Exodus, I took a deep breath, for this was the beginning of the Law of Moses, or the Mosaic

Law, or what we sometimes simply called the Law with a capital L. God introduced His Law with the well-known introduction to the Ten Commandments to remind the Israelites of their indebtedness: "I am the LORD thy God, which have brought thee out of the land of Egypt, out of the house of bondage" (Exodus 20:2).

As Christians, we had heard a lot about the Law but always in a negative sense, how it was binding and tiresome, a drudgery and severe restriction to life. Jesus had freed us from the Law and we only had God to thank for sending His Son to do so.

But when I read the Law that God gave to Moses, I questioned the way Christians viewed it. There was something clean and pure, fair and right about it that drew me to it, even making me want to observe it. After all, this same God who sent Jesus to save us also gave the Law to Moses. Many of the things written in the Law Christians were expected to observe anyway and some Laws were long forgotten that I thought should have been reintroduced.

The Law instructed the children of Israel what God expected them to do to be righteous but He also was aware that the Israelites were going to sin. Sin could only be paid for by death and, because God loved His people, the sin was paid for, not by the person, but by an animal substitute. Because animals at that time were a person's livelihood, killing an animal to pay for sin was probably equivalent to today's practice of paying a fine. This act of giving up something to make up for a sin was where the idea of a sacrifice began. Different sins demanded different types of animal sacrifices, according to their worth, from pigeons to oxen. I immediately made the connection between the animal sacrifices according to the Mosaic Law and the ultimate sacrifice of Jesus Christ, the Great Sacrifice, who was able to die once for all the sins of eternity.

The ritual of sacrifice needed a priesthood to conduct it but, strangely enough, although Moses was the great prophet who led the Israelites out of Egypt, it was his older brother, Aaron, who was blessed with being the father of the Jewish priesthood. To become a priest, one had to be a descendant of Aaron. And because Aaron was a descendant of Jacob's third son, Levi, this priesthood was also called the Levitical Priesthood, and it was for this reason that the English name of the third book of the Old Testament is Leviticus.

The ritual of sacrifice needed a Temple but, because the Israelites were wandering around at this stage, a mobile temple, called the Tabernacle, which was just a temple made of tent material, was erected which could be pulled down when the Israelites were moving on. The Tabernacle was encircled by a courtyard, bordered by a fence that was too high for anyone to see what lay within. Within the courtyard on the eastern side was the altar of sacrifice, facing towards the front entrance of the Tabernacle where the sacrificial animals were burnt before the Lord.

The Tabernacle itself was divided into two parts, the Holy Place, where only the priests could enter, inside being the seven branched Candelabrum, the symbol of Judaism that we are familiar with today, a table with twelve rolls of bread called the showbread, to represent the Twelve Tribes of Israel, and an altar of incense. The Holy Place was separated by a veil from the most holy place in the Tabernacle, the Holy of Holies, where the Ark of Moses was placed, where only the high priest could enter once a year. God spoke to Moses via the Ark and inside the Ark were the Ten Commandments engraven in stone.

God told Moses to tell the Children of Israel that when they entered the Promised Land, they were to place the Tabernacle in the one location that God chose and it would be there and there only where they could offer up their sacrifices. The original place that God chose was a town called Shiloh.

But although Moses was a great man of God, he never entered the Promised Land. The story has it that one day the Israelites complained to Moses that they were thirsty and there was no water. God told Moses to speak to a rock and out of it would come water. But in anger towards the complaining Israelites, Moses struck the rock with his rod and, because he did not obey God explicitly, his punishment was that he would not enter the Holy Land but only see it from a distance. This seemingly small sin was so great in the eyes of God that it eclipsed all the great works of Moses, which meant that God had to punish Moses so severely. This was where the first five books of Moses ended.

The Book of Joshua tells the story of how that it was Joshua who was chosen by Moses to lead the children of Israel into the Promised Land, kill all the former inhabitants and divide the land into twelve portions for each of the Twelve Tribes.

Once settled, so the Book of Judges tells us, the Israelites forgot God and sinned. God punished them by bringing foreign nations to oppress them. The Israelites repented, God raised up a leader who was called a Judge and through this Judge the yoke of the oppressor was overthrown. But once settled again, the Israelites forgot God and so the cycle continued.

Eventually, so the books of I & II Samuel tells us, the Children of Israel wanted to have a king to rule over them like all the other nations and not be ruled by a Judge or Priest. Although offended by the idea (for He was the great King), God gave in to their wish and gave them a man called Saul as their first king.

Saul started out as a very good and righteous king. But as time passed by, he began to make some really stupid mistakes and commit some serious sins. He had a son called Jonathan who was the rightful heir to the throne after him but, because of Saul's behaviour, God told Saul that the kingship would be taken away from him and his descendants.

At this point, the Bible says that "the Spirit of the Lord" left Saul and "an evil spirit from the Lord" troubled him, which we might say today that Saul began suffering bouts of depression. The only way Saul could find comfort was through music and so the king needed a good musician to soothe his heart. A young shepherd boy by the name of David, who was described as both an excellent harp player as well as a fearless young man, was chosen for the task. David was therefore brought to the king each time the king was afflicted by the evil spirit and David's harp playing drove the evil spirit away.

During this period of Israelite history, the Philistines were a menace to Israel and were set on taking over the country. One day, the Philistines decided to put the Israelites to a contest and, instead of going into open battle, the Philistines suggested a representative from each nation be brought together to fight it out like an Olympic Games wrestling match. The Israelites were at first happy to comply but then their hearts sank when they saw that the representative for the Philistine team was a giant called Goliath. However, it was this young shepherd-cum-harpist who took up the challenge and miraculously killed Goliath with a sling and a stone.

King Saul therefore made David a permanent resident at his palace and both Saul, and Saul's son, Jonathan, loved him. Jonathan loved David so much that it was the most intimate relationship between two men you can ever read about in the Bible.

In the end, Saul and Jonathan were killed in battle and David was proclaimed king.

The books of I & II Kings and I & II Chronicles tell us the story of the dynasty that was established by King David which was to have great significance to Christianity. King David was, as the Bible tells us, a man after God's own heart. God promised that not only would David be king but also all his descendants forever.

Although David was a good king in God's eyes, ensuring that the people continued to keep the Law of Moses, David made a big boo-boo by committing adultery with a married woman, Bath-Sheba, which was made complicated when Bath-Sheba found out that she was pregnant. David was duly punished but he never wavered from his devotion to God.

King David brought in many reforms, conquering a Jebusite city called Jerusalem, making this city his capital and bringing the Tabernacle to this city to be the new place where the Children of Israel were to offer up their sacrifices to God. Because they were no longer wandering, some of the priests' functions had to change accordingly and King David brought in many priestly reforms. Although David wanted to get rid of the Tabernacle and build a permanent dwelling place for the Lord, it was his son, Solomon, who received the fame for building the Temple.

If God loved David, the Bible is clear that He loved Solomon even more, for He told a prophet to call Solomon *Jedidiah* meaning 'beloved of the Lord'. Solomon had seven hundred wives and three hundred concubines but it was when he began to worship other gods that God condemned him.

In order to strike a balance between punishing Solomon but still keeping the promise He made to David that one of David's descendants would be king, God allowed the kingdom of Israel to split in two. When Solomon died, the northern part of Solomon's kingdom became the Kingdom of Israel and was ruled by a man called Jeroboam, and the southern part of the former kingdom became the Kingdom of Judah, ruled by Solomon's son, Rehoboam. The Kingdom of Judah was so named because it was populated by the descendants of Jacob's fourth son, Judah, the only tribe that Solomon's descendants ruled, whereas the northern kingdom gained the other ten tribes. (As an aside, this was always a mathematical problem I could never figure out. Originally there were twelve tribes but when the kingdom split, one tribe went to Judah and ten to Israel. One and ten make eleven, so what happened to the twelfth?)

Once king of Israel, Jeroboam decided to build rival temples of his own. It is quite understandable why he did so because the temple to which all the descendants of Abraham were to offer their sacrifices was in Judah, and Jeroboam felt that his new kingdom was threatened if all his subjects were still religiously bound to Jerusalem, within the Kingdom of Judah. Thus, he built two places of worship in the Northern Kingdom, one in a city called Bethel and the other in a city called Dan. Jeroboam made a city called Samariah his capital and it was from the name of this city that the later race of the Samaritans came, who later became famous in the story of the Good Samaritan.

Eventually with each succession of kings, the inhabitants of both kingdoms sinned, but throughout this portion of history more focus was placed on the kingdom of Judah for this was where the Temple of Solomon was. After all, God lived only in this Temple and only Jerusalem was His city.

The kingdom of Israel sinned almost immediately after the split and so God sent the Assyrians to take the Israelites away so much so that the Israelites became absorbed into the vast Assyrian Empire, and thus began the enigma of the Lost Ten Tribes of Israel.

The people of Judah, who were now called Jews, lasted longer but they eventually sinned themselves. So God sent the Babylonians to take them away and had the Temple destroyed. The promise of God to David that there would always be one of his descendants ruling over Israel finally came to an end.

So mighty and important was the kingship in Judah that to see the termination of it was a real blow to the Jews and their faith. God, however, was not going back on His promise. Rather, it was the sins of the Jews that caused God to end the great Davidic dynasty. Nevertheless, when the Jews returned their hearts to Jehovah, God would return the Jews back to their land. Prophet after prophet arose and assured the people that the kingdom would be restored and a king of the line of David would resume the throne. This would be a kingship that would never end, unlike the former.

This awaited king was referred to as the Messiah, the Anointed One, who would restore the kingdom in much the same way as David had established it in days of yore. The Messiah would also rebuild the Temple as David's son, Solomon, had done. The Messiah would restore Israel to its former glory as it was in the days of King David, where the Twelve Tribes of Israel would be united once more and the Law of Moses would again be brought back in righteousness and truth. And thus ended the Old Testament.

After reading the Old Testament, I felt as if I had been reading the New Testament under a dim lamp because suddenly so much more of the New Testament made sense. What the New Testament writers tried to prove over and over again was that Jesus was the awaited Messiah and that He had heralded in a new era, just as the prophets had prophesied. Even the death and resurrection was a part of this plan, it was just misunderstood by God's people before it came to pass. The more I read the New Testament after reading the Old, the more I realised that Christianity was not really a separate faith from Judaism but was a branch of Judaism, where the believers believed that the Messiah had come.

This was a wonderful moment in my life for now I understood the full story. Although as a child I had been told that the story of Jesus Christ was about God seeing that we were miserable sinners who needed deliverance from our sins and so God sent His Son to die for us, I now realised that this was not the original story – Christianity was based on the belief that the Messiah, for whom the Jews were waiting, had finally come. The significance for me was that this meant that through Jesus Christ, the Messiah, Jews were no longer the exclusive people of God. The awaited Jewish Messiah also brought salvation to the Gentiles.

Because I now saw a connection between Judaism and Christianity, I began to develop a desire to meet a Jew. In my nightly prayers, I included the chance to meet a Jew because I felt that having contact with the

Jews would give me some sort of evidence of and contact with the authors of the entire Bible.

My reading of the entire Bible also gave me a holistic view of the universe and for the first time I strongly disagreed with our church's teaching that the Old Testament was irrelevant. The Old Testament was absolutely necessary if one wanted a complete understanding of the Christian faith in its entirety. And, hence, at a moment when I needed it, my faith was revitalised.

Chapter 10

And now a new phase had begun in my life. It was time for me to take off my school uniform, put on working clothes and join the ranks of the common employee. But if it felt like a great transition when I went from Year 10 to Year 11, going from being a school student to a nine-to-five worker was a transition into another dimension.

A daily routine began consisting of waking up in the wee hours of the morning, shoving down breakfast with a coffee chaser, walking to the station, commuting to work, starting work, morning tea, work, lunch, work, knock off, walk to the station, commute home, eat dinner, go to bed, and then be rudely awaken by a cheery voice over the radio telling me that it was a beautiful morning at 6 am, to begin the routine all over again. It was a wonderful experience in the beginning because I felt that I was now entitled to be called an adult, but the glow eventually died away as the routine took on its true blandness.

When my HSC results came in the mail, I was bitterly disappointed with my marks as they were much lower than I was hoping for, preventing me from pursuing the career in Speech Pathology I had strived to obtain. Deep down I knew those marks were obtainable and if it had not been for the conflict between my faith and sexual orientation, my mind could have been more focused on my studies than on these external issues. My father surveyed my results with me and saw that I had obtained a good mark in chemistry and thus advised me to study to become an industrial chemist.

My father also wanted me to have a head start in life. Instead of going to university full time and then hoping to get a job with no experience after I graduated, he advised me to obtain a traineeship with a company and study part time. This, he explained, would give me the best of two worlds, to enable me to begin earning an income and become familiar with the responsibility employment brings while getting a university education which would broaden my horizons and future prospects in the company and in my employment life in general.

At the time this sounded excellent but the reality was further from the truth than I could imagine. Included in my daily routine were three evenings and one half-day at university, only to be followed by nights poring over lecture notes and textbooks, and weekends spent writing up reports. It was like studying the HSC all over again except that now there were six years of this to look forward to and not two whereas, if I had studied full time, I would have completed the degree in three years.

After my third year at university, I watched all the full timers complete their degrees, get jobs and begin to climb the corporate ladder while I was left behind to finish off the next three years because I was still classified as a trainee until I had graduated despite the experience I had gained in the company over that time. Part time study was not the head start my father had promised after all but a handicap which I would grow to resent.

Studying to become an industrial chemist meant looking for a job in a laboratory and at the time there were quite a number of placements for trainee chemists available. I was able to get employed quite soon after I had received my results and thus my life as a worker began. But my success at the interview in my mind was not due to the way I presented myself or my school record. Rather, out of all the jobs that I had applied for, it was God's design to place me in the one of His choosing, to preach the gospel and as a soldier of Christ conquer the devil by saving as many souls as possible in the place of His appointment.

The position I eventually obtained employment in was as Trainee Research and Development Chemist in a company called Zenith Chemical Products. Zenith Chemicals manufactured cleaning products for both domestic and industrial use. It was quite a fascinating job really because it brought out a lot of what chemistry was all about. In the cleaning products profession, dirt, grime and stains are all chemicals, and there are certain chemicals that remove them. It was thoroughly interesting for me because I began to understand the intricacies of household products that we buy at the supermarket and what they were really all about.

It also brought chemistry alive as a subject. No longer was chemistry simply a subject to study at school just to make up enough subjects to get a final

HSC mark, chemistry was a subject which tried to give meaning to the physical universe.

There were two main chemical divisions in the company: the Quality Control Department and the Research and Development Department. The Quality Control Department was a laboratory where routine chemical analyses were carried out. Something like 5,000 L of cleaning product were made at one time and before it could be bottled and sent to the market, the contents had to be analysed to ensure that each constituent that made the product work was present in the correct proportions. I began to realise, then, that what was written on labels about the constituents of a product were obtained by the analyses carried out by routine quality control chemists.

However, because this job was so routine, eventually it became rather tiresome. Quality control chemists tended to be people who had only completed a chemistry certificate and hence the job was particularly suited for people who wanted to do something a little more than work in a factory but yet maintain a regular routine worker's life.

The Research and Development Department was much more interesting. Here, the constituents of the products were analysed and then other chemicals were studied to see if they could be used as cost effective alternatives or improvements over competitive products. Research and Development was much more exciting and required continually asking questions and searching for new challenges in the overall goals of progress. Each day was different because it delved into the nature of chemical ingredients and brought new challenges into understanding what makes products clean better. Only qualified chemists from university worked in the Research and Development Department as they were supposedly better trained and disciplined in the scientific approach, specialising in chemistry, to do the type of work that such a position demanded.

It was company strategy to begin chemist trainees in the Quality Control laboratory for at least a year so that they became familiar with the constituents of the products and how the presence of these constituents were analysed. It was believed that this gave a budding new research chemist the basis necessary before embarking on developing new ideas for improving products. So, I began my full time employment life as a quality control chemist trainee in one of the laboratories that made up this vast complex that made a company.

There were two of us who worked here, me and another guy, an Australian born Italian guy named Giuseppe, who preferred to be called Joe. He was a tall and lanky guy, quite smart, but with a weird sense of humour, with a drain-pipe laugh to match. When I found out that he had an Italian background, I assumed rightly that he was a Roman Catholic and so I wasted no time refreshing my arguments I had used on Ruth to convert him. But he was a real hard nut to crack, not agreeing with any of my arguments, infuriating me with his raucous laughter whenever he disagreed on a point. I argued with him for months but got nowhere, especially because he did not believe the Bible was divinely inspired. This surprised me no end and I was unable to fathom how he could believe the Bible contained errors and yet he could still claim that he was a Christian. Eventually I reached a stalemate and stopped preaching to him. But as a fellow worker, he was agreeable and, as soon as I gave up with my sermons in the laboratory, I discovered that he was enjoyable company as a fellow worker.

Joe and I reported to the QC supervisor, a woman called Tracey. Her job was to collect samples of the different products from the manufacturing site and bring them to the laboratory where Joe and I would then take turns in performing different analyses. Her job was also to collect the results and write a report, a part of which would end up on the labels with the strange chemical names and the amount of each in them.

Despite the fact that Joe was Catholic, I still remember that he was a nice guy. He taught me a lot about what it was to be Italo-Australian. I have only a vague memory of the stories he told me about growing up in a predominantly Anglo-Celtic culture and coming to terms with the differences between the culture he was born in and the culture of his parents, trying to strike a balance between being Italian and Australian, until he came to the realisation that he was, after all, simply Italo-Australian.

Despite our different views of God and the universe, we both shared a deep fear of the person we had to report to, Tracey. Tracey was the dragon lady who with one swipe of the tongue could have you cringing in the corner. She made the teachings of "love your enemies" the greatest challenge to my Christian upbringing. The sound of her footsteps in the laboratory made my heart beat wildly even when she was just coming in to drop off another sample. But did she teach me to be real sharp where my analyses were concerned. Her philosophy was "To Err Is Impossible" and I always felt a flush in my face whenever even the slightest thing went wrong. If any of us made the slightest mistake in our work, she came down on us with one crack of the whip and we felt as if we had to seek absolution for even the slightest analytical or mathematical error we committed. She was certainly ill-placed as a QC supervisor and would have been more suitably employed as a high ranking officer in one of the armed forces. She made life hell for me all the time I was there and I was certainly all the happier that this was only a temporary arrangement.

The Research and Development Department was in a completely different part of the company, a good 10 minute walk away. It was to this laboratory that I would end up and, all the while that Tracey was our boss, I counted the seconds until I was transferred to it.

However, as part of my training, every Friday afternoon I was sent to this laboratory to work as an assistant to one of the R&D chemists, Markus, to help him work on any project that he had been assigned. Markus was from Sri Lanka and he explained to me that he was a burgher, part native Sri Lankan, part European. He had strikingly beautiful features, a permanent dark tan, a generous serving of body hair and a wonderful physique. He was a rather intelligent man, well-organised with his work, and his methodical work style gave me the impression that I was working with an Isaac Newton or a Michael Faraday. And yet, he had a very casual, somewhat relaxed way about him as well that stood in direct contrast to my first impressions of him.

Morning tea was a social gathering where the QC and R&D chemists, the QC supervisor, and the chief chemist all came together and socialised for twenty minutes in another "seniors'-room-sized" tea room. I was very timid in the company of these strange adults and for a long while only listened to their conversations on politics, company structure and a variety of other subjects that were at first so foreign to me. It was the first time that I socialised in any sort of way with anyone who was much older than me, especially in the secular world. It was such a different world to school and the social make-up of a group of adolescents on park benches in the school yard.

During these short break periods, conversations flourished on a wide range of topics that were so different to what I discussed on the seniors' lawn that it was as if they were speaking a different language. It took me quite some time to get adjusted to this new way of viewing the world, the world of family life, night clubs, investing money and company politics. I realised in my little insular world of the church and family that I had been ill-prepared to understand what it was that they were talking about. The world of the Bible and the real world seemed so incongruent that it took me quite some time to try and make these two worlds a unified reality.

I was a good listener which I needed to be because it took me quite a long time to feel that I had anything to contribute to any of their conversations. I also realised that my ability to get a word in and therefore steer the conversation to a point that I could preach Jesus was very difficult indeed. But I knew I had to eventually because that was my mission. God had sent me to this company to be a light to these people who had been so long kept in darkness.

One particular morning in the tea room, a heated conversation ensued over a bomb attack in Tel Aviv. I had not heard the news on the radio but apparently it was the big news of the moment. There was great fear that this bomb attack could spark World War III if it escalated out of control. You could almost taste the fear in the staff room that such an event could have global repercussions.

The conclusion that was reached was the problem of religion. Both the Jews and Muslims felt that they held claim to this small area of the globe. As the conversation progressed, all religions were blamed for the problems of the world. After all, if we looked at all the fighting that was going on, it was all because of religion: Muslims fighting Hindus in India, Catholics fighting Protestants in Ireland, Armenian Christians fighting the surrounding Muslim states. Each religion assumed righteous authority over the others and hence bloody conflicts broke out between them contrary to each religion's teaching of love and peace. Religion, they argued, was the cause of our present day instability and if only the religious could see reason the world would be a better place.

At first I just listened but eventually I was not able to sit there and allow my precious faith to be unjustly criticised so I just burst out with, "I don't agree. The reason why there are wars in the name of religion is because Satan wants us to question all faiths. Satan wants you to think that all religions are the same and all wrong, and therefore reject the true and only God, Jesus Christ. If everyone believed in Him, the whole world would be at peace because Jesus is the Prince of Peace."

The whole tea room just went silent and all eyes were poised on me for some moments. Everyone had become totally still, probably shocked by the naiveté of the statement, especially when what I had to say was a perfect example of what they had just been talking about. No-one dared move for what seemed an eternity. But, quite expectedly, Tracey was the first to attack.

"You mean to say that Jesus Christ is the only God and all other religions are wrong, do you?"

"Yes," I replied boldly.

"But how can you say that? I mean, this is the type of one-eyed attitude that is causing all these religious wars in the first place. The Jews say that Jehovah is the only God and all other gods are the handiwork of the devil, the Muslims believe the same about their god, Allah. That's why they're all fighting."

"No, that's not true. All these religious people think they are worshipping the true God but they are living in ignorance. If they really were searching for the true God, they would eventually discover that it is Jesus Christ they are seeking."

Everyone smiled condescendingly at me, not the least Tracey. She was not one for letting a statement go unproven.

"Then all the other gods are deceptions created by the devil, I suppose," she said.

"Yes," I replied confidently.

"But, Michael, what makes you so sure that Jesus Christ is the true God and all the others are wrong?"

"Because the Bible says so!" I said.

"Well, of course, this is all the proof we need, isn't it, Father Farril," Tracey said sarcastically.

I could see that this argument was in no way convincing and so I decided to play an old card that had won me this argument at school to silence my opponents.

"Tracey, what year is it, this year?" I asked.

"Nineteen eighty-four. So what?"

"And what does that mean?"

"It's supposed to refer to how many years ago Jesus was born."

So far so good, I thought.

"And what does AD mean?"

"Anno Domini. It's Latin for *The Year of the Lord*. So what?"

I sat back in confidence to declare the logical verdict.

"Well, every time you write the date, you are actually confessing how long ago the Lord was born. That's how I know Jesus is the Lord and true God."

I sat there smugly, assured that Tracey would not be able to answer me. But she leant forward and looked me straight in the eye.

"Michael, what day is it, today?" she asked.

"Thursday," I replied.

"And what does that mean?"

"It means Thor's Day, Thor being the Norse God of Thunder."

"Therefore, do you believe that Thor is still the God of Thunder? Because, every time you use the term 'Thursday', you are confessing that you believe it is Thor's day which proves that the Norse gods still exist."

I thought I was going to choke on my tongue.

"Yeah, but no-one believes in the existence of the Norse gods anymore," I spluttered. "The names of the days of the week date back to an old convention."

"And that's my argument, too. Using the terms BC and AD to me are only an old convention, which convinces me as much that Jesus is the Lord as the Norse gods exist."

"But, Michael," Markus added, "you need to realise that the dating system we use in Australia is based on the European system which comes from the Christian view of the world. Not every country recognises it as *the* dating system, although they now use it because it was forced on them by the western world. According to the Hindus, this year is 2041, because they use a dating system called the Vikram

Samvat which begins at the time when King Vikram ascended the throne two thousand and forty-one years ago. The Muslims also have their own dating system which begins from the time that Mohammed left Mecca to go to Medina. According to them, this year is 1371 AH, where AH is Latin for *Anno Hegirae*, loosely translated as *The Year of the Migration*. To the Jews, this year is 5744 because they claim that their dating system begins at the first day of creation. And in China and Japan, counting the years is based, or at least at one time was based, on the reign of the emperor. So your argument to support Jesus' divinity on the dating system is based purely on a Christian convention, not a universal one."

"Not only that," Tracey threw in, "nowadays, historians tell us that there was an error in the calendar and when they updated it, they found that Jesus was born somewhere between 6 and 4 BC. So now they use a new convention, BCE meaning *Before the Common Era* and CE meaning *The Common Era*. So, your proof amounts to nothing."

I didn't know what to say or where to look. But I needed to support my statement and so I reached for the first thing that came to mind.

"Yes, but what makes Christianity unique is that God appeared on earth as a man, talked and spoke with men. That's why John wrote in his first letter, 'That which was from the beginning, which we have heard, which we have seen with our eyes, which we have looked upon, and our hands have handled, of the Word of life.' This is the only God who has ever come to earth so we know for sure who He is and what He expects of us. The gods of Judaism, Islam, Hinduism and the like are just inventions of those who call themselves prophets for they have never really known or seen God in person. But the followers of Christ had first hand experience with God because they talked and communed with the Creator of this world and the Christians are the only ones who can make this claim about their god."

"Oh, Michael, that's not true," Tracey retorted. "In the *Iliad*, the Olympian gods and goddesses came down from heaven in the form of humans during the battle between Agamemnon and the city of Troy."

"Yes, but no-one believes in these gods and goddesses anymore," I replied.

"But, Michael," Markus threw in again, "the Hindus believe that God, in the incarnation of Krishna, appeared to the chariot rider Arjuna and talked with him. His dialogues are recorded in the Hindu holy book, the Bhagavad-Gita, just like the New Testament records the sayings of Jesus Christ. And there are millions of Hindus who believe that today."

Again, I was beaten. But I had one more hand to play and I thought it was a royal flush.

"That may be so. But there is one distinguishable difference between Christianity and other religions. All other religions teach that salvation comes by works. You have to spend your life trying to do enough good works so that they will outweigh your bad works on the Day of Judgement. All religions talk of reaching up to God to win his favour.

But Christianity is different. Jesus recognised that spending all our lives trying to do good works won't achieve anything because we sin all the time, sometimes without realising it. So, Jesus came down and paid for the crime by His death and resurrection. By this loving act, we don't have to spend our lives trying to be good, living in fear that we haven't done enough to make it to heaven. Because of this, Christians don't have to fear hell because they have accepted that Christ has paid for their sins and we are assured of our salvation from that moment on. All our sins are forgiven, past, present and future."

"You can't say that," Tracey blurted out. "Christianity is not like that. You can't say that if someone believes in Jesus Christ they are saved from that moment, even though they sin!"

"No, I can't," I replied confidently and proudly. "But God can. That's why the Bible says in Romans 10:9, 'if thou shalt confess with thy mouth the Lord Jesus, and shalt believe in thine heart that God hath raised him from the dead, thou shalt be saved.' The Bible doesn't say, 'if thou shalt confess with thy mouth the Lord Jesus, and do good works, and do this and that, thou shalt be saved'. If good works saved us, it would have been completely unnecessary for Jesus to have died for us.

But God knows that humans are sinful creatures. The Bible says that 'there is none righteous, no, not one' and points out that all of us are sinners. God would have had no choice but to throw us all into hell because we are all miserable sinners getting nowhere. However, because He loves us, God paid for the crime. Other religions offer a false hope, enslaving us to rites and rituals to win God's favour."

The whole tea room had gone quiet during my sermon. I thought they were all sitting there pricked in their hearts from what they had heard, ready to ask the question, "Men and brethren, what shall we do?" But nothing could have prepared me for what Tracey had to say in reply.

"Oh, okay, if that's all I need to be saved, then, heck, why not? I'll believe that Jesus died on the cross for my sins and rose again from the dead. Now I'm saved! What do you think, Markus? Do you believe Jesus died for your sins and rose from the dead?"

Markus just smiled and Tracey said, "Just say 'yes', Markus."

Markus nodded.

"How about you, Joe? Do you believe that Jesus died and rose again from the dead for your sins?"

"Of course, I do," Joe hawed. "I'm a Roman Catholic. I believe that, too."

Tracey asked everyone around the room and everyone replied that they believed.

"Well, there you go, Michael. We're all Christians now and going to heaven. No more argument."

I was shocked. I knew that this was just mockery.

"But it's not that straight forward," I protested. "You have to repent from your sins first. You can't just say you believe and that's that. You have to turn away from your sins."

"But, Michael," Tracey said. "You just said that we are all sinners, including yourself, and because

214

we are all sinners, Jesus paid for our sins. I believe, now I'm saved. I'm a Christian and I don't have to repent from anything because Jesus has paid for my sins. As a matter of fact, I should become even more sinful to make Jesus' suffering all the more worthwhile. It would be pointless of Jesus to have died for the petty things that we do wrong."

I just opened my mouth in horror. I knew Tracey didn't believe in Christ at all but was making a mockery out of me.

"But, you can't believe in Christ and keep on sinning. You have to turn from your sins or you could lose your salvation," I protested further.

"What? You mean that you're now perfect?" Tracey asked.

"N…no, but I try to be good…" I said, but I could feel how trapped I was in my argument and how it didn't have a consistent flow.

Here I was boasting about the superiority of Christianity because we are saved by faith only but when faced with the reality of the doctrine, I couldn't accept that Tracey could be saved in this way. Once she said she believed, I was expecting a change in her conduct or else she would lose her salvation, which just sounded like all the other religions that required a life of having to do good works to be saved.

But then I was going a step further. By saying to Tracey that she had to repent from her sins meant that I was assuming that I had completely turned away from mine and was no longer sinful. But because I believed I still sinned despite the fact that I was a Christian, what I was more or less saying was that my sinfulness was not as bad as hers and she had to aspire to my height of righteousness, which I admitted was not perfection, to accept her as a sister in Christ. But to say this was stepping beyond what the Bible said, and what she had to say in reply was, according to the Scriptures, quite justifiable.

That afternoon, while setting up some glassware to do a distillation, Tracey wandered over to me and said, "You know, Michael, I feel really good that I'm going to heaven. Don't you? Just think! We'll see each other there, Markus will be there, Joe will be there, the factory workers, the managers, and none of us will have to worry in the meantime about doing good works to make it because we are saved by the faith in Jesus Christ. And we'll all probably be working in the same laboratory in the sky."

And then she walked off.

And she didn't stop there. The next day at morning tea, Tony was reaching over to the biscuit container when Tracey smacked his wrists and said, "Uh, uh! We have to say grace first. Everyone close your eyes so we can say it. Michael, would you like to say grace for us and thank Jesus Christ for saving us?" and everyone laughed.

For days I had to put up with Tracey's snide comments and there was nothing I could say. It was a real nightmare. However, she would never have stopped if Markus had not intervened. In the middle of one of her jibes, he turned to her and said quietly but firmly, "Tracey, I think enough is enough. I think you've proved your point. There's no need to go overboard."

Ah, there he was, my knight in shining armour, riding in full strength to rescue me in my time of need. Because I knew that it had started again. Clumsy cupid had shot his arrow and here I was, smitten again.

This simple event brought out feelings that must have been lying dormant inside me, waiting for the spark to set it all alight. For, as it was with Troy, I knew that I had fallen in love with a man when the world was telling me that this was evil. Love was evil. That was the message I was receiving.

I knew if I had gone home that day and told my parents that I thought I had fallen in love and it was a girl I was talking about, my parents would have been happy and would have begun to talk of marriage and my joy would have been shared by all. But if I had gone home and said I was in love with this guy at work, Markus, happy would be the most inappropriate emotion to describe the way that they would have reacted.

It was beautiful and awful at the same time. The sensation of falling in love went beyond what words could describe but there was no-one with whom I could share these beautiful feelings. That I had them for a man was a curse and so they had to be bottled up inside of me. And so the merry-go-round was coming around again. What was wrong with me? Why did I have these feelings for a man when we had been indoctrinated that it was only good if I or Markus were a woman? And how could these feelings be evil? Because I was filled with love for Markus, I wanted to spread this beautiful feeling around and be good to everybody. Wasn't this the whole objective of the Christian faith, to promote love, to promote God, for "God is love"? And if God is love, how could these feelings come from the devil, the antipode of the embodiment of love?

But because of my love for Markus, Friday was my favourite day. As I became more and more accustomed with my work in R&D, my conversations with Markus slowly changed from professional to social. Markus began to tell me about his family, his home country, that he had come to Australia when he was seven but had been back to Sri Lanka many times for holiday. He told me about his time at school and what he did on the weekend. I, in turn, shared my life with him, obviously having quite a different and what I considered a very boring story in comparison. We delved deep into a variety of topics and despite the embarrassment in the tea room not so long before this time, I alluded to Christianity in some of our discussions and Markus seemed to listen, although more just to be polite than because he particularly agreed with my views.

I felt close to Markus. I tried to convince myself that the way I felt for him was purely platonic but deep down inside, I knew that my feelings for him were overstepping those allowed according to my belief.

All was well between us until one particular Friday afternoon. I was setting up the glassware as I always did while Markus was busily writing. Every now and again I threw a glance at this man I loved when he suddenly sat up as if he had been pricked in the derriere.

"Hey, Michael, I've been meaning to ask you. What're you doing next Friday night? Got any plans?"

"I don't think so. I'll probably be just studying. Why?"

"Why don't you give your studies a break and come with me to the Pink Slipper? It's a really nice night club, and there's an Australian band playing there and I hear that they're really good. You can sleep over at my place afterwards and I'll drop you off home the next day."

My heart must have skipped a beat. Wow! Markus was inviting me out and asking me to stay over at his place. What more could I have asked for! But while I let the idea sink in, I began to see the real reason why Markus was inviting me out. Satan was speaking through Markus, enticing me with earthly pleasures, to lead me to an eternity in hell. So, after a long fight within my soul, I turned the offer down.

"Oh, why not?" Markus asked, openly disappointed. "I'd really love you to come. You'd have a great time."

"I don't believe that's a place a Christian should go."

Markus looked at me with a crooked smile.

"Well, one of my friends who's going is a Christian just like you. And he enjoys himself there, and doesn't feel that it clashes with his faith."

That seemed strange to me. But again, the thought that went through my mind was that this

Christian had either taken the bait that Satan had fished out to him or he was just a decoy to suck me in.

"No, thanks, Markus," I replied. "As a Christian, I believe I should abstain from such sensuality."

"Michael, what's wrong with it? Don't you, as a Christian, believe that God wants you to be happy and enjoy this life?"

"Yes," I said affirmatively. "But the Bible forbids this type of pseudo-pleasure."

Markus was quite shocked by that statement and the expression on his face openly portrayed that he was very hurt. But as much as I didn't like to hurt his feelings, I felt that it was more important to honour God.

Markus sat there for a second and then commented.

"Michael, you put too much faith in that book. And that's all it is, a book!"

That was it! I now knew that Satan had placed Markus here to deceive me away from God's Holy Word.

"It's the Word of God!" I said coldly and curtly.

Markus rolled his eyes. I finished fidgeting with the experiment. I had to wait thirty minutes before the distillation was complete and so I turned around with my arms folded and leant my back on the bench. Markus looked at his report, put his pen down and then looked at me.

"Michael, how do you know that the Bible is the Word of God, anyway?"

The question was like a clanging gong in my head. This was the second time I had been asked that question and it was the second time I did not have an answer. So, I decided to throw the ball back into his court, not realising that he had perfected his backhand.

"How do you know that it isn't?"

"Because it contradicts itself."

I could feel the blood rush to my head and I knew for the first time how religious wars started. Markus had made a statement and I hadn't even asked him to justify his claim. I felt that I could have jumped across the room and strangled him to death for saying something as blasphemous as this without allowing him the opportunity to explain his viewpoint.

"Where does it contradict itself?" I asked acidly.

Markus took a deep breath.

"Let's take the four gospels for a start. All of them relate the same stories but they don't always agree in detail."

"Where?" I asked.

"When you read the last chapters of each of the four gospels, for example, they all tell the story of the resurrection but the stories are slightly different. I mean, irreconcilably different."

"They are not!" I said. "They all testify to the same story, just said a different way."

"Oh, do they? You're so sure of that?" Markus asked.

"Where do they differ?" I asked, thinking confidently that Markus was just being pedantic.

"Let me ask you, who visited the tomb on the day that Jesus was supposed to have resurrected?"

"Mary Magdalene, Mary, the mother of Jesus, and some other women."

"And how many angels were at the tomb when the women arrived?"

"Two."

"Then, why do Matthew and Mark mention only one?"

"Because...because only one spoke to them, I guess."

Markus looked at me in deep thought.

"Mmmm. That's a point, I suppose," Markus said. "But, then, tell me, where was the angel, or the angels, when he spoke to the women?"

"In the tomb."

"Then," returned Markus, "why does Matthew say that the angel spoke to them while sitting on the stone after he had rolled the stone away?"

"It doesn't say that!" I retorted.

"Oh, then you must have read it in another Bible."

I was getting furious but Markus kept on.

"Not only that, in Matthew, Mark, and Luke, it says that Mary Magdalene and the other women arrived at the tomb, and the angel, or the angels, told them that Jesus had risen and they were to go and tell the disciples. They were so excited to hear the news that they did what the angels had told them to do. But in the fourth gospel, John writes that it was only Mary Magdalene who went to the tomb and, when she had arrived, she found it empty. But instead of meeting angels, she saw no-one, and thinking the body of Jesus had been stolen, she ran back to tell the disciples. Peter and John went with Mary to the tomb and found it empty just as Mary had said. Peter and John then left but Mary Magdalene hung around long enough for two angels, and then Jesus Himself, to appear. Jesus, according to John, was the one who spoke to Mary, not the angels."

"You're wrong!" I yelled.

"Michael! Don't yell at me. If I'm wrong then prove it by all means."

I stood there for a moment and thought about what Markus was saying but I couldn't let it go just like that.

"I don't agree that the gospel stories of the resurrection of Christ are different. On the contrary, there are four gospels which relate the same thing, that Jesus did rise from the dead."

Markus shrugged and then crossed his arms.

"That may be so. But remember that four Christians wrote that. What testimony is there from other sources written at the time and their opinion of the resurrection?"

"What do you mean?" I asked.

"Michael, I really question what happened. The whole scenario surrounding the resurrection story leaves one very suspicious. I mean, why did Jesus only appear to a chosen few, namely, His followers, when He rose from the dead? Why didn't He just roll the stone away, stroll into Jerusalem and say to everyone there, to Caiaphas, to Pontius Pilate, the priests and the scribes, 'See, I told you I would rise from the dead. And despite the fact that you crucified me, your sins are forgiven, too'? Wouldn't that have made a greater impact than just revealing Himself secretly to His closest followers that He had risen from the dead? Isn't that the whole reason why Jesus died and rose again from the dead, to save everybody, and don't you think that He would have wanted to make His suffering worthwhile by saving as many people as He could, making the event of His resurrection as obvious as possible?

And if it was such a miraculous event, why don't we have secular sources from the Romans of the time who were so meticulous at recording everything?"

I didn't know what to think or where to look. Again, I wanted to kill him for his blasphemy but I didn't have a good reason to do so.

"You're just being picky!" was all I had as an answer.

"And you're not being picky when you find fault with other religions and try to prove that Christianity, and moreso, your version of Christianity, is the only way to heaven?"

I stood there dumbfounded and angry. There was a slight pause. But then Markus toned down and spoke softly and tenderly to me.

"Michael, you're throwing your life away over a book. There's nothing wrong with believing in God or the Bible but be reasonable about it. Life is here to live and enjoy. Don't throw it away because once it's gone, you can't get it back."

I was hostile but I relaxed a bit when I consoled myself that it was Satan speaking through Markus to tempt me away from the Bible.

Suddenly the laboratory telephone rang. Markus answered it and then left. But his words rang like chimes of an old church in my head.

That evening I attended lectures. But while my lecturer rambled on, my mind was concentrated on Markus' words. And that night on the train on my way home from university I decided to read the four gospel stories of the resurrection. And I didn't like what I read either. To clarify it, I got my lecture pad out of my bag and drew up a table with the four gospels along the top and wrote out the major differences between the four. What Markus had said was true. There was a discrepancy between the four versions.

But there was one particular contradiction that stood out which Markus hadn't even mentioned. In Matthew 28:9, when the women were running from the tomb to tell the disciples that Jesus had risen, Jesus appeared to them, and they worshipped Him, holding His feet. But in John 20:17, Jesus told Mary *not* to touch Him because He had not yet ascended to the Father.

When I arrived home, even though it was late, I decided to check whether this was a mistranslation from the Greek but to my dismay I found that these verses were translated correctly. Thus, if there was a disparity between the four Gospels, they could not have been written by a perfect, omniscient God.

And then I thought further about Markus' doubts concerning the resurrected Christ. Why didn't the risen Christ walk into Jerusalem and prove beyond a doubt that He had resurrected? Why did He only show that He had resurrected to His disciples only? Jesus had performed so many amazing miracles, even raising someone else from the dead in front of everybody. Why not this last and greatest miracle which was the cornerstone of the Christian faith?

I lay in bed and stared up at the ceiling in the dark. As exhausted as I was, I couldn't sleep. Something was wrong with my perfect view of the Bible. It was like Galileo viewing the moon for the first time through his telescope and seeing that the Church's teaching of a smooth, spherical object with no imperfections was in fact wrong.

But unlike Galileo, I wasn't prepared to accept this. All my indoctrination had told me that to question the Bible was satanic and was an immediate ticket to hell, where we would not pass Go nor collect $200. Satan had tried through Markus to tempt me with life's pleasures and when that hadn't worked, he had spoken like he had through the snake in the Garden of Eden, saying to Eve, "Yea, hath God said?" and then Eve was tricked into believing that God really didn't mean what He said, and she was punished for questioning and doubting God's words.

No, I had to believe in the truth of the resurrection story by blind faith. I could not let Satan have a foothold over me. If I questioned the Bible further, I would probably give up the faith. Satan would then have me where he wanted me and the next thing I would be dead and on my way to eternal damnation.

What Markus had said was wrong. There were answers in the Bible and I would eventually find them.

Chapter 11

For some time after this, I tried to avoid this discussion I had with Markus. I didn't even tell Markus that what he told me was right, and Markus never pursued the topic either. And I was more than happy that he said nothing more about it.

But still, all these problems about biblical doctrines lay dormant in my subconscious. I felt that as long as I did not question my faith and just believed in Christ and the Bible by blind faith, I was avoiding trouble in my life. I thought that if I simply ignored the contradictions, they would eventually explain themselves away. After all, I had now read the entire Bible and this collection of books which had accumulated over the centuries flowed through history like the dauntless river of time. From Genesis to Revelation was a natural, consistent flow of thought where even the transition form Judaism to Christianity was beautiful and complete, like the transition from winter to spring. That was my initial general view after my first reading of the entire Bible.

My parents were oblivious to all the questioning that was going on inside me, the doubts about my faith and the conflict over my sexuality. According to them, I was standing on a stable rock and all inside was at peace with Jesus Christ the Lord.

Because of the knowledge that I was accumulating from my studies of the entire Bible, I was able to explain a lot more of what the New Testament was about. My knowledge of the Greek enlightened not only myself but also my listeners at the Friday night Bible Study group we attended. Everyone marvelled at my knowledge and always asked why I hadn't entered the ministry but I could not find a reason to satisfy myself why this vocation had not called me. All considered me a diligent student of the Bible and placed me on a pedestal. But I couldn't see myself like they did. My homosexual desires gnawed at my soul and made me feel less than human and barely better than Satan.

When the Friday evening Bible Study was over and we had come home, my parents would stay up a little longer and we would chat. My mother generally went to bed early and so she would soon leave my father and me alone in the loungeroom. My father would sometimes open up a bottle of port and we would savour a couple of glasses together.

I treasured these evenings with my father. This was when I knew how much my father and I had in common. We particularly loved to philosophy, I think simply because it was such a common enjoyable mental exercise. We talked about work, our Bible Study group, politics, relationships, marriage, sex, other religions and so on, all within the framework of our understanding of the Bible.

My father taught me a lot about marriage and relationships, and what it took to maintain them and keep them healthy. His views, of course, were based on a relationship between a man and a woman but I later discovered that these same principles were just as important to hold a gay relationship together.

But although we spoke about many things, I avoided raising the issue about my homosexuality. So many times I wanted to open up to him and tell him how I really felt inside and ask him if he had an answer. But the courage wasn't there. I knew my father would not be pleased, let alone be able to understand my attraction to other men. He knew also what the Bible said about the cause and fate of homosexuals, and nothing was said in the Scriptures about a possible escape from this sexual attraction. So, how could I open up to my father? All I could do was keep my feelings wrapped up deep inside, hoping that just by ignoring them they would eventually go away. Struggling forth, I assured myself that the answer lay in the Bible but I had not as yet discovered it.

All my life revolved around my faith in Christ, my family and my church. Only in my work life was it permissible to step out of this religious, holy world and into the secular, for we believed that we were in the world but not of it. This was why, although Markus had raised the question concerning the different resurrection stories and the secrecy surrounding the resurrection itself, I couldn't imagine it being otherwise. If Jesus was not whom I claimed Him to be, my whole world would have crumbled around me.

In the first year of my degree, although my major was chemistry, I had to do one extra subject which had no bearing on the rest of my course. I had a choice between geology and biology and I chose the latter. I was very happy with this choice because out of all the subjects I did that year, this subject was my favourite. And it showed in my marks because I performed well. Because I was so good at the subject, every time we did an experiment, I was able to waltz through it without any trouble at all and soon I was renowned throughout the class.

One evening as I was doing an experiment and writing down my findings, one student kept coming over to my desk to have a look at what I was writing. He would then copy what I had written when I wasn't looking. But one time he stayed too long. I saw him scribbling down notes that he obviously was copying from my work and so I came right up behind him and yelled in his ear, "Sprung!"

He jumped with a start.

"I…I wasn't copying," he said with a peculiar accent. "I just wanted to check something."

I just smiled.

"Look, mate. If you're having problems, just ask me. I won't bite. Nor will our lecturer, for that matter. Copying my work won't help you understand, okay?"

This guy just smiled politely and thanked me. But I was taken aback by his features and his accent. He had olive skin and a dark beard but it was the accent that made me extra curious.

"Hey, mate, I hope you don't mind me being really forward but what nationality are you?"

The guy looked at me cautiously.

"I…I'm from Israel."

When he said that, I was delighted!

"So, you're Jewish, then?"

"Well, yes," he replied hesitantly.

"Oh, how exciting! I have always wanted to meet a Jew. I prayed at the beginning of this year to meet a Jew and God has answered my prayer. Wow! I can't believe it! What's your name?"

"Joseph. Joseph ben-Moshe."

"Oh, Joseph, you don't know how happy a man you've made me tonight! My name's Michael Farril, and I'm really glad to meet you."

Joseph stared at me a little perplexed while I quivered with excitement, laughed, and touched him delicately as if he were an object of adoration. Poor Joseph didn't know what to think of me, he must have thought he had stumbled across a real loony!

At the break, we went to the canteen together. I was so excited, I had a hundred and one questions I wanted to ask at the one time and poor Joseph wasn't sure how to approach me. So, I explained that I was a Christian. I was worried how he would take this information because I was aware of the suffering that Jews had undergone at the hands of Christians but I wanted him to know up front. Then I explained how I had read the Old Testament and from this had developed a love for Jews and Judaism. Having said this, Joseph's facial expression relaxed and he half smiled and half laughed.

"Oh, now I understand," he said with relief. "I must say, though, I've never met anyone who was so excited to meet me before."

I asked him about Israel and was surprised to hear that the national language was Hebrew and not

Yiddish. I had always thought that Hebrew, like Latin and Classical Greek, had left the realms of the secular and was only spoken and studied among the scholastics, intellectuals and the religious.

Joseph told me little bits and pieces about Israel from what he could remember since he'd left there when he was thirteen. He told me about his family and why they had moved to such a far away country like Australia.

But talking to Joseph was for me more like speaking with a historic relic than another human being. His people were so steeped in ancient history that it was difficult for me not to view Joseph as a part of that historic flow that began at the Creation of God.

But Joseph was more than of historical significance. In him I could see his ancestors at Mt Sinai when Moses came down from the mountain holding the Ten Commandments written by God. I could see Joshua at the Battle of Jericho and the miraculous victory of the Israelites. I could see in him the calling of David, to whom God promised a continual line of kings ruling in Jerusalem. I could see in him the line of kings from David to Jehoiachin and the final Diaspora of the Jews under King Nebuchadnezzar, King of Babylon. I could see the birth of Christ and the ensuing conflicts caused by this new version of Judaism. Joseph was held with awe in my eyes and because of my understanding of the plight of the Jews at the hands of the Christians, I did not want to preach to him Jesus Christ from the outset. I didn't want to mar our relationship or cause Joseph to be at enmity with me but instead wanted to gain a voluminous amount of information of Judaism from him.

I saw Joseph often at university. He was in my physics class as well and he was brilliant in this subject. He attacked the subject as if each lesson were to him an intellectual banquet to get his intellectual teeth around. But in biology he was hopeless. He often complained how he wanted to major in physics and couldn't understand why in the first year he had to do biology only to make up the subjects for his degree. He had no end of trouble remembering terms, understanding lectures or writing up reports or assignments for this subject. In contrast, I found biology easy. Remembering terms was as easy as English because so many biological terms were of Greek origin.

Joseph was so worried that he was going to fail biology that I eventually volunteered to help on the weekend. He knew by this stage my express interest in Judaism and in turn told me that he could teach me about his faith and answer my questions. If there were things he did not know the answer to, his father no doubt had answers because he was a rabbi.

Joseph lived in Dover Heights, one of the eastern suburbs of Sydney, in an area where was and still is a large Jewish community with a number of synagogues and Jewish schools. But before I had met Joseph, I didn't even know that this part of the world actually existed and this was quite a treat for me in itself. I knew Joseph's stance regarding the Sabbath and I knew that the Jewish Sabbath was Saturday. And I respected his belief. In Romans chapter fourteen, Paul argued that we should respect those who observe the Sabbath even if we now view all days equally. Hence I chose to help him out one Sunday afternoon after church.

I remember driving to East Sydney for the first time. Prior to this time, my knowledge of Sydney was the western extremity, Emu Plains and Penrith and the surrounding areas, and the Central Business District of the city itself where I had gone a few times on day trips. The drive from the city towards the eastern suburbs was just amazing, with winding roads that opened out onto splendid views of bays crammed full with yachts. It was obvious that the rich lived in these areas and it appeared as if the wealth was just oozing out everywhere. Many of the houses were old but stylish, displaying a rich grandeur that I thought only existed in Jane Austen's novels. The people were well dressed in fashion and style as if they were forever going to a ball, which was in such stark contrast to jeans and T-shirts that I was so used to in my local area.

I finally found Joseph's house, a grand modern building, with two storeys, an imposing balcony and a wonderful front garden. I was so daunted by the place because I had never seen such wealth so openly displayed.

When I came to the door, Joseph greeted me with great joy. He then led me through the front door and on the lintel was the Hebrew letter Shin hanging on a plaque.

"See that?" Joseph said. "That's to ward off evil spirits."

That took me quite by surprise. I thought Jewish philosophy was like my Christian philosophy where they believed only the Old Testament Scriptures. I had never read in the Law of Moses or anywhere in the Old Testament about such a superstitious practice.

Joseph's parents were lovely. Mr ben-Moshe greeted me as soon as I entered like a long, lost relative, shaking my hand with his left hand on my elbow. I could feel the love and sincerity flowing like a mythical river from his heart into mine. But Mr ben-Moshe could barely speak English so communicating with him was very difficult indeed. But Mrs ben-Moshe spoke English fluently and she welcomed me with lovely compliments because I had wanted to help their son. Mrs ben-Moshe sat me down to some Arabic coffee and various cakes which were typical of the Middle East. We sat there for a moment and made our acquaintance.

While we were having coffee, I looked around the room. Just like the Carpenters' house, this house was permeating with religious motifs but this time from a different religion. There was a silver candelabrum, the Menorah, sitting on the table, there were Stars of David in various guises around the room, and a plaque on one wall containing the Ten Commandments in Hebrew, in this strange but beautiful squarish Semitic script.

After coffee, Joseph and I struggled through experiments and assignments for most of the afternoon. When we had finished, Joseph took me down to the end of the road which terminated with a sheer cliff face. Standing here one could hear the waves smashing against the rocks way below and feel the strong breeze blowing against our faces. I stood there and looked out to sea and smelt the fresh air. With Joseph by my side, I could feel God's presence in all Creation, the seagulls flying by, the clouds puffed up like oversized cotton balls. But most of all, I was standing in the presence of a descendant of Abraham, a descendant of the man whose seed bore the Christ.

That evening I had dinner with the family. It was an interesting and great evening. Because of the language barrier, Mrs ben-Moshe and Joseph acted as translators between me and Mr ben-Moshe. But I was in my element that night. I asked all about the Jewish festival days like Passover, Yom Kippur, Sukkoth, and what they all meant. The question was translated into Hebrew and the answer brought back to me in English.

I expressed my interest in Judaism and how I wanted to learn Hebrew. Because of this Mr ben-Moshe loaded me up with books. One was a history of the Jews starting with Abraham right up to the present state of Israel. He also gave me a couple which taught the Hebrew language. And last of all, he gave me a copy of the Old Testament in Hebrew and said, through Joseph, that if I had any trouble reading it, he'd be more than happy to help. On the spine of the book were written three words. I asked what they meant. Joseph read them in Hebrew first and translated them for me.

"'Torah, Nevihim, Uchtuvim'. In English, it means, The Law, The Prophets and the Writings.

Sometimes we just say 'The Law and the Prophets' or even just 'the Law' and sometimes we use the acronym 'Tenach'. But they all mean the same thing."

I was very touched by their generosity.

Joseph accompanied me out to the car. Before I got in, Joseph thanked me profusely for my help.

"Joseph, it was no problem at all. I want to thank you for all the information. I enjoyed your parents' hospitality and your father's generosity for giving me these books to read. But one thing I have to ask. Do your parents know that I'm a Christian?"

"Of course they do," Joseph said laughing. "I told them that ages ago and told them of your interest in Judaism. But that doesn't worry my parents or me at all."

I smiled at that. I shook Joseph's hand again and jumped into my car. As I left, I watched Joseph wave good-bye and I replied with a hoot of my horn and zoomed off home. This was a very fulfilling experience. My adventure among Jews filled me with an inexplicable joy.

My association with Joseph and his family highlighted my original feelings towards Jews after reading the Old Testament, and Mr ben-Moshe's books helped very much. I read the book about the history of the Jews in a couple of hours. I loved it. It repeated the stories in the Bible that I already knew but it also spoke a lot about the history of the Jews I didn't know before

The Old Testament ends with the story of how the Persian kings allowed the Jews to return to rebuild the Temple in Jerusalem and the New Testament begins with the Roman oppression of Judea. In our church, this interim period between the Testaments was called the Silent Years because no books of the Bible were written at that time which meant that God did not speak to the world through His prophets during these four hundred years.

But this book explained what happened during the intertestamental period, how that the Persians were eventually conquered by the Greeks and during this time many Jews became merchants. A large Jewish community developed in Alexandria, in Egypt, and around 280 BC, the Bible, which had up to this point in time only ever been in Hebrew, was translated into Greek to form the famous Septuagint. The Septuagint, meaning *seventy* in Latin, was so named because, so it is believed, seventy rabbis were involved in the translation. It was the first time that the Bible appeared in a foreign tongue. I was so intrigued that I bought a copy from the Christian Bookshop.

But with the Greeks came new persecution. The Greek kings encouraged the world to be as one and to believe and sacrifice only to the Greek gods and goddesses. But what the Greeks also brought along with them was culture: poetry, theatre and gymnastics, and philosophy: the works of Plato and Aristotle. This caused a spiritual battle within the Jewish community because many of the Jews questioned the traditions of their forefathers and wanted to abandon their faith and adopt a Greek lifestyle. Many Jews went so far as to participate in the Olympic Games but to do so they had to compete naked. But the uncircumcised world did not like the appearance of these circumcised men and so, to be more aesthetically pleasing, the Jews artificially uncircumcised their flesh, rejecting the physical sign of their covenant with God.

But bad came to worse when one Greek king, Antiochus Epiphanes IV, unified all nations by force, commanding them to abandon the faith in their nation's heritage on pain of death. Antiochus marched into Jerusalem and entered the Temple, taking practically all the Temple furnishings of gold and silver, and then left, leaving the Temple in shambles. Antiochus soon returned to erect an altar, sacrificing a pig in the Temple precinct. All the books of the Law and the Prophets Antiochus could lay his hands on were burned, and anyone possessing a copy or practising the Law such as circumcision and the observation of the Sabbath was slaughtered. All dedicated Jews went into hiding.

But there was one man, Mattathias, who would not follow the King's decree to abandon the ancestral practices, and he led a revolt against the Greeks. This revolt was continued by Mattathias' son, Judas Maccabeus, and eventually the Jews' land was delivered from the Greeks.

Years later, the Romans came conquering all that the Greeks had established in the Mediterranean and the Holy Land came under possession of a foreign nation once again. The name of the kingdom of Judah was latinised to Judea and Herod was made a puppet king of this area. Herod wanted to gain the favour of the Jews and so he rebuilt the Temple and adorned it in gold and splendour. But despite this, the Jews hated being oppressed by the Romans and it was against this backdrop that Jesus was born.

This book followed on from where the New Testament left off, telling the story of a Jewish uprising in 66 AD which was concluded with a retaliatory attack by the Romans under General Titus, later to become one of the Roman Emperors, an attack which ended with the Temple being destroyed in 70 AD.

I read also that Jesus was not alone in saying that He was the Christ. In 132 AD, a man called Simon bar-Kochba claimed that *he* was the Christ. At this stage, I did not really understand what it meant to be called the Christ and so thought Simon bar-Kochba was being blasphemous. I therefore felt that he was justly punished for his blasphemy. He led a revolt against the Romans but his mission failed and eventually the Jews were banned from coming within sight of the Holy City.

I read about another branch of Christians living side by side with the Pauline Christians. From this I discovered that the Pauline Christians were those Christians who believed in Paul the apostle, whose letters make up much of the New Testament. I discovered that not all Christians at the time acknowledged Paul as an authority on Christian issues. One important group of Christians who did not believe in Paul were the Ebionites, who believed Jesus was the Messiah but also believed in observing the Mosaic Law. I guessed that the leader of the Ebionite Christians was James whose epistle is included in the New Testament.

I learned in later history about the persecution of the Jews in the East by the Muslims and in the West by the Christians. I learned about the origin of two classes of Jews called Ashkenazi and Sephardi, the former being Jews from central Europe, the latter from Spain and northern Africa. I read that in the fourteenth century, Jews in Europe were forced to wear a yellow circle on their clothes to distinguish them from the rest of society, a practice which was repeated under Hitler's regime during the Second World War where they had to wear a yellow Star of David.

I was horrified at the forced baptisms and the Inquisition in Spain and how that many Jews finally found refuge in 1492 when Christopher Columbus discovered the Americas which opened the way for many Jews to flee European persecution and find respite in the New World.

I read about the Jews finally winning back their land in 1948, which seemed to be a fulfilment of the Old Testament prophecies. I read how a small pocket of Jews had been living in Yemen whom the world had forgotten about for centuries and who were flown back to the Promised Land on the "wings of eagles" as it was prophesied in the Old Testament so long ago, and how they spoke untainted Hebrew. I read about current Judaism and how the name *Pharisee*, which is used as a derogatory term by Christians, came from the Hebrew word *perushim* meaning "pious" and that the modern day Pharisees are represented today by the Hassidic Jews.

As for the Hebrew language, the book I used was well set out that in a week I knew all the letters and vowel points of the Hebrew language.

But studying the Hebrew gave me the greatest delight. This was the very language in which God spoke to Abraham, Moses, David, and all the prophets and great men of the Bible. I did not view Hebrew as just another language like French, or German, or even Koine Greek. Hebrew was more sanctimoniously romantic for me that, even before I knew many words, I read aloud passages from the Hebrew Old Testament, just listening to the sound and rhythm of this strange tongue as if there were something holy and godly in them, as if I could hear God Himself speaking.

The more I studied the Hebrew, read the Septuagint and read the New Testament in Greek, I began to see yet more Jewish overtones in the early Christian faith. But I also began to see how that because the Bible was originally written in Hebrew, then in Greek, then translated into English, sometimes via Latin, many terms today had been obscured or had lost their real meaning in the translation. This was particularly noted in the terms Ark, Tabernacle, Bishop, Church, Baptism, LORD, God, The Wise Men, and even the name Jesus Christ.

I was first struck by the word Ark. In Sunday School, we learned about two Arks, the Ark of Noah and the Ark of Moses. One was a large boat and the other was a small box. As a child, I could never see the connection. However, in Hebrew and Greek, the word used for both Arks was *ahron* and *kibotos* respectively, both words meaning *box*. This became *arca* in Latin, but instead of being translated, it was anglicised, and by so doing, the meaning was lost.

But by going back to the original languages, the connection between the two Arks became evident. They were two boxes, one a gigantic box (and not the traditional boat-shaped object as it is often depicted) used to house Noah, his family, and two of every animal, and seven of every clean animal, against the ravages of the Deluge, the other a comparatively small box in which contained the Ten Commandments. Of course, translating the word into English would make these mystically religious items sound very plain and common indeed! No Christian would like to tell the story of Noah's Box or the Box of Moses because it would sound vulgar, despite that it would be a more precise understanding of the word.

The word *tabernacle* was another such elevated term for something which had a common meaning. The original languages, Hebrew and Greek, used the words *mishkan* and *skaenae* respectively, which were translated into Latin as *tabernaculum*. But instead of being translated into English, it was anglicised to *tabernacle*, robbing the real sense of the original meaning of *tent*. By using the English word which translated the original would again make this special set up sound vulgar and common, and rob it of its religious connotation. But any boy scout or girl guide could justifiably go camping in their two-person tabernacle and be linguistically correct.

The term *bishop* was another word which had lost its real meaning and given an elevated religious meaning to describe an office held in the Catholic and Anglican churches. But this word came from the Greek *episkopos*, latinised to *episcopus*, and anglicised to *bishop*. This same word had come from the Greek into English in other ways, one via Latin, and another a complete translation from the Greek, in the forms of *supervisor* and *overseer* respectively, these two other words having no religious connotation at all.

But what was more striking was how this meaning and function was consistent in Greek but was translated differently in the King James Version which made it look like a part of the hierarchy of the church. But, in fact, the terms *bishop* and *elder* both referred to the same person in the early church. There was no minister or priest who had been to college and then laymen who were elders. In the early church, to be a bishop or an elder was to simply be a leader of a local church, there were originally a number of elders elected for each church and not just one, and to be an elder was not viewed as an earthly profession as it later became.

The word *church* in the Bible does not have anything to do with buildings as we understand it today. The etymology of the English word begins with the Greek word *kuriakon*, "house of the Lord", and finally comes into the English as *church* via the German *Kirche*. But the word used in the Greek New Testament is not *kuriakon* but *ekklesia*, from whence come the Spanish and French words *iglesia* and *église* respectively. The word *ecclesiastical* is one relic in the

English language that is derived from this biblical word.

But the *ekklesia* did not originate with the Christian Church of the New Testament but had already been established centuries earlier in Classical Greek times to describe the secular assembly of voting citizens in the city-states. It was by the *ekklesia* that laws were made for the citizens and the fate decided for those who were brought to trial. Those who did not abide by the rules of the *ekklesia* were sentenced to death. Socrates himself was tried and condemned by the *ekklesia* to drink hemlock because it was thought that he was corrupting the minds of the youths by questioning the established religions and beliefs of the time. The *ekklesia* was made up of all the free voting citizens of the city-state, which excluded women and slaves, and it was upon this form of assembly that the New Testament church was formed.

This explained why, then, Jesus told His followers in Matthew 18:17 that if a brother sins against you, you are to first tell him privately, then before one or two witnesses, and if he still does not listen, "tell it unto the church (*ekklesia*): but if he neglect to hear the church (*ekklesia*), let him be unto thee as an heathen man or a publican". Because murder was a sin, and the church was more of a spiritual city-state than a physical one, the severest punishment that could be imposed on a member was to be excluded from the church, later known as excommunication. And like the Greek counterpart, Paul instructed women to keep silent, forbidding them to have any involvement in church matters and affairs.

The term *baptism* which has so many different understandings among Christians is an anglicisation of the Greek word *baptizo*. *Baptizo* had no religious connotation in its original form but simply meant *immerse* or *submerge*. In II Kings 5:14, as an example, we read how a man called Naaman was suffering from leprosy and so he sought help from the prophet Elisha. Elisha told Naaman to dip himself seven times in the Jordan River at Elisha's command. The word in the Septuagint translated as *dipped* in English is in fact *ebaptisato*, "baptised".

The word LORD intrigued me. It was written in two forms in the King James Version. When written as *Lord*, that is, beginning with a capital letter and the rest in lower case, it was a translation of the Hebrew word *adonai* which means exactly that: *Lord*. However, when written with four capital letters, that is, LORD, it refers to the holy name of God that the Jews believe is too holy to pronounce: *Jehovah* or *Yahweh*.

In fact, we really don't know exactly how to pronounce the word at all because the word has only reached us in the twentieth century in its written form. One of the features of the Hebrew language which is quite different from English, or any European language for that matter, is that only the consonants are written and the vowels are filled in by the reader from their knowledge of the pronunciation of the word in speech. So, because the Jews never said the name aloud, God's holy name in Hebrew has reached us only in the form of YHWH.

What exactly, then, is God's name? Or is it really a name? In Exodus 3, we have the story of God speaking to Moses from the burning bush. God told Moses that he was to go to Egypt and tell the Children of Israel, who were still slaves there, that He would deliver them from the Egyptians. Moses asked God that, if the Israelites asked him who sent him, God said to Moses to tell the Israelites that I AM sent him. The word for I AM in Hebrew is similar to the word YHWH and all the conjugations of the verb "be" which led me to the conclusion that it was possible that the name YHWH was not some special, secret codeword but simply a version of the word "be". YHWH probably meant something like, "he who exists", "the existing one", "he who is" or "the being". It made sense because it meant that God's name, YHWH, meant that He alone existed and all other gods and goddesses were simply fantasies in the minds of those who believed in them.

This, coupled with the word *God*, surprised me. In the opening lines of the Bible, the word in Hebrew for *God* is *elohim*. What intrigued me was that it was a plural word, the singular being *eloha*, cognate with the Arabic *Allah*. The plurality of the term was more pronounced when viewed in the opening lines of the Ten Commandments in Exodus 20:2, 3 where the Bible says, "I am the LORD thy God (*elohim*), which have brought thee out of the land of Egypt, out of the house of bondage. Thou shalt have no other gods (*elohim*) before me." The same word was used in the two verses but translated differently, one in the singular when referring to YHWH, and the other in the plural when referring to other gods.

This was further highlighted in the first three chapters of the Bible when YHWH set out to create man, for He speaks in the first person plural saying in Genesis 1:26, "Let us make man in our image, after our likeness", and later, after the Fall, God says in Genesis 3:22, "Behold, the man is become as one of us". I felt that, linguistically, it was quite plausible to translate these verses as, "And the gods said, Let us make man in our image, after our likeness," and "And the gods that be said, Behold the man has become as one of us."

But in Jewish tradition and indeed throughout the Bible, we read always about the existence of one God only. This revelation filled me with great joy for it was astounding proof that the idea of the Trinity existed right at the beginning of God's Word. Through translation, this evidence had been lost. But such an understanding of the original text therefore made room for the belief of three gods in one. This, then, was a wedge that I could use to preach to Joseph about Jesus Christ.

But there were two terms which caused great consternation in my soul when viewed in the original languages. The first was the term translated as *Wise Men*. Christians at Christmas time honour the Three Wise Men (although the Bible doesn't specify how many men there actually were, only that there were three gifts) because they recognised Jesus as the king of the Jews, and because God spoke to them in a dream and protected them from Herod by telling them to return to their home country via a different route than by the way they originally came. But the term used in the Greek was *magoi*, which in Latin is *magi*, which comes into the English language in words such as *magic* and *magician*. This same word, *magoi*, so I discovered, is later translated as *sorcerer* when referring to a man called Bar-jesus in Acts 13:6.

But I had more to learn of the magoi than I was willing to discover. First of all, they came from Persia, which was why the Wise Men came from the East. But most importantly, the magoi, in fact, were the sacerdotal class of the Zoroastrian faith, the Zoroastrian religion being the established religion of the Persian Empire. As a part of the religion, the magoi used the stars among other things as a means of predicting the future. In other words, the magoi were astrologers. This, then, gave a greater significance as to why the Wise Men followed the Star and why they saw in the Star the significance of the birth of a Jewish king.

Putting it into an Australian context, it was like saying Athena Star Woman and various other astrologers went to Bethlehem because they had read that Saturn was in the sign of Scorpio which indicated the birth of the king of the Jews. It was shocking enough that the magoi were astrologers because astrology to us was satanic, but they were also worshippers of a different god and followers of another prophet called Zoroaster. According to the Christian God, anyone worshipping another god was accursed, for after all YHWH was a jealous God, but here we have a story of a group of astrologers who believed in another god and yet God protected them from harm.

But what troubled me more than ever was the name of the Saviour, Jesus Christ, for I discovered that neither of these two terms uniquely belonged to Him. The name *Jesus*, so I discovered, was a hellenisation of the Hebrew name *Yeshua*, the name by which the Jews call Jesus today and a name which comes into English in the form of *Joshua*. In other words, *Jesus* and *Joshua* are really the same name.

But the term *Christ* had completely lost its significance through the centuries when it came into the English language untranslated. Many Christians today believe that the term uniquely belongs to Jesus but I discovered that this was not the case.

Another term which Christians associate with Jesus and generally see as distinct from the word *Christ* is the term *Messiah*. But by studying the Bible in the original languages, I discovered that *Christ* was simply the anglicisation of the Greek word *christos*, and *christos* was the Greek translation of the Hebrew word *moshiach*, or better known in its anglicised form as *messiah*, and both terms mean *anointed one*. *Anoint* is a word which refers to the action of pouring oil over someone's head which symbolises that that person has been chosen by God to carry out a particular function. Therefore, someone who was called *the Anointed One* was someone who had had oil poured over his or her head to carry out a special function that God wanted him or her to fulfil.

What opened my eyes was that all the kings of Israel and Judah were anointed before they began their kingship, and they were all called, according to the King James Version, *the Anointed One*. The interesting thing was that when I read these verses in Hebrew and Greek, the words in the originals were *moshiach* and *christos* respectively.

I found that when I used the term *Christ* or *Messiah* in certain Old Testament verses instead of *the Anointed One*, as was the translation, it made the sense of the verse sound blasphemous, for the first regal Christ in the Bible was not Jesus, but King Saul. David recognised this because he was frightened to cause harm to King Saul even though the prophet Samuel had prophesied that David would be the next king. By translating the Hebrew word *moshiach* by the anglicised word *Christ*, I Samuel 24:5, 6 would read

> *And it came to pass afterward, that David's heart smote him, because he had cut off Saul's skirt.*
> *And he said unto his men, The LORD forbid that I should do this thing unto my master, the LORD's Christ, to stretch forth mine hand against him, seeing he is the Christ of the Lord*

Here David admitted that King Saul was God's Christ about one thousand years before Jesus was born. When David became king, he was referred to as the new Christ who took the place of Saul.

When the last king of Judah was finally deposed, the Jews lived in expectation of a Christ whom God would raise up to return the Israelites back to their land and rebuild the Temple and it was expected that this Christ would be a great figure if he had to defeat the great empires that surrounded this small pocket of land.

I had no problem understanding this concept of Christ. It explained to me the significance as to why Jesus was called the Christ and why many referred to Jesus as the son of David in the Gospels. It also made sense why Matthew chapter one opens with a genealogy of Jesus through David's line to prove that Jesus had a legitimate right to be called the Christ.

But what puzzled me, or moreso, shocked me, was that one Messiah or Christ recognised by the Jews during the Diaspora and recorded in the venerable Word of God was neither a descendant of David, nor a Jew, neither by race nor religion. If we once again substitute the word "anointed" with the word used in the original languages, we discover that Isaiah, who the Christians and Jews and even Jesus Himself uphold as a spokesperson for God, says of Cyrus the Great, King of the Medes and Persians, in Isaiah 45:1

Thus saith the LORD to his Christ, to Cyrus, whose right hand I have holden, to subdue nations before him.

I discovered from both Christian and secular sources that Cyrus was never a Jew, nor did he ever regard Jehovah as God, but had always worshipped Ahura Mazda, the great Lord, and Zoroaster, his prophet, just like the Wise Men had. He was a worshipper of another god, which to us was an incarnation of the devil, and yet, Isaiah called Cyrus Yahweh's Christ. I could understand why the Jews

viewed Cyrus as such because one of the expecta-
tions of the Messiah was that he would rebuild the
Temple in Jerusalem, and King Cyrus allowed the
Jews to return to Palestine to do just that.

But this revelation I did not like at all. Why did
Almighty Yahweh, who can do anything He likes,
choose a Gentile, who was not even a descendant of
Abraham, nor a descendant of David, to be His
Christ? But further, why did a jealous God like Yahweh choose a man who worshipped another god to
subdue the nations before him when there were no
doubt thousands of Jews at that time, especially true
davidic descendants, who could have easily been
chosen for the task?

This troubled me no end. I thought that by studying the original languages of the Bible my understanding of God would be enhanced. In a way it was
but was not leading me in the direction I thought it
would. On the contrary, it was like opening a Pan-
dora's Box as far as my faith was concerned.

But again, Mr Norman's words came to mind:
this was the work of Satan. Lucifer was trying to
make me doubt the validity and consistency of the
Bible and drag me in chains into the dungeons of
hell. There were definitely explanations to account
for all this new information coming to hand. If I
sought God for guidance, everything would all iron
itself out.

I asked Joseph if I could go to the synagogue with
him one Sabbath day. I always thought that the
synagogue was forbidden to Gentiles like the Temple
was in Jerusalem and Joseph just laughed.

"Of course you can. Can I attend a church service with you although I'm Jewish?"

I got his point. I remember dressing up ready to go. I had asked my parents if they wanted to come because I thought they would be as interested as I was in Judaism but they were satisfied with their Christianity as it was. So I went alone. I brought along my Hebrew Old Testament which I left in the car once I had arrived at Joseph's house. When I went inside, I discovered that Mr Ben-Moshe had already gone but Joseph and his mother were waiting with breakfast for me. I thought we would be late but Joseph assured me that we weren't.

Before we left, Mrs ben-Moshe brought out an assortment of kippahs, the skull caps the Jews wear, and I chose one that made me look the most Jewish. When I looked in the mirror, I felt quite proud of myself.

When Joseph and I went out the door and began walking onto the footpath, a lady walked past and politely said to us, "Shabbat Shalom", and I responded proudly.

I went to my car, fetched my Bible, and Joseph and I walked to the synagogue. Just before we entered, I asked Joseph why he hadn't brought a Bible with him to the synagogue.

"On the Sabbath Day, we're not allowed to carry anything. Anyway, there are Bibles there."

"Why didn't you tell me that when I was at the car?" I complained.

"It doesn't matter. They'll still welcome you."

But I was embarrassed and when we entered I quickly placed the Bible on the pew.

Inside the synagogue there were two floors like in a theatre. I noticed that the central focus was a raised platform and all the pews formed a U-shape around this. On the platform was a middle aged man rocking back and forth on his heels chanting in Hebrew. To me, it sounded weird but godly and sanctimonious at the same time and the atmosphere caught me up into another dimension.

On the second floor were all the women. They sat in silence. It was really strange. All the men were wearing kippahs (there was even a guy wearing an Akubra hat!) and half of them were chatting as if they were at a football match, not in a holy place. Mr ben-Moshe came over and greeted me while the man chanted in the background.

I noticed that the men wore something on their head while the women didn't. This was quite striking to me because St Paul, being a Jew, had reversed this commandment saying that women should wear coverings and men shouldn't.

Finally the man finished chanting. The ark at the front of the synagogue was opened and the Torah was brought out. While the Torah made its way to the platform, some men kissed it as it passed by.

The Torah was opened and then one of the men from the congregation came up and read a portion. Joseph explained to me that seven men read from the Torah each Sabbath. The Torah was so divided that in a year the entire five books were read. Each Sabbath Day reading was further divided into seven portions which were read by seven different men. The first man to read was a descendant of Aaron, the second was a Levite, and the other five were anyone else. This was fascinating stuff.

After synagogue, the rest of the day I spent with Joseph and his family. I asked questions about the Law I didn't understand. Joseph translated my questions to his father, his father answered them in Hebrew and then Joseph translated them into English. There was one particular question I asked concerning a certain verse which for me was particularly memorable because I was expecting an esoteric significance in a verse which had a base meaning. I said to Joseph, "Ask your father this. It says here in Exodus 20:26, 'Neither shalt thou go up by steps unto mine altar, that thy nakedness be not discovered thereon'. What does this mean?"

Joseph asked his father. As his father was telling him the answer, suddenly both Mrs ben-Moshe and Joseph just burst out laughing.

"What did he say?" I asked impatiently.

"Dad said that they weren't to make steps up to the altar because then the congregation could look under his garments and see his bum!"

I had a pleasant afternoon and evening with Joseph's family. I enjoyed it so much that I didn't want to go home. If the ben-Moshes were a representative sample of all the Jews in the world, it was obvious why God loved the descendants of Abraham.

Chapter 12

My association with Joseph affected me greatly. Because the entire Bible, both the Old and New Testament, was so Jewish, I failed to see why the Jews had been pitilessly persecuted throughout antiquity at the hands of the Christians. I couldn't help but notice, like I never had before, how Jewish the New Testament and Christianity was, and the history of the Church persecuting the "Christ-killers" made less sense. When we read the Gospels, it is quite clear that all Jewry were not responsible for the death of Christ and it certainly wasn't only Jews who wanted Jesus killed. It was true that the established religious leaders of the Jewish faith found Jesus a threat to their religion because He claimed to be the Messiah contrary to their expectations. But it was also true that the ruling power of the time, the Romans, wanted to dispose of Jesus because, by declaring that He was the Christ, Jesus was declaring that He was the King of Israel. As far as the Romans were concerned, there was only one king, Caesar, and for Jesus to make the claim that He was a king was, in the eyes of the Romans, a threat to their grand empire. In this light, if Jews were considered as Christ-killers, then, by the same token, all descendants of the Roman Empire should equally be condemned to wear this name.

From a Christian standpoint, I could not see how all Jews in general were despised by the Christians when not all Jews wanted Christ dead. On the contrary, Paul asks a very poignant question in Romans 11:1, 2

> *Hath God cast away his people? God forbid. For I also am an Israelite, of the seed of Abraham, of the tribe of Benjamin*
> *God hath not cast away his people which he foreknew*

Here, Paul explains that contrary to what later Christians assumed, God did not cast away his people, the Jews, after Christ had come, and answers this question by explaining that he himself was a Jew. How, then, the Roman Catholic Church could be renowned for its history of hatred towards the Jews was beyond my comprehension because Catholics to this day venerate Mary, the mother of Jesus, and her husband, Joseph, the Twelve Apostles, St Paul, St Silas, St Barnabas, St Luke and many other saints when they were all Jewish. Even the first Pope, St Peter, was a Jew.

And, in a similar vein, I could not understand how the Protestants could run around Europe condemning Jews when every New Testament book was written by a Jew. It was a Jewish book as much as the Old Testament was.

What was unusually revealing was that the first Christians were all Jews. Further, these Christian Jews did not even consider the Gentiles worthy of having any part of this faith. When we read the Acts of the Apostles, we read of thousands upon thousands of Jews becoming Christians.

When the first Gentiles finally did become Christians, this was, at first, a culture shock to the Christian Jews, that they should share their holy Messiah with uncircumcised Gentiles. But finally they were able to bring themselves to praise God by saying in Acts 11:18

Then hath God also to the Gentiles granted repentance unto life

What was most striking from my study of the New Testament was that these Jews who believed that Jesus was the Christ did not think of themselves as members of a new faith. Acts 11:26 tells us that the term "Christian" was given to them from outsiders. Rather, these Jews considered that anyone who became a member of this new faith became a Jew, despite whether they were true descendants of Abraham or not. Paul argues this in Romans 2:28, 29 where he writes, "For he is not a Jew, which is one outwardly", one who is physically a descendant of Abraham and circumcised, "But he is a Jew, which is one inwardly", that is, those who have accepted Jesus as the Messiah. And Paul later writes in Galatians 3:29, "And if ye be Christ's, then are ye Abraham's seed", which means that if you are a Gentile and you become a Christian, you become in a way an artificial but legitimate descendant of Abraham, and ultimately a Jew.

Paul writes in Romans chapter 11 that natural Jews can no longer be considered Jews if they reject Jesus as Messiah but Gentiles who believe in Christ immediately become adopted sons of Abraham. Paul uses the analogy of a tree where Abraham is the trunk and all the natural Jews are like the natural branches of this tree. Jews who do not believe that Jesus is the Messiah are like dead branches that are removed and Gentiles who do believe are like fresh branches from another tree that are grafted into this trunk. By extension, this meant that all the promises and commandments made to Abraham and his descendants before Jesus came applied to Abraham's physical descendants but after Jesus came the promises fell on all believers, whether natural descendants of Abraham or not.

Even those things that were considered important or even vital to the Jewish faith retained their importance in this new version of Judaism, namely, the Temple and the Mosaic Law.

The Temple at Jerusalem features prominently in the New Testament. Jesus upheld it and berated the Pharisees in Matthew 23:16, 17 because the Pharisees considered the gold that made the Temple important whereas Jesus insisted that the Temple itself was the central focus, not the material that made it.

Jesus, before He was crucified, preached in the Temple and even cast the money changers out of the Temple, saying in Mark 11:17, "Is it not written, My house shall be called of all nations the house of prayer?" Here Jesus quoted Isaiah 56:7 to prove that there would come a time when the Temple would not be just for the Jews but for all nations.

Even after the resurrection of Christ, the apostles preached and prayed at the Temple in Jerusalem, even performing the first miracle there.

As for the Law of Moses, which the Christians say that we are no longer under, I found verses which seemed to say the opposite. For example, Jesus Himself said in Matthew 5:17:

Think not that I am come to destroy the law, or the prophets: I am not come to destroy, but to fulfil.

Jesus then went on to say that the Law and the Prophets, which Joseph ben-Moshe had explained was the Jewish expression used to describe what we called the Old Testament, would not change even in the slightest until the end of the world. Jesus then went on to say that if anyone breaks even the least of these commandments, that person will be punished.

This became more obvious in verses like Matthew 7:12 where Jesus says, "Therefore all things whatsoever ye would that men should do to you, do ye even so to them: for this is the law and the prophets." How could this be clearer? Jesus was stressing one of the fundamental commandments that Christians should observe: "Do unto others as you would have them do unto you," saying that we should observe this, not because it is something new that Jesus said, but because it was the embodiment of the Mosaic Law.

It says in Matthew 22: 36 – 40 that when Jesus was asked which was the greatest commandment in the Law, Jesus replied, "Thou shalt love the Lord thy

God with all thy heart, and with all thy soul, and with all thy mind...And the second is like unto it, Thou shalt love thy neighbour as thyself. On these two commandments hang the law and the prophets". These two commandments Christians consider still the most important commandments in their creed. But what was striking was that Jesus said that Christians should observe these commandments because all the Old Testament hung on these two commandments. They were not new precepts that Jesus was advocating.

Jesus was not alone with his views of the Old Testament Law. Paul wrote in Romans 7:12

> *Wherefore the law is holy, and the commandment holy, and just, and good*

putting a positive light on the Mosaic Law.

Not only so, many of the New Testament writers said that we should obey certain precepts because they were written in the Old Testament. For example, the basis of Paul's argument in I Corinthians 14:34 that women should be silent in the church was because the women "are commanded to be under obedience as also saith the law" which was based on Eve's condemnation in Genesis 3:16.

Peter wrote in I Peter 1:16 that Christians should be holy because it says in Leviticus 11:44 that God expects us to be holy.

James wrote in James 2:8 that Christians should obey the Royal Law and "love thy neighbour as thyself" because it says so in Leviticus 19:18.

All this sounded beautiful. The only difference between a natural Jew and an "adopted" Jew was that the former was waiting for He whom the latter believed had come. Christianity did not rob a Jew of his or her Jewishness, at the same time it allowed a Gentile to have a common faith with the Jews without making him or her a stranger. It was such a wonderful revelation.

Until one morning, on my way to work while the train jostled and jolted unrepentedly, I was reading the Bible very intently like I had done faithfully every morning. I was reading the story about Abraham and the covenant God made to him regarding circumcision when the smooth, purring engine of reading jolted to a sudden stop when I read the following verses from Genesis chapter 17:

> *This is my covenant, which ye shall keep, between me and you and thy seed after thee; Every man child among you shall be circumcised...*
> *...and my covenant shall be in your flesh for an **everlasting** covenant.*
> *And the uncircumcised man child whose flesh of his foreskin is not circumcised, that soul shall be cut off from his people; he hath broken my covenant.*

> *(emphasis mine)*

I took a deep breath and sat back when I read it. I read it again. Yes, God gave circumcision in the flesh as an everlasting covenant. The word *everlasting* meant going on forever and ever, never ceasing, or so I had always thought. I looked out the window and watched suburbia zoom by but my mind was in shock. The ritual of circumcision was everlasting.

It was shocking because I was sure that the New Testament writers indicated otherwise, and yes, I found the verses. In the Acts of the Apostles, chapter fifteen, we read about Pharisee Christians (which illustrates that some Pharisees were believers at the time which means that not all the Pharisees were against the Christians) who believed that circumcision was still a requirement for those who became Christians but Paul and Barnabas disagreed. Paul and Barnabas went down to Jerusalem to speak with the apostles and elders and had the argument out. After a long dispute, all concluded that circumcision was no longer necessary.

But what Peter had to say as his final argument against circumcision horrified me, for he said to the assembly in Acts 15:10, "Now therefore why tempt ye God, to put a yoke upon the neck of the disciples, which neither our fathers nor we were able to bear?" I was absolutely stunned at the way Peter called the everlasting covenant of circumcision a yoke, a burden that they could not bear, and to continue observing Yahweh's covenant with Abraham and his descendants was tempting God. I was horrified and disgusted. What Peter was saying in effect was, "this commandment is just too intolerable and difficult to observe, so let's not keep it. Anyway, if we continue to keep it, this will make God angry."

Paul had argued in Romans that only those who believed in Jesus were Abraham's descendants which meant that circumcision should now apply to Christians if the covenant was everlasting. But, contrary to his own line of argument, Paul says circumcision is now meaningless for Christians in I Corinthians 7:19 and in Galatians 5:2 he writes, "Behold, I Paul say unto you, that if ye be circumcised, Christ shall profit you nothing", this last quote coming from the same letter in which Paul writes, "And if ye be Christ's are ye Abraham's seed".

I couldn't cope with the disparity between the two thoughts. When I read the story of Abraham, I couldn't help but feel the same reverence that every Christian and Jew had for the covenant made by God through circumcision, and I was proud to be circumcised and felt no burden being so. If God wanted me to be circumcised, because of my love for Him, it was such an insignificant thing to do compared to His suffering for me.

What made the matter more confusing was the outlook on circumcision in Australia. I had been circumcised because doctors in the nineteen sixties had advised my parents that it was healthy for boys to be circumcised to prevent diseases of the penis later in life. And I knew that my father was circumcised and his parents weren't even Christians.

I also remembered a documentary on television about the argument over the necessity of circumcision in the twentieth century. Some doctors said that circumcision was unnecessary as long as boys were taught how to clean themselves properly and to pull the foreskin back from time to time so that the foreskin grows properly. But many Christian doctors were all for circumcision because it was biblical.

Even my parents were pro-circumcision because it was a commandment by God to Abraham.

It was a grand disparity, a contradiction. But my indoctrination told me that to question the Bible was wrong. If you see something which doesn't make sense, it is Satan trying to deceive you into thinking that the Bible is not the Word of God in order to drag you to hell. As much as these verses disturbed me, I put them aside out of my mind until I could find an answer.

But it didn't go away. Because when I read further in the Bible, I found more things to highlight this inconsistency. While reading the Book of Exodus, I came across the story of Moses who kept telling Pharaoh to let his people go. Pharaoh said no and then Moses brought on a plague. Pharaoh then begged Moses to stop the plague in exchange for letting the Israelites go. When the plague was stopped, Pharaoh changed his mind.

But the last plague was the one to force Pharaoh to let the Israelites go and this is the origin of the Jewish Passover. In this story, God told Moses to tell the Israelites to put the blood of a lamb or goat on the lintel of the door on a particular day. That evening, the Angel of Death would pass through the land of Egypt and kill every firstborn child from Pharaoh down to the animals. If the Angel of Death saw the blood on the lintel, he would pass over that house and the firstborn in that house would be spared. Hence the name Passover, which is a memorial feast celebrated by the Jews even to this day in remembrance of this event. The way that this festival was to be celebrated was described in great detail in Exodus chapter 12 but there were some parts of the description that hit me off balance:

> *And this day shall be unto you for a memorial; and ye*
> *shall keep it a feast to the LORD throughout your*
> *generations; ye shall keep it a feast by an ordinance **for***
> ***ever**...*
> *And ye shall observe the feast of unleavened bread;*
> *for in this selfsame day have I brought your armies out*
> *of the land of Egypt: therefore shall ye observe this*
> *day in your generations by an ordinance **for ever**...*
> *And when a stranger shall sojourn with thee, and will*
> *keep the passover to the LORD, let all his males be*
> *circumcised, and then let him come near and keep it;*
> *and he shall be as one that is born in the land: for no*
> *uncircumcised person shall eat thereof.*

(emphasis mine)

It hit me like a hammer in the face. The keeping of Passover and the Feast of Unleavened Bread, which are two Jewish holy days, were ordinances to be kept forever by all the generations of Abraham, and seeing again that Christians are Abraham's seed, it should still apply to us. Not only so, it was accepted that strangers, that is, Gentiles, could keep the Passover but they first had to be circumcised which opened up this argument again.

And so it was with the keeping of the Sabbath day for it was written in Exodus 31:16

> *Wherefore the children of Israel shall keep the*

sabbath, to observe the sabbath throughout their
*generations, for a **perpetual** covenant.*

(emphasis mine)

This was all terribly distressing because, again, I knew what Paul had to say about the Jewish holy days (to which Passover and the Feast of Unleavened Bread belonged) and the Sabbath Day. In Romans 14:5, Paul argued

One man esteemeth one day above another: another
esteemeth every day alike. Let every man be fully
persuaded in his own mind.

Here Paul was saying that one person may view the Sabbath Day and all the Jewish festival days as special days whereas another person can look at all the seven days of the week, three hundred and sixty-five days of the year equally. Whatever way a person viewed the days of the year was a personal choice. Paul was discrediting all these precious covenants which God had said were everlasting to all the descendants of Abraham.

On top of that, the argument about the Sabbath was confusing among Christians. Mainstream Christians view Sunday as the Sabbath Day. To work on Sunday was viewed in our church as sacrilegious. I remember arguments at church when fellow members were criticised for working on Sunday. It was one thing that the Bible was divided on this opinion, another that the Christians were in disharmony with the Bible's indecision (if that's possible!).

This shocked me for some time but I decided that there must be an answer to this confusion that I was missing. My parents were so much older than me and hence I reasoned that they were familiar with this dilemma and knew the answer.

One night after our family Bible Study around the dinner table, I decided to quiz my parents about the matter. When my father had closed in prayer, before leaving the table I threw him the question.

"Dad, why don't we observe the Sabbath Day anymore?" I asked.

My father looked at me a bit perturbed but provided me with the first unsatisfactory answer.

"Because we are no longer under the Law but under grace," he replied.

"But, Dad, God told Moses that it was a covenant between Him and His people forever."

My father looked at me with a deep furrow.

"Where does it say that?" he asked.

I quoted the reference and watched my father open up to the passage and read it.

"Yeah, so?" I heard him say with a hint of anger in his voice. This made me feel uneasy but I had to continue.

"Well, it says there that the Sabbath is an observance forever. That means that Christians should still be observing it."

With this, the conversation only began to highlight the confusion that Christians bring to the issue.

"Well, aren't we?" my mother said. "We go to church on Sunday, so we are observing the Sabbath."

I paused and swallowed for I knew that I was walking on tender ground.

"But in the New Testament, Paul says we are no longer required to keep the Sabbath Day."

My mother never opened her Bible but she was ready with an answer.

"The Sabbath Day is for the Jews. We are Gentiles and we don't need to observe it any more. The Jews might have to keep it but we don't because we are free. Jesus wasn't against the Sabbath anyway but against the Pharisees who had made up so many laws about what you could and couldn't do on the Sabbath Day that Jesus had to come down from heaven and set them straight. Anyway, we are no longer under the Law but under grace, because we are saved by faith, not works."

I sat for a moment trying to digest the information but nothing in their answers had any solid ground but was rather like a shifting platform.

"But God says it is a law forever," I replied. "Not only so, Paul says that all Christians are the descendants of Abraham which therefore should mean that any promises or laws made to Abraham and his descendants should apply to us, which includes these everlasting commandments."

My mother broke out in a fury.

"Are you saying the Bible is contradicting?" she said with a cold stone glare. My mother then followed with her spiel that this is how Satan gets in, he starts with little doubts and finally we come to Satan's finished work as a drug-addicted alcoholic with a major sex problem. So after that I decided not to

271

ask any more questions. But my father lightened the blow a bit by trying to find an answer to the question.

"Son, you know how in Australian laws that once they are made they are the law forever until someone changes it? Then the new law becomes binding forever. So it is with the transition from the Old Covenant to the New. In the case of the Mosaic Law, Christ could change it because He is God and hence greater than Moses. Does this answer your question?"

I nodded my head but inside I was furiously shaking it. If anything, the question I had asked had now blossomed and bloomed into more confusion. For a start, Jesus had never discredited the Sabbath Day. He upheld it but tried to bring it back to its pure simplicity of being a day of rest. I could see that the Jews really had turned it into a cumbersome day because there were so many rules and regulations one had to observe to comply with this commandment that it was difficult to view it as a day of rest.

But the way my parents answered my question showed that they had neither read the Bible thoroughly nor did they have a consistent view on this point themselves. When I originally asked the question, my father said we didn't have to observe the Sabbath because we were under grace. When they saw the verse in the Old Testament, my mother said that we still were observing this precept because we went to church on Sunday. But when I mentioned the New Testament said we were no longer to observe it, my mother drew a line between Jews and Christians, saying that the Sabbath Day was only for the Jews and that, anyway, we were saved by faith and not by works. When I tried to show them that we as Christians were Jews according to the New Testament, which showed the inconsistency of the argument, my mother exploded with threats of Satan and hell. If anything, this made it clear to me that there was a problem, an inconsistency in Bible doctrine.

What made it all the more confusing was that in the Law it said that if the descendants of Abraham did not observe circumcision, the Sabbath or the Jewish holy days, they would be "cut off from my people", which was the Old Testament way of saying that we wouldn't be saved. But Paul said that if you *did* observe all these precepts, you would not be saved. I couldn't content myself with the statement that we are saved by faith only because Jesus said that only those who did the will of the Father and kept the commandments would go to heaven, and James said we were saved by faith accompanied by works because faith without works is dead.

My hope lay in the meaning of the words *forever, perpetual* and *everlasting* used in the Hebrew. My father used the analogy of Australian laws (even though, as I was to find out later, that his analogy of Australian laws wasn't quite correct). Was this justified in the word used in the original?

I looked up all the verses in the Hebrew and discovered that the word used in each account was the Hebrew word *olam* which actually means something like *concealed* or *a vanishing point*, implying a time so far in the future or the past that was hidden from view, which for all intents and purposes is eternity.

So, I thought, the problem lies with the understanding of the word. This gave me new hope. What my father had said was right because it was possible to interpret the word *olam* to mean that a time would come in the very far away future when these ordinances would cease. The time between the establishment of these ordinances and the death of Christ was about a thousand years which for all intents and purposes was a time in the future so far away that it was concealed. So, yes, there was consistency in the Bible. Although these verses indicated that these perpetual commandments would continue forever, it was also possible to interpret this Hebrew word in a way that meant that these precepts may finally come to an end after all.

But what continually troubled me was how my parents said that because we were Gentiles, we were free from the commandments of the Law. This was confirmed by Paul who wrote in Galatians 3:10, "For as many as are of the works of the law are under the curse", and in Galatians 4:9, "But now, after that ye have known God, or rather are known of God, how turn ye again to the weak and beggarly elements, whereunto ye desire again to be in bondage?" Here Paul calls the Mosaic Law "a curse", "weak and beggarly elements" and "bondage". With such a view of the Law, it made me question what type of god would introduce His people to His Law by saying in Exodus 20:2

> *I am the LORD thy God, which have brought thee out*
> *of the land of Egypt, out of the house of bondage*

when, according to Paul, the Law was bondage. This Yahweh did not bring the Children of Israel out of bondage at all – He merely changed its form.

Chapter 13

I did finally come to a happy medium to appease the confusion, accepting that if Jews became Christians, there was no reason for them to stop observing Jewish practices, but for Gentiles who are foreign to them, following these practices was unnecessary, as long as they were doing what Jesus said.

But Jews who did not accept that Jesus was the Messiah were going to hell. And I didn't want Joseph to go to hell so it was time to preach to him Jesus. I had found and memorised many of the Old Testament prophecies that proved Jesus was the Messiah so my argument was ready. But when could I tell him? And where?

My biology class was on a Tuesday evening. But one evening our lecturer didn't show up because she was sick and so the class was cancelled. But instead of going straight home, Joseph suggested that we go for a drink at a favourite drinking hole of his in the city.

I wasn't really keen on the idea myself because I knew these were worldly places into which I shouldn't venture but at the same time I saw this as a golden opportunity to preach to Joseph in a more re-laxed atmosphere with time on my side.

The place that Joseph took us to was an outdoor café on the walkway between Circular Quay Station and the Opera House. It was the perfect spot to sit and drink. Although cool outside, it was worth it to see the city of Sydney lit up like a Christmas tree, to be sitting with a grand view of the harbour, listening to the water lap against the wall of this peninsula.

This was also a frightening time for me because this was the first night I had ever gone for a drink in a public place. We had always been discouraged to go out into the world like this because the world was full of sinners. Because the general population did not believe in Jesus, they did not believe in morals. Without morals, they could murder, steal, rape and commit any atrocity, and even a simple drink in a worldly place made me a target for their despicable acts. The only consoling thought was that this time was being used for God to preach the gospel and, because this was a good deed, the Holy Spirit would protect me from the evil one.

Joseph disappeared for a moment to buy the beers while I looked pensively around. It was a splendid evening. There was a lot of animation, people walking past, others sitting at adjacent tables just chatting, ferries coming and going from the quay, a gentle hum of traffic as commuters came and went over the Sydney Harbour Bridge. There was a gentle breeze which blew an aroma of salt water. It was a great feeling for me. But what struck me the most was the moderate rumble of conversation, people together talking and socialising. Everyone seemed relaxed and it was difficult for me not to feel the same with this spectacular view before me. I sensed no evil lurking in the shadows around me, everyone seemed quite normal.

Joseph finally returned and sat down with me, stretching out his legs.

"If only we could do this all the time instead of studying biology!" he said and smiled.

For a long while we chatted. As the beers began to take their effect, we became more relaxed and Joseph began to tell me in greater detail about his past. He told me that he was born in Tel Aviv and how he used to play soccer with his friends on small playing fields that were fully asphalted unlike our large grassy stretches of land that we take so much for granted. He compared the openheartedness of the people there, how he knew all the neighbours within about a two hundred metre radius whereas here in Sydney where he was currently living, he didn't really know the neighbours in the adjacent houses. He explained that because of the instability of his home country, his parents had decided to leave and move to a country which was politically stable, and had been attracted to Australia because of its relaxed lifestyle, freedom and general acceptance of foreigners. But then he related a story of how he took up soccer here and once he was tripped up by an opponent who called him a Jewish dog. His parents had taught him at an early age not to allow these insults to hurt him because the world hated the Jews and there was nothing he could do to stop it.

Somewhere near the end of his soliloquy he began to reminisce about Israel and told me that one day he would like to return to the Holy Land to work and hopefully settle down.

"Do you think you will ever return to Israel and live there?" I asked.

Joseph sighed.

"I'd love to, yes, that's my home. But there's so much trouble there at the moment. But one day I will return to my homeland."

Joseph looked into the distance and I had the impression that he had flown in spirit to the other side of the world as he contemplated the land of Israel, the land that God had promised to him and the descendants of father Abraham. I wondered what it was like to have a piece of earth that was given to me and my people by God.

"When do you think you'll go back and live in Israel?" I asked.

Joseph sighed.

"Mmmm. Not now. In the future, for sure. Maybe I will have to wait until the Messiah comes. Who knows?"

As soon as Joseph mentioned the Messiah, it filled my heart with sorrow. How hard it must be to be a Jew, to hopelessly wait for the Messiah when He has already come and yet His own people did not recognise Him.

"When the Messiah comes, what do you expect Him to do? How will you know when He has come?" I asked.

Joseph turned towards me and stroked his glass in deep thought.

"The prophets say that he will restore the Kingdom of Israel and build the Temple, just like David established the Kingdom and Solomon built the Temple. That's how we will know."

"Do you think there is a possibility that Messiah has already come?" I asked rather cautiously.

Joseph picked up his glass and took a mouthful, all the while his big, round, brown eyes looked disturbingly at me.

"You mean to say that Yeshua is the Messiah, aren't you!" he said, but smiled to take the bite off the statement.

I didn't say a word. Joseph leaned forward.

"Michael, I think you are a very nice person and my parents have said a lot of good things about you. They even say things like 'this Michael acts like a Christian should' and really appreciate your interest in Judaism. And you have to admit that if it weren't for Judaism, there would be no Christianity. However, this doesn't make Christianity true."

I agreed with him on that point.

"One thing I cannot accept about Christianity," Joseph continued, "is that you say that Yeshua is the Messiah, and then at the same time that he is God, then you say that he is the second person of the Trinity, making out that there are three gods when the Tenach says that there is only one. Don't you see how blasphemous this is?"

I was ready for such a comment. And I knew how to counter it.

"But, Joseph," I said by way of reply, "isn't the word for 'God' in the Tenach *elohim*, and isn't this literally a plural word?"

"Yes, that's true," Joseph said.

"Why is that, then, if you only believe in one God?"

Joseph laughed a bit and sat back in his chair.

"I know what you're going to say. But the reason is that God is the most supreme and so we talk about Him in the plural."

"Does that make sense to you?" I asked.

"I know what you think. You're going to say that it means that what the Christians say about the Trinity is true because we use the word 'God' in the plural."

"Well, it does seem like strong evidence that you refer to God as 'gods' and mean only one, which is more or less what Christians mean when they talk about the Trinity."

"And that's the only way you can view it, isn't it?" Joseph asked.

"Well, yes, there is no other way you can view it."

"But, Michael, how can you say that? I mean, doesn't the Queen when she addresses the public use the Royal 'We'? You know, like, 'we are not amused'?"

I sat and thought about it for a moment.

"And," Joseph continued, "doesn't the Pope in his edicts say 'we' and 'us' and not 'I' and 'me'? What they obviously mean is that they are the most supreme. The Queen is the head of the Church of England and of the British Empire, and the Pope is the head of the Roman Catholic Church. But there is only one Queen and only one Pope."

"Yes, but how the Christians view God as a Trinity and the use of the word 'God' in the plural in Hebrew seems more than coincidental, doesn't it?" I argued.

"No, it's not. I mean, both you and I say that we believe in one God but you believe in three gods at the same time, which really makes you a polytheist."

"No," I said, "that's why I believe 'God' in Hebrew is in the plural form."

"Well, I think you're reading into that to try and make Yeshua the Messiah and then make him God, when he is neither. Does it really make sense to you that the Almighty God who fills the universe can and will at one time occupy a small point in space? A man being God? Does that make sense to you?"

I sat and paused for a moment. In my mind I understood why Paul had said that a veil covered the eyes of the Jews concerning something I found so obvious as Jesus' claim to being the Messiah.

"But, Joseph, Yeshua was the awaited Messiah," I said quietly and firmly.

Joseph rolled his eyes and sat back in his chair with a humph.

"Yeshua was *not* the Messiah. I mean, how can you believe that he is? The Messiah, when he comes, will build the Temple, free Israel from the *goyim* and rule as king in Jerusalem forever. Yeshua did none of these things. He came, he died and he rose again from the dead so you say, but he did not fulfil the prophecies of the awaited Messiah."

I sat back in my chair in comfort, feeling the presence of the Holy Ghost come upon me, preparing me for all the arguments I had learned to use when speaking to the Jews.

"Joseph, what you don't understand is that the Tenach speaks about the Messiah coming twice."

Joseph smiled condescendingly and took another sip from his beer.

"There is nowhere in the Tenach which says that Messiah would come twice. Messiah will return and build the Temple. Yeshua didn't do that."

"I believe Messiah *will* do all those things when He comes again. What you fail to realise, Joseph, is that there are two sets of prophecies concerning the Messiah, one that He would be a suffering servant, the other that He would be a conquering hero of the Children of Israel. You see, no-one understood these prophecies of Yeshua's suffering until after the resurrection. Everyone failed to understand that the Messiah had to fulfil these prophecies first before He could fulfil the latter prophecies when He comes again."

Joseph laughed and placed his elbows on the table.

"Do you seriously believe that?" Joseph asked.

"Of course!" I said confidently.

Joseph sat back in his chair.

"But doesn't that seem strange to you? Everyone understood the prophecies of the Second Coming before the event but not the First Coming until after the event? It sounds more like a way of making Yeshua the Messiah when he failed to fulfil what he claimed to be, by making up this idea that Messiah will come twice."

I looked at Joseph a bit perturbed.

"What do you mean?"

"Well, think of it this way. Prior to Yeshua, we were waiting for the Messiah. This man, Yeshua, comes claiming that he is the Messiah. All the Jews knew what it meant to be the Messiah so they were waiting for Yeshua to fulfil the prophecies, to march into Jerusalem, take the throne of David, build the Temple, free Israel and give her back her land. However, when Yeshua arrived in Jerusalem, he was arrested by the Romans and crucified as a criminal. But those Jews who believed he was the Messiah, who happened to be fishermen, not rabbis or educated men, couldn't let go of this belief. So, they looked for prophecies in the Tenach and built up a story of a twice-coming Messiah, something no-one had ever heard of before until that time."

I could see that Joseph had a point but I didn't agree with him. The overwhelming evidence of the prophecies in the Law and the Prophets seemed to weigh against what he was saying, moreso, it was Satan placing a veil over his eyes.

I pulled my Bible out of my briefcase.

"Joseph, if this is the case, who is Isaiah speaking about when he writes in Isaiah 53:5, 6, 'But he was wounded for our transgressions, he was bruised for our iniquities: the chastisement of our peace was upon him; and with his stripes we are healed. All we like sheep have gone astray; we have turned every one to his own way; and the LORD hath laid on him the iniquity of us all.' Who in all history was chosen by God to bear our sins? No-one in the Tenach was called by God to fulfil this role. But Yeshua did. He fulfilled this Scripture. Can you think of anyone in the Tenach who was chosen to bear the sins of Israel?"

But instead of sheer silence from Joseph, which is what I expected, Joseph just looked straight at me and said, "Yes, Ezekiel. Ezekiel fulfilled this Scripture."

My blood boiled. I wanted to yell on the top of my voice in front of everyone in this café that Joseph ben-Moshe was a blasphemer. But while the thought was there, Joseph took my Bible and flicked through the pages and then read the following passage from Ezekiel 4: 4 - 6 out loud:

> Lie thou also upon thy left side, and lay the iniquity of the house of Israel upon it: according to the number of days that thou shalt lie upon it thou shalt bear their iniquity.
> For I have laid upon thee the years of their iniquity, according to the number of the days, three hundred and ninety days: so shalt thou bear the iniquity of the house of Israel.
> And when thou hast accomplished them, lie again on thy right side, and thou shalt bear the iniquity of the house of Judah forty days: I have appointed thee each day for a year.

When I heard him finish, I snatched the Bible from him and read it for myself. I wanted to rip the page from the Bible I was so horrified. Why was this verse there to give Joseph an edge against my belief?

"But Ezekiel was not the Messiah!" I protested.

"But who says that the servant that Isaiah speaks about is the Messiah? It just says that God would raise up a servant to take away the sins of Israel and Ezekiel clearly fulfilled this prophecy as it is clearly written in the Tenach."

I was horrified but what could I say? It sounded like blasphemy but after all it still was a fulfilment of the prophecy written in Isaiah.

Joseph looked lazily around while he rubbed the side of his glass with his finger. I believed that he was reading something else into this prophecy in Ezekiel but he still had a valid point: Ezekiel was chosen by God to bare the sins of Israel in fulfilment of Isaiah's prophecy.

"But Yeshua *is* the Messiah," I more gasped than said. "I'm not that good at explaining it but I know that if you read the New Testament, you would understand that Yeshua fulfilled the prophecies of the suffering Messiah."

Joseph leaned forward.

"The New Testament is *not* the Word of God. It was written by Jews who were deceived by the devil. I don't want to be deceived by the devil and so I am not going to read it."

"But how can you say that when you've never read it?" I asked. At this stage, my back had stiffened and my limbs trembled for I felt that I was now talking to Satan embodied in this innocent human being.

"I don't have to read it. We already have the Tenach so why do we need another book to tell us about God? If Yeshua was the Messiah, it would say so in the Tenach. And, anyway, if Yeshua was the Messiah, why don't you observe the Law?"

I looked at my half-empty glass of beer.

"Because, when Yeshua came, He introduced a new covenant with His people, which included us, the Gentiles, and with a new covenant came a new Law."

Joseph looked at me with a crooked smile.

"A new Law? What was wrong with the Law that Moses gave us?"

"It didn't save us," I replied. "God saw that all the Law was doing was showing what we were doing wrong, but it couldn't save us. So, God made a new covenant."

"So, God didn't know what He was doing when He gave Moses the Law? This perfect God gave Moses the Law and then said, 'Gee, there's something wrong with this Law. I think I'll make a better one.' If this is what the New Testament says, then I know it's wrong because it makes out that a perfect God makes mistakes and my God doesn't make mistakes."

I was stunned. What Joseph said was quite right and I didn't have an answer.

But Joseph didn't stop there. He explained to me that he could not accept the New Testament as the Word of God because it contradicted the Old Testament concerning certain details. For example, he told me how that when Jacob's son, Joseph, was in Egypt, his father, Jacob, and his eleven brothers came down to Egypt during the famine. Genesis 46:27 summed up the number of Jacob and his family as seventy people whereas in Acts 7:14 it said seventy-five. He explained also that there was a story in Numbers 25 which spoke about the Israelites committing sin and how God killed twenty-four thousand of them, whereas in I Corinthians 10:8 it says twenty-three thousand. Although I argued that this was petty for it was only a matter of a number, Joseph explained that a perfect God makes no mistakes and hence for the New Testament to be inspired by the God of the Old Testament, everything had to be accurate.

"Not only that, I don't believe Yeshua is the Messiah because he said that he would return during the lifetime of his apostles. Somewhere in the New Testament I know Yeshua says to the apostles something along the lines that there would be some apostles still alive when Yeshua returned when obviously they're now all dead and Yeshua has still not yet returned."

I was shocked by that. I knew he was referring to Matthew 16:28. But I didn't have an answer and I was more than happy to change the subject.

Pretty soon after this, Joseph expressed how tired he was and decided that it was time for us to leave. As soon as we stood up, I glanced across at a table in the far corner and who else was there but Markus. Our eyes met and, with a beaming smile, Markus got up from his seat and walked over to me.

"Hey, Michael! What're doin' here?"

"Oh, I'm with a friend of mine, Joseph."

I introduced Markus and Joseph to each other and they shook hands. But Joseph again excused himself and left. Markus withheld me for a moment.

"You're not in a hurry, are you?"

"Ah, well, it is late and I've gotta long drive home."

"Why don't you stay for another drink and you can sleep at my house tonight. You can go to work from my place in the morning."

"I don't know," I said hesitantly. "My parents are expecting me."

"Just give 'em a call, tell 'em your car has broken down and a Christian friend from work said you can stay at his place tonight."

"I dunno," I said. I didn't want to turn down the offer but at the same time I didn't want to tell a lie and was worried that I would be in big trouble with my parents for residing in the house of one common and unclean.

"Go on," Markus pushed. "Just relax for the night a bit, hey?"

Markus pushed hard enough and soon I was on the phone to my parents. I spoke with my father and to my surprise my father said that all was fine and he complimented Markus for his hospitality.

When I returned, Markus was really pleased, and so was I! I pulled up a chair at the table next to him and he introduced me to the friend of his that was there with him. I was a bit shy at first but soon was joining in the conversation.

While we chatted, I looked around. There were various groups of people talking and laughing and the place was half full. But there was something so gripping and different about this atmosphere. There was no-one drunk or unruly, although there was a guy in the corner who laughed really loudly and boisterously. But still I couldn't get over the friendly, normal atmosphere. I saw a girl and guy talking to each other but no girl was coming up to me, pressing her breasts into my face saying, "Well, do you want it or not?" All I could see was a relaxed atmosphere. There was something about this entire atmosphere which was more relaxing and more honest than the rigid lifestyle of church and Bible Study.

I couldn't help seeing a further error message in my parents' description of the world which contrasted with what I was seeing here. I was constantly told that because non-Christians don't believe the Bible, they have no morals, but I saw nothing immoral going on in this place. But I was still on my guard. Perhaps Satan was showing me something innocent at first, but later, if I took the bait, I would end up in the street in rags, looking for my next fix, or another bottle of methylated spirits to cure my craving and satisfy my addiction.

Soon Markus' friend left, and Markus and I were alone.

"What's the time?" Markus asked.

"Ten o'clock," I said after looking at my watch.

"Well, it's getting late, then. Have you eaten?"

"No, I usually wait till I get home."

"Michael, you must be starvin'! C'mon, let's go home. My mother made me something last night and I've got a lot of it left over."

Markus didn't have his car so I drove him to his place, since by this stage I had bought a car. I was extremely excited, frightened, unsure of myself, shy, being with Markus and going to his place.

Markus lived in Ashfield, a suburb about a ten minute drive west of the city. My initial appreciation of Ashfield was Parramatta Road which is the main artery that leaves the city to head west to where I lived. I had always thought that Ashfield was an ugly, dirty concrete jungle but I had never driven within the side streets that led to Markus' home. I was amazed by the tree lined streets and the grand old buildings that made this suburb. It wasn't grandiose like the eastern suburbs but it held a certain charm that was quite unexpected from my initial appreciation of the place.

We finally arrived at his place which was a building that I guess was originally a large house in a former epoch that had since been divided into four flats. We got out and walked inside. I took all my books and my briefcase with me. Markus opened the door and let me in. Immediately the strange odour of a foreign residence and the warmness of the flat hit me. It was a moderately furnished flat, not plush, but comfortable and very well kept. All the essentials of a twentieth century residence were there, a lounge, television, video recorder and stereo. I walked in and Markus led me to one of the rooms.

"You can put your books and bag here if you like."

Markus sat me down in the loungeroom and disappeared into the kitchen. I heard him open the refrigerator, followed by the sound of beeps and clicks and the whirring sound of the microwave oven. While he fiddled around in the kitchen, I looked around the room feeling very nervous and excited, like a five year old.

"Would you like a beer?" Markus yelled from the kitchen. I answered in the affirmative.

Soon Markus came out with the meal and the drinks and sat down with me. The food was delicious and I thanked Markus for it.

"Thank my mother!" he said with a laugh.

And I was hungry! I hadn't realised that the time had flown and I hadn't eaten anything since lunch, so I wolfed the meal down as if it were my last. When I had finished, I sat back in the chair bloated, nursing my beer.

"Do you live by yourself?" I asked.

Markus looked up at me smiling.

"Oh, well, yeah!"

"Don't you get lonely?"

"Oh, no. Usually I'm out with friends. Some nights I stay home on my own. But I don't mind. I can read or watch a bit of telly."

"Do you like living on your own?"

"Oh, yes. It's great. I can do what I want, when I want. I'm my own boss!"

There was some silence and then Markus turned to me.

"By the way, why were you out drinking tonight? I thought you didn't go to places like that because they're against your beliefs."

"Yeah, they are. But it was an opportunity to discuss with Joseph, my friend, about Jesus. He's Jewish."

Markus looked at me squarely.

"You're trying to convert a Jew to Christianity? C'mon, what'd you say?" he said with a cheeky grin on his face.

"You want me to tell you what I was discussing?"

"Sure, why not?"

I placed the empty plate on the coffee table and took a sip from my beer while I gathered my thoughts together.

"Well, I've started learning Hebrew and I discovered that the term for 'God' in Hebrew is *elohim*. This is really a plural word which means 'gods', not 'God'. As a Christian, I believe in three 'gods', so to speak, which are in fact one, and I tried to show Joseph that the belief in the Trinity was always in the Bible."

"Yeah?" Markus said. "And what did Joseph say?"

"Well, he said that it could also mean that God is supreme like the Queen and the Pope when they address the public saying 'we' and 'us' and not 'I' and 'me'."

"Yeah! Fair enough. Your friend's got a point there," Markus said.

"Well, I said that it could just as possibly refer to the Trinity being viewed as three gods in one as we Christians confess."

"Oh, yeah? And what did Joseph say to that?"

"He didn't agree. But I know it is possible and I know for sure that the reason why the Hebrew uses a plural word to refer to a single deity is to marry the two ideas that I, as a Christian, believe, that there is only one God, manifested in three persons. People find this concept so hard to understand but I don't see why."

Markus smiled.

"So, you believe in three gods, God the Father, God the Son and God the Holy Ghost, which are all one God. This one God has existed for all eternity and He is everywhere, permeating every part of existence."

"Yeah, that's right," I agreed.

"This triune God has manifested Himself as the man, Jesus, who is an incarnation of one of the three gods, and who lived as a man to give His teachings to the world."

"Yes, you obviously know a lot about Christianity."

"Who doesn't? Anyway, this is a belief that the Jews can't cope with because they believe in only one God in its absolute sense, and that God, who always has and will occupy a timeless and spaceless dimension, would not become a finite mortal, occupying a finite space for a finite time and then return to this timeless and spaceless dimension."

This required digestion and it was obvious that Markus was leading somewhere.

"What do you mean?" I asked cautiously.

"Don't you see how markedly different Christianity and Judaism are concerning their views of God?" Markus challenged.

I bit my bottom lip and thought about it. It was a valid point but what was he getting at?

"And, yet," Markus continued, "the Christian view of God bears more similarities with Hinduism than with Judaism from where it is supposed to be derived."

I scorned the thought.

"That's not true. Hindus believe in many gods."

"No," Markus said sharply, "*that's* not true. That is a Christian's view of Hinduism. You see, Jews and Muslims claim that you are polytheistic because they believe in one God in its absolute sense, whereas you deny this claim, even though you believe in three gods. But, like the Christians, Hindus believe in only one God, Brahma, who has existed from eternity and always will, that he is in everything and everything is in him.

But, at the same time, the Hindu God is really a Trinity, consisting of Brahma, Vishnu and Shiva. They believe that at one point in time, Vishnu took on the form of a man, under the name of Krishna."

"Oh," I said a little perturbed.

"Not only that," Markus continued, "the Hindus consider Krishna and Christ to be one and the same person. *Krishna* is supposed to be the Sanskrit version of the Greek *Christos*. You'll find some of their functions similar, particularly the part about bearing the sins of the world. What is most striking is that the Hindus believe that Krishna did all this at about the same time that Christ is supposed to have suffered."

I sat and stared at Markus while he told me all this but I thought he was just making it up to make me doubt the Bible and the uniqueness of Christianity. Markus must have realised my disbelief.

"Believe me, it's true! In my country and from what I've read, I've been exposed to all this and that's how I came to realise that the Christian view of God shares a lot more in common with Hinduism than Christians realise, almost as if Christianity is a splinter religion from Hinduism more than Judaism. If you talked to a Hindu, you would even find the teachings of Hinduism and Christianity strikingly similar. It's a wonderful comparison, a beautiful communion of faiths."

I did not like what Markus was telling me. I could see the serpent curled up around the trunk of the Tree in the garden, polishing the fruit so that it looked more enticing than ever. Then the revelation came to me. Satan had set up this counterfeit religion to confuse future generations into believing that Hinduism and Christianity borrowed from a common source. But then, what was this about the communion of faiths?

"Don't you get it, Michael?" Markus said full of excitement.

His excitement was frightening me because I did not understand what he was talking about and his attempt to find a common ground between Christianity and Hinduism was to me like trying to show that God and Satan were one and the same. He must have read the misunderstanding in my face.

"Don't you see that Christianity and Hinduism are both leading us to the same God?"

Blasphemy! Heretic! That was all I could think. This was horrible what he was telling me. But he continued.

"Examine all the religions, philosophies and ideologies in the world and what are they trying to tell you? All of them without question are trying to say that all humankind is equal, all are acceptable to God, and telling us all to love one another. That all of these religions bear similarities is because God is showing them all the same message. But the reason why they differ in their views of God is because God does not reveal Himself and we are groping around like blind people trying to see what He looks like. But God doesn't want us to try to work Him out. God's main purpose is to teach us to love one another, to develop human relationships with all races and creeds, not to find out His name, or what He looks like, or if He has offspring, or helpers, or has the form of an elephant or a person with four arms or what not. What God looks like or what form He takes, these things are irrelevant to God in comparison to the teachings of love and equality towards each other."

I sat there in utter silence. There was something deep in what Markus said and I wasn't sure I grasped it or liked it. Markus paused while he allowed me to digest what he was saying. And then he continued.

"All religions are a part of the whole picture. There are differences between them but there are similarities as well. I mean, consider the sacred places in which believers of the different faiths gather together, synagogues, mosques, churches and temples. On the surface they point towards a different god, but when you look deeper, you can see they are still buildings, they have a roof to protect the believers from the elements, it's quiet inside, the ceremony is ritualistic and repetitious, the devotees say prayers and sing hymns or chant. In other words, they share many elements in common, which means they must really be leading to the one and same God. So it is with the beliefs of the religious systems."

I sat there in total disbelief, trying to make out whether this person sitting across from me was of God or Satan. From my limited Christian point of view, Markus had to be the devil because he was trying to unite two different and opposing religions and make them one. But from a rational point of view, I could see that there was an element of truth in what he said.

He then moved on to the further comparisons between Hinduism and Christianity: baptism, the forty day fast we call Lent, and the incarnation of the second person of the Trinity who ended His life on earth by dying for ours sins. All these were common to both faiths.

But not only so, there were similarities between each religion's understanding of the concept of God and the Godhead. Where the Hindus believe that the personality of the godhead dwells within Lord Krishna, Paul wrote in Colossians 2:9 that the Godhead dwells bodily within the Lord Jesus. And just as the Hindus believe that Lord Krishna abides in all parts of creation, so Paul wrote in Colossians 3:11 that this was the same about Christ.

But it wasn't just Hinduism. Christianity had absorbed a taste of the essence of the Chinese belief of the Tao, the Way, which is why Jesus said that He was the Way in John 14:6 and why believers were said to belong to the Way in Acts 9:2. Like Krishna and Christ, the Tao was in all things and all things were in the Tao, and we are individual manifestations of the Tao just like the Jews and Christians believe that each human being is a physical manifestation of the image of God.

But Christianity, Markus explained, also shared many ideas that were common with Zoroastrianism, the ancient Persian faith which had stepped out of the polytheism and mysticism of antiquity to believe in the Great Lord, Ahura Mazda, and the six great spirits, the Amesha Spentas, who together formed the great heptad, where Ahura Mazda was father of them all.

"This is where the idea comes from that the number seven is holy in Judeao-Christian belief. Seven was holy because of the divine heptad. And the Zoroastrians believe that the seven wandering luminous bodies in the heavens are a reflection of the divine heptad, that is, the sun, the moon, Mercury, Venus, Mars, Jupiter and Saturn. These seven luminous bodies move independently to the other stars in the night sky which led the Zoroastrians and later the Jews and the Christians to believe that the number seven is holy."

I sat there dumbfounded, trying to absorb all this new information. I wasn't sure what to make of it all, but Markus continued.

Markus explained that to the Zoroastrians, Ahura Mazda was light and there was no darkness in him in the same way that John described God in his first epistle. Both the gods of Zoroastrianism and Christianity were gods of truth and goodness. Zoroaster was the one who introduced the idea of dualism, the belief that there are two fundamentally opposed forces at work in the universe, where Lord Mazda is in conflict with the "anti-god", Aingra Mainyu, a powerful but opposite force, the Christian Satan. Markus explained that this same idea of God and Satan that was so much a part of Christianity did not enter the Jewish faith until quite late in the development of Judaism.

"But what about Satan in the Garden of Eden?" I interjected.

"Where does the Bible say that Satan existed in the Garden of Eden?"

"Right at the beginning of the Bible, in the form of a serpent," I stated as if it were obvious.

"But does the Bible tell you that the snake was Satan? From my understanding, the Bible teaches that a snake with legs tempted Eve and we know that the ancients who wrote that story did not entertain the notion that the snake was Satan in the form of an animal. Rather, the Bible says that the snake, the actual animal, tricked Eve into eating the fruit, implying there was direct communication between animals and humans before the Fall.

When the Great Sin was committed in Eden, three of God's created beings were cursed: the man, the woman and the snake. If the original story entertained the idea that Satan was in the form of a snake, snakes as an entire class of animals would not have been cursed for the evil committed by an impostor of their species. But the snake and its generations to follow were cursed to go legless and eat the dust of the earth just as they do today and nothing is said of the condemnation of a devil."

I pondered on that thought for a moment. I wanted to say something but I had nothing to say in reply. What Markus had said was right. The Creation Story said nothing of Satan. Rather, the Bible says in Genesis 3:1 that in the Garden of Eden, the snake "was more subtil than any beast of the field which the LORD God had made." We had been so indoctrinated that whenever we read this story, we immediately interpreted the snake as being Satan in a serpentine disguise. But, in fact, the story on face value meant that what caused the first humans to sin was simply a common animal. The implication was that snakes, in the beginning, were creatures with legs, just like many of the other animals, and that they all talked like humans did. It was, therefore, simply an animal that spoke to Eve, not some mystical evil angel. This meant that, if I had to believe the Bible was infallible, whenever I saw a snake slithering along the ground, I had to believe that this same creature once talked like humans and was the cause of humankind's demise. Further, looked at in this light, there was absolutely nothing to suggest in the original Creation Story that such a creature as Satan actually existed.

I just stared at Markus for a moment without saying a word. So, Markus continued where he had left off.

Markus explained that Zoroaster also was the first to propose the idea of the resurrection from the dead, the end of the world and the Last Judgement, concepts that were absent in early Judaism. For the blessings in the Pentateuch were a long and happy life on earth if the commandments were observed and there were no blessings of eternal bliss in the next life. But the idea of the resurrection and the Last Judgement must have appealed to the minds of the Jews, particularly during the Diaspora when the Jews were forced to live among the Persians where the Zoroastrian faith was prominent.

Later under Greek and Roman rule, many Law-abiding Jews were slaughtered at young ages by the Gentiles, which seemed like an injustice on Yahweh's part. The idea of a long life in the realms beyond the grave then made the promises in the Law sensible in the light of the troubles the Jews were going through.

It was certain, Markus said confidently, that the Jews gave their blessing to absorb ideas from the Zoroastrian faith when Isaiah's writings were elevated to the ranks of Holy Writ, announcing that King Cyrus of Persia, the king of the empire built on the faith of Zoroaster, was looked upon as the Messiah or Christ. Cyrus, no doubt, received this title from the Jews because he held a policy of tolerance to all faiths and allowed the Jews to return and rebuild Solomon's Temple, the rebuilding that was prophesied to take place under the auspices of the Messiah.

The finality of history according to the Zoroastrians was that another great prophet would be born of a virgin, just as it was predicted about Jesus, who would herald forth the Last Days of history, the Final Conflict between Good and Evil, between Truth and

Lies. This prophet would be the great King and Saviour of the world, leading the righteous ones to triumphantly destroy forever all that was evil in the universe.

"Don't you see?" Markus said excitedly. "Jesus wasn't only the Messiah of the Jews. He was also the promised Saviour of the Zoroastrians."

"That's impossible!" I stated emphatically.

"But can't you see? Don't you know that the priests of the Zoroastrian faith, the Wise Men, went to Bethlehem to worship He that was born of a virgin according to the Zend Avesta, the Zoroastrian Scriptures? Don't you realise that the Magi followed the Star to Bethlehem to worship the great King, the Saviour, as a fulfilment, not of an Old Testament prophecy, as there is no such prophecy in the Old Testament, but as a fulfilment of prophecies about the coming Saviour as recorded in the Zend Avesta?

Don't you understand the uniting principle of the Christian faith? Through Jesus Christ, all faiths are united, for He is the incarnation of the Second Person of the Trinity in accordance with the Hindu faith, He is the manifestation of the Tao, the Way, He is the awaited Messiah according to the Jewish Scriptures, and He is the Lord and Saviour of the world born of a virgin and visited by the Magi in answer to the Zoroastrian expectation. Can't you see how through Jesus Christ all faiths have been united?"

The whole idea was absolutely preposterous. And how dare Markus syncretise all these devilish faiths and use the Lord Jesus Christ as the linchpin that binds them all together.

"It's not true! It's not possible!" I cried out in despair. Markus' great speech stirred me up emotionally that I just burst into tears. I just couldn't cope with all this information. It was as if my head were about to explode as I tried to absorb it all.

While I sobbed, Markus came over, sat next to me and held my hands to console me, apologising if he had caused me so much distress. That touch of affection reached well into my heart and I just bent over and hugged him and cried into his chest. He held me close and stroked my back. It felt so comforting, this man I loved, holding me so close to him.

While holding me close, he told me that he could see that I was searching for something but he could see that I had not found what I was looking for. As much as it hurt to hear him say it, he told me plainly that the Bible alone was not the answer. It was a part of it but was not the whole and until I realised that the Holy Scriptures were only another imperfect way of understanding the spiritual world and that the importance of the Bible was its teaching of love towards other people, I would always end up frustrating myself.

At that time, I didn't understand what he meant nor did I want to. We had been indoctrinated so much that anything that wasn't Christian was satanic and we had to have nothing to do with it because it would be evil. And the very thought of seeing the Bible in any other way than the way we had been brought up to view it was apostasy.

But the peace, confidence and love in Markus' voice was so striking. My soul was at war but his was at peace. And I wanted to have the peace together with the man himself. But the clutches of the Bible over my mind and my life were still weighing me down. The foundation of my faith had yet to be shaken even more thoroughly and be completely brought down before I was able to begin restructuring my whole philosophy of life and enjoy the peace that it would bring.

Markus did not say any more about religion after that. Instead, he turned me around and began to massage my shoulders to make me feel better. It felt great. The feeling of his hands touching my shoulders, back and neck was just great. While my limbs loosened to the great artwork of his hands, he commented that I needed to relax and not let the world get on top of me. He massaged my back for quite some time and it was great.

That night I slept in the spare bed that was in Markus' room, across from Markus. Markus was quickly sound asleep but I couldn't sleep. Not immediately. Being with Markus made me feel warm and fuzzy inside. Not once in my Christian experience could I remember having such strange beautiful feelings flowing inside me like this, like the gentle flow of a warm stream of water. Just the sound of Markus breathing heavily in sleep across the room felt soothing and comforting. Each breath he took made me feel so good and right but at the same time conflicted with my world view. But my world view felt so cold and sterile in comparison to the warm feelings flowing deep inside me that night.

Chapter 14

Some days later, I had a chance to meditate on what had occurred the Tuesday evening that had passed. Back in the holy solace of my family who believed that only Jesus was the answer, I simply rejected all that Markus had said to me out of fear of going to hell. It just couldn't be possible. I knew damn well that if I had told my parents what Markus had told me, they would have thought he was the devil incarnate.

But what was I to make of Joseph's critique about God's perfection? If God is perfect and makes no mistakes, why did He give Moses the Law and then one thousand or so years later replace it with a better one? Can a perfect God better Himself? When I read through the Book of Hebrews, I found the words of Joseph hard to cope with for, throughout chapters seven and eight, the author keeps saying that God found fault with the Old Covenant established through Moses and the Law, and replaced this with a better covenant through Christ. The verses that particularly struck me were found in Hebrew 8: 6, 7 where it said

> *But now hath he obtained a more excellent ministry,*
> *by how much also he is the mediator of a better*
> *covenant, which was established upon better promises.*
> *For if that first covenant had been faultless, then*

should no place have been sought for the second.

Joseph had a strong point against our view of God. Our perfect God delivered a Law and a Covenant to Moses which He found fault with but under which He subjected the Children of Israel for over a thousand years. But how could this perfect God find fault with something that He had created? And if He knows everything and knew this first covenant that He delivered to Moses was faulty, why didn't He just send Jesus from the outset if the second covenant was better?

But what about what Markus had to tell me about the communion of faiths? What did he mean? Was it possible? But how? What gripped me about his soliloquy was how what he had to tell me beautifully united all the religions of the world to a point that they had a common link between them. This message was so much more beautiful than the raw Christian message. Markus' view of Jesus was that Jesus brought the world together under an umbrella of unity. This meant that we could view all humans equally and not elevate born-again Christians as being special humans above the rest of humanity.

But what Markus had to say about the Bible being incomplete and imperfect penetrated to the very depths of my being. Although we had been indoctrinated about the perfection of the Bible, my experience and my own reading of this book agreed more with what Markus had to say than what my parents or the minister ever told me.

Markus' critique of the Bible being only a dim, vague, shadowy view of the spiritual world was only the more borne out when I attended Friday Night Bible Study. Here was a group of twenty-odd Christians who gathered together, all holding fundamentally the same belief that Jesus died for their sins and rose from the dead, and that the Holy Ghost dwelt inside them, the same Holy Ghost who wrote the Bible. And yet, I don't remember one issue that did not cause dissension and opposing views. It struck me as extremely odd. If the Holy Ghost dwelt in all of us, wouldn't we all read the Bible and understand the text in exactly the same way as each other?

Sometimes the arguments became quite heated and there were times when certain members stormed off never to be seen again while others had to patch up the argument by means of Christian love and forgiveness. But what amazed me the most was that none of these issues were ever resolved because each side had verses to back up their arguments.

But that's all Bible Study was, an intellectual battlefield for Christian issues, and I had the impression that we were all spiritual lawyers, fighting cases where the world was on trial. Why the dissension? Why couldn't these Christians, filled with the one and the same Holy Ghost, ever come to unanimous conclusions?

But there was definitely one issue that everyone agreed with: that homosexuality was very wicked. Homosexuality was evil and it was not possible for a man to find another man physically attractive or two women the same. God had made sex purely for procreation. But many Christians in our Bible Study group believed, despite what it said in Paul's letter to the Romans, that homosexuals deliberately perverted the natural design of sex as an outward expression of their hatred towards God. For in reality, so they claimed, homosexuals did find the opposite sex attractive but, because Satan hated God and everything good that God had made, Satan distorted even the natural sexual union between a man and a woman out of spite. And those non-Christians who hated God the most used this as the ultimate visual form of their spite for God. I was aware that homosexuals did, in fact, have an outward hatred towards the Church and the Bible, and this was obvious whenever we saw the news broadcast of the Gay Mardi Gras every year. But looking back I can understand why: Christians have been so intolerant of this sexual phenomenon that homosexuals have simply rebelled against the Church.

In light of what the Christians said at Bible Study, I constantly asked myself, then, why I had these feelings towards men. I didn't hate God or His Word but at the same time men physically turned me on in a way a woman could never do.

It was understandable why those in the church hated homosexuality because they believed it was wrong in the eyes of God. But what about the non-Christians? In John's first general epistle, chapter four and verses five and six, John wrote that "They", that is, the non-Christians, "are of the world: therefore speak they of the world, and the world heareth them. We are of God: he that knoweth God heareth us; he that is not of God heareth not us." This means that the world revels in the lust of the flesh and in all that is evil and depraved because the world does not believe in the pure righteousness and truth of the Bible. Christians hate homosexuality because it is anti-God and only those who know God share this view of homosexuality. And so it followed that if Christians hated homosexuality so much, then the non-Christians must absolutely love it and wallow in it because it is so anti-God and anti-Christian. But this I found not to be the case. Both Christians and non-Christians hated homosexuality equally. It seemed that homosexuality was a sin so evil that even Satan himself did not like it.

I remember that as part of my job I was required to go down to the factory from time to time. The part of the factory with which I dealt was full of men. But they were real ocker, macho, stereotypical masculine men. They were rough, a real motley crew of guys, most of them did not look after their physical appearance and thought having a beer gut was the epitome of their manhood.

Walking into their office was like entering a shrine dedicated to sex. Plastered on the walls in this little office were pages from centrefolds full of naked women in all sorts of poses which highlighted their sexual parts. I found entering this little room so repugnant and it only highlighted to me ever strongly my sexual orientation. I wanted to find these women titillating, to awaken a sexual desire that I would then have to try to resist in order to obey the Bible when it told me not to lust. I certainly had no lustful thoughts when I saw these women, which was a real bitter-sweet feeling.

The guys in the factory were nice guys deep down. But their conversations consisted mostly of those things that were considered manly such as cars, football, beer and women. None of these things interested me at all and I was always at a loss to communicate with them beyond work related issues.

But through the conversations they had with each other and with me, I learned that they also hated homosexuals and homosexuality. A man having sex with a man was so repugnant to them that they would be happy to beat the shit out of a poofter if they ever came across one. Poofters were not quite men, only possessing those parts that made them males, but they wore women's clothes, minced as they walked, swivelled their hips and spoke with a lisp which showed that they were in a mean between the two sexes.

I remember the leading hand, Stephen Stoneletter, was really homophobic. He told me a story of a friend of his who had been in the vicinity of Oxford Street one night. While getting into his car, he saw an effeminate poofter walking home alone from one of the Oxford Street bars. He followed him into a dark street, cornered him and then beat him up. Stephen told this story with a lot of bloodthirsty fervour as if causing brutal, bodily harm to a person had greater moral value and caused less harm to society than two men who consented to having sex together. How this gay-basher was never caught for this act I will never know, although I had the impression that Stephen was making the story up – and it also raised the question as to why this friend of his was in this area in the first place. Even so, I knew of the phenomenon of gay bashing which was quite rife at this time.

And there was more to it that I could not quite understand. It was alright for a heterosexual man to have multiple female partners. This was considered the ultimate success of the Aussie male, to have had sex with as many women as possible. The man who achieved this was a stud, a hero, a real man. But if a man had sex with another man, even if he only did it once, he was looked on as a pervert and immoral. It always struck me that these factory guys viewed homosexuality as immoral and even used this word when they were the roughest and basest people you could meet and certainly not shining examples of pure morality. I especially found it odd in the extreme that they stated that homosexuality was immoral when sex outside of wedlock is considered immoral in all religions and cultural contexts I am familiar with. However, even when confronted with this argument, they were able to shrug that off by saying that even the best of us can slip because sex was a strong, natural and uncontrollable urge – as long, of course, as it was channelled towards the opposite sex.

But that a man could find another man sexually attractive they considered immoral. But they also often said that homosexuality was unnatural. I was never able to understand what that meant because my sexual attraction was very much a part of me. I wanted to know what it was like to lust women. But I didn't. My attraction to men was spontaneous even if I hated the fact that men were physically attractive to me and women I found sexually repugnant. Whatever determined my sexual orientation did so without my control which meant that my attraction for men was natural. It certainly wasn't man-made or artificial. So what did they mean that homosexuality was unnatural?

But hating myself did not stop these feelings I had for Markus. But why did I have them when I didn't hate God? I loved God, adored God and passionately read His Word. So what was I to make of my feelings for Markus? I tried to appease my mind by thinking my feelings were merely platonic for I certainly had not had sex with Markus and he had not given me any signs that he liked me physically. The difficulty was that there was no-one to whom I could turn, to talk about how I felt. If what I felt within was a deliberate expression of my hatred towards God, how could I approach my parents for help? It would be natural for them to conclude that I hated God and my destiny in hell would be already sealed forever. So, I was forced to suffer in silence, thinking that I was the only Christian in the entire universe who had these terrible desires.

Apart from Bible Study and church, all that was left of my life other than work and studying for my degree was an empty void. Those who attended Bible Study were much older than me and their children were very young.

My alternative for a social life with Christians of my age group was Sunday Night Fellowship after the evening church service. "Fellowship" was simply a term used to describe a social gathering of people, usually those in their late teens and early twenties, who got together and socialised within the church precinct. I had been once or twice but didn't like it. Next to the church was the church hall where Fellowship was held. These young Christians were supposed to have set their lives apart from the world but I saw little difference between them and my non-Christian associates. I couldn't relate to any of them due to my radical beliefs because these people were much too worldly for me. Sunday Night Fellowship was not a gathering of young soldiers for Christ but a hang out for young adults to let their hair down from the rigours of the religion they found so hard to maintain in their lives. Even the Fellowship leaders supported this attitude, for salvation came by faith and not by works. So if everyone at Fellowship acted so unchristian-like, they, after all, still believed in Christ, and God would still forgive them because He loved them the way they were.

What I resented about these people was that they swore, told foul jokes and dressed in their daggiest clothes even when they attended the church service, with ripped jeans, and jumpers that fell down around one shoulder. Some of the guys even wore earrings which was, at the time, a very sinful thing. But what I hated the most was that the Fellowship seemed like the Lonely Hearts Club where young men and women met prospective partners, broke up and then went out with somebody else. For me, in my good clothes, sometimes I even wore a tie, interested only in God and everything that glorified Him, I just did not fit in.

In other words, these young Christians at Fellowship were simply ordinary people. My critical view of them was brought about by my extremism. In contrast to those who attended Fellowship, I could not relax and be a human being. As far as I was concerned, if I was going to be a Christian, I had to be a Christian to the nth degree, which meant that I had to do everything the Bible said to the letter and try to be as close to perfect as was possible according to the Bible's view of a perfect man. Because of this extremist approach to Christianity, it made me look down on the other members of Fellowship with disgust and I suppose with arrogance because I felt that I was better than they were in spirituality, even though I admitted that I was still a sinner. I could not view these people at Fellowship as simply human beings, they were too beneath me. Imagine, then, how I viewed people outside the faith!

Looking back on this now, I understand the source of religious extremism and intolerance because I had become the birth-child of such a radical philosophy. But I could not be a Christian in any other way. As far as I understood what Protestant Christianity was all about, if we were to obey the Bible, we had to obey all of it, there were no half measures. And if we had to obey all of it, we had to read it, every word from Genesis to Revelation, and yet, I didn't know one member of my church who was familiar with what was written within the covers of the

Bible, and worse, anyone who showed any interest in finding out.

Tuesday night, however, was the night that I was me. I could not be the extremist that I was at Fellowship when I was with Markus because I viewed Markus as being more spiritual than me. I looked up to Markus almost as if he were a spiritual leader of a not so clearly defined religion.

But moreso, Markus had explained to me, which was supported by what I had observed amongst other Christians, that the Bible was not the complete picture but was only part of the whole. This meant that it was futile to try to live up to biblical righteousness in his presence. But this was also unnecessary. Because Markus had wonderful characteristics that I admired, I didn't feel the need to live up to the righteousness we were expected to according to the Bible. In Markus' presence, I was relaxed and felt that I did not have to put on a show of perfection.

When class had finished, I couldn't get to my car quick enough to be at Markus' place since going to Markus' place on a Tuesday night had become a regular occurrence. I thoroughly enjoyed being with Markus because I could relax and just be me. Markus liked me for what I was and I liked him in the same way. Sometimes we would talk and sometimes watch television together. While watching TV, we took turns massaging each other's backs or Markus' would lie with his head on my shoulder or I would lie with my head in his lap and he would comb my hair with his fingers.

There was something simple and pure about being with Markus. An aura of peace and wholeness surrounded him which attracted me to him like a moth to a flame. It is true that there was a physical attraction. But there was something more. It was also a mental attraction. Although not a Christian, I viewed Markus as religious and found what he had to talk about on a religious and philosophical bent was profound. He had a love for humankind that I felt was so absent from the Christians with whom I associated, and a breadth of knowledge of Christianity and other religions that was extremely far reaching. Despite the fact that he did not embrace the Christian faith as closed-mindedly as I did, it was his view of Christianity and the unity of all beliefs that was extremely bewitching.

I observed Markus intently at work. He was an excellent worker, not only in his abilities to carry out his work but the way he interacted with other people as well. He had a gentle, helpful sort of character and reacted to mistakes I made as a step within a learning process. This was so different to the reign of terror I experienced in the QC laboratory with Tracey who reacted to mistakes as an opportunity to put me down.

Markus was always courteous with the workers as well which came in striking contrast to Tracey's reaction to them. Tracey treated the factory workers as beneath her for, after all, she had qualifications but the workers did not have certificates or degrees so she was above them. Tracey, however, only had a chemistry certificate whereas Markus had a degree and yet, he treated the factory workers as his friends, as helpers towards achieving a common goal.

Another striking feature was Markus' language. I never heard a swear word ever come out of his mouth. He also never talked about other people behind their backs. If there was something that someone did or said to him that he didn't appreciate, he told the person straight to their face. Other members of staff took delight in gossiping about other staff members if ever they were disgruntled over something they did or said. Even I was guilty of that. When I started working with Markus, I began to tell him that I didn't like Tracey and things that she said or did that I found extremely unpleasant. Markus' only reply was a question, "Have you told her?" When I answered in the negative, Markus' next question was, "Then why are you telling me? What will that achieve?" It was the philosophical bent in his question that was so striking. It wasn't said in accusation but for me to reflect on it. But I knew why I didn't say anything directly to Tracey. I was terrified of her. But Markus wasn't. Tracey could snap at him about anything but he would stand there calmly and answer her back.

I remember an event in the tea room during the break. Tracey had brought into the tea room her latest laboratory report and placed it on the table. Markus brought his coffee to the table and placed his cup down, not realising that there was a pen in the same place. The cup tilted, then fell, and the contents poured like a running stream of muddy water all over Tracey's paperwork. When I saw it, I gasped in horror, knowing exactly how Tracey would react. And she reacted precisely the way I thought. She really flipped her lid, abusing Markus because it had taken time for her to prepare correctly.

Markus didn't say a word immediately. He grabbed a sponge and began cleaning up the mess, trying his best to absorb the water out of the report. Unfortunately, the report was now coffee stained throughout and had to be reprinted. The tea room was silent but when Markus had finished, he looked at Tracey and said, "I do apologise, Tracey. However, it was an accident. When I took up the job here, I did not claim as one of my attributes that I am devoid of spilling coffee over others' reports. This was an accident. However, the way you reacted, your tone and your language was your *choice* and was inappropriate. I did not do this deliberately so your anger was ill-placed. And if it is such a difficult task, I can always go over to your computer and print out another copy, which will probably take no more than about two minutes."

There was no anger in his voice but a complete assuredness of his position of this situation. And sure enough, he left the room and about two minutes later, which I checked by looking at my watch, he was back with a pristine copy of the report.

Later that day, when I saw Markus, I began talking about this event and wanted to use it as a pretext to highlight another of Tracey's faults. But Markus stopped me in my tracks, making the comment that this event was resolved and finished and did not need to be discussed again. Markus did not say this with an accusative tone but I felt very ashamed, knowing that I had committed the sin of gossiping and I never did it again with Markus.

Markus' whole character disturbed me. He was not a Christian and yet he followed certain ethics and moral values. This did not make sense according to my world view. The Bible divided the world into two groups: the believers and the unbelievers. The believers were presented in a favourable light because they believed in the God of the Bible. Because God was love and good, and God lived within the heart of the believer, the believers, by logic, were also good. The unbelievers, by contrast, did not believe in this God of love and goodness, so God did not live inside these people, and therefore, these people could not be good. In fact, because these people did not believe in God, the alternative was that they followed Satan, and because Satan was evil, unbelievers were therefore evil.

By following this line of argument, it should have been easy to determine who was a Christian and who was a non-Christian simply by observing a person's conduct. As Paul put it in Romans chapter 8, Christians are dead to sin because they do not live according to the flesh but according to the spirit. Paul also says in Galatians chapter 2 that Christians are "crucified with Christ" and therefore, although alive, it is Christ who lives in them. Because Christ is perfect, Christians must also be perfect.

But this description of humanity did not reflect what I observed around me. There were, I could agree, good people who were Christians, and there were people I considered as evil who were not Christians. But I also knew that there were some good people, and in particular, Markus, who were not Christians, and I knew some people whose conduct was questionable, and yet they claimed the name of Christ.

It was all terribly confusing. It was as if the Bible were talking about a world in a non-existent place or, at least, not in the world of my immediate reality. I can understand now, looking back, why we were encouraged not to have non-Christian friends because, as long as we didn't know anyone personally, it was such an easy task to consider anyone not of the faith as evil. We could take on a clinical, sterile, negative approach towards unbelievers as long as we had no association with them and did not have any personal feelings for them.

Once we established a close relationship with someone outside the faith, particularly if we liked this person because of his or her qualities, we were forced into a predicament. If this person had good reasons for not believing in the faith but still had qualities as a person that we admired, we were forced to question why God would put this person in hell in the next life.

And this is what had happened to me. I did not consciously go out of my way to form any sort of friendship with Markus. It just happened through a series of events. Despite the encouragement from our church to not become emotionally involved with non-believers, it was too late for me to change my association with Markus. There was now an emotional attachment. And despite the fact that he was not a Christian, I could see he was a good man. The last thing I would have wanted to do to him was cause him physical pain, even for a second. If I, a sinful mortal, could see his goodness and didn't want to cause him pain, couldn't an omniscient and loving God also see his goodness? So how could God still put such a nice guy in a place of utter torment for the rest of eternity?

How would I cope on the Day of Judgement if both Markus and I were standing before the Lord, and God said to me, "Enter thou into the joy of the Lord" and to Markus standing next to me, "Depart from me into everlasting fire"? Simply being separated from Markus for eternity would be bad enough, but knowing that this God of love was sending this good man to eternal torment would fill me with anguish beyond what words could describe. These feelings of anguish would only be exacerbated if, while on the way to eternal bliss, I met up with Christians from the Fellowship who I knew were not really good people, who I didn't like as people on earth, knowing I would have to spend the rest of eternity with them, whereas Markus, who I loved because of his qualities as a person, would be sent to endure the horrors of hell forever. Eternal paradise would become an eternal torment for me.

Of course, the only course of action was to try to convince Markus that the Christianity I adopted was the only way to escape the horrors of the after-life. But Markus had raised valid points as to why he did not believe, and I had no answers for his skepticism.

If God wanted Markus to be saved, why didn't the Holy Spirit, who was supposed to dwell within me, give me the answers I needed to win him over to Christ?

But despite all these questions, I still visited and stayed over at Markus' place on Tuesday night. Every now and again, Markus would meet me at the university and then we would go out to a restaurant. This was when my soul and my world view really clashed. In contrast to my days with Ruth, being with Markus felt right and agreed with the person I felt I was despite what my indoctrination in the Christian faith dictated to the contrary. This little part of the week my parents knew nothing about. I had told them Markus was a Christian for I knew if they found out that he wasn't, they would not have let me stay there. I told them that we discussed the Bible together, for this was not a lie, but I did not divulge what the discussions were all about. Markus was very liberal as far as the Bible was concerned.

But these two worlds I kept well apart, my Christianity and my love for Markus. It was a strange game that I played, a hypocritical game, trying to be two people at the one time. I knew that my homosexuality was not, as I had been taught, due to my turning away from God, and so the best way for me to deal with these contradictory versions of life was to pretend that my feelings for Markus didn't exist. Committing double-think strangely enough worked for a long while, as long as our relationship towards each other was not expressed in words or actions.

Markus was the only one who really made me feel human and alive. I just loved being with him, seeing his smiling face, watching him joke around, the way he looked after me when I was with him. He may have had too liberal a view of Christianity but he was not evil. He entertained a view of Christianity and all religions that, although was quite profound and filled with a love of all humankind beyond what Christianity had to offer, I still was not prepared to accept whilst my mind was chained to the belief in the Bible.

I adored Markus. He made me feel good and alive. He was my *raison d'être*, love of my life, light of my soul. All through this twisted confusion, I didn't want him to go to hell and every now and again I tried to convert him, but to no avail.

But there was one unforgettable night that changed everything. We were watching a movie at his place. I was massaging Markus' back as was now commonplace while Markus was talking. The movie wasn't really very interesting and Markus was making smart quirks about the events in the film. He had become really cheeky that, when an advertisement came on television, he just blurted out, "Oh, Michael! That feels just great! Take me, I'm yours!" and then he grabbed my head and pulled me down. I thought he was going to break my neck.

I was excited, nervous, titillated. Then Markus grabbed my head in his hands and gave me a big, wet kiss on the lips, and then he laughed. He sat up again. I recoiled back in disbelief and sat there with my hands half in the air, not knowing what to think.

"Michael, loosen up a bit, why don't you?" Markus said with a big Cheshire grin on his face. I just sat and stared at him in confusion, so Markus reached for the closest cushion and hit me over the head with it. That brought out the child in me and so I grabbed another one and hit him across the chest.

Markus laughed, jumped up over the lounge and began hitting me with the cushion while I covered my head with my arms. Then he just disappeared out of the room. There was dead silence. I got up quietly out of the lounge and tiptoed towards the hall, holding my cushion ready to attack. I got to the door. Markus was behind it, saw me coming and bopped me right in the face. He was killing himself laughing while I staggered around, dazed for a second, with a tingling sensation in my face. Then, bang, his cushion hit my legs.

"Right! This means war!" I said laughing.

Markus then grabbed my wrists and my cushion fell to the floor. He stuck his leg behind both of mine and pushed me forwards. I lost my balance and, with that, I was on my back and Markus was lying on top of me. I could feel his heart beating against my body, his chest rubbing against mine. Both of us were breathing heavily.

"What was that you said?" Markus said panting with a cheeky look on his face.

We lay there for a moment, just puffing away. Markus just lay on top of me, waiting to catch his breath. But once his breathing was back to normal, he pushed himself on his hands. His facial features had changed completely from cheekiness to a stern, serious expression, as if something were troubling him. With a quivering breath and a deep sigh, he reached his left hand and placed it on my forehead, pushing my hair back to expose my forehead. He just stared at me for a moment. I was completely unsure of what was going on. He was looking straight into my eyes and I could see a gentle sparkle and a yearning in those deep, brown eyes. Without warning, he brought his head close to mine, pressed his warm cheeks against my face and rubbed gently back and forth. And then he kissed me. It was such a soft, gentle, caress of the lips. He gazed into my eyes. Those craving eyes. He looked as if he were really desperate for something and he left it no secret.

"I love you, Michael," he said so quietly, with a tremolo in his voice, as if he were about to cry. It was such a contrast from what he was doing only five minutes earlier.

"I love you, Michael," he said again, "and I really want you to love me, too."

The following night when I drove home from work, the look in Markus' eyes and those words that were spoken from his soul haunted me: "I love you, Michael, and I really want you to love me, too." All throughout the next day, I couldn't look at him. It was so disturbing what he had said to me the night before. It went over and over in my head, the statement, and the look in his eyes: "I love you, Michael, and I really want you to love me, too".

There was something strangely correct that remarkably matched up in my soul but contradicted my world view, that a man was in love with me and I was in love with him. It troubled me so much, causing me to tremble down to my foundations. The statement went further than the physical, as if he wanted his soul to be knit with mine. Phrases from the Bible containing the word love kept coming to my mind: "God is love", "Love is of God", "Everyone who loves is born of God." My mind was yet in confusion. Markus didn't say to me, "Hey, Michael, let's bonk!" He said that he loved me, but it was followed by such a desperate plea from the heart: "I really want you to love me, too."

What did he mean? It confused me because we had been so indoctrinated that homosexuality was a mere physical element, an animalistic craving, that a man only had sex with a man to fulfil the lust of the flesh. But for Markus to say that he loved me like he did filled me with confusion. There was such a deep communion of our souls when he said it.

I could remember when I told Ruth that I loved her. I felt nothing. They were merely words that were traditionally correct for a boy to say to his girlfriend. But I had no physical feelings towards her and thus had reasoned that love didn't necessarily have to have an emotional nor spontaneous physical element. After all, God told us to love one another and it was true that some people were hard to love. Love, therefore, was a duty, not an emotion.

But Markus had merely said thirteen words and yet I could feel an ocean of emotions which flowed with it. It troubled me so much for I did not know what to think about it. What did it mean? Didn't I feel the same way towards him? Why, then, couldn't

I say these same words back to him? Because it was wrong to have these feelings for him? But why?

But moreso, I knew that sex with Markus that night was not purely due to his physical appearance, although that was partly true, but moreso because it was the most intimate I could be with him. Yes, it was the first time that I had ever had sex and it was with a man.

What were these feelings that I was experiencing towards Markus that expressed themselves with such intimate physical contact? I knew that this was the same type of feelings that my father had explained to me when he had spoken about sex and marriage, and how sex was the most intimate one can be with a person. In its proper place, sex is a beautiful thing, but my father had never told me that it was possible for me to have the same feelings towards a man for it was beyond his comprehension that a man could possibly have these same feelings for the same sex.

But I did not have them for the opposite sex. I could like a woman, even love a woman, but I could not imagine doing with a woman what my father did to my mother. The mere thought of it was disgusting. Watching a woman take all her clothes off and wanting me to touch her body was just too dreadful a thought for me that I was prepared to remain a celibate for the rest of my life.

But when Markus removed all his clothes and allowed me to touch him all over, and when he touched me in the same way, it was the most beautiful, romantic, the most intimate thing I had ever experienced. During the whole time of this beautiful moment, I did not allow my Christian objections interfere with what Markus and I were doing. What was wrong with it? I didn't feel evil doing it, nor immoral. It felt right, it felt good, it felt like heaven. It made me feel the closest I could ever be to Markus than was ever possible. To touch his body, his arms, his legs, his chest, his neck was wild and enchanting, that I did not want to stop. When the moment had reached its climax, we sailed down slowly to the land of reality, my head on his shoulder, my arm on his chest.

But the next day when I returned home, back into my sacred home of Christ and the Bible, the guilt was overwhelming. The burden of guilt hung heavy on me like the Mariner's albatross. What was wrong with me? Why did I have these feelings for Markus that God said were wrong and said that He only gave them to me because I had turned away from Him? Why me? As irreverent as the thought was, I entertained the notion that when God assembled my parts together in the womb, by some misadventure, He accidentally placed the diode of sexual attraction that He usually put in women into me and, not realising the mistake, allowed me to be born as I was. Where was this diode? Why wouldn't God pull it out and place the correct one inside me?

But the more I thought about it, the more it troubled me, so I tried to push it out of my mind. But I couldn't because every day I saw Markus at work. What was wrong with me? Why did I have these physical desires for a man and not for a woman?

Why was it impossible for me to even imagine going through this same event with a woman that came so easily with Markus?

Chapter 15

This was one of the most confusing parts of my Christian experience but still I continued to believe that Jesus was the only way to heaven and that the Bible was what it claimed to be. Despite the contradictions that I had discovered in the past which had troubled me, I continued to believe by blind faith.

But what was I to do with Markus and my relationship with him? One half of me wanted to stop it all while the other wanted this to go on forever.

But there wasn't a lot of time reserved to analyse all that was going on inside me. For another event arose to further complicate all that was going on in my head. There were two seemingly unrelated events which occurred that would later become intertwined.

The first began with a simple knock at the door. I was studying in my bedroom at the time. As soon as I heard the knock, I began making my way to the door. When I arrived at the diningroom, I heard my father answer the door before me and so I stopped and waited to hear who the visitors were.

"Good morning," I heard a young male American voice say. "My name's Elder Macklan and this is Elder Maysfield. We're from the Church of Jesus Christ of Latter Day Saints and we would like to speak to you about the gospel of Jesus Christ."

"No, thank you," my father returned acidly. "We're Christians and we don't believe in your heresy."

"We don't preach heresy," Elder Macklan replied. "We want to preach to you the truth."

I heard a crossfire of words and very soon the Mormons were gone. My father closed the front door and when he came into the diningroom he met me there standing in anticipation.

"Who was that?" I asked.

"Oh, it was just the Mormons."

"What did they want?" I asked.

"To convert us to their heresy."

"What heresy?" I asked.

"They believe the Book of Mormon is part of the Bible. But there is no addition to the Bible because the Bible is complete as it is."

"Why?" I replied. "What is it about the Book of Mormon that makes it heretical?"

At this stage, my mother walked in and asked my father my initial question. My father again replied that it was the Mormons. My mother just said, "Did you tell them that they're going to hell unless they repent?"

"Repent from what?" I asked.

"From their heresy!" my mother exclaimed.

"What heresy?" I asked trying not to become exasperated.

"They teach that the Book of Mormon is the Word of God," my mother said, beginning to raise her voice in anger.

"Why, what is it that the Book of Mormon says that is so heretical?" I asked mystified.

"They preach another doctrine and another Jesus. Paul warns us in Galatians 1: 8, 9 that if someone brings another gospel, you are not to believe them."

"Oh," I agreed. "But what's the other gospel they bring?"

My mother was becoming particularly aggravated by my questions.

"They preach that the Book of Mormon is the Word of God, equal to the Bible," my mother snapped.

I paused for a moment. My mother's reaction terrified me but my curiosity was much too strong to allow me to leave this conversation so much up in the air.

"What is the Book of Mormon anyway?"

"It's a book written by a man called Joseph Smith who claimed that God told him to write it," my father explained. "He claimed that it was a missing part of the Bible."

"But what does the Book of Mormon say which is wrong?" I asked hesitantly.

"You don't need to read the Book of Mormon to know that it is not the Word of God," my mother exploded, almost screaming. "We have the Bible which contains all that God ever wanted to say to us. Why do we need another book to tell us that Jesus died on the cross for our sins? That's how we know that the Book of Mormon is not the Word of God. If you read the Book of Mormon, Satan will try to convince you that it is true and you will be tempted to become a

Mormon. You'll become so engrossed in the religion and then Satan will have you where he wants you. The Book of Mormon is just another bait of Satan to lure you into his trap. But the Book of Mormon contradicts the Bible so it cannot be God's Word."

With those words, I knew that question time was over. But they were frightening words. The Book of Mormon went from being just another book to a book written by Satan with inbuilt clutches that if I were to begin reading it, Satan would grab me and pull me like a spider into his web and I wouldn't escape. Hence, if I were to come across the Book of Mormon, I was not to read it or even be tempted to touch it, it was so dangerous.

With that, I returned to my room to resume my studies. But I couldn't study. As I thought of my mother's condemnation of the Book of Mormon, I couldn't help but see how her words aligned in unison with the words of my former Jewish friend, Joseph ben-Moshe, and his objection to the New Testament as viewed against the Law and the Prophets. My mother said that the Book of Mormon could not be God's Word because we already have the Bible and we don't need another book. But Joseph ben-Moshe had said that the New Testament could not be a part of God's Word because we already have the Torah, the Prophets and the Writings and, seeing these are complete, we did not need any other book.

My mother said that the Book of Mormon could not be the Word of God because it preached another gospel which differed from the Bible. But Joseph said that the New Testament could not be a part of God's

Word because it preached a new law and a new way to heaven which superseded the Mosaic Law, implying that God had made a mistake the first time around.

My mother said that the Book of Mormon was written by Satan, but Joseph also had said that the New Testament was written by Jews who were deceived by the devil and he would never read it.

But lastly, my mother made the statement which should have ruled the death sentence to my faith. The Book of Mormon could not be a part of the Bible because it contradicted the Bible. Joseph also had said, and went so far as to prove, that the New Testament contradicted the Old Testament and it was for this reason he was convinced that the New Testament was not a part of the Bible.

The confusion that was now spinning around in my head! I felt like I was standing between a rock and a hard place. It was a world of double standards. And the verse in Matthew 7:2 came straight to mind: "For with what judgement ye judge, ye shall be judged: and with what measure ye mete, it shall be measured to you again."

In the past I could content myself that despite the contradictions I saw, the Bible had to be the Word of God. But now I was forced into a predicament. There were now certain criteria to reject the Book of Mormon's claim to divinity. But if I had to reject the Book of Mormon by this measurement, the Bible had to pass these criteria before we could accept it as divine. I could no longer just accept the contradictions in the Bible. If I saw verses which seemed to contradict, there now had to be an answer for them for, otherwise, how was I to judge what books should be considered as part of the Bible and those which should be rejected?

The other event occurred right in our church. I decided to attend Fellowship again. I hated going to Fellowship because I couldn't cope with the misbehaviour of these Christians, falsely so called according to my zealous view of Christianity. But at the same time, the loneliness I experienced drove me here because as far as my parents were concerned, although they would never admit this, this was the only congregation of believers going to heaven. Thus I could only associate with these people if I wanted to associate with anyone because the Bible said in II Corinthians 6:14, "Be ye not unequally yoked together with unbelievers." My parents backed this verse with force and had always said that we could only associate and have friends with those who believed the Bible was the Word of God and, intrinsically, believed it the way we viewed it.

This night I went like always but felt so uncomfortable around this unruly mob. I knew most of the people here at least by name but couldn't say I was close, nor did I feel that I wanted to be yoked with any of them. I went inside and headed straight for the kitchen to make myself a cup of coffee and to hide behind a biscuit.

I watched with contempt as these people mucked about, running around, yelling and screaming like six year old children, or couples sitting in corners pashing each other off as if this were a brothel, not the House of God. But while I cowered away in safety, I saw a stockily set, well-dressed girl standing over on the other side of the hall who was with Susan Norman, the Minister's daughter, and Trevor Buchanon. My first shock was the contrast between the two girls: Susan was dressed like a tart, loud mouthed, and laughed loudly and coarsely, mouth wide open. The girl standing with her, whom I had never met before, was rather quiet, nodding politely from time to time.

Susan turned to the new girl at one stage and, after pointing in the general direction of the kitchen, the new girl left Susan and Trevor. I saw the perplexed look on the new girl's face as she marched across the floor and disappeared into the kitchen. I felt so sorry for her that I decided to introduce myself, using the need for a second cup of coffee as an excuse.

I found her in the kitchen putting hot water into her cup. She turned and saw that I was after the same thing and politely asked me if I wanted the water. I replied in the affirmative and she smiled, poured hot water into my cup and gave me back my cup. I thanked her kindly and used this as a means for beginning a conversation.

"Hi, I'm Michael. I see that you're new here."

"Oh, hi," came the strikingly obvious New Zealand accent. "I'm a friend of Susan Norman. My name's Rosemary."

"So, what brings you here tonight?" I asked.

"Well," came the accent, "I am a Christian but I haven't been to church for years. I work with Susan and she invited me to come along. She said it was a good Christian church."

"I can hear that you have a Kiwi accent," I said with a smile.

"Yes, I'm from over the Tasman," she said with a grin.

"Where from?"

"Auckland. My parents migrated here with the family about five years ago."

"I hope you don't mind me saying but I really love your accent," I said.

Rosemary blushed.

"Why, thank you. Usually Australians don't like it at all."

"Ooh! I do. I love how you have a 'chet' with people, and eat 'fesh and cheps' which are 'rech, theck, and crimmy'," I imitated and laughed. "I'm serious! It's a nice accent."

Rosemary just smiled.

"Is this your first time here?" she asked.

"Oh, no. I've been attending this church for years."

"I've never seen you here before," Rosemary said.

"No, I don't come to Fellowship that often. I wouldn't say that I was a regular," I replied.

We moved out of the kitchen and returned to the hall, found a seat and sat down.

"So, where do you work?" Rosemary asked.

I told her about my work, what I did, who I worked for, that I was also a part-time student and hated every minute of my degree. I hadn't got far when the Youth Leaders called the Fellowship to gather for Devotion.

We began with singing a few choruses, opened with a word of prayer and then one of the Youth Leaders gave a talk. All the young Christians of the Fellowship listened intently as if they really believed what was being said, that we all should be devoted to Jesus Christ and love one another. But once the last prayer had been said, the spell was broken and all the wild animals returned to their gibbering and chattering, running about, screaming and yelling.

Rosemary and I resumed our conversation where we had left off. We talked about neutral subjects for some time. I wanted to know more about Rosemary's work, what New Zealand was like, if she liked living in Australia and so on. Eventually the conversation moved mutually onto the subject of Jesus and the Bible, two subjects which were strangely avoided at Fellowship. As soon as we had arrived at this subject, Rosemary became very keen. We chatted for quite some time but it was Rosemary who was asking a lot of questions about the Christian faith. I was proud of myself because I was able to answer all of Rosemary's questions which strengthened my faith all the more and my spirit was soaring to the seventh heaven. I raved on and on about what I knew and Rosemary listened intently to what I had to say. I was in my element. Somebody at Fellowship actually found talking about the Bible fascinating!

The evening dragged on and finally came to a close. Rosemary didn't want to leave but she said something a little distressing as well.

"You know, Michael, I've never heard much about the Bible except from my sister, Helen, and she's a Jehovah's Witness. Because your church is like most other Protestant churches, I thought it'd have the truth. The people at this church say they believe the Bible but these people don't seem interested in the Bible or living up to their beliefs. But you're the first person in this group I have found who really seems to believe and want to pursue their faith."

I was taken aback but I had to agree when I observed this unruly mob.

"Can I see you and talk to you more?" she asked.

Rosemary came across as a starving soul looking for the truth and I believed I possessed it. She did say she was a Christian but I took that to mean she was a Christian in name only. I told her I would be very happy to talk more but it would have to wait until the following Sunday because I was busy with my studies. I invited her to come to Friday Night Bible Study but she turned the offer down as she was busy herself on that night. We parted ways but the week was so long. I couldn't wait to see her again. Speaking with Rosemary renewed my faith in Christ and the Bible because, by answering all her questions, I could see some sort of coherency that I thought was missing.

The following Sunday night, after the church service, Rosemary appeared just as she said she would. While we sat and talked, everybody around us was like a herd of animals let loose. Rosemary asked if I knew many of the people there and I said I basically knew them but they were so worldly that I didn't have much to do with them.

"Why do you come, then?" Rosemary asked.

"Because my parents come to this church and I feel if they come here then the teaching must be correct, and even though these people at Fellowship muck up, they still are at the right church."

"I don't know," Rosemary said. "My sister is a Jehovah's Witness and she has been wanting me to join her church for a while now. I always said no because it didn't seem right. I was brought up as a Christian but I've kind of strayed over the years. But after a number of conversations with Susan, I felt I should believe again. I told Susan that my sister is a Jehovah's Witness and wanted me to join her church but Susan said Jehovah's Witnesses don't preach salvation by faith and so they are wrong."

Jehovah's Witnesses. I was vaguely familiar with this organisation. But that's about all. I knew about them because of a joke I was once told at school where a woman comes up to a man on the street and says, "Hello, I'm a Jehovah's Witness." The man then replies, "Well, goodness, laudy me! I didn't even know there'd been an accident!"

And I was at least familiar with their practice of going door to door selling *Watchtower* and *Awake* magazines. So I needed Rosemary to explain to me more of what they believe.

"They don't preach believing in Christ and you'll be saved?" I asked.

Rosemary looked nervously around the room, then into her cup and then back at me.

"Well, I don't really know. My sister just tells me that she knows that she has the truth and that I won't find it unless I come to her church. She says that the Jehovah's Witness Organisation is the only church which follows the Bible correctly."

"Well, what do they teach?" I asked.

Rosemary smiled shyly and shrugged her shoulders.

"To be honest with you, Michael, I really don't know. Whenever we get onto the topic of religion, I usually change the subject."

"Well, what made you change to become interested in religion again?" I asked.

I could see Rosemary starting to display signs of discomfort as she looked in her cup and shuffled her feet slightly. She looked up at me and then said, "Can we go outside?"

I nodded in agreement. We went outside and started going for a walk in the cool of the night.

We strolled along a bit and there was a bush in someone's garden that was pouring over the front fence, with lots of pretty pink flowers on it. Rosemary picked off a flower, put it to her nose and sniffed it, commenting on its pleasant aroma and appearance, and then threw it gently to the ground.

"Michael, that flower will die now because I've just picked it from the bush. But no-one will care because there are plenty more on the bush to replace it, and there are plenty more of these bushes around.

But when we die, although there are many of us around, we are not like identical flowers. I can enjoy this flower I threw on the ground and later pick another one and enjoy it as much as the first. But in this world of people, there are only certain people whose company I can enjoy. When they die, they're gone forever. What's the point of it all?

But more than that, when I die, what will happen to me? Is there a heaven and a hell like the Bible says? I know I'm not a bad person but would God think I was good enough to go to heaven if I were to die tonight?"

I looked down at the flower and then back at Rosemary.

"If you believe that Jesus Christ died for your sins, you will go to heaven," I replied softly.

"Is that all?" she asked.

"Yes, that's all," I replied. "That's the beauty of being a Christian and the demonstration of God's insurmountable love, that we cannot do good to save ourselves. All one needs to do is believe in Jesus and from that moment you are saved."

"And that's all? You mean therefore I'm saved?"

"Yes," I said in such a manner as a loving father would tell his dear daughter.

"So, all these people at Fellowship will go to heaven because they believe in Jesus?"

"Yes," I replied.

"Then why don't you act up like them?"

"Because Jesus expects better conduct from us."

"Does that mean that you will be more saved than they?" Rosemary asked.

I hated the question but I had to follow the argument.

"No," I hated admitting. "We'll all go to the same place."

"Michael, I can't believe that. My sister, her husband and her children are all well-behaved. And my sister keeps begging me to join her church because she says she knows and is convinced that she has the truth. So, her behaviour alone is convincing enough.

Where I work, there are also some really lovely, genuine people but they all have varying views about religion. Some say they are religious, others say they're not. But apart from that, they would go out of their way to help someone, are courteous on the phone and don't swear.

And then there are other people at work who are rude, boisterous, they swear and carry on. Susan is like them. She herself swears, tells the boss off and flirts with the men. According to what you just told me, only those who say they are Christians, including Susan, are going to go to heaven because they believe that Jesus died for their sins, and all these nice people who don't believe are going to be tormented in hell, irrespective of how selfless they are, all because they don't believe in Jesus. But can you blame them for rejecting Jesus, if Susan is an example of a Christian, especially when they know she's the minister's daughter? This does not prove that God is just at all, does it?"

Wow! What a statement! How could I argue against that? I was really stuck for words. I was, therefore, mystified as to why Rosemary criticised Susan's behaviour and yet agreed to come to her church. But Rosemary had also raised a number of objections that I had already thought about and did not have a satisfactory answer to them. So, I threw the ball back into her court.

"What do the Jehovah's Witnesses believe?" I asked.

Rosemary just smiled.

"I really don't know. My father was so much against my sister joining their church in the first place because he said that their organisation was run by the devil. My sister still joined and so my father didn't speak to her for years. Because of my father's dominant influence over the family, I didn't talk to her either.

Now that I'm older, I thought it was such a silly thing to do. She is still my sister after all and can believe what she likes and so I got back in contact with her. She has tried a couple of times to preach to me but I don't listen much to what she has to say, at the moment, anyway, because of the stigma I've had against it for years. But, at the same time, I find the Jehovah's Witnesses very militant and don't really seem to love but spend more of their time trying to convince you by some sort of intellectual argument that they are right. I think that's why my father hated the Jehovah's Witnesses so much."

"Well, what does your father believe? Why don't you go to the same church he goes to?" I asked.

Rosemary looked up at the stars, down at the flower and then back at me.

"My...my father and my mother died in a car accident some months ago – " and then she began to sob. I took her into my arms and tried to console her. Now I could understand all her questioning.

"I'm sorry," I said.

Rosemary pulled herself together.

"I'm alright," she said with a teary smile and wiped her eyes gracefully with a handkerchief.

We walked back to the church hall without saying a word. When we walked past the hall, there was a girl trying to get out the door while a guy was holding her jumper, and she was screaming and laughing.

I walked Rosemary back to her car.

"Michael," she said. "I'm really glad to have met you. And I'm glad to talk to you because you are one of the few here who acts like a Christian should. I'd like to talk to you more. Will you be here next Sunday night?"

"Of course. As long as you come, it will be a pleasure."

With that, she smiled, started the car and drove off into the night.

As I drove home, I thought about Rosemary's sister being a Jehovah's Witness. What was a Jehovah's Witness? They must have been some sort of Christian faith because when Rosemary talked about them, she referred to them as having a belief in Jesus. But what were they?

When I arrived home, it was late. My parents, as usual, were sitting watching television. As I walked in and sat down on one of the chairs, my parents greeted me and asked how Fellowship was. It was not a place that I spoke about in glowing terms and, with the comments Rosemary had to make about the attendees, I was as critical as ever. But Rosemary's sister was on my mind at the same time and I wanted to know about this other sect that claimed to be Christian and yet was foreign to mainstream Protestantism. And so, I just promptly asked without introduction.

"What do Jehovah's Witnesses believe?"

"What made you ask that?" my father asked inquisitively.

"Well, there's a girl at church called Rosemary, who has a sister who is a Jehovah's Witness, and she wants to know if she should join their church."

"They aren't a Christian church!" my father said bluntly. "They have their own Bible."

"Their own Bible, like the Book of Mormon?" I asked.

"No, they say they have our Bible. But when you read their Bible, the translation puts the meaning out of context."

I sat there for a moment. I must have had a perturbed look on my face. So my father gave me his undivided attention and turned to me.

"The Jehovah's Witnesses go around door knocking. They've been here once. We chatted with them for a while but when we read verses from their Bible, their version was quite different."

"What like?" I asked.

"Well, they've added an extra letter in John 1:1 and it has changed the meaning completely. Instead of saying that Jesus was God, it reads that Jesus was *a* god."

"Oh," I said with interest. "So, they're polytheists?"

"Well, of course they are but they won't admit that. They don't believe in salvation by faith either but that you must work for your salvation," my father concluded.

"They don't even believe in heaven or hell," my mother added.

"But they still believe in the Bible?" I asked.

"Yes, but in their Bible, the translation is wrong!" my mother exclaimed.

I found it interesting that my mother was so sure that the King James Version was translated correctly when she couldn't read a word of Greek. So how would she know which version was correctly translated and which one wasn't? However, this was not the time to challenge my parents over something that seemed so trivial.

"Why do they call themselves 'Jehovah's Witnesses'?" I asked puzzled.

"Because Jehovah is God's name," my father replied.

"Why don't *we* call God 'Jehovah', then?"

"Why don't you call me Alan? Why do you call me 'Dad'?"

"Because that would be disrespectful."

"That's correct."

"But why do we call God 'Jesus' if it's disrespectful to call God by His first name?"

"Because Jesus is the Son of God," my father replied.

"So, He's not Jehovah?"

My father stopped in his tracks and my mother began to get cranky.

"Jehovah is God's name. Like the word God, it refers to the Father, to Jesus and the Holy Ghost. Jehovah is God's name!"

"So, is Jesus Jehovah or the Son of Jehovah?" I asked, trying to make sense out of it all.

My mother was again about to explode.

"There are three in one. There is the Father, the Son and the Holy Ghost, and these three are one. It's a mystery which can't be explained until we get to heaven and see it!"

My mother looked at me with daggers in her eyes.

"I'm surprised God doesn't strike you down with lightning with all your questions!"

I was taken aback and too dumbfounded to ask for clarification.

My father came to the rescue somewhat to help me understand the concept.

"Think of it this way, Michael. The sun is one but it is made up of three things: light, heat and radiation. But it is still one sun. Does that make sense?"

I nodded my head, only to save myself from more sermons of damnation. But my father must have sensed my lack of comprehension and fear of admitting that I didn't understand.

"Look at it another way. There is one God, who is the Father, the Son and the Holy Ghost. Now I am a father, a son and a friend, but I'm still the same person and there is only one of me. Does that make sense?"

Again, I nodded. I was too frightened to do otherwise. But that evening in the safety and privacy of my bedroom, I thought about my father's two analogies. My father said that the sun was one thing made up of light, heat and radiation, but it was still one sun. But the analogy didn't fit when I considered our understanding of the Trinity. We referred to the Trinity as God the Father, God the Son and God the Holy Ghost, who were all one God. Concerning the sun, we didn't say, "sun the light, sun the heat and sun the radiation, and these three suns make up one sun." We said the sun was one thing, made up of three different and distinct properties which when combined made the sun.

As for my father's second analogy, he said that he was a father, a son and friend, all at the same time but he was still one person. But my father ignored the fact that "father", "son" and "friend" were relative terms, which showed his relationship to other people. My father was called a son because he had parents and a father because he had children. He was called a friend because he had at least one friend. For my father to bear all these titles required that other people existed around him. In comparison, I was called a son because I had parents, but could not be called a father because I had no children. My father was not a father to himself but to me, for he was a father to one person and a son to another.

The same with the Trinity. If God was called Father, it was because He had at least one child. If He was called Son, it was because He had parents. Hence, if both analogies fit the Trinity, we were left with three personages: one who was the Father, one who was the Son and one who was the Holy Ghost.

I pondered on this and on the word *elohim* used in its singular sense. It seemed, therefore, that what the Bible was alluding to was that each of the persons in the Trinity were separate identities but so equal in power and thought that they were for all intents and purposes one God, and it was only necessary to see the three individually when one of the persons left heaven and lived on earth, died and rose again.

Rosemary came to Sunday Night Fellowship again. When I spied her, I went straight over to her. She was pleased to see me as I was to see her. While the rabble around us carried on, we talked about nothing else but the Bible. Both of us sat in a corner and we chatted, and Rosemary wrote down verses in her notepad as I presented her the beliefs that we adopted.

Every now and again, other members of the Fellowship looked on. But the scorn they had for what we were doing really surprised me a great deal. There were quite a number who said to me how religious I was and that religion isn't what will get us to heaven but faith in Christ only. Others said things like that you cannot have religion twenty-four hours a day and the reason why there was Fellowship after church was to relax after the church service with fellow Christians of the same age. I felt the scorn of many of the members of the Fellowship but I also took it as a sense of guilt, as if they knew that they should all be more diligent in studying the Bible like Rosemary and I were doing.

But I didn't receive just scorn. Some of the leaders of the Fellowship asked me why I had never decided to attend Bible College in view of my knowledge of the Bible. The thought had never crossed my mind for I felt that one could just as well study the Bible alone, for it was only a matter of reading it. After all, the New Testament books were written by ordinary people who held occupations unrelated to religion. Peter and John were fishermen, Paul was a tent-maker, James, the writer of the epistle that bears his name, was a carpenter, Matthew held a profession that was something that resembles a modern day accountant, and Luke was a doctor of medicine. If the writers of the Bible were common employees with no theological qualifications, why did the readers of the Bible need special training?

But I could see how uncomfortable Rosemary was here and disappointed at all those around us who professed to be Christians and yet poked fun at us. This practice went on for months. There were times when I would arrive in the Fellowship hall and those at the Fellowship would say, "Here comes Pastor Michael. Going to preach again this evening?"

What a twisted sort of events. I could easily understand this attitude at school and work, but at the church that I was attending? This seemed so odd indeed. Rosemary's objection to faith only as a means of salvation began to rub off on me because I could not equate these people as equal in the faith.

Our friendship was going well for months when one Sunday evening, without warning, Rosemary didn't show up. As the evening rolled on I waited and waited but she never came. It seemed highly unusual that Rosemary would not attend without letting me know. I decided to ask Susan if she knew if Rosemary meant to turn up or just couldn't make it that night. Amongst the rabble I found her.

"Susan, do you know where Rosemary is tonight?" I asked.

Susan turned around.

"Oh, she's not coming anymore," she replied.

I was hit stone cold.

"What? Why not?" I asked a little distressed.

"She said she didn't feel right here. She felt we were too worldly," Susan said with a bit of scorn in her voice.

"Well, what did you say to her?"

"I said that Christianity is not a religion of dos and don'ts. I said we are saved by faith, not by works, and that Christians aren't perfect, just forgiven. We got into an argument so she said that she was going to attend another church."

"What? The Jehovah's Witnesses?" I asked.

"I dunno. I suppose. One of those weird religions. She was always raving on about how her sister is a Jehovah's Witness and was well-behaved. But she won't find the truth there."

"But didn't you try to stop her?"

"Yeah, I tried. But she argued that they held the truth and we didn't. She began showing me all these verses from the Bible but I didn't have a clue what she was talking about, especially from her weird viewpoint. She said we didn't know our Bibles very well and that her sister did and that was more convincing because she could answer a lot of her questions. I just said, if that's what she wants to do, then she can do it. But she's a prude anyway, a boring, little, old prude," and this last sentence was said with a lot of sarcasm and she spoke with a tone which clearly illustrated that she was quite happy that Rosemary had left.

"Oh, and she said you were the only person here who knew the Bible well. But you're too stuffy and boring yourself. We're all enjoying ourselves and having a good time. But you're so legalistic with your list of dos and don'ts."

I was hurt by Susan's comments about me but I fought back.

"But, Susan, God expects us to be better behaved than this."

"The Bible says we are saved by faith, Michael. Doesn't John 3:16 say that? So, who are you to go beyond the Bible and tell me that John 3:16 says more than that?"

I was horrified and at that instant left. Here was a Christian, someone who was supposed to believe in the same God as myself therefore behave and act somewhat the same as me and yet we were worlds apart. Susan went so far as to insult me, a fellow Christian, and Rosemary, someone who was hungering after the truth. But Susan didn't really like Rosemary which was obvious from her comment nor did she seem to care that Rosemary was going to hell. Susan's attitude was more one of, "Well, I'm going to heaven, who cares about the rest of the world? I'm saved by faith, so why should I have to be a good girl?"

That night I went home distressed. I knew that this was the attitude of most of those who attended the Fellowship. These people thought they were going to heaven but, apart from that, they really didn't care much about what the Bible said except that Jesus died for their sins. They acted as if God handed out tickets to heaven to whosoever believed and, now that they had one, God couldn't refuse them because they just had to show their tickets at the foyer and walk through the pearly gates.

But what made it worse was that Susan backed herself from a verse in the Bible and it further accentuated the confusion in the Bible about being saved by faith and being saved by faith and works. But as for Rosemary, she was trying to show herself approved of God and trying to find out what God had to say to us in this book which claimed to be His very words. When I asked Susan what verses Rosemary quoted, Susan just replied that she didn't know because she wasn't a preacher. But her father was. She could have asked him.

I couldn't sleep that night. Rosemary was not some person I discussed religion with, she had become a friend who was searching with me for consistency in what it meant to be a Christian.

But Rosemary didn't leave me in the dark. Some weeks later she rang me at home.

"Michael," she asked over the telephone.

Oh, it was so great to hear her voice.

"Oh, Rosemary, I miss you! Where are you? Are you okay?" I said with great excitement.

"Yeah, I'm okay. Are you busy?" she asked.

"N...no. I'm just studying. Why?"

"I'd like to talk to you. But not over the phone. And just to you. Can I pick you up and go out somewhere so we can talk?"

"Sure. Okay," I said, hung up and waited pensively for her to arrive.

She picked me up and drove us up to Springwood, a town in the Blue Mountains, about twenty minutes drive away from where I lived.

I was familiar with these towns in the Blue Mountains because they weren't far from Emu Plains. It was always a pleasure to escape Emu Plains, which received the brunt of Sydney pollution because of its geographical location, to be elevated into the cleaner air of the mountains.

The townships of the Blue Mountains were quite different to the suburbs of Sydney. They were cleaner and more modern, and the locals took much more pride in the natural surroundings and in nature itself, which was illustrated by front yards filled with flowers and trees, and by many houses made of stone and not artificial brick.

We went to a large café-restaurant called Eucalyptus House. It was a pretty place. The restaurant inside was set up like an outback scene with waggon wheels and a colonial-style veranda in one corner with eucalyptus trunks for pillars. There were candles on each table displayed in the shape of an open Waratah flower, the state flower of New South

Wales. The entire atmosphere of the place made it appear that we had stepped back into the simplicity of the colonial times and away from the artificial world that makes the twentieth century.

We found a table and sat down, and Rosemary slung her bag over the chair she was sitting on.

"This is really a pretty place," I said. "I've never seen this before. I never knew it existed. How did you know about it?"

"Oh, I've come here with some friends before."

We began a general conversation with no real relevance to anything and I felt as if Rosemary was avoiding the real issue or at least trying to build up the courage to tell me something that she felt she needed to tell me. We ordered coffee and the coffees finally arrived. As we sipped on the coffee, Rosemary suddenly went deathly silent as if she were in deep meditation. The suspense was mounting. At first, Rosemary was a bit hesitant but then she finally dropped the bombshell. She smiled as she said it.

"Michael, I've become a Mormon!"

Oh, my God! I thought. She was talking about her sister being a Jehovah's Witness and now she had become a Mormon. I had obviously missed something but in any case I wasn't happy. All I could think of was my mother's warning about reading the Book of Mormon but Rosemary had done it and now she was caught in Satan's snare, hook, line and sinker. She looked so happy and serene like I had never seen her before and I wanted to share her happiness. But I just couldn't.

"But, why?" I asked. To me it was as if she had told me she had killed somebody or robbed a bank, and now was sitting there smugly as if she were proud of her achievement.

"Because they are the closest church to perfection. They have the Word of God and could answer a lot of my questions."

"But, Rosemary," I said, "The Book of Mormon is an addition to the Bible so it can't be the Word of God. Even Solomon said in Proverbs 30:6, 'Add thou not unto his words, lest he reprove thee, and thou be found a liar.' So it is obvious that the Book of Mormon is not the Word of God, nor a part of it."

"Yes, that's true," Rosemary replied. "King Solomon said that don't *you* add to God's Word. If what you're implying were true, then you could not include the New Testament because it was written after King Solomon wrote this. Only God can add to His Word. But anyway, the Book of Mormon is not an addition. On the contrary, the Bible itself prophesied that there was another part of the Bible missing and that in the Last Days it would be reunited. Let me read it to you."

Rosemary took her Bible out of her bag and opened up the passage and then read it.

"It says here in Ezekiel 37:15 - 17, 'The word of the LORD came again unto me, saying, Moreover, thou son of man, take thee one stick, and write upon it, For Judah, and for the children of Israel his companions: then take another stick, and write upon it, For Joseph, the stick of Ephraim, and for all the house of Israel and his companions: And join them one to another into one stick; and they shall become one in thine hand.' What this passage of Scripture is saying is that a prophet was going to join the stick of Judah, which is the Bible, because it is the book of the Jews, and another stick, which is the stick of Joseph, that is, the Book of Mormon, and join them to make one book. This happened in 1820. God raised up a prophet, Joseph Smith Jr, to finally perform this task which is now complete because now the sticks are joined together and only one church believes it, the Church of Jesus Christ of Latter Day Saints. But the Book of Mormon doesn't take away from the Bible, it clarifies things which were mysteries in the Bible but now are revealed."

I could feel the anger building up inside me. I wanted to jump across the table and kill the devil in Rosemary for speaking such blasphemous words, even bringing the Bible into it. To me, it was as if the devil personified were speaking to me across the table. My parents were right. Satan was the author of this book.

"These verses in Ezekiel don't mean what you say they mean," I said indignantly.

"Well, if they don't mean that, what do they mean?" she asked peacefully.

"I don't know but it doesn't mean that," I snapped.

"But that's not an answer. You can't say this is wrong and not show why," Rosemary responded quietly

I couldn't resist the peacefulness that she displayed as if all the warrings of her soul had finally been quieted. That only made me all the angrier.

"I don't know but I'll find out," I replied in despair.

"Michael, please don't be angry," Rosemary beckoned.

This was a jolt back to reality and I immediately calmed down.

"I'm sorry," I half whispered. I took a few breaths.

"Well, tell me, then," I continued, "what else does the Mormon Church teach that clarifies something that remains mystified in the Bible?"

"Well, you know how Paul talks about baptism for the dead? In I Corinthians 15:29 he says, 'Else what shall they do which are baptized for the dead, if the dead rise not at all? why are they then baptized for the dead?' No-one in any other church and nowhere in the Bible is this properly explained. But the Mormon Church can explain it. The baptism for the dead means that we can be baptized for someone who died before being saved. So, I could be baptized for my parents. They didn't have the truth but now they won't go to hell because I have been baptized for them."

This was outrageously blasphemous to my ears.

"Your parents weren't Christians?" I asked.

"Well, they said they were. But they didn't go to church or read the Bible. I don't believe they ever were."

"So, unfortunately, they've gone to hell," I said coldly.

"And that's what I thought," Rosemary continued. "But can't you see the love of God, how that He can still save us even after we have died? It is no longer a helpless situation that my parents died unsaved but I was able to save them by being baptized for them."

Again, the blood boiled within me and all I could think of was how blasphemous she was. But what made me just as angry was how the religion I believed in left no opportunity for a lost soul after death whereas hers did. Mormon teaching seemed to show the love of God deeper than what I had ever known.

Christians always boasted that Christianity was so much better than all other religions because all one had to do was believe in Jesus and entrance into heaven was granted at that moment. I had always thought that the love of Jesus in the Bible far surpassed all other gods living and dead.

But now I was listening to someone preach to me about another gospel, and another Jesus, whose love was deeper than the Jesus I knew because, according to my theology, once you were dead, your destiny was sealed forever. And they were the cold facts. But according to the Mormon belief, even if you had died and went to hell, if some living person loved you enough, this loving God had provided a means whereby your destiny could be reversed, and by this loving act, you had another chance of eternal bliss.

"You're wrong! It's not true!" I exploded.

"Then what does it mean?" she asked peacefully.

"I don't know but I'll prove you wrong," I said angrily

I was in a panic and a frenzy. What Rosemary had told me was creating a lot of confusion in my mind. None of the Protestant Churches taught this type of theology so it had to be wrong. But Rosemary had quoted the Bible to support her answer and so it was possible that it could be correct. I had nothing to prove that the way Rosemary understood these verses was wrong and therefore blasphemous, and yet the anger inside wanted me to slap and kick her to death.

The two of us had gone silent. I stared at Rosemary and saw an aura of tranquillity emanating from her countenance. My mind was swimming. So, I picked up my coffee, which had fortunately cooled down enough, swallowed the contents of the cup with one gulp and then asked Rosemary to take me home.

All the way home, neither of us said a word. While Rosemary drove, I stared out of the window of the passenger side of the car in deep reflection. My mind was numb. I didn't know what to think.

Rosemary dropped me off at my house but, before I got out of the car, she detained me for a moment.

"Michael, please don't be angry with me. Look, I've got a copy of the Book of Mormon for you. Please read it. You'll find the truth inside."

I was going to blurt out that I would not read it but I couldn't help hearing Joseph's words to me when I asked him to read the New Testament. This hit me so strongly that I just smiled at her.

"I'm sorry, Rosemary. Yes, okay, I'll read it. But I'll be honest with you. I won't be able to read it without a critical eye. I'm sure it will contradict the Bible and, if it does, I'll definitely show you."

Rosemary just smiled.

"Keep in contact, then, will you?"

I smiled in agreement, hopped out and waved good-bye. But my heart just sank when I thought how Rosemary was now a daughter of Satan.

Chapter 16

That Rosemary had become a Mormon caused great consternation in my soul. When I finally related the story to my parents, they were just as sorry as I was. But being sorry didn't do anything. Something had to be done about it.

"What can I do?" I asked perplexed.

My father ran his finger over the rim of his glass of port.

"Well, the only obvious thing to do is to show Rosemary that the Book of Mormon cannot be a part of the Bible. The Church of Jesus Christ of Latter Day Saints is based on the Book of Mormon and on Joseph Smith whom they think is a prophet of God. I'm sure the Book of Mormon is full of errors," my father said confidently.

"It's an addition to the Bible," my mother added. "That's evidence enough. We don't need any other book to teach us about Jesus dying on the cross for our sins. And, anyway, if she wants to be swept along by the Mormon religion and go to hell, then that's up to her. She'll find out when she's up there on Judgement Day what a big mistake she made!"

I was horrified by my mother's callousness. To her, Rosemary was just a statistic, just like my school friends were, someone to add on her tally of those who are going to hell. But to me, Rosemary was my friend. If she had been drowning in a lake, I certainly would have jumped in to save her. In this case, in the next life, she would be drowning in the Lake of Fire and it was only in this life that the opportunity existed for me to fish her out.

"Rosemary gave me a copy of the Book of Mormon and I'm going to read it so I can find the errors in the book."

My mother's eyes almost plopped out of her head.

"You've got that devil's book here, in this house?" she shrieked. "You're bringing the devil into the house? Don't you know that the devil is powerful and can lure you into his trap?"

"Dear, he's not going to fall for the stupidity of the Mormon Church," my father said dryly. "Michael is a diligent student of the Bible and is grounded in his faith in Christ. Do remember that Rosemary has only been on the milk of the word which is why she was easily misled. Personally, I believe the Holy Spirit is leading Michael in this area so that he can show not only Rosemary but all the Mormons the error of their way."

"Well, I don't like it one bit," my mother huffed. "Satan is very deceitful and you can't imagine how subtly he can trick you into turning away from the truth. You make sure that before you read the Book of Mormon that you pray to God to bind the evil spirits so they can't touch you."

My mother's words were strong and, from her standpoint, it was logical and rational. If the Bible was the Word of God, any book which claimed to be so but was not God's Word had evil spirits hovering around it, like vultures around a carcass. So, naturally, I prayed to the Father, the Son and the Holy Spirit of the Bible to bind Satan and his angels while I read.

I started from the beginning, at the first book of the Mormon Bible called The First Book of Nephi, or I Nephi. I tried reading I Nephi but found it so difficult to read, the style was so awkward. In fact, it didn't matter where I read in the Book of Mormon, after reading a couple of verses, my mind seemed to twist out of shape because I couldn't quite follow the sense of the passage. So, I decided to consult anti-Mormon material. The Christian Bookshop contained a vast array of books to help in my search against the teachings of Joseph Smith, Jr.

During my study, I discovered the origins of the Book of Mormon and of the Church of Jesus Christ of Latter Day Saints. It all began in the early 1800s. The founding father of this church, Joseph Smith, Jr, was born in 1805 in the state of Vermont, in the USA, but later moved to the state of New York. Joseph noticed an unusually high religious feeling among the Christians at this stage and noticed that there were three main contenders for this fervour: the Methodists, the Presbyterians and the Baptists. What troubled Joseph was that, although all these different religions claimed to be Christian and believed the Bible was the Word of God, they were divided. But he also noticed that even within the churches, individuals were divided among themselves over many issues. Joseph was caught up in the confusion but favoured the

Methodists. But still, he wasn't sure who was right and who was wrong.

One evening, he was reading the Bible by candle-light where it said in James 1:5

If any of you lack wisdom, let him ask of God, that giveth to all men liberally, and upbraideth not; and it shall be given him.

This verse seemed to be the answer young Joseph was looking for and so one day he went into the woods to do as this verse beckoned: ask God. Joseph relates that while praying in this isolated place, he was seized by some supernatural power that paralysed him so that he was unable to move or speak. Everything went dark around him and he was overwhelmed with fear, thinking that this was the last moment of his life. Soon the darkness was replaced by an exceedingly brilliant light, the source of which were two personages hovering above him in the air. One of them pointed to the other and said, "This is my beloved Son. Hear him!"

At first, Joseph was afraid to move or talk. But soon he was able to get a grip on himself and ask the question that was foremost on his mind: which of all the sects was right and which should he join? One of the personages replied that all of them were wrong and all their creeds were an abomination in His sight, and that Joseph would be given more instructions in the future.

Later, one evening, a messenger, or angel, or some supernatural being of some description by the name of Moroni, appeared beside Joseph's bed. Moroni told Joseph that God had a work for him to do. There was a book buried somewhere written on gold plates which told of the former inhabitants of the Americas, and which contained the gospel delivered by the Saviour to the former inhabitants of the New World. Joseph's task was to find these golden plates and translate them.

Eventually Joseph Smith Jr found everything he was told to find and translated the golden plates. What was written on this gilded document was a record of the inhabitants of the American Continent prior to the arrival of Columbus.

The first arrivals in America, according to these documents, were the descendants of a man called Jared. Jared and his family were originally the inhabitants of the city of Babel at the time God confounded the languages of the people. These Jaredites lived for many years on American soil but eventually died out. The significance of this story was not clearly explained and I didn't study it long enough to find out.

Then later, in about 600 BC, the year indicated quite clearly in my copy of the Book of Mormon, some Israelites of the Tribe of Joseph left Israel and went to the American Continent as God had bidden them. They recorded their travel and eventual habitation of the New World. This, then, explained the Mormon interpretation of Ezekiel 37:15 – 17, for the stick of Joseph did not refer to Joseph Smith Jr, but to the Tribe of Joseph.

Another messenger of the Lord conferred on Joseph and his followers the restoration of two priesthoods mentioned in the Bible but which were not present in any modern church: the Aaronic Priesthood, which in the Bible is known as the Levitical Priesthood and was originally made up of the descendants of Aaron, and the Melchizedekan Priesthood, a priesthood mentioned in the Bible but rather vague in its description and significance. And so started the Mormon movement.

But as the church grew, so did the opposition. Joseph Smith Jr was finally imprisoned and in 1844, two hundred people stormed the jail where Joseph was being held and shot this modern day prophet to death.

Now that Joseph was dead, someone had to take over Joseph's leadership. This fell to a man called Brigham Young.

Brigham Young was led by the Lord to lead a westward march to a place that God would tell him. This march led ultimately to Utah, to Salt Lake City, where the Mormon Church settled, and a new Holy City established in the world, the first in North America. Brigham Young introduced new teachings into the church such as the belief in many gods and the acceptance of polygamy.

But not everyone agreed with Brigham Young nor thought that the westward march was a calling from God. Splinter groups formed such as The Reorganised Church of Jesus Christ of Latter Day Saints, the Church of Christ Temple Lot, the Church of Jesus Christ and the Stangite Church of Jesus Christ of Latter Day Saints. But out of all these churches that trace their origins to Joseph Smith Jr, only the group that made the westward march to Salt Lake City, The Church of Jesus Christ of Latter Day Saints, had the best marketing staff, who were able to successfully spread their doctrine beyond the shores of the American Continent and greet us in our homes in Australia.

I discovered also that the Book of Mormon was not the only additional edition of God's Word advocated by the Mormons. Other literature with an equal footing was the *Doctrine and Covenants* which were revelations from God to Joseph regarding doctrines for the Mormon Church as well as another piece of Mormon literature called the *Pearl of Great Price*. And then there was a large collection of books called the *Journal of Discourses*.

I was overwhelmed by the volumes of books purported by the Mormon Church as written revelation from God and I wondered how anyone could be able to ever obtain an overall view of what God expected of them within this sea of words. The Bible itself was voluminous enough without adding extensively lengthy additions to His Word. It seemed that to be a Mormon, one would have to spend time doing little else but reading!

I knew an exhaustive display of contradictions would be too complicated. But if I could show Rosemary enough inconsistencies between the Bible and Joseph Smith's literature, this would be evidence enough to convince her.

Chapter 17

"Good evening!" Rosemary said when she greeted me at the door. She was all smiles and still had that aura of peace that seemed ever glowing from the new person she'd become. But with Rosemary was a sister in her new found faith with whom Rosemary flatted, a very beautiful blond girl called Tanya. Both welcomed me as their special guest and sat me down in the loungeroom.

Rosemary offered me a cup of coffee but both girls drank warm Milo, for according to Mormon belief, one is not allowed to drink tea or coffee nor anything too hot, for it says in the Scriptures in Proverbs 20: 1, "Wine is a mocker, strong drink is raging." "Strong drink", according to the Mormons, encompasses beverages that are too hot or contain chemicals like caffeine and hence are not permitted for Mormons.

All three of us sat down in the loungeroom and even though our conversation touched an area of no real consequence, my heart ached for the mistake Rosemary had made in following this apostate church. But she seemed so much at ease. This was not the same woman who had attended the Fellowship at my church, questioning and torturing herself with beliefs that contradicted the reality of the people around her at the time who said they based their conduct, or lack of it, on the same foundation as myself. There was a peace in this room, so gentle, so serene that was as warm and gentle and soothing as no peace I had ever known.

But it was a false peace, I thought, a counterfeit peace brought about by Satan. How illogical when I think about it now! Jesus, so we believed, was the Prince of Peace, and Satan could only bring disharmony and discord. And yet, my soul was filled with the antipode of peace, and yet I believed Jesus dwelt within me. How could I explain to myself that the warring of my soul was from the Prince of Peace and the gentle peace demonstrated by these two young women was a deception created by the devil?

Rosemary had found her niche in life, making her bed in the bosom of hell, and it was pressing that she came out. It was of great importance that I unmask the devil and let them both see him as the Angel of Light. The same pressure rested on my shoulders when I wanted to tell Ruth the error of Catholicism. This was my Christian duty. But it was Tanya who brought the question out.

"So, did you read the Book of Mormon at all? Did you find it interesting?" she asked.

"In the light of the Bible," I replied, "I found it more than interesting. Tanya, the Bible and the Book of Mormon don't agree on various points."

Tanya smiled peacefully. "No, the Bible and the Book of Mormon do not contradict at all. It is purely our lack of understanding of what God is saying to us that makes us doubt the validity of the Book of Mormon's claim to divinity. But I'd like to hear why you feel this way."

I breathed a deep sigh. It was time to begin.

"For a start, Tanya," I asked. "Does it make sense that there should be an addition to the Bible in the nineteenth century after so many years? I mean, Jesus was the last and greatest prophet, being more than a prophet. Why would God send another prophet after Him and bring us an additional book when the Bible is enough as it is?"

"Michael, it's not ours to ask questions about God or how God does things," Tanya replied. "God only asks us to do as He says in pure obedience. We cannot tell the Holy Spirit what we want revealed to us, it's the other way around. We have to accept when the Holy Spirit reveals something through His Word and through His prophets.

But God saw in advance that there would be resistance to His prophet, Joseph Smith, which is why it was prophesied in the Book of Mormon in II Nephi 29: 2, 6, 7: 'And because my words shall hiss forth – many of the Gentiles shall say: A Bible! A Bible! We have got a Bible, and there cannot be any more Bible. Thou fool, that shall say: A Bible, we have got a Bible and we need no more Bible. Have ye obtained a Bible save it were by the Jews? Know ye not that there are more nations than one? Know ye not that I, the Lord your God, have created all men, and that I remember those who are upon the isles of the sea; and that I rule in the heavens above and in the earth beneath and I bring forth my word unto the children of men, yea, even upon all the nations of the earth?' God said that there were other Bibles because there were more nations than Israel."

This obviously was not going to be easy. It was clear that Joseph Smith had been aware of the same argument I proposed against having additional books to the Bible and so he wrote something to defend his position. So, without going any further in trying to show that we didn't need additional books of the Bible after the New Testament was established, I decided to go straight into debating the central issues I had come to argue.

"Tanya, if the Book of Mormon contradicts the Bible, don't you agree, then, that we must reject the Book of Mormon?"

"Well, of course. But I know that the Book of Mormon doesn't contradict the Bible, so I know it is from God."

"I see," I said.

Rosemary sat and watched this contest of words, resting both her Bible and the Book of Mormon on the coffee table, ready to take notes in her pad as if she were the Hansard.

"Well, let me start with something straight forward. Where was Jesus born?"

"In Bethlehem," Tanya replied.

"Well, Tanya, the Book of Mormon doesn't agree with your answer because it says in the Book of Alma 7: 9, 10, 'for behold, the kingdom of heaven is at hand, and the Son of God cometh upon the face of the earth. And behold, he shall be born of Mary, at Jerusalem.' In the Book of Alma, it says that Jesus would be born at Jerusalem, which clearly opposes the New Testament teaching. Not only that, to be the Messiah, Jesus had to be born in Bethlehem to fulfil the prophecy in Micah 5:2 which clearly states that the Messiah would be born in Bethlehem."

Tanya looked at the passage of Scripture and said with a lot of gentleness, "Michael, I think you're being too rigid in your approach here. Do you really think that a difference in the town where Jesus was born affects the gospel of salvation through Jesus Christ? You mean that Jesus cannot save if He was born at Jerusalem and all His good works and miracles are denied on this small, insignificant thing?"

"Yes," I replied militantly. "Jesus could not be the Saviour if He had been born in Jerusalem because then He could not have been the Messiah."

"I think you're being too legalistic and judgemental, Michael. But there is an answer. Bethlehem, when you look at a map of Israel, is very close to Jerusalem and so it is obvious that it was probably a part of Jerusalem like Penrith is a part of Sydney. If I said I was born in Penrith and then said I was born in Sydney, I haven't contradicted myself because Penrith is within the Sydney metropolitan area. Of course, you could say I was contradicting myself because, technically speaking, Penrith is 60 km away from the city of Sydney. But if you look at the spirit of what I am saying, you would realise that I'm basically saying one and the same thing. So it is here."

I wasn't sure what to answer right away. But then the story of the Wise Men came to mind.

"Tanya, what you say about Jerusalem and Bethlehem, I don't agree with you from the Bible. The Wise Men followed the Star because they knew that the Star led them to where the King of the Jews was born. Because Jerusalem was the Jewish Holy City, naturally they assumed that the King of the Jews would be born there. However, when they arrived in Jerusalem and asked King Herod where the King of the Jews had been recently born, the scribes found the prophecy in Micah 5:2 and the Wise Men were redirected to a highly unlikely birthplace of a Jewish king, a little town called Bethlehem. The way the story is presented in the Bible, it is as if Bethlehem was a completely separate town and not simply a suburb of Jerusalem."

Tanya just smiled peacefully.

"Michael, you're too exacting. I mean, do you believe the New Testament is the Word of God?"

"Of course!" I stated.

"But sometimes there are slight differences in stories in the gospels. If we were to apply this exacting attitude you display, we'd not only have to reject Joseph Smith as a prophet, we would have to dispense with the New Testament as well."

"That's not true," I said. "The New Testament does not vary in its accounts."

I knew I was lying. I thought Tanya was referring to the resurrection story like Markus once had and I was at pains to make her leave that alone. I thought that this was the only story which had minor differences.

"But, Michael, that's not true at all," Tanya said. "There's a story in Matthew 8: 5-13 which is retold in Luke 7:1-10 about a centurion whose servant was sick. In Matthew, it says that the centurion came personally to Jesus to beg of Him to heal his servant but in Luke it says that the centurion felt too unworthy to speak to Jesus himself and so he sent messengers to speak to Jesus on his behalf. Now, this is a minor contradiction, but you wouldn't say the New Testament should therefore be rejected as God's Word on such a petty issue, would you? And so it is between the Bible and the Book of Mormon."

But the way that Tanya explained this was neither derogatory nor condemnatory. There was an overwhelming peacefulness in the way she explained her answer, a pacific confidence in her speech.

But it stirred up the war in my soul and enflamed the confusion. There was now another discrepancy between two gospel stories which again proved that a perfect God was not involved in the writing of the Bible. And Tanya, whether she realised it or not, had me in a bind: if I reject the Book of Mormon because of a contradiction, I reject the Bible because of a contradiction. But if I overlook this seemingly trivial contradiction in the Bible, it was possible for me to accept the Book of Mormon, despite that it contradicted the Bible on a seemingly trivial issue. So, I had to end that point.

"I understand your point, Tanya, but I don't agree."

Tanya showed no resentment nor did she show a smug look of an attitude as if to say, "Get out of that one, you smart Alec." It was an air of confidence that she was sure of her unshakable faith. But I had to plough on. This was as much an exercise to prove that the Book of Mormon was not the Word of God to Tanya and Rosemary as it was to me.

"Another thing about Mormon teaching is about polygamy," I continued. "Are you aware, Tanya, that in the early years of Mormonism, many of the men practised polygamy?"

"Yes, of course," Tanya replied. "There's nothing wrong with a man having more than one wife. Many of the Old Testament figures had more than one wife, like Jacob, who had two wives who were sisters, and their handmaidens, and God did not tell them that this was wrong.

David and Solomon and many of the other kings of Israel also had many wives. In II Samuel 12:8, it says that God gave David his wives. If God gave David more than one wife, and God is eternal, then naturally a man can still have more than one wife to-day."

Good, I thought. She has caught herself.

"Well, if that's so, then why does it say here in the Book of Mormon in Jacob 2: 24-27, 'Behold, David and Solomon truly had many wives and concubines, which thing was abominable before me, saith the Lord…Wherefore, I the Lord God will not suffer that this people shall do like them of old. Wherefore, my brethren, hear me, and hearken to the word of the Lord: For there shall not any man among you have save it be one wife; and concubines he shall have none'. Your polygamous forefathers were transgressing, not the Bible, but the Book of Mormon."

But Tanya just smiled and Rosemary just wrote.

"I can't help you there, Michael. But I know that the Book of Mormon is the Word of God and there is definitely an answer. It is not my position to question

God. This may look like a contradiction but I believe the Book of Mormon is the Word of God so there must be an answer and I'm confident that there is one."

I didn't know what to answer and it further enflamed the feelings of confusion in my soul. I could hear Tanya saying about the Book of Mormon what I had been told about the Bible. If we saw contradictions in the Bible, we weren't to question them. She no doubt was taught the same concerning the Book of Mormon. This was making me all confused and dizzy so that I could no longer think straight. I completely lost my line of argumentation. But it also made me question to what extent I was supposed to accept the Bible despite the contradictions I saw in it. Christians condemn the Mormons for believing in the Book of Mormon by blind faith but it was obvious that I was doing the same with the Bible.

Eventually I pulled myself together. I tried to think of something concrete and fundamental of the Judaeo-Christian faith that the Mormons taught contrary to and I finally came up with my next argument.

"Tanya, in Christian belief, there is only one God, for it is written in many places that there is one and only one God. But according to the Mormon belief, Jesus is the Son of Jehovah, and Jehovah is the son of another god, and this god is the son of another god, and this goes on *ad infinitum*. Is this what the Mormon Church teaches?"

"Yes," Tanya confessed.

"Now, I believe that in one of Joseph's *Journal of Discourses* it says, 'In the beginning, the head of the Gods concocted a plan to create and populate the world and people it,' and in another Mormon book, the Book of Moses, the first chapter is a direct quote of Genesis chapter one, but instead of saying 'In the beginning God' it says 'in the beginning the gods', implying a plurality of gods, whereas the Bible only uses the singular. Jews and Christians have always maintained the belief in one and only one God. So this is extremely strong evidence that the Book of Mormon is not of God but of Satan who wants to take your eyes off the one true God.

Not only so, the Book of Mormon contradicts this teaching of Joseph Smith by saying in another part of the Book of Mormon, in Alma 11:26-29, 'And Zeezrom said unto him: Thou sayest there is a true and living God? And Amulek said, Yea, there is a true and living God. Now Zeezrom said: Is there more than one God? And he answered, No.' Even the Mormon teaching does not have a consistent view of God. One minute there is only one God, the next minute there are many. Can't you see the confusion?"

Tanya smiled placidly. "Michael, you're really taking everything well out of hand. I mean, don't you believe that there are three gods, so to speak, the Father, the Son and the Holy Ghost, and in another breath say that there is only one God? On that statement, I could use your foolproof, logical argument and say that the Bible has an inconsistent view of God because at one time you say there is only one

God and in another breath you say that there are three. But you have to remember in what context you are viewing these points when you confess how many gods there are. Now, as far as this world is concerned, there is only one God, Jehovah. He watches over this world. But there are many worlds and many gods who preside over these different worlds. But in each case, to the inhabitants of these worlds, there is only one God.

But the Bible does tell us that there is more than one God. Not only does the belief in the Trinity tell us this but also the Hebrew word for God is not a singular word but a plural word. That's why the Book of Moses and Genesis are really identical because in the Old Testament when it says 'god' the Hebrew word is consistently the plural 'gods'. That's why it says in Genesis 1:26 that God said, 'Let us make man in our image, after our likeness', which is in accordance with the Council of Gods in the *Journal of Discourses*.

Eventually, we humans can become gods, for as it is also written, 'As Man is, God was; As God is, Man may become'. This actually happened because, after the Fall, the Council of the Gods said, 'Behold, the man is become as one of us' in Genesis 3:22. Man has begun that journey to be like the gods, like Jehovah."

I was outraged. The violent turmoil in my soul wanted to walk across the room and rip her limb from limb. How dare she imply that God was once a man like us and that man one day may become a god like Him. But yelling blasphemy would not help at all because I couldn't show that Tanya was wrong.

She had confirmed her belief on the very Bible that I believed was the Word of God.

But I still had to prove that this whole idea of a genealogy of gods was entirely unscriptural and a verse came straight to mind.

"Tanya, you said that Jehovah had a beginning, being the descendant of another god. But it clearly says in the Bible that God has always existed from eternity, for it says in Psalm 90:2, 'even from everlasting to everlasting, thou art God'. If God is from everlasting, how can He have a beginning?"

But Tanya didn't have to answer that one. She made an attempt but I wasn't listening because of my own conviction. I was certain that the word *everlasting* used here would be the Hebrew word *olam*, and later discovered that I was right. *Everlasting* in this verse could be interpreted *from a time concealed* in the same way I had used this interpretation to justify that the everlasting commandments made to Abraham and his descendants came to an end with the death of Christ. This allowed Mormons to interpret this verse of the Bible as meaning that God's beginning was so far in the past that His existence began in a time concealed.

I was completely in a daze. It was as if my mind were weighed down with concrete blocks that prevented me from moving freely from one argument to another. But even as I tried other arguments to show the inconsistency of Mormon teaching and Protestant Christian doctrine, each argument only highlighted inconsistencies within the Bible itself.

By the end of the night, I was mentally exhausted. But Tanya showed no signs of fatigue at all. She had been a restful soul throughout the whole exercise, like a soft feather resting on a pillow.

Tanya had an end comment to make. "Michael, there is something I see in you. You have an extremely restless soul. I wonder if you really believe yourself that you have the truth. But let me help you. You will never find the truth without having the Spirit of God. From the way you were arguing against the Book of Mormon, I could see that you were using reason and your intellect and it is no wonder that you have found fault. You cannot grasp God's truth by the intellect, you have to have God's Holy Spirit in you to lead you to all truth. Until you can see that Joseph Smith Jr was a prophet of God, you are always going to be searching and finding fault."

I didn't know what else to say. All I wanted to do was go home. I closed all my books and went to give back the copy of the Book of Mormon that Rosemary had given me but she told me to keep it. But as she gave it back to me, she placed a card inside.

"Here, keep this. This is my address and phone number in New Zealand if you ever come across the Tasman."

"What do you mean?" I asked.

"I…I'm going back home…to New Zealand. I'm going to begin my mission there," she said with half a smile, half a frown. Her lips quivered as she said it, as if she knew what this really meant, that our friendship had come to an end.

My heart sank down into my feet.

"I...I'd better go," I said. "Thank you, Tanya and Rosemary, for having me."

"It was a pleasure," Tanya said. "I'll still be here if you ever want to call in and talk again. And it doesn't have to just be on a religious topic. The door is open at any time."

I walked out the door but, before going, I gave one last look at Rosemary and then left.

My feelings for Rosemary were complicated. Not only was a friend of mine leaving me for good on the physical plane, in the spiritual plane she was swallowed up by Satan and this evil church and now I couldn't help. All those conversations we had had at Fellowship to show her the truth seemed like a great waste of time and effort, and the wasted effort was accentuated by the way Tanya was able to confidently squash every argument I had against this apostate church.

Chapter 18

I still write to Rosemary from time to time and have told her all that has happened in my life. I was expecting her never to reply after that but she eventually did. Her letter was filled with sadness and disappointment when she found out but she did not forsake me as a friend. She had learned what it was like for the universe in her mind to change and how it felt to be rejected by those she loved because of it.

Her sister, Helen, has not had anything to do with her for years because she believes that Rosemary has now been caught up in an apostate church like I once thought. Helen maintains that the only true voice of God is the Jehovah's Witness Organisation. Rosemary told me that this made her really sad because she thought that her sister would have had more sympathy and understanding, seeing Rosemary had rejected her when she joined a new faith and still wanted to be accepted as her sister regardless. Now the table had turned. Helen was now the staunch, unforgiving one contrary to the teachings of the Bible.

But Rosemary still keeps up the communication between us. She told me that I never forsook her as a friend when she became a Mormon and, despite that my letters contained condemnations against this modern-day prophet, I maintained the contact with her. Now it was her turn to be shocked and sad at my change and yet, she told me that she does not love me any less, she never stops praying for me and I will always be a welcome visitor in her house when and if I take the trip to New Zealand.

Years later, I thought again about the Mormon Church and from a completely non-religious viewpoint. I could sympathise with Joseph Smith Jr. First of all, during his time, he had difficulty trying to make sense out of all the Christian factions in North America which were claiming that they had the Word of God and yet they were all divided. Each of them, the Methodists, the Presbyterians and the Baptists, all claimed that Jesus was the Way and the Bible was the Word of God but they still were separate entities. I was faced with the same problem.

But Joseph Smith, no doubt, had another difficulty to contend with. Why did Christians believe that the Bible revealed all truth and all that there was to know about the universe and yet said nothing about the Americas? Prior to Columbus' epic journey in 1492, Christian Europe believed that there existed only three continents: Africa, Asia and Europe, a reflection of the three gods in one. But on his westward journey to China, Columbus unwittingly bumped into a large landmass that extended from the Arctic to Antarctica which no-one in Europe ever knew existed. Why hadn't the Bible spoken of its existence?

No doubt in Joseph's mind, the developing North America must have filled him with pride, seeing this great new land leap forward in great strides with the Bible at the helm, and yet, the land that the God of the Bible loved was not America, but a tiny, poky, insignificant little piece of real estate on the east coast of the Mediterranean. It must have tormented his mind. But Joseph provided a solution. Uniting, as best he could, the promises of God to Abraham, he developed a story built around certain of Abraham's descendants who were led by God to go to another promised land: the United States of America. Now the United States was part of Bible history and, when Jesus returns, He will begin His new rule there.

But arguing with Tanya was supposed to show her the confusion of the Mormon belief and the unshakable soundness of the Bible. But instead, more incoherence was discovered within the pages of the Bible.

And what of the interpretation of the word *olam*? It helped when justifying the everlasting covenants, giving them an end, but it also gave the Mormons the liberty to believe in a descendancy of gods. I was caught in a tight squeeze – if I said "everlasting" had no end, Christians could not be saved unless they were circumcised, kept the Sabbath and the Jewish holy days, and kept the Mosaic Law. But if I allowed *olam* to have an end, I could not use Psalm 90:2 as evidence of God's eternal existence.

And what of the plurality of gods? *Elohim* literally means *gods*, even though the whole Judaeo-Christian belief was founded on the existence of only one God. But the Mormons have as much right to translate and understand this word as *gods* and moreso because it is linguistically correct.

But what ate at me the most was how well Tanya argued for the Mormon belief and used the King

James Version of the Bible to support it. She did not, at any time, disregard the infallibility of the Bible, but upheld it, and used it as a foundation stone for her faith. And yet, Mormonism and Protestantism are two entirely different beliefs. How can this be?

I was sick for days after that. The next day I had symptoms of influenza and the day after I was in bed. My body ached with fever and all I could do was toss and turn because of the pain in my back and limbs. I couldn't sleep, and what little sleep I did have was filled with weird dreams about the Mormons, Rosemary, Markus, Joseph, Ruth, Troy, my parents, the church and Jesus Christ Himself.

I was bedridden for the entire week and on the Friday an unusual surprise awaited me. I heard the doorbell ring but was too sick to care who it would be. Not long after that, my mother appeared in my room.

"Er, you have a visitor," she said with a smile.

What followed my mother into the room was a bunch of flowers with legs, but the visitor could not hide his hands and I recognised them immediately.

"Markus! What are you doing here?" I asked with a feverish groan.

"We heard you were sick and we bought you these," Markus replied.

"My goodness," my mother said. "That's nice of you all. Maybe I should work where you guys work so that when I'm sick, I'll get a nice bunch of flowers."

"Well, Mrs Farril, whenever you're sick, I'll remember to bring some for you," Markus replied.

My mother was taken aback by Markus' statement and commented on his hospitality and good-breeding. Within the next couple of moments, the comments my mother made and her subtle body language made it apparent that my mother took a liking to Markus. His physical beauty coupled with his gentle voice and his confidence no doubt captured her attention. Despite my throbbing headache, I listened to the casual conversation that was developing between them, cautious and worried of what may come out of it, what personals would be accidentally disclosed. I was in no fit state to try and explain anything if the requirement arose but this passing fear was uncalled for and finally my mother concluded the conversation with an offer of some refreshments. Markus dutifully and politely replied in the affirmative and my mother then left the room.

Once my mother had completely disappeared, Markus turned to me and smiled.

"Where can I put these?" he asked, moving the flowers around in the air as if they were about to topple over. I just pointed to the desk and Markus obeyed by just lying them down. He then hastily removed a card from his pocket and walked over to me and sat on the bed, handing me the card.

"Before your Mum comes back, I'd just like to tell you that the flowers are from me only! You know how stingy the company is! Hide the card and read it later when no-one's around."

The warmth of his body as he sat on the bed next to me was homely. Nobody's body heat brought the same delight as his. But at the same time, it was unnerving to have Markus in the same house as my parents. Despite how sick I felt, I was really on my guard.

"When I heard you were sick, I was so worried," Markus further said. "I missed you all week at work and missed you coming over on Tuesday night."

I told him I missed him, too.

"So, how are you feeling now?" he asked and stroked my hair back. I was feeling extremely uncomfortable that he was expressing physical affection so obvious as this in my room when my mother was likely to walk in at any minute.

"I'm fine, now," I groaned. "I still get a bit dizzy when I walk around and I have a rotten headache. I should be back at work by Monday, though. And how's work?"

Markus sat up.

"It's work! Tracey's still Tracey, Joe's still Italian, coffee tastes the same."

"Here you are," my mother said to Markus as she walked into the room and offered him a cup of coffee. "I hope this coffee is better than the one you drink at work!"

Markus smiled and thanked her.

"Well, I think it was really sweet of you to bring these for Michael from your work. It's nice to know that there are still people in this world who have manners. You know, we're Christians, and we believe in these values because Jesus taught us this in the Bible."

When my mother said that, I could have died. My mother didn't know to whom she was talking. But Markus surprised me further still.

"Yes, I'm a believer, too. That's why I maintain these values."

I didn't know where to look. But I also knew that Markus was playing with the word "believer" which meant one thing to him but another to my mother.

"Oh, are you?" my mother said with facially expressed delight. "I think that's really good to have a friend at work who's a Christian. Oh, yes, come to think of it, I know who you are now. You're the boy that lets Michael stay over on Tuesday nights. I'd just like to say that we are pleased that you are so hospitable."

"Oh, thank you," Markus said. "It's no problem. I like Michael staying. He's really good company and I know it must be a drag for him to drive so far so late at night. Just coming here I realise how far you live from the city! I don't go this far for my holidays!"

My mother was well taken aback by Markus and she sat and talked with Markus at length. My mother weaved into her conversation many religious topics that did not dance around sensitive issues and Markus was able to share in the conversation without my mother knowing any better. I was amazed at the way the two got on so instantly. In the end, my mother invited Markus to stay for dinner and he obliged.

That evening around the dinner table, Markus stole the show. He chatted to my father about work, to my mother about cooking hints. He joked, he was serious, he was the perfect guest.

My parents embarrassed me by having our family Bible Study while he was there. But Markus participated, expounding a point of view that my parents had never seen before, something that my mother quoted forever afterwards. He helped with the dishes, had another cup of coffee and chatted some more. I couldn't help but see that neither of my parents wanted him to go.

To me, this was the strangest feeling in the world. It was as if I had brought home the life-time partner of my choosing to visit my parents and this was the test to see if he fit in with the family. And he passed in every way.

And when he left, my parents spoke about him in glowing terms. My word, if my parents had only known who they were liberally giving their praises to!

But the glow of happiness that my parents liked Markus was soon replaced by guilt. My parents' perception of him was only partly true. They thought he was thoughtful, hospitable, courteous and polite, which were true of him. But they also thought that he was a born-again, heterosexual Christian. But he wasn't. He was my lover. And his views of the Bible, had my parents ever had time to discover them, would have been considered too liberal for their liking as Markus always told me that the Bible was only a part of the whole. Had my parents ever discovered that Markus, like me, was a homosexual, their whole perception would have entirely changed when the only thing different about him was that he preferred me to a woman. He would have become in one fell swoop a deviate, a pervert, a slimy, detestable thing, all because his sexual orientation was different.

And it ate at me. I loved Markus. I loved him to the full extent of what it meant to love another person, that special person most of us search for to spend the rest of our lives with. But Jesus, the Saviour, who died for my sins, got in the way, telling me from His Word that I would be tormented in the flames of hell in the next life if I did not end all that was going on between Markus and me.

I had seen enough contradictions, inconsistencies, false prophecies and double standards in the Bible and among the various groups of people calling themselves Christians. But indoctrination is not an easy thing to escape. The fires of hell singed my soul whenever I thought of Markus. The tug-o-war between my fear of God and my love for Markus were both strong opposing electromagnetic forces ready to split me in two.

Chapter 19

I don't know what ever happened to Markus. It was in a way my first relationship and I will never forget him as long as I live. Had it not been for my faith, I guess I would still be living with him and would have been very happy. But as much as I loved him at the time, I couldn't cope with the conflict in my soul and so I decided to abort the entire relationship I had with him. After the night he had come to my place, it brought it out plainly and clearly to me what I really was, what I did not want to be: a homosexual. I couldn't cope with it. The social stigma and, more importantly, the fear of God were such great influences against this unholy alliance and the only way I could live with myself was to make a complete break from him.

But this was no easy task. Going to Markus' place after lectures bearing these sad tidings weighed heavily on my heart. My feet felt like lead as I walked from my car to his flat as the war in my soul fought a bitter struggle over the move I was about to make.

Markus was his noble self when he greeted me at the door, served me dinner and then we chatted like we always did. We eventually made our way on the lounge in front of the television and he began to massage my back. It felt so good. I knew that by breaking up with him I would be forfeiting the pleasure of being looked after by that one special person in life of my choosing, to be touched, to be handled, to belong to one other person and he belong to me.

Markus suspected that something was wrong.

"Michael, is everything all right?" he asked so softly.

I bit my bottom lip to prevent myself from bursting into tears. How could I tell Markus that this was over, our relationship together, in the name of a book? Markus stopped and turned me around to face him and looked into my eyes. He must have read something really bad in them.

"Michael, what's wrong?"

"Markus, this is wrong. How can we commit sin in the eyes of God?"

To me, that was what it was but I was surprised with Markus' answer to this.

"Michael, what's wrong? What is it that makes you think we're sinning?"

"Markus, two men cannot love like this. You might not believe in the Bible, but I do, and the Bible forbids what we are doing. The Bible says that this type of love is reserved only between a man and a woman."

As much as my lips were saying this, my heart was filled with acid when I thought of having to exchange this relationship for a relationship with a woman in order to please God.

"Michael," Markus said with a hint of anger in his voice. "If this is true, then what about the relationship between David and Jonathan?"

"What of it?" I asked.

"The Bible says that David and Jonathan had a relationship just like ours."

"Where does it say that?" I snapped.

Markus asked me to get my Bible which I dutifully obeyed. On returning, I handed the Bible to him. He took it from my hands and began flicking through the pages until he reached the passage he was looking for.

"Look here. Read II Samuel 1:26."

He passed me the Bible and I read it. This verse was part of the lament that David made for Jonathan, King Saul's son, when Jonathan was killed in battle at Mount Gilboa. This verse was near the conclusion of this lament and it said:

> *I am distressed for thee, my brother Jonathan: very pleasant hast thou been unto me: thy love to me was wonderful, passing the love of women.*

I gasped when I read the passage. How was it that I had read this verse many times before but had never seen it? The whole expression was quite peculiar except when viewed in the light of Markus' inference: David and Jonathan were lovers. What else did it mean? Why was Jonathan's love for David more wonderful than a woman's love? How could David compare Jonathan's love to the love of a woman if a man cannot love a man like a woman loves a man? And it shook me down to the very foundations. The Bible subtly implied concerning the man after God's own heart that the beginning of the line of kings into which Christ would be born, the great King of Israel, David, had a male partner.

"But that's not all," Markus said. "Remember when Jesus prophesied of his Second Coming? Here, read Luke 17:34."

I read the verse aloud: "'I tell you, in that night there shall be two men in one bed; the one shall be taken, and the other shall be left'".

After I had finished reading it, Markus continued. "What else does that mean but that two men were in love with each other and lived together? If Jesus condemned such love, why didn't he say 'a man and his wife will be in one bed'?"

"But what about Romans chapter one?" I objected. "It says that two men cannot love one another because this is evil."

"Michael, Romans chapter one tells you that when someone turns away from Jesus Christ to worship idols, God makes them a homosexual. Tell me seriously, is this true of you? Do you believe that Jesus is something else other than God? Do you worship idols?"

I just shook my head.

"And what about me? I never was a Christian and yet I'm a homosexual. So, what does that tell you about the accuracy of Romans chapter one?"

I was completely dumbfounded. It was the first time I had ever heard Markus use the word to describe us and our relationship and it affected me right down to the bone.

I stood up and cried out in despair.

"But God hates homosexuality and homosexuals! It's a sin. Jesus doesn't want us to be this way. It's wrong! It's evil!"

"If Jesus was so adamant against this form of love," Markus cried back at me as he stood up, "then why does the Bible say that John was the disciple whom Jesus loved, and why did John recline on Jesus' chest at the Last Supper in much the same way as we lie on each other's chests at night here on the lounge? If Jesus was so much against this form of love, why did He have it for John?"

That was the last straw. I couldn't cope with the implication. I just slapped Markus across the face for such a blasphemous statement.

Markus was going to hit me back but he took control of himself not to do so. He clenched his fists and closed his eyes in despair.

"Why can't you see it, Michael? God has brought us together and you're going to throw it all away over a book. Why does the Bible have such a hold over your mind that it prevents you from seeing reason?"

He reached down for my Bible and shoved it in my face.

"Here, love this. Go on, kiss it, fondle it, caress it and show how much you love it! Have a romantic dinner with it, hold it in your arms and tell it you love it, massage its back, lie with your head on its shoulder, make love to it, do all those things with it that we have done together and tell me if it's worth it.

Don't you see, Michael? This book has taken complete control of your mind when it is only an object. Your obsession for this book verges onto idolatry. You would rather love this object of paper and ink than a human being, someone with a human touch, someone who deeply loves you and knows how to show it to you."

Markus was trembling and I was frightened. But he hadn't finished. After a slight pause, Markus looked up at the ceiling, took a deep breath as if he had just surfaced for air and then turned to me and said, "How much does it take to tell you that I love you, that my feelings for you are so strong that I can't stand the thought of you never being around? If God is love, aren't my feelings for you a reflection of His very essence?"

There was utter silence for some time after that last statement. Those last words plunged deep down into the very depths of my being. It was as if Markus had unsheathed his steely sword and pierced deep into my seat of reason.

Eventually I was brought back to my encapsulated view of the universe. Reason was not the issue in this case, the Bible was, and eventually I expressed this. When Markus saw that I was strong and final with my decision, he just burst into tears. It was heart-wrenching to watch a grown man cry and to be the cause of it all. There were tears on both sides. It was a painful experience, a great loss. It was as if a piece of my flesh had been ripped from my body. I knew that from that time on, Tuesday nights would never be the same, life would never be the same.

Markus sealed the end of our relationship when not long after this event he resigned from work. It stirred my heart to know that even work that had forced us to be together would lose its sweetness now that Markus was no longer going to be there. At the farewell speech, many of the women shed a sorry tear because of Markus' departure because he was much loved by everybody. The chief chemist gave a glowing farewell speech, presented him with a parting gift and wished him all the best in the future.

"Satan is the cause of all this," I said under my breath, full of guilt, knowing that the reason why Markus was leaving was because there was no way we could continue to work together like this when all things beautiful between us had come to an end all in the name of a book.

It was a tragic loss, no doubt as much on his side as it was on mine, for I had never felt this close to anyone before, neither to my parents, my sister, to any of those at church nor to this invisible God I worshipped.

Markus had one last thing to say to me before he left my life forever. As he stood there, I could see that the bright sparkle in his eyes had been lost to a dull sadness.

"Michael, we could have made it together. Life would have been a wonderful experience with you around. But the Bible has won. But not forever. The time will come when the Bible will let you down with one *coup de grace* which will hurt you more than anything because the Bible is not what you think it is.

But I still love you, Michael, and I always will. You'll always hold an important place in my heart. I just hope you find the happiness you're looking for to release you from your struggle against yourself."

These words were branded into my brain and I never forgot them.

My parents were totally unaware of what was happening inside me and what had really been going on between Markus and me. They later learned that Markus had left the company and that I no longer saw him but it did not seem to trouble them in any way. Rather, my home life remained totally the same: mundane, predictable, boring, Christian.

It was an empty time. The vacuum left by Markus gasped mightily for something to fill it and it was the Bible and my study of it that I used to try to cover the hurt that I felt inside. But the loneliness was very biting. My friendship with Joseph had faded away, dying a natural death. Rosemary had returned to New Zealand. And I no longer attended Sunday Night Fellowship out of disgust towards Susan and these lukewarm Christians. It was a very lonely existence I led, trying to sustain my relationship with a god who existed in another dimension, communing with Him in silent contemplation, trying to cover the pain I brought on myself and on Markus.

It was a strange psychology. Markus had taught me many things to free me from the chains that the Bible held over me and to accept my nature for what it was without shame or remorse, but strangely, Markus' teachings forced me to clutch tighter to the Bible. His last words were haunting and I wanted to prove him wrong. The Bible had to be the answer and Jesus alone had to be the way.

But if the Bible was the answer, why hadn't I changed? Why did I still have these feelings towards men and how could I continue to love this book which condemned me for them? Didn't it say in I John 5:14, 15, 'And this is the confidence that we have in him, that, if we ask anything according to his will, he heareth us: And if we know that he hear us, whatsoever we ask, we know that we have the petitions that we desired of him'? If heterosexuality was according to the will of Jesus, why, when I had begged God for years to change my sexual orientation, I remained the same? Where was this confidence? If these desires were inflicted on me because of the evil one, why didn't God avenge me speedily like He promised in Luke 18:8 but rather He had allowed me to go on for years, dragging myself around ashamed of these feelings I had for men and not for women?

It was strange that I thought that homosexuality was from Satan because the Bible is absolutely clear in saying that homosexuality is a punishment inflicted by God on those who first believed in Him but then turned away to worship idols. But I knew this wasn't true. But to admit that this was untrue then meant that I had to finally admit that the Bible had made a mistake. But to even entertain the thought that the Bible could be wrong meant utter torment for eternity. So it was easier to blame Satan for both my homosexual feelings and the guilt I experienced because of them, even though this was totally unbib-

402

lical. After all, how could I blame a perfect and powerful God for anything, even when the blame was rightfully directed at Him? God had the power over our eternal destiny, and He threatened a nasty and horrible one of utter pain and torment for those who entertained the notion that maybe His book wasn't perfect after all, even if there was clear evidence that what was written in His book was obviously not true.

In the last year of my degree, I remember going to the library one Saturday morning to do some research on an assignment I had to finish for the following week. While searching for the relevant books for the topic, I accidentally found myself in a completely unrelated section of the library.

Along one of the shelves I saw the Encyclopaedia Britannica's Great Books of the Western World series but there was one volume that seemed to stand out. It was the complete works of Plato in one volume. As soon as I saw it, it was as if it were calling me to read it. I removed it from the shelf and began flicking through the pages. There was nothing there that struck my interest but I decided to borrow it that afternoon anyway. Even to this day, I still cannot remember what made me borrow it in the first place.

I did not let my parents know that I had this book in the house because my parents would have gone completely berserk. But when they had gone to bed, the works of Plato became my night time reading.

Throughout my life I had regarded the Greek philosophers as writers of a whole lot of mumbo jumbo and had only heard of them in conversation.

Like any non-Biblical authors, they were viewed with scorn and derision because they did not talk about God or Jesus. These thoughts about the Greek philosophers floated in the back of my mind as I opened to the first page of this vast volume.

But my initial negative thoughts of Plato's works were completely squashed when I read the first three parts of this book: *Charmides, Lysis* and *Laches*. Instead of a dull commentary, Plato discussed his ideas in the form of a dialogue between various characters, Socrates being Plato's chief speaker and the hero of the discussion. It appeared that Plato wrote down Socrates' words in the same way as the apostles wrote down the sayings of Jesus.

These dialogues were very heavy reading but were spiced with a lot of wit and humour to keep the reader interested. What struck me at first was that Socrates, through Plato, expressed the view that the Greek philosophers were searching for Reason as the ultimate goal of life which could only be obtained through wisdom and virtue. Wisdom and virtue enhanced one's character, producing an upright and respectable citizen in this life and in the hereafter. How then, I reasoned, could Satan be working through Socrates if Socrates sought the noble characteristics of virtue, justice and truth, the same ideals that the Christians strove towards, when Satan was the epitome and embodiment of all that was evil?

The ultimate goal of the Greek philosophers, as borne out by Socrates, was the search for Reason. This Reason, in classical Greek, was called *logos* and the Greek philosophers believed that this was their lifetime goal and those who sought after the *logos* were on their way to eternal bliss. *Logos*, it must be added, has come into the English language in the form of the word *logic* and as the suffix to many branches of science that end in *logy*.

Immediately I saw a connection between the Greek philosophers' search for Reason and the message of John's gospel. For John opens his gospel with

> *In the beginning was the Word, and the Word was with God, and the Word was God.*

There were many interpretations floating around to explain what this meant. The meaning that was highly favoured in our church was that Jesus was the human, fleshly manifestation of the Law and the Prophets because, while He was on earth, He lived a sinless life in accordance with the Mosaic Law which at the time was God's Word. But the word that was translated as *Word* in English was not the Greek word *nomos*, "law" but *logos*, "reason". The *logos*, the Reason, according to John, was found in the person of Jesus for Jesus was the Reason made manifest in the flesh, and John must have been writing his gospel with the Greeks in mind to show them that this was the *logos* that they were looking for. This meant that, if Jesus is the embodiment of Reason, Christians are required to use their intellect and reason to search for God.

And contrary to my understanding of the Greeks, the philosophers believed that they obtained favour from the gods without the necessity of religious rites and practices necessary towards the Greek pantheon. And what was also striking was that Socrates eventually confessed to a belief in one God, in a society that believed in many gods, which was borne out in his *Apology*.

Socrates intrigued me even more because he claimed to have received wisdom directly from heaven. At certain moments, he would enter some sort of trance during which time he claimed that God had spoken to him. The western world has always viewed Socrates as a philosopher but is it possible that we could call him a prophet? What makes prophets different to the general religious laity is that prophets claim that God spoke to them directly and Socrates himself made this claim.

But what made Socrates different to other prophets, if we could call him one, was his message. He did not receive messages from God which he then commanded those around him to follow. He claimed that God was telling him to tell the world that it was up to each individual to search for God through the *logos* and not just accept blindly the set traditions and beliefs that society imposed on them. This is what made Socrates such a problem to the Athenians because he made the youths question the established religion of the time, the belief in the Olympian gods and goddesses and the inconsistencies contained within this belief, which led these youths to reject it. Rejecting the Olympian deities was about as equal as rejecting the Athenian authorities and so Socrates was condemned to death as a result.

But what struck me the most was how the flavour of Plato's works seemed familiar in style to the writers of the New Testament, mainly St John and St Paul, as if these two saints had drawn from Plato's ideas when developing the new faith.

I could see in particular how Paul was influenced by the teachings of Plato. For through Plato, I could see how Paul was able to dispense with the perpetual rites of the Mosaic Law and still maintain the integrity of his Jewishness and the Jewishness of the Christian faith, for Plato's *Republic* held the key.

In *Republic VII*, Plato presents an allegory of all humanity. All humans are like people in an underground cave, chained up in such a way that they cannot move their legs and necks but can only look forward. Behind these prisoners, somewhere in the distance of the cave, a fire is burning, and between the fire and the prisoners is a wall along which run all sorts of statues and figures of animals and people.

The prisoners, because of the restriction of their movement, cannot see the objects or the wall behind them but can only see the shadows displayed on the opposite surface of the cave ahead of them, the shadows of the images caused by the fire. This, therefore, becomes their perspective of reality and the prisoners believe that the shadows are real figures.

One of the prisoners is then released by an instructor. At first the prisoner turns around to see the source of the light and the images moving across the wall. The instructor leads the prisoner to the wall and asks the released prisoner to name the objects. But the prisoner, being accustomed to viewing the objects only as mere shadows and not in their true form, at first becomes perplexed and considers the shadows to be the truer form than the actual objects themselves. And because he is unaccustomed to looking at the light in its full strength from the standpoint at which he now is, he finds it hard to focus on these real figures and thinks that the shadows are much clearer than the actual objects dancing on the wall.

Eventually the prisoner is led out of the cave and for the first time he sees the light of day and many new and unusual objects that surround him, trees, flowers, birds, animals, mountains and the sea. Because of the dimness of the cave to which he has been accustomed, it takes some time before he is able to get used to his new surroundings.

The allegory concludes with the prisoner returning back to his former state chained up again against the wall, trying to explain to his fellow prisoners all he has seen, attempting to explain that the shadows on the wall are simply that, merely shadows of the true objects. This in itself is difficult to explain, let alone what he has seen outside the cave. His companions, however, who have always remained chained up, think he is completely out of his mind.

Paul uses this allegory in an attempt to explain to the contemporary Jews that the rites of the Mosaic Law are also simply shadows of the true realities, which is why he writes in Colossians 2:16, 17

Let no man therefore judge you in meat, or in drink, or in respect of an holyday, or of the new moon, or of the sabbath days:

> *Which are a shadow of things to come; but the body is of Christ.*

And why he writes in Hebrews 10:1

> *For the law having a shadow of good things to come, and not the very image of the things*

Here, then, was how Paul was able to make the Jewish faith universal, doing away brilliantly with the perpetual Old Testament rites and practices by making them merely shadows of the true realities. Circumcision, Passover, the Sabbath Day and all the other eternal observances demanded of the children of Abraham are readily dispensed with because they are merely shadows of the true realities, the true Circumcision, the true Passover and the true Sabbath, the true images being perpetual and eternal. This paved the way for Paul to mould out of the religion of his ancestors an alternative version of Judaism which was convincing to the Jews and palpable to the Gentiles, allowing him to create a uniting principle which gave Jew and Gentile a common ground.

But the *Republic* had more to offer Paul. For what Plato was trying to establish in this great work was the ideal State or ideal *ekklesia*. In his creative style, Plato introduces this work by an argument about justice between various people and Socrates, which leads Socrates to use the ideal State as a means of describing the ideal human. Socrates argues that for a state to be successful, every member must perform a particular function that they are best suited for, whether they be a carpenter, cobbler, farmer, poet, musician, soldier, guardian or ruler, just as in the human body, there are different members such as the eye, the ear, the hand and the foot. Each member of this well-organised State has its proper place, all performing their duties to the benefit, not of themselves, but of the State as a whole inasmuch as various members of the human body work in harmony in order to preserve the entire body and not for their own individual interests. At the head are the guardians who, being at the top of this hierarchy, are given the responsibility of ensuring that the entire State is served equally well and that every member is educated only in those things that produce noble characteristics in each individual to the benefit of the State and the individuals themselves.

So, too, in Paul's church, or his *ekklesia*, every member has a particular function to play and Paul also compares the Church to the human body in I Corinthians 12 and Ephesians 5. But unlike Plato's State, the Church is a spiritual entity and each member is endowed with spiritual abilities. For cobblers and artisans, musicians and soldiers have no meaning in a spiritual State to fight against the spiritual enemy. Paul writes in I Corinthians 12 that each member of the Church is empowered with a miraculous spiritual gift such as wisdom, faith, the power to heal, the ability to perform miracles, speaking in tongues, the interpretation of tongues and the gift of prophecy. And in answer to the secular guardians in Plato's perfect State, Paul places the apostles and prophets as the guardians of the spiritual state. Each member is imbued with different spiritual gifts, just like the body is made up of different limbs and organs to the benefit of the Church as a body.

But for the State to hold soundly together, each member must have a respect and love for the other members so that if one member is down or injured, the others feel the pain with them, just as it is in the human body. For Plato writes in *Republic V*

> *When but a finger of one of us is hurt, the whole frame...feels the hurt and sympathizes with the part affected* *

which is echoed in Paul's account of the spiritual State where he writes in I Corinthians 12:26

> *And whether one member suffer, all members suffer with it*

The ultimate goal of each member of the State is to be perfect in word and deed. Each member should continue towards virtue despite what troubles lay in their way for, as it says in *Republic X*

> *All things will in the end work together for good to him in life and death: for the gods have a care of any one whose desire is to become just and to be like God...by the pursuit of virtue* **

---

* *(Reprinted from the Great Books of the Western World,* © *1952, 1990, 2005 Encyclopaedia Britannica, Inc., p. 363*

** *(Reprinted from the Great Books of the Western World,* © *1952, 1990, 2005 Encyclopaedia Britannica, Inc., p. 437*

which only differs from the spiritual State in that the members in the latter are already saved by God, for Paul writes in Romans 8:28

> *And we know that all things work together for good to*
> *them that love God, to them who are the called*
> *according to his purpose*

But the dialogue that most intrigued me, and at the same time frightened me, was Plato's *Symposium*. In this dialogue, Socrates and various companions assembled together at a banquet and decided to give praise to a deity that formerly knew no praises, the god Love. Although viewed as one of the many gods and goddesses within the Greek world, the deification of Love seemed to have a similar ring to John's first general epistle, except that John singles out the one and only true God, Jesus Christ, as being this very God of Love.

For Jesus, the God of Love, and His relationship to the Father, according to the Christians, differs greatly from the unified Jewish view of Jehovah and the Messiah that was to come. To the Jews, the great God Jehovah promised that a great figure of the line of King David would be born to deliver the Jews from the Gentiles and return the Holy Land to the Children of Israel and build the Temple of Solomon. This was the Messiah the Jews were waiting for, a heroic, fighting figure bearing arms for a victorious deliverance of the Jews and their homeland.

In contrast, in the epistles of Paul and John, we read how Jesus the Messiah is mighty in power, that He is wonderful in His birth and that He is the only begotten of the Father, being born only of a male deity. In the *Symposium*, the god Love is strikingly presented in exactly the same way, using almost precisely the same words.

But although God, Paul also argues that Jesus has a position between God and men as he writes in I Timothy 2:5

> *For there is one God, and one mediator between God*
> *and men, the man Christ Jesus*

which is a whole new approach to the expectations of the Jewish Messiah, a concept which seemed not to come from the Old Testament but has more in common with what Plato wrote in the *Symposium*

> *Love...interprets...between gods and men, conveying and*
> *taking across to the gods the prayers and sacrifices of*
> *men, and to men the commands and replies of the gods;*
> *he is the mediator who spans the chasm which*
> *divides them, and therefore in him all is bound together.**

Here was another concept of Jesus, for not only was He the Jewish Messiah, the Zoroastrian Saviour, the Hindu incarnation of Vishnu and the Tao of the

Reprinted from the Great Books of the Western World, © 1952, 1990, 2005 Encyclopaedia Britannica, Inc., p. 163

Chinese, He was also the Reason of the Greek philosophers and Plato's deity of Love.

This new revelation about the similarities between Plato and the apostles was troubling enough. But Plato, in the *Symposium*, gives a different reason for the origins of sexuality. Speaking through Aristophanes, one of the guests at the banquet, Plato presents a picture of humankind at the beginning of time, consisting of two faces facing outwards, four hands, four legs and two sets of genitals. There were three types of human beings: male, female and androgynous. The males had two penises, the females had two vaginas and the androgynous beings had one of each. Procreation was not by means of sexual intercourse but was carried out like grasshoppers, where the female placed the eggs in the earth and the males fertilised them without the need for any physical contact between them.

These primeval humans were so strong and their heart lifted up with pride that they made an attempt to overthrow the gods on Mount Olympus. In punishment, and to diminish their power, Zeus cut them all in half and Apollo healed the two halves, moulding what was left of their bodies to form the present state of humankind.

Now that these beings were only half of their original selves, in some sort of panic or anguish, the opposite parts came together, embracing each other, trying to get as close to each other as possible in an attempt to be joined together as they were before. Men, who were originally a section of primeval man, sought other men, women who were originally a section of a primeval woman, sought a woman, and men and women, who were originally a section of a primeval androgynous being, sought after someone of the opposite sex.

It was such a shock to me. Plato, so long ago, gave an origin of sexuality which was so unlike the view that had permeated the thoughts and beliefs of the western world. Instead of being perverts, homosexuals were attracted to their own sex like heterosexuals were attracted to the opposite. It wasn't a sin, it simply just was. Plato's explanation of the origins of sexuality seemed to be more in accordance with reality than the Christian view.

But Plato went a step further. He claimed that homosexuality was purer than heterosexuality because the fruit of heterosexual sex was the continuation of one's genes which, he seemed to indicate, was a form of selfishness. By contrast, homosexuality was noble because this form of love depended on the way two people viewed each other and there was no ulterior motive behind the sexual act.

I couldn't cope with this information. On the one hand, it filled me with great hope. But on the other, it was the Great Hypocrisy. Paul and John were inspired by Socrates and used his teachings in their letters that make our New Testament. And yet, Paul reversed Socrates' view of sexuality making heterosexuality noble and homosexuality despised. And for the millennia to follow, homosexuals were crushed and condemned by a Church which hated them, when the book that this same Church claimed to be inspired by God had absorbed the teachings of one of them.

And it wasn't just Paul. Many of the early Christian writers in the early centuries after the resurrection, who Christians call the Church Fathers, spoke of Socrates with great admiration as a holder of Christian beliefs about 400 years before the advent of Christ and Christianity. The Church Fathers must have also been aware of Socrates and his acceptance of homosexuality because it is brought out clearly in almost every dialogue of Plato. And I had ended my relationship with Markus over a book which condemned me for my natural state, a book inspired by a man who viewed our relationship as noble.

It filled me with anger and hatred towards the Bible and Christianity, for if everything else Socrates had to say was good enough for Paul and the later Christians to borrow and plagiarise, why not this idea that homosexuality is a pure form of love?

Chapter 20

This was the final blow, the *coup de grace* that Markus had promised. Going to church on a Sunday morning was most uncomfortable and I could no longer tolerate Mr Norman's sermons. Every time I heard him say something negative about the non-Christian sinners in the world or something positive about the uniqueness of Christianity or that only by believing in Jesus could we be saved, it made me writhe in my seat when I thought of all that I had learned from Markus and what I had read in Plato. When Mr Norman talked about the love of God, I could still see Markus shoving the Bible in my face and hear those words from his lips, "If God is love, aren't my feelings for you a reflection of His very essence?" And whenever I heard Mr Norman say that the Bible only is the Word of God and we must obey everything it commands us to do, I would glance at Trevor Buchanon, the unmarried deacon, and my mother, wearing a hat in church. In the past, I wanted to stand up and scream "Blasphemy!" against those who did not believe the Bible but now I wanted to stand up and scream "Hypocrisy!" at those who said they did.

But it took a long while before I could come to terms with my feelings for the Bible and my sexuality. Even though my feelings for and understanding of the Bible were changing, I was often overwhelmed with a sense of guilt for entertaining thoughts that the Bible was only a book written by men and not a revelation from God. It was a conflict between reason and indoctrination. I finally came to accept that the idea of Satan tempting us away from the belief in the Bible's infallibility was a kind of propaganda introduced into the Christian faith to enslave our minds and our reason so that the church, under whatever guise, had the licence to control us, just as Markus and Troy had once told me.

But then, how was I going to tell my parents how I felt about the Bible? I still loved my parents despite the fact that they still followed the erroneous belief of the Bible's divinity. But I knew how they were going to react when they discovered that I no longer shared their views. I had already been educated in this area, witnessing Ruth's move from Catholicism to Protestantism, hearing from Rosemary how her sister had nothing to do with her. I knew my parents would be no different and they weren't.

I didn't come straight out and say it like that. Rather, it was a slow process. At first, I simply raised questions that were rather difficult for my parents to answer and to which they ended up admitting that they had no answer for. I did this slowly and deliberately in a way that I knew my parents would begin to see how critical of the Bible I was becoming. Whenever we read something during our after dinner Bible Study, I became more and more critical until I came to a point where I was openly admitting that I couldn't help but see that some things just didn't add up, or that they didn't make sense, or they just could not be true. Whereas my parents had earlier in the part coolly admitted that they had no answer to my questions, soon the conversations were turning into mild conflicts as my questions and statements became more and more obvious as to the stance I was taking. It reached such a point that Bible Study finally became a heated intellectual battle ground, ending with the curses my mother could dream up against me for questioning the venerable Word of God.

But it came to a head when one evening we read Matthew chapter sixteen. The last two verses of this chapter were like the death blow through the heart of any shred of belief I had left for the Bible because here Jesus is recorded as saying

For the Son of man shall come in the glory of his
Father with his angels; and then he shall reward every
man according to his works.
Verily I say unto you, There be some standing here,
which shall not taste of death, till they see the Son of
man coming in his kingdom.

There was no way I could contain my sentiments. I just blurted out that if Jesus said this, He was a false prophet because this verse was so clear in prophesying His return within the lifetime of His contemporaries, when in reality this was not true.

My parents argued back. My mother's argument was all the more ludicrous because she shouted at me that the Bible is true and therefore some of the apostles must still be living in a secret place in Israel that we don't know about.

I knew this was a stupid response which made me all the more enflamed to let all my feelings out, showing them that this verse was not the only Scripture that held this opinion. I explained that in Matthew chapter twenty-four, Jesus foretells the events that would lead up to the end of the world, punctuated by His Second Coming, to which Jesus says in verse thirty-four, "Verily I say unto you, This generation shall not pass, till all these things be fulfilled". The generation of people living at the time of Jesus, according to this passage of Scripture, would not all die out before the Lord returned, which in reality was not the case.

I told them that Jesus even said at His trial in Matthew 26:64 that those who tried Him would see Him again in the future coming in the clouds of heaven. In context, Jesus meant that the members of the Sanhedrin, Pilate and the centurions would see this glorious event while still alive in their bodily form. And this was echoed by John the Revelator who said in the first chapter of the Book of Revelation, "Behold, he cometh with clouds; and every eye shall see him, and they also which pierced him," which implied that those who were responsible for putting Jesus to death would one day in their lifetime look up to heaven and see this same Jesus returning in His glory.

I went on to explain that Paul even believed that Jesus would return within the lifetime of his contemporaries, for he wrote in I Corinthians 15:51, "Behold,

I shew you a mystery; We shall not all sleep, but we shall all be changed", and in I Thessalonians 4:15, "For this we say unto you by the word of the Lord, that we which are alive and remain unto the coming of the Lord." Paul wrote these letters, not to all Christians in future times, but to those living in his time. In other words, Paul believed that some members of the Corinthian and Thessalonian congregations to whom he wrote during the first century would still be alive when Jesus returned. This same Paul, who wrote Romans chapter one, was wrong.

An argument broke out between my parents and me, my parents telling me that Satan had polluted my mind and me telling them that the church had stolen theirs. It was very messy and ended with my mother smacking me across the face, followed by me getting into my car and driving off into the night and not returning till the following afternoon after work.

My parents were distraught and the relationship between us was strained. I stopped going to church and my parents made the wise decision of allowing me to leave the dinner table without having to read the Bible with them because all the time they made me read it, I just pulled it apart. In a way it disturbed me that I was hurting my parents for not believing in the Bible anymore. From time to time I tried to explain that just because I didn't believe in Christianity anymore, it did not mean that I did not love them. But this they could not grasp and felt as if my disbelief was a direct affront against them. To them, I was now a victim of Satan and no longer had the God of love living inside me so how was I capable of loving?

I remember times when I would come home from work and my mother would have red, swollen eyes and a distraught look on her face and I knew she had been crying. It caused a swell of feelings inside, of anger, hate and sorrow, all because the universe in my mind had changed and my parents felt sad because of it.

However, for the first time in my life, I felt free. I could now make friends with anybody irrespective of what they believed. The world just seemed to open up before me. I could listen to whatever music I liked, I could read what I liked and I could believe what I liked. And most of all, I didn't feel guilty.

And the first person I thought of was Markus. The excitement that filled my heart to know that I could resume my old friendship with him now that I was no longer shackled down by the Bible was indescribable. From the time I had left him to when I told my parents I no longer was a believer, two years had elapsed. Would Markus still want me back? I had not stopped thinking about him all that time. I hoped desperately that his feelings towards me had remained the same.

I decided to go to his place one day after work and had decided that I would stay that night if he let me. When I arrived in front of his block of flats, the old memories rushed in like a mighty wind and filled me with great expectations. My feet felt as if they were shod with Mercury's winged slippers as I ran up the stairs to his apartment. But instead of being greeted at the door by the face I longed to see, a grumpy, old man with a beer gut and a cigarette hanging out of his mouth opened the door and grunted, "Whatta ya want?" It was definitely Markus' old apartment but he no longer lived there. The new occupant told me that he had been living there for over a year and a half. My heart just sank into my shoes. I apologised for disturbing and sulked back down the stairs.

At work the next day I asked my colleagues if Markus had ever been in contact with any of them, only to discover that my colleagues did maintain some contact for a while but soon Markus just disappeared. It was speculated that he went to Melbourne, or to Perth, or even back to Sri Lanka.

Every means I used to find Markus was futile. After months of trying, I gave up. It hurt to know that I had tried to hold onto the Bible, a book, a mere object, because I thought Jesus loved me, all at the cost of a person who demonstrated his personal love for me. And now I had lost him. I became so bitter against the Bible and against my church which had indoctrinated me into believing in it in the first place. Everything I had been brought up to love and cherish had become something I completely despised.

Chapter 21

My faith in the Bible was completely shattered like a dropped piece of intricate glasswork. I had crossed one hurdle. Despite all I had learned from Socrates, and despite my relationship with Markus, the social stigma of being gay kept me in the closet. Because I had never had sex with a woman before, I thought that this was the reason why I had homosexual tendencies. Now that I did not believe the Bible, I was no longer inhibited by the modest, strict view that the Bible and Christians have of sex, and I was now free to find out what having sex with a woman was like.

Markus' replacement in the laboratory was a guy called John. He was anything but your stereotypical image of a scientist, of someone wearing a suit and tie, glasses, and with a short back-and-sides hair cut. Within a week he was able to wear clothes that came in all shapes and in all the colours of the rainbow, and he wore a different earring each day with a different gemstone in it. The bosses didn't care because his job did not entail customer contact. John was very cluey where product development was concerned so as long as he was improving productivity, the chief chemist didn't care if he came to work naked.

Now that I wasn't a Christian, it was a real relief to know that I was able to get to know John as a person and not view him as a target for salvation. Because of his outrageous appearance, I immediately thought he was gay. After all, he had all the external trimmings of being so. And I wasn't alone in my analysis of him. Even the guys in the factory made fun of him because they thought the same. But John was so cool about it and he didn't care what they thought of him to the point that he and the guys in the factory soon became very good friends, despite what he did in his private life.

John was also great company in the laboratory. Although so unlike Markus in his work, very sloppy, disorganised, writing things on pieces of paper and then losing them, somehow he was able to get all his work done properly and correctly. We started to become friends and not long after that I was going out to nightclubs with him and meeting his friends. In a matter of months, I learned what it was to have a great time, to drink, to smoke and to party. My life was turned completely upside-down. Coming home in the wee hours of a Saturday or Sunday morning drunk, sleeping until midday and waking up with a throbbing headache and throwing up every half hour, becoming an outright rebel to my whole Christian upbringing, all this must have really broken my parents' hearts.

John introduced me to life in the fast lane. And soon I had my first and only sexual experience with a woman, although I would tell John later that I had had more encounters with women than one. It was a very unpleasant and uncomfortable feeling and it only spelled it out clearer to me that I was gay. But I was too scared to tell John that I liked men and not women in this way because of the social stigma against homosexuality and because I thought John would reject me because of it.

In the meantime, I knew this reckless life I was leading distressed my parents and so I decided to leave home. But they would have none of it. My parents believed that a child stays in their parents' home until the day they marry, and my parents threw at me the guilt trip whenever I made the suggestion of moving out. So I decided to stay. If they wanted an outright anti-Christ living under their roof, I wasn't going to complain. I suppose they didn't want me to leave home because they felt that they could still keep an eye on me and maybe reconvert me.

I remember one afternoon when my parents came into my room. I hated the depressed looks on their faces. It ate at me because their hearts were heavy because I had left the faith and they were afraid that Satan was just biding his time, enticing me with the pleasures of the world, waiting for the right moment to terminate my life and seal my eternal destiny in hell.

My father asked me if I found the life I was living fulfilling to which I replied in the affirmative. He could not understand. Why had this life of drinking, smoking and sex made him feel empty, and becoming a Christian had given him meaning to his life, when the reverse had happened to me?

"What has Satan done to you to make you hate God so much?" my father asked pitifully.

"Satan? Why is Satan to blame? What about the Bible? Why don't you blame the Bible?" I retorted.

My father recoiled back in horror.

"But the Bible is the Word of God without error!" my father exclaimed, almost pleading.

"No, it isn't, Dad. It's full of errors and contradictions. So how can it be the reflection of the mind of a perfect God?"

My father sighed and put his hand to his face. My mother's eyes swelled with tears.

"Then, if it's not the Word of God," my father continued, "you believe you don't have to obey it anymore."

"That's right, I don't," I snapped.

"But, son, if you don't believe the Bible, then you're free to sin. You'll start committing little sins, then bigger ones, and soon you'll not even think that killing and stealing are wrong. You won't feel guilty about this because Satan will convince you that there is no God, no Last Judgement and no hell."

I just stood up in anger.

"Do you really believe that those who believe in the Bible are not capable of committing these same sins? Don't you know that the believers in the Bible have a track record of committing these atrocities and are blameless? Read the stories in the Bible, like the story of the Israelites when they entered the Promised Land. The Land of Israel was already inhabited by the Canaanites before the Israelites arrived and the Israelites believed that God had given them this land, which gave them the licence to butcher the Canaanites and steal everything they owned. At that time, there were many other places of vacant, inhabitable land in the world that God could have given them, so why did He give them this one?

And the Israelites are not alone. What about the Spanish Inquisition when all those innocent Jews and other non-Christians were hacked to death or burnt at the stake all because they didn't believe Jesus was God or the Bible His Word?

This is the hypocrisy of the Christians. For the first three centuries they were persecuted by the Romans, being thrown to the lions and burnt at the stake, while Christian apologetics pleaded the Caesars not to be so cruel. Justin Martyr and Tertullian begged the Roman Emperors to see what the Christians were really like, that they were nice people, good people, kind people, see how bright their smiles are, hear how sweetly they sing, they arrive at work on time and always say 'please' and 'thank you'.

But, gee, when the tables were turned and the Christians held the reign of power, their whole attitude changed. They took over where the Romans left off, leaving a trail of bloodshed and misery in their wake. At no time did they reflect back to the early centuries of Christian persecution and say amongst themselves, 'Hey, you know? When the non-Christians were in power during the time of the Roman Empire, we hated being persecuted simply because our beliefs were different to theirs. So, maybe we should learn from this and be tolerant towards people who don't share our views of God and the heavens but who are otherwise good citizens.' Quite the contrary! They showed that their feigned meekness and their apparent call for tolerance hid their real intentions and that their real objective was complete domination and control. And they certainly achieved this. They adopted the philosophy that anyone who didn't believe in Jesus was damned and they decided to give the unbelievers a head start by making their lives hell on earth, persecuting and torturing them, finishing them off by hacking them to death or burning them at the stake so that God could finish up the work they had left off by sending them to eternal torment.

Take a quick flashback into history and recall the bloody battles and wars in Europe between Catholics, Protestants, the Huguenots, the Anabaptists, the Calvinists, the Cathars, all of them believing that Jesus died and rose again for their sins and all believing that the Bible is God's Word. Why didn't their belief in the Bible prevent them from such inhumanity?

And they weren't satisfied with creating havoc in their own backyard but decided to spread their reign of terror to the rest of the world, taking the Bible to the new countries that had been discovered together with the squabbles and contentions that came with it. They stole the land from the original inhabitants and killed any of the natives who put up any resistance.

And what about here in our own country, when Christian England descended on the original inhabitants of Australia, justifying the murder of thousands of the men and women who had been living in this land for millennia, and considering it righteous to steal children from parents so that their children could be brought up as Christians? And you're telling me that by not believing in the Bible, I will become a thief and a murderer?"

My father's eyes began to water.

"But these people were not Christians, then," my father said almost whispering, "if they did these things. They were not doing the will of God and so they will go to hell."

"But, Dad," I said, "these people believed that Jesus died and rose again from the dead, which according to the Bible is the only prerequisite for becoming a Christian and being saved. And the Bible is clear in saying that Jesus forgives all sins, which means that, according to the Bible, these butchers and thieves will enter eternal bliss because all these will be forgiven them.

But getting back to what you said, believing the Bible doesn't make us good. Look at Ruth's parents and how they threw Ruth out of her home the night they found out she did not believe the Bible in the same way as they did. And look at Rosemary. Her sister, Helen, won't have anything to do with her because Helen believes her interpretation of the Bible is superior to Rosemary's."

"But the Bible says in II Peter 1:20 that 'no prophecy of the Scripture is of any private interpretation'," my mother cried.

"In your dreams, Mum," I said in anger. "The Bible might like to say all it likes that it is of no private interpretation but we all understand it differently. Just look at the contentious issues within our own church over what the Bible says and doesn't say. If you believe the Bible is not to be privately interpreted, then the only conclusion you can come up with is that the way *you* understand what the Bible says is the right understanding and everybody else is wrong. But Mr Norman thinks the same thing and so do the Catholics, and the Mormons, and the Jehovah's Witnesses, and the Christian Scientists, and the Christadelphians, and the Jews, and the Seventh Day Adventists, and any other religion that believes the Bible is the Word of God. They also believe that the way they understand the Bible is the only true and right way. So, why should I believe you and not them?"

My parents no longer tried to convert me back to the faith after that. And our relationship was as strained as ever. It was really difficult coming home at night and so I generally stayed out as long as I could and came home when my parents had gone to bed or I stayed over at John's place.

My friendship with John became more intimate but, no, there were no fireworks and champagne glasses. I was never in love with John in that way but I did become close enough to be able to open up my heart to him. I told him all about my life as a Christian and the torturous road it led me along until I came to the realisation that it was not true.

Eventually I told him about Markus and my feelings towards men. John looked at me puzzled and I was afraid he was going to call me a faggot and tell me to leave his house immediately. But instead, he said, "But what about all those girls you said you had slept with?"

I was unable to answer him right away. I mumbled something and then just said, "But I thought that would please you! I thought that you would hate me for being gay!"

"Please me? Oh, Michael, you don't need to do anything to please me. Just be yourself. But for God's sake, why didn't you tell me before? Why would I hate you for being gay? I think you're a nice guy, and just because you're gay, this doesn't change anything."

This was the first time in my life that from my lips I had told someone that I was gay. It was such a relieving experience, like a weight off my shoulders, like being unburdened by a load of guilt. And it was the first time I had heard the voice of tolerance and understanding, and it surprised me even more coming from a straight guy because I didn't know before this that there were heterosexuals in the world who had so much understanding. John then told me how members of the group of friends we went out with were also gay and sometimes went to Oxford Street, the major street in Sydney renowned for its gay nightclubs.

"Paul's gay? But he doesn't act gay!" I commented.

"How does a gay man act? What did you expect him to do? Swivel his hips, speak with a lisp and wear women's clothes? And what about Linda? Did you expect her to shave her head, wear leather, roll her own Drum cigarettes and act real butch? Michael, being gay is not that clear cut."

And so I discovered for myself when John eventually took me to Oxford Street. I remember first going with him to a bar called the Oxford early in the evening and seeing all these very masculine men standing there, drinking, chatting and laughing. They were really rough, ocker, macho guys and looked just like the guys in the factory at work. Because of the stereotyping, at first I thought that these men were heterosexual and as the evening progressed, they would slowly be replaced by the homosexuals. But it wasn't until about thirty minutes had elapsed when it dawned on me that these guys were gay!

Being introduced to Oxford Street was like letting a child loose in a lolly shop. For, yes, I let my hormones loose for a long time after that. All that pent up sexual frustration that I had bottled up inside for all those years was let out in one moment.

But what amazed me the most was that there were homosexuals from every country of the world. In time I would meet Aboriginal Australians, Italians, Greeks, French, Estonians, Swedes, Turks, Indians, Chinese, Iranians, Japanese, Fijians, Tongans, Lebanese, Egyptians, Tanzanians, Nigerians, Sudanese, Moroccans, who had been believers of as many religions and ideologies: atheists, Catholics, Mormons, Muslims, Zoroastrians, Hindus, Buddhists, Communists, Jews. It was like a League of Nations united under the same sexual orientation. Each of them had a story to tell about the extent to which they had come out of the closet and how homosexuality was viewed in their country, in their society and in the belief systems from whence they had come. It was becoming more and more obvious to me that homosexuality was just a variant of sexuality which constituted a part of the human species.

My parents did not know that I went to Oxford Street. Rather, they were always making comments, asking what I'd do if I got a girl pregnant. I replied that there was no possibility of this happening. My father particularly told me that I was arrogantly confident and that he would force me to marry if I got a girl in that state. My poor parents!

But there was no way I was going to tell them. I knew that telling my parents I was gay would be like smoking a cigarette in front of an open LPG tank. I would have kept this information from my parents but the information reached my parents without my consent. But it was the way it reached them that was the most ironic.

One night I was at the Oxford Bar with Paul and John. We were drinking and laughing and really enjoying ourselves when over on the other side of the room in the crowd were two men kissing. There was something familiar about one of these men and when they finally stopped to take a breath, I realised I knew him. There in this den of iniquity and house of immorality was Trevor Buchanon, checking out another man's tonsils with his tongue. Trevor both saw me and recognised me. He ran out and the other guy followed him chasing him with an expression on his face which suggested that he didn't know what was happening. And that spoiled my evening. I told John and Paul that I wanted to go home, and so I did.

Trevor must have panicked and thought I would divulge his Saturday night whereabouts to my parents which would then reach the rest of the church and, to prevent this from happening, he managed to spread a story about how he was trying to preach to some of those perverse homosexuals on the gay scene and had seen me kissing another man, which was not true. He spread this story through the church so that it would eventually end up in the ears of my parents. And when my parents found out, the powder keg exploded. When I asked them how they found out, I screamed out that it was Trevor kissing another man, not me. But that made them all the more infuriated, telling me not to be so blasphemous about one of the deacons of the church. Ah, now he was worthy to wear the name "deacon", a title my parents would not use to describe him in the past because he was not married.

They asked me if it was true that I was gay and I realised that it was no use hiding it. My mother just burst into tears and walked out of the room, and my father hit me fair and square across the face.

"If this doesn't convince you that the Bible is true, I don't know what else will. It says in Romans chapter one that if you turn away from God, God will make you a homosexual. And He has. So it's over. You've lost your salvation forever. Pack your bags and get out. I want you out of this house in an hour."

Chapter 22

I had fulfilled the Scriptures in my parents' eyes because never in the past had I ever told them that I had homosexual tendencies but had done my utmost to try to act like a heterosexual man. No doubt this worked because my parents were not, and to this day are still not, convinced that I was ever gay all the time I had been a Christian but rather believe I only became gay the day I turned away from the Christian faith.

One of the greatest ironies of the story was my sister, Karen, and her husband, Peter. My parents told Karen what had happened and about a week or so after I had left home, Karen rang me at work.

"Michael, I just want to tell you that despite who or what you are, I still love you. You're still my brother," she said full of love.

I was speechless. I thought she must have given up Christianity but she told me that she hadn't. She told me that just because I was gay, this did not constitute a reason for not loving me, for Jesus taught all Christians to love one another, Christian or non-Christian, for God Himself made the rain fall and the sun shine on the evil and the good. These evildoers and sinners who the Christians were commanded to love and do good to included homosexuals as well as heterosexuals.

I was touched to the very heart. This was the daughter of another God and another Christ. But most of all, I was surprised at her willingness to openly talk about it, and we discussed it in great detail.

It was because of my sister that I did not become completely iconoclastic. Because my sister is a Christian and a good person, this reality indicated to me that there are Christians who are good people. Karen didn't try to convert me back to the faith. She only ever said once that she did not approve of my life but then it was not for her to judge me. She also said that if I ever fell in love and lived with a man, my partner would be just as welcome into her house as I was because he would be an important part of my life.

My sister's open-heartedness allowed me to continue to see the beauty in some of the teachings of Jesus and of the Bible, even though I now no longer view the Bible as infallible. Jesus' whole message was about love and forgiveness, not judgement and self-righteousness.

By contrast, my parents don't speak to me to this day. As far as they are concerned, eventually they will hear about me in the news, how a man robbed a bank or committed mass murder and was sentenced to life imprisonment, and then they will see my face broadcast on national television. They would probably be disappointed with the result which contrasts strongly with their expectations because I finally settled down with a man who I have now been living with for many years. I live in a flat in the suburbs and carry on life like an average suburbanite.

And contrary to what they expected, I don't feel a compulsion to go out and murder or steal. But nor do my non-religious friends either. I realise now that people have some sense of morality and that this idea that morality is a derivative of religion is a simplistic and specious view of humanity. Rather, humanity has managed to survive because we all seem to contain an inbuilt sense of morality, the origin of which we can't explain. So religion is used to give a reason for the origins of morality. But where religions go wrong is that the founders of these religions include amongst those things they claim to be moral or immoral those things they personally like or dislike, such as what foods we can eat, what clothes we should wear and, of course, who we are allowed to be intimate with.

Whereas in the past religions were able to survive in isolated pockets in the world, today we are constantly in contact with people with different beliefs. Hence, for the modern world to get along, there needs to be a lot of respect towards those of alternate views of the universe. And people have to ask themselves, do they dislike what someone else does with their lives because it is inherently wrong or simply because they themselves would not like to indulge in such an activity which causes no harm to those around them?

What is important is that we need to become more aware of different views and why people hold these views. I can see that as we increase our knowledge, we are more capable of making wise decisions about our lives and our conduct. It also increases our acceptance of others who have belief systems different to our own, and that we should adjust our beliefs to fit reality and not confine our reality to a belief system that does not allow for alternative views.

Contrary to what I had been taught when I was young and growing up, Christianity doesn't necessarily make a person good or bad. In fact, there is no link between goodness and Christianity. Christianity teaches goodness but it doesn't follow that a person will become a good person if they follow the Christian faith. Christianity in the hands of a good person will certainly result in a person doing wonderful things for humanity. Mother Theresa easily brings out this point. But religion in the hands of those bent on achieving their own ends can have catastrophic results. One only needs to look at modern day Ireland and the constant conflict between Catholic south and Protestant north to see the evidence of this.

Having accepted my homosexuality for the simple fact that it is has made me reflect on why Christianity is opposed to this sexual phenomenon, particularly because much of the Christian faith is built on Socrates, the greatest homosexual of all time. But moreso, why has the western world, which builds its entire way of thinking on Socrates' philosophy, been so savage towards homosexuals when two men or two women having sex together is such a private affair?

Not only so, why have other cultures and countries around the world which are based on other religions and philosophies had such a negative view of this sexual phenomenon? Because Sydney is a multicultural city, it is easy to meet gay men and women from all the countries of the world and as a result I have discovered that Christians are not alone in their hatred towards homosexuals – this hatred is almost universal.

A picture began to form in my mind when I put all these facets together. Most societies around the world today have one thing in common: they are male dominated. Men are viewed as superior and dominant, and women as inferior and subservient.

Christianity supports this stance from the Bible because of the story of Adam and Eve. Eve's punishment for eating of the forbidden fruit was that the man would rule over her. Therefore, men are superior to women, reflected by a woman's subservient role in the Church. According to the New Testament, women have to be silent in the church (I Corinthians 14:34), women have to wear a covering when they pray or prophesy to show their subjection to men (I Corinthians 11:3-15), wives have to obey their husbands (I Peter 3:6), and women cannot "usurp authority over man, but...be in silence" (I Timothy 2:12). Although women are human beings and necessary for the continuation of the human species, women are, according to the Bible, lesser humans than men. Simply being born with a penis gives the male human being his birthright to dominance.

Homosexuality, however, makes this otherwise clear demarcation between men and women blurred. If two men have sex with each other, at least one of them takes on the receiving role, that is, one "plays the woman" so to speak. If a man, therefore, takes on the role of a woman in the sexual act, in a male-dominated society, this man has practically demeaned himself. He has somehow "feminised" himself and therefore lowered himself into the ranks of the subordinates. If men are superior to women, how do those in a male-dominated society view this man? Is he still a man, because he has the physical attributes of a man, or a woman, because he takes on a woman's role during sex? In some ways, this man has somehow betrayed his manhood by being submissive in the sexual act.

And if one man can do it, it means that all men have the physical potential to do it. This means that simply having a man's body no longer makes the distinction between men and women clear. If a man can "be a woman" during sex, then a man can "be a woman" in other areas of life. This then makes a man's superiority over the woman farcical. Therefore, male homosexuals are a threat to male dominance.

Lesbianism also has its part to play. One of the major ways a man proves his masculinity is through the sexual act. The more women he has sex with, the greater the evidence of his virility and therefore his importance. But if women can find sexual gratification without the man, the man loses one of the fundamental means of proving his manhood. It is a blow to a man if his position as the dominant "actor" in the physical union is replaced by a subordinate of his species to the point that he is no longer needed. But further, if a woman can "play the role of a man" in the sexual act, she can play the role of a man in other areas of life as well.

It seems more than mere coincidence that women's fight for equal rights in the western world was followed by the gay rights movement. If women and men are now equal, it is no longer imperative to look down on women. If women now stand on an equal platform with men, gay men and gay women are no longer defiling the unequal gender stratification. There is no longer a man's role or a woman's role in the home or in society and, therefore, everything is shared equally, including the sexual act.

The idea that a gay man demeans himself by "playing the woman" in the sexual act is brought out when we examine words in different cultures to describe homosexuals. In modern English, we use the word "gay" but this word is relatively modern and came out during the gay revolution in the seventies. The term "gay man" simply means a man who has sex with another man, irrespective of what they do to each other.

However, prior to this, the derogatory word *poofter* was used. *Poofter* comes into the English in a round about way from a derogatory French word to describe a woman's genitals. That is, it was surmised that homosexuals were only passive, therefore, submissive and womanlike.

This became more evident when I discovered the words used to describe homosexuals in many other languages. I remember once talking to a Tanzanian who explained to me that there are two words in Swahili which are translated as "gay man": *basha* and *msenge*. *Basha* really means "active homosexual" and *msenge* means "passive homosexual". There is no single word in Swahili that simply means "a man who has sex with another man". In Tanzanian society, a *basha* is not looked on any differently from a dominant, masculine man who has sex with women within their society because a *basha* plays the "active" and therefore "masculine" role in the sexual act. By contrast, a *msenge* is viewed with contempt because he becomes a woman in the sexual act. What was also degrading about the word was that *msenge* originally meant a man who was a slave to a woman. In a male dominated society, what could be more demeaning for a man!

In Mauritian Creole, "gay man" is translated as *pilon*. But again, a *pilon* refers only to a man who "takes on the female role" in the sexual act. One Mauritian explained to me that the real meaning of *pilon* is "a man who cannot get an erection and therefore derives pleasure from men who do". There is no term to describe an active male homosexual because such a man has not betrayed his masculinity.

This is the same in Farsi for the words *bache-bas* and *koni*, the former meaning "active homosexual" and the latter meaning "passive homosexual" and no word exists in Farsi which correctly translates the English word "gay". And I am sure if I were to examine the words used in other languages, I would come up with the same result.

This, then, made me reflect back on the stories of Sodom and Gomorrah, and the Levite in Gibeah, and understand the real message behind these stories. If Lot had sent out the angels or the old man had sent out the Levite so that the men of these cities "may know them", the angels and the Levite would have been raped, that is, forced into the position of a woman. This was the sin the inhabitants of these cities wanted to commit, to bring down a man from his superior position and force him against his will into the subservient woman's role. This is why Lot and the old man were willing to send out their virgin daughters instead of the men under their protection, and why the Levite's concubine was in the end sent out. Neither Lot nor the Levite was condemned for their acts because they maintained the status quo of the dominant man.

In the Jewish religion, it is understandable why women have been in subjection to men because of Eve's condemnation in the Garden of Eden. However, this is yet another inconsistency within the Christian faith. Although Christians include the Jewish Scriptures within their creed, Christians also have the New Testament which makes alterations to the sins of Adam and Eve.

When we read the story of Creation, we read how God made both man and woman in His image. It was not only the man who was created in God's image but the woman also. The woman may have been made from Adam's rib but she was still a part of man and therefore equal to man. As it is written in Genesis 1:27, "So God created man in his own image... male and female created he them". The word "man" in this verse appears to mean humans, not males. In other words, both man and woman together, like the two halves of a whole, are the image of God. God, therefore, is not a male being. He is a completion and unity of the two sexes. Religions, therefore, that are based on the supposition that God is purely masculine are lopsided. These religions are worshipping only half a god. If God is the Supreme Being over both men and women, God must also be both male and female.

According to the Bible, in their sinless state, neither the man nor the woman had the authority over the other. It was only when man and woman fell from their sinless state to become sinful beings that the man ruled over the woman.

Although the Old Testament tells us that the first humans brought sin on all humankind, the New Testament tells us that this situation has now been revoked. Despite Paul's view of women's subservient role to men, Paul proposed an opposite view of men and women in the new faith. Paul, in his letter to the Corinthians, in chapter 15, tells us that the first man, Adam, became a sinful being and therefore passed on sin to the rest of humanity. However, Jesus Christ was the "second Adam" who passed on sinlessness to the rest of humanity. If Jesus restored humanity to its original, sinless state, then Christianity should be based on man and woman's original situation: equality. Paul does support this argument when he writes in Galatians 3:28 that through Christ, "there is neither male nor female" and it appears that, in the early Church, women were originally restored to equality when they were assigned special functions in the Church on an equal footing with men, with the specific example of Phebe, the deaconess. Somewhere in the development of the Christian Church, women once again lost their equal status.

But it still surprises me how Paul had no difficulty in taking many ideas from the great homosexual of all time, Socrates, and used his ideas to develop the Church, but still condemned homosexuals and kept women in a subservient role. For not only did Socrates put homosexuality in a favourable light, this same Socrates attempted to bring in equality between the sexes in the male-dominated world of Greek society. Socrates, through Plato, argued in the *Republic* that women should be allowed to partake in everything that was at the time limited to men, including being rulers of society. One did not need a piece of flesh to hang between the legs to achieve this end. One simply needed the *logos*, and women had a soul just like men did that had the capability of attaining the *logos*.

Socrates even admitted being taught by a woman called Diotima as is recorded in the *Symposium*. If this great and wise philosopher could receive wisdom from a woman, then it was only logical that women could impart wisdom to the rest of the world as equally as men. In a world ruled by men, this teaching was no doubt threatening, and it is no wonder that Socrates was put to death by the *ekklesia*.

But what surprises me even to this day is how much the New Testament is built on much of what Socrates said and Socrates is still venerated in the western world as the wisest and most moral man who ever lived. Yet, his message of equality between the sexes and his positive view of sexuality has been passed down through the centuries entirely unnoticed. Socrates' sayings, through Plato, have managed to survive into the twenty-first century and his works are still studied, and yet the western world is generally quite ignorant of his teachings.

What is also peculiar in this modern, overpopulated world is that homosexuality is badly perceived in much of the world when the sexual union between two men or two women is a natural contraception. If overpopulated countries allowed homosexual couples to have an equal standing with heterosexual couples, there would be no need to resort to artificial methods of family planning or make policies which limit the number of children a heterosexual couple can have. After all, the command to "be fruitful and multiply" might have been appropriate when the planet was occupied by only two people, but in a world of six billion, it is wise to apply the brakes to human fruitfulness. It may be that God, in His wisdom, introduced homosexuality to keep the population growth in check.

The beauty of Socrates, at lest for me, is that Socrates has become a role model. At least there is one man in history who claimed God spoke to him and therefore in some ways has the right to join the ranks amongst the prophets. Socrates' message is that we can be gay and still be good and acceptable before God. But further, Socrates' message is that we all have a mind and we should use our intellect to free ourselves, and not bind ourselves to belief systems which cause dissension and conflict. I am a believer in Socrates, not to the extent that I believe I should go out and proselytise, because I know that many people live their lives in much the same way and have no idea what Socrates ever said. It's the principle that is important, not who said it.

And if Jesus Christ is the *Logos*, the Reason, then Jesus expects of us to use reason ourselves to find the truth, which means we should view the Bible from a rational point of view and accept what is reasonable and reject what is not. In this way, the Bible still maintains its integrity as a special book.

And, so, I am Michael and this is my gospel, that sex and sexuality have absolutely nothing to do with righteousness. Irrespective of what our sexuality is, I believe that our time on earth is the pursuit of noble characteristics and of knowledge because these are common in all religions and philosophies. God has given us a free mind, not to believe in the bad, but to believe in the good, to pursue it and to follow it wherever it leads us. This has freed me from feeling guilty for something about myself when there is no reason for feeling guilty, and has allowed me to re-turn to reading the Bible, not as a book that I must believe without error, and therefore torture myself with guilt and shame, but as a guide that contains in many ways good teaching and philosophy.

www.ingramcontent.com/pod-product-compliance
Lightning Source LLC
Chambersburg PA
CBHW030646120726
47905CB00001B/77